STUART NEVILLE

Ratlines

VINTAGE BOOKS
London

Published by Vintage 2013

2 4 6 8 10 9 7 5 3 1

First published by Harvill Secker in 2013

Vintage
Random House, 20 Vauxhall Bridge Road,
London SW1V 2SA

www.vintage-books.co.uk

Addresses for companies within The Random House Group Limited can be found at: www.randomhouse.co.uk/offices.htm

The Random House Group Limited Reg. No. 954009

A CIP catalogue record for this book is available from the British Library

ISBN 9780099552581

The Random House Group Limited supports the Forest Stewardship Council® (FSC®), the leading international forest-certification organisation. Our books carrying the FSC label are printed on FSC®-certified paper. FSC is the only forest-certification scheme supported by the leading environmental organisations, including Greenpeace. Our paper procurement policy can be found at www.randomhouse.co.uk/environment

Typeset in Sabon MT by Palimpsest Book Production Limited, Falkirk, Stirlingshire

Printed and bound in Great Britain by CPI Group (UK) Ltd, Croydon, CR0 4YY

For Isabel Emerald Neville

War-battered dogs are we,
Gnawing a naked bone,
Fighting in every land and clime,
For every cause but our own.

President John F. Kennedy
Wexford, Ireland, 27 June 1963

Author's Note

THIS IS FICTION, NOT HISTORY. ALTHOUGH THIS NOVEL IS inspired by real people and locations, all of the events herein are entirely imagined.

These things are known to be true: Dozens of Nazis and Axis collaborators sought refuge in Ireland following the Second World War; in 1957, Otto Skorzeny was welcomed to a country club reception by the young politician Charles Haughey; Otto Skorzeny purchased Martinstown House in Kildare in 1959; in 1963, in response to a question by Dr Noël Browne TD, the Minister for Justice Charles Haughey told the Irish parliament that Otto Skorzeny had never been resident in Ireland.

The rest is just a story.

I

SOLDIER

1

'YOU DON'T LOOK LIKE A JEW,' HELMUT KRAUSS SAID TO THE man reflected in the windowpane.

Beyond the glass, rolling white waves threw themselves against the rocks of Galway Bay, the Atlantic glowering beyond. The guesthouse in Salthill was basic, but clean. The small seaside town outside Galway City hosted families from all over Ireland seeking a few days of salt air and sunshine during the summer months. Sometimes it provided beds for unmarried couples, fornicators and adulterers with the nerve to bluff their way past the morally upright proprietors of such establishments.

Krauss knew so because he had enjoyed the company of several ladies in guesthouses like this one, taking bracing walks along the seafront, enduring overcooked meals in mostly empty dining rooms, then finally rattling the headboard of whatever bed they had taken. He carried a selection of wedding rings in his pocket, alongside the prophylactics.

This dreary island, more grey than green, so choked by the godly, provided him few pleasures. So why not enjoy the odd sordid excursion with a needful woman?

Perhaps Krauss should have allowed himself the luxury of a decent hotel in the city, but a funeral, even if for a close friend, did not seem a fitting occasion. The security might have been better, though, and this visitor might not have gained entry so easily. For a moment, Krauss felt an aching regret, but immediately dismissed it as foolishness. Had he been the kind of man who submitted to regret, he would have hanged himself ten years ago.

'Are you a Jew?' Krauss asked.

The reflection shifted. 'Maybe. Maybe not.'

'I saw you at the funeral,' Krauss said. 'It was a beautiful service.'

'Very,' the reflection said. 'You wept.'

'He was a good man,' Krauss said. He watched gulls skate the updraughts.

'He was a murderer of women and children,' the reflection said. 'Like you.'

'Murderer,' Krauss said. 'Your accent is British. For many people in Ireland, you British are murderers. Oppressors. Imperialists.'

The reflection swelled on the glass as the man approached. 'You hide your accent well.'

'I enjoy the spoken word. To a fault, perhaps, but I spend time refining and practising my speech. Besides, a German accent still draws attention, even in Ireland. They shelter me, but not all make me welcome. Some cling to their British overmasters like a child too old for the teat.'

Krauss had felt the weight of his age more frequently in recent times. His thick black hair had greyed, the sculpted features turned cragged. The veins in his nose had begun to rupture with the vodka and wine. Women no longer stared at him with hungry eyes when he took his afternoon walks through Dublin's Ringsend Park. But he still had good years ahead of him, however few. Would this man steal them from him?

'Have you come to kill me too?' he asked.

'Maybe. Maybe not,' the reflection said.

'May I take a drink, perhaps smoke a cigarette?'

'You may.'

Krauss turned to him. A man of middle age, between forty and forty-five, old enough to have served in the war. He had looked younger across the cemetery, dressed in the overalls of a gravedigger, but proximity showed the lines on his forehead and around his eyes. Sand-coloured hair strayed beneath the woollen cap on his head. He held a pistol, a Browning fitted with a suppressor, aimed squarely at Krauss's chest. It shook.

'Would you care for a small vodka?' Krauss asked. 'Perhaps it will steady your nerve.'

The man considered for a few seconds. 'All right,' he said.

Krauss went to the nightstand where a bottle of imported vodka and a tea-making set waited next to that morning's *Irish Times*. The front page carried a headline about the forthcoming visit of President John F. Kennedy, a story concerning a request by the Northern Irish government that he should venture across the border during his days on the island. The Irish worshipped the American leader because he was one of theirs, however many generations removed, and anticipation of his arrival had reached the point of near hysteria. Krauss intended to avoid all radio and television broadcasts for the duration of Kennedy's stay.

Not that it mattered now.

Krauss turned two white teacups over and poured a generous shot into each. He went to soften one with water from a jug, but the man spoke.

'No water, thank you.'

Krauss smiled as he handed a cup to the man. 'No glasses, I'm afraid. I hope you don't mind.'

The man nodded his thanks as he took the cup with his left hand. Undiluted vodka spilled over the lip. He took a sip and coughed.

Krauss reached into the breast pocket of his best black suit. The man's knuckle whitened beneath the trigger guard. Krauss slowed the movement of his hand and produced a gold cigarette case. He opened it, and extended it to the man.

'No, thank you.' The man did not flinch at the engraved swastika as Krauss had hoped. Perhaps he wasn't a Jew, just some zealous Briton.

Krauss took a Peter Stuyvesant, his only concession to Americanism, and gripped it between his lips as he snapped the case closed and returned it to his pocket. He preferred Marlboro, but they were too difficult to come by in this country. He took the matching lighter from his trouser pocket and sucked the petrol taste from its flame. The set had been a Christmas gift from Wilhelm Frick. Krauss treasured it. Blue smoke billowed between the men.

'Please sit,' Krauss said, indicating the chair in the corner. He lowered himself onto the bed and drew deeply on the cigarette, letting the heat fill his throat and chest. 'May I know your name?' he asked.

'You may not,' the man said.

'All right. So why?'

The man took another sip, grimaced at the taste, and placed the cup on the windowsill to his left. 'Why what?'

'Why kill me?'

'I haven't decided if I'll kill you or not, yet. I want to ask a few questions first.'

Krauss sighed and leaned back against the headboard, crossing his legs on the lumpy mattress. 'Very well.'

'Who was the well-dressed Irishman you spoke with?'

'An insultingly junior civil servant,' Krauss said.

Eoin Tomalty had given Krauss's hand a firm shake after the ceremony. 'The minister sends his condolences,' Tomalty had said. 'I'm sure you'll understand why he was unable to attend in person.'

Krauss had smiled and nodded, yes, of course he understood.

'A civil servant?' the man asked. 'The government actually sent a representative?'

'A matter of courtesy.'

'Who were the others there?'

'You already know,' Krauss said. 'You know me, so you must know them.'

'Tell me anyway.'

Krauss rhymed them off. 'Célestin Lainé, Albert Luykx, and Caoimhín Murtagh representing the IRA.'

'The IRA?'

'They are fools,' Krauss said. 'Yokels pretending to be soldiers. They still believe they can free Ireland from you British. But they are useful fools, so we avail of their assistance from time to time.'

'Such as arranging funerals.'

'Indeed.'

The man leaned forward. 'Where was Skorzeny?'

Krauss laughed. 'Otto Skorzeny does not waste his precious time with common men like me. He is far too busy attending society parties in Dublin, or entertaining politicians at that damn farm of his.'

The man reached inside his jacket pocket and produced a sealed envelope. 'You will pass this message to him.'

'I'm sorry,' Krauss said. 'I cannot.'

'You will.'

'Young man, you misunderstand me,' Krauss said. He downed the rest of the vodka and placed the cup back on the bedside table. 'I admit to being verbose at times, it is a failing of mine, but I believe I was clear on this. I did not say "I will not". I said "I cannot". I have no access to Otto Skorzeny, not socially, not politically. You'd do better going to one of the Irish politicians that gather to his flame.'

The man got to his feet, approached the bed, keeping the Browning's aim level. With his free hand, he opened Krauss's jacket and stuffed the envelope down into the breast pocket.

'Don't worry. He'll get it.'

Krauss felt his bowel loosen. He drew hard on the cigarette, burning it down to the filter before stubbing it out in the ashtray that sat on the bedside locker.

The man's hand steadied.

Krauss sat upright, swung his legs off the bed, and rested his feet on the floor. He straightened his back and placed his hands on his knees.

Fixing his gaze on the horizon beyond the window, Krauss said, 'I have money. Not much, but some. It would have been enough to see out my days. You can have it. All of it. I will flee. The rain in this damn place makes my joints ache anyway.'

The Browning's suppressor nudged his temple.

'It's not that simple,' the man said.

Krauss hauled himself to his feet. The man stood back, the pistol ready.

'Yes it is,' Krauss said, his voice wavering as he fought the tears. 'It *is* that simple. I am nothing. I was a desk clerk. I signed papers, stamped forms, and got piles from sitting on a wooden chair in the dark and the damp.'

The man pressed the muzzle against the centre of Krauss's forehead. 'Those papers you signed. You slaughtered thousands with a pen. Maybe that's how you live with it, tell yourself it was just a job, but you knew where—'

Krauss swiped at the pistol, grabbed it, forced it down, throwing the other man's balance. The man regained his footing, hardened his stance. His countenance held its calm, only the bunching of his jaw muscles betraying his resistance.

Sweat prickled Krauss's skin and pressure built in his head. He hissed through his teeth as he tried to loosen the man's fingers. The man raised the weapon, his strength rendering Krauss's effort meaningless. Their noses almost touched. Krauss roared, saw the wet points of spittle he sprayed on the man's face.

He heard a crack, felt a punch to his stomach, followed by wet heat spreading across his abdomen. His legs turned to water, and he released his hold on the barrel. He crumpled to his knees. His hands clutched his belly, red seeping between his fingers.

Hot metal pressed against Krauss's temple.

'It's better than you deserve,' the man said.

If he'd had the time, Helmut Krauss would have said, 'I know.'

2

ALBERT RYAN WAITED WITH THE DIRECTOR, CIARAN FITZPATRICK, in the outer office, facing the secretary as she read a magazine. The chairs were creaky and thin-cushioned. Ryan endured while Fitzpatrick fidgeted. Almost an hour had passed since Ryan had met the director in the courtyard surrounded by the grand complex of buildings on Upper Merrion Street. The northern and southern wings were occupied by various government departments, and the Royal College of Science resided beneath the dome that reached skyward on the western side of the quadrangle. Ryan had expected to be ushered into the minister's presence upon arrival, and by the look of him, so had Fitzpatrick.

Ryan had left his quarters at Gormanston Camp as the sky lightened, turning from a deep bluish grey to a milky white as he walked the short distance to the train station. Two horses grazed in the field across from the platform, their bellies sagging, their coats matted with neglect. They nickered to each other, the sound carrying on the salt breeze. The Irish Sea stretched out beyond like a black marble table.

The train had arrived late. It filled slowly with tobacco smoke and slack-faced men as it neared Dublin, stopping at every point of civilisation along the way. Almost all of the passengers wore suits, whether dressed for their day's work in some government office, or wearing their Sunday best for a visit to the city.

Ryan also wore a suit, and he always enjoyed the occasion to do so. A meeting with the Minister for Justice certainly warranted the effort. He had walked south from Westland Row Station to Merrion Street and watched the director's face as he approached. Fitzpatrick had examined him from head to toe before nodding his begrudging approval.

'Inside,' he'd said. 'We don't want to be late.'

Now Ryan checked his watch again. The minute hand ticked over to the hour.

He'd heard the stories about the minister. A politician with boundless ambition and the balls to back it up. The upstart had even married the boss's daughter, become son-in-law to the Taoiseach, Ireland's prime minister. Some called him a shining star in the cabinet, a reformist kicking at the doors of the establishment; others dismissed him as a shyster on the make. Everyone reckoned him a chancer.

The door opened, and Charles J. Haughey entered.

'Sorry for keeping you waiting, lads,' he said as Fitzpatrick stood. 'It was sort of a late breakfast. Come on through.'

'Coffee, Minister?' the secretary asked.

'Christ, yes.'

Ryan got to his feet and followed Haughey and Fitzpatrick into the minister's office. Once inside, Haughey shook the director's hand.

'Is this our man Lieutenant Ryan?' he asked.

'Yes, Minister,' Fitzpatrick said.

Haughey extended his hand towards Ryan. 'Jesus, you're a big fella, aren't you? I'm told you did a good job against those IRA bastards last year. Broke the fuckers' backs, I heard.'

Ryan shook his hand, felt the hard grip, the assertion of dominance. Haughey stood taller than his height should have allowed, and broad, his dark hair slicked back until his head looked like that of a hawk, his eyes hunting weakness. He had only a couple of years' seniority over Ryan, but his manner suggested an older, worldlier man, not a young buck with a higher office than his age should merit.

'I did my best, Minister,' Ryan said.

It had been a long operation, men spending nights dug into ditches, watching farmers come and go, noting the visitors, sometimes following them. The Irish Republican Army's Border Campaign had died in 1959, its back broken long ago, but Ryan had been tasked with making sure its corpse remained cold and still.

'Good,' Haughey said. 'Sit down, both of you.'

They took their places in leather-upholstered chairs facing the desk. Haughey went to a filing cabinet, whistled as he fished keys from his pocket, unlocked a drawer, and extracted a file. He tossed it on the desk's leather surface and sat in his own chair. It swivelled with no hint of creak or squeak.

An Irish tricolour hung in the corner, a copy of the Proclamation of the Irish Republic on the wall, along with pictures of racehorses, lean and proud.

'Who made your suit?' Haughey asked.

Ryan sat silent for a few seconds before he realised the question had been spoken in his direction. He cleared his throat and said, 'The tailor in my home town.'

'And where's that?'

'Carrickmacree.'

'Jesus.' Haughey snorted. 'What's your father, a pig farmer?'

'A retailer,' Ryan said.

'A shopkeeper?'

'Yes,' Ryan said.

Haughey's smile split his face, giving his mouth the appearance of a lizard's, his tongue wet and shining behind his teeth.

'Well, get yourself something decent. A man should have a good suit. You can't be walking around government offices with the arse hanging out of your trousers, can you?'

Ryan did not reply.

'You'll want to know why you're here,' Haughey said.

'Yes, Minister.'

'Did the director tell you anything?'

'No, Minister.'

'Proper order,' Haughey said. 'He can tell you now.'

Fitzpatrick went to speak, but the secretary bustled in, a tray in her hands. The men remained silent while she poured coffee from the pot. Ryan refused a cup.

When she'd gone, Fitzpatrick cleared his throat and turned in his seat. 'The body of a German national was found in a guesthouse in Salthill yesterday morning by the owner. It's believed he died the previous day from gunshot wounds to the stomach and head. The Garda Síochána were called to the scene, but when the body's identity was established, the matter was referred to the Department of Justice, and then to my office.'

'Who was he?' Ryan asked.

'Here, he was Heinrich Kohl, a small businessman, nothing more. He handled escrow for various import and export companies. A middleman.'

'You say "Here",' Ryan said. 'Meaning elsewhere, he was something different.'

'Elsewhere, he was SS-Hauptsturmführer Helmut Krauss of the Main SS Economic and Administrative Department. That sounds rather more impressive than it was in reality. I believe he was some sort of office worker during the Emergency.'

Government bureaucrats seldom called it the war, as if to do so would somehow dignify the conflict that had ravaged Europe.

'A Nazi,' Ryan said.

'If you want to use such terms, then yes.'

'May I ask, why aren't the Galway Garda Síochána dealing with this? It sounds like a murder case. The war ended eighteen years ago. This is a civilian crime.'

Haughey and Fitzpatrick exchanged a glance.

'Krauss is the third foreign national to have been murdered within a fortnight,' the director said. 'Alex Renders, a Flemish Belgian, and Johan Hambro, a Norwegian. Both of them were nationalists who found themselves aligned with the Reich when Germany occupied their respective countries.'

'And you assume the killings are connected?' Ryan asked.

'All three men were shot at close range. All three men were involved to some extent in nationalist movements during the Emergency. It's hard not to reach the logical conclusion.'

'Why were these men in Ireland?'

'Renders and Hambro were refugees following the liberation of their countries by the Allies. Ireland has always been welcoming to those who flee persecution.'

'And Krauss?'

Fitzpatrick went to speak, but Haughey interrupted.

'This case has been taken out of the Guards' hands as a matter of sensitivity. These people were guests in our country, and there are others like them, but we don't wish to draw attention to their presence here. Not now. This is an important year for Ireland. The President of the United States will visit these shores in just a few weeks. For the first time in the existence of this republic, a head of state will make an official visit, and not just any head of state. The bloody leader of the free world, no less. Not only that, he'll be coming home, to the land of his ancestors. The whole planet will be watching us.'

Haughey's chest seemed to swell as he spoke, as if he were addressing some rally in his constituency.

'Like the director said, these men were refugees, and this state offered them asylum. But even so, some people, for whatever reason, might take exception to men like Helmut Krauss living next door. They might make a fuss about it, the kind of fuss we could be doing without while we're getting ready for President Kennedy to arrive. There's people in America, people on his own staff, saying coming here's a waste of time when he's got Castro in his backyard, and the blacks causing a ruckus. They're advising him to cancel his visit. They get a sniff of trouble, they'll start insisting on it. So it's vital that this be dealt with quietly. Out of the public gaze, as it were. That's where you come in. I want you to get to the bottom of this. Make it stop.'

'And if I don't wish to accept the assignment?'

Haughey's eyes narrowed. 'I must not have made myself clear, Lieutenant. I'm not asking you to investigate this crime. I'm ordering you.'

'With all due respect, Minister, you don't have the authority to order me to do anything.'

Haughey stood, his face reddening. 'Now hold on, big fella, just who the fuck do you think you're talking to?'

Fitzpatrick raised his hands, palms up and out. 'I'm sorry,

Minister, all Lieutenant Ryan means is that such an order should come from within the command structure of the Directorate of Intelligence. I'm sure he meant no disrespect.'

'He better not have,' Haughey said, lowering himself back into his chair. 'If he needs an order from you, then go on and give it.'

Fitzpatrick turned back to Ryan. 'As the minister said, this is not a voluntary assignment. You will be at his disposal until the matter is resolved.'

'All right,' Ryan said. 'Are there any suspects in the killings?'

'Not as yet,' Haughey said. 'But the obvious train of thought must be Jews.'

Ryan shifted in his seat. 'Minister?'

'Jewish extremists,' Haughey said. 'Zionists out for revenge, I'd say. That will be your first line of inquiry.'

Ryan considered arguing, decided against it. 'Yes, Minister.'

'The Guards will give assistance where needed,' the director said. 'We'd prefer that be avoided, of course. The fewer people involved in this the better. You will also have the use of a car, and a room at Buswells Hotel when you're in the city.'

'Thank you, sir.'

Haughey opened the file he had taken from the cabinet. 'There's one more thing you should be aware of.'

He lifted an envelope from the file, gripping it by its corner. One end of it was a deep brownish red. Ryan took the envelope, careful to avoid the stained portion. It had been cut open along the top edge. He turned the envelope to read the words typed on its face.

Otto Skorzeny.

Ryan said the name aloud.

'You've heard of him?' Haughey asked.

'Of course,' Ryan said, remembering images of the scarred face in the society pages of the newspapers. Any soldier versed in commando tactics knew of Skorzeny. The name was spoken with reverence in military circles, regardless of the Austrian's affiliations. Officers marvelled at Skorzeny's exploits as if recounting the plot of an adventure novel. The rescue of Mussolini from the mountaintop hotel that served as his prison stirred most conversation. The daring of it, the audacity, landing gliders on the Gran Sasso cliff edge and sweeping Il Duce away on the wind.

Ryan slipped his fingers into the envelope and extracted the sheet of paper, unfolded it. The red stain formed angel patterns across the fabric of the page. He read the typewritten words.

SS-Obersturmbannführer Skorzeny,
We are coming for you.
Await our call.

'Has Skorzeny seen this?' Ryan asked.

Fitzpatrick said, 'Colonel Skorzeny has been made aware of the message.'

'Colonel Skorzeny and I will be attending a function in Malahide in a few days,' Haughey said. 'You will report to us there with your findings. The director will give you the details. Understood?'

'Yes, Minister.'

'Grand.' Haughey stood. He paused. 'My tailor,' he said, tearing a sheet from a notepad. He scribbled a name, address and phone number. 'Lawrence McClelland on Capel Street. Go and see him, have him fit you up with something. Tell him to put it on my account. Can't be putting you in front of a man like Otto Skorzeny wearing a suit like that.'

Ryan dropped the bloody envelope on the desk and took the details from Haughey. He kept his face expressionless. 'Thank you, Minister,' he said.

Fitzpatrick ushered Ryan to the door. As they were about to exit, Haughey called, 'Is it true what I heard? That you fought for the Brits during the Emergency?'

Ryan stopped. 'Yes, Minister.'

Haughey let his gaze travel from Ryan's shoes to his face in one long distasteful stare. 'Sort of young, weren't you?'

'I lied about my age.'

'Hmm. I suppose that would explain your lack of judgement.'

3

THE SUN HUNG LOW IN THE SKY BY THE TIME RYAN DROVE into Salthill. His buttocks ached from the journey. Cutting west across the country, he'd paused outside Athlone to relieve his bladder by the roadside. On three occasions he had to stop and wait while a farmer herded cattle from one field to another. He saw fewer cars as he travelled further from Dublin, driving miles at a time without seeing anything more advanced than a tractor or a horse and cart.

He parked the Vauxhall Victor in the small courtyard adjoining the guesthouse. Fitzpatrick had handed him the keys along with a roll of pound and ten shilling notes, telling him not to go mad on it.

Ryan climbed out of the car and walked around to the entrance. A hardy wind carried salt spray up from the rocks. He tasted it on his lips. Gulls called and circled. Their excrement dotted the low wall that fronted the house.

The sign above the door read ST AGNES GUEST HOUSE, PROPRIETRESS MRS J. D. TOAL. He rang the bell and waited.

A white form appeared behind the frosted glass, and a woman called, 'Who's there?'

'My name is Albert Ryan,' he said. 'I'm investigating the crime that occurred here.'

'Are you with the Guards?'

'Not quite,' he said.

The door cracked open, and she peeked out at him. 'If you're not the Guards, then who are you?'

Ryan took his wallet from his pocket and held up the identification card.

'I'll need my glasses,' she said.

'I'm from the Directorate of Intelligence.'

'The what?'

'Like the Guards,' he said. 'But I work for the government. Are you Mrs Toal?'

'Yes,' she said. She looked back to the card. 'I can't read that. I need to find my glasses.'

'Can I come in while you look for them?'

She hesitated, then closed the door. Ryan heard a chain slide back. She opened the door and allowed him to enter.

'I don't mean to be rude,' she said as he followed her into the dim hallway. 'It's just I've been plagued with all sorts of people since the news got out. Newspapermen, mostly, and others who just want to see if the body's still here. Monsters, all of them. Ah, here we are.'

She lifted her spectacles from a table and perched them on her nose. 'Let me see that again.'

Ryan handed her the card. She studied it, reading every word, before handing it back.

'I've already told the Guards everything I know. I'm not sure I can tell you anything different.'

'Maybe not,' Ryan said. 'But I'd like to speak with you anyway.'

He looked into the room to his left where a middle-aged couple and a young priest took their leisure. The lady read a paperback book, while the gentleman smoked a pipe. The priest studied the racing pages of the *Irish Times*, marking the listings with a stubby pencil. Mrs Toal reached in and pulled the door closed.

'I'd rather you didn't disturb my guests,' she said.

'I won't. Perhaps I could take a look at the room where the body was found. Then maybe we could have a chat.'

She turned her gaze to the stairs, as if some terrible creature listened from the floors above. 'I suppose.'

Mrs Toal went ahead. Old photographs of Salthill and Galway City hung on the walls alongside prints of Christ and the Virgin, and what appeared to be family portraits of generations past.

'It's a shocking thing,' she said, her breath shortening as she climbed. 'He seemed a nice enough man. Why someone would want to do that to him, I really don't know. He may have been a foreigner, but that doesn't account for it. And there's me all booked out for next month, all them people coming in to see President Kennedy when he visits – they're landing the helicopters just up the road, you know – and now I've got blood all over my carpet. I'll have to do that room top to bottom. How can I expect anyone to stay in there with blood on the carpet? Here we are.'

She stopped at a door bearing the number six and fished a ring of keys from a pocket in her skirt. 'I'll not go in with you, if you don't mind,' she said as she turned the key in the lock.

'That's fine,' Ryan said.

He put his fingers to the handle, but Mrs Toal seized his wrist.

'I'll tell you one thing,' she said, her voice dropping low. 'There was drink taken. I found a bottle on the bedside locker.

I don't know what sort of drink it was, but they'd been at it when it happened.'

'Is that right?' Ryan asked.

'Oh, it is. And he wouldn't be the first man to meet his death when drink was taken. I know. My husband was one of them. He died right outside my front door. He had a bellyful of whiskey and porter one night, then he fell on those rocks out there. Split his head open and drowned when the tide came in.'

'I'm very sorry to hear that,' Ryan said, meaning it. 'I'll come and find you when I'm finished here.'

'All right, so.' She nodded and went to the stairs. 'Call me if you need anything.'

Alone, Ryan turned the handle and entered the room.

The smell came first, like metal and meat gone bad. He coughed and brought one hand up to cover his nose and mouth. With the other, he felt for the light switch and flicked it on.

A simple guesthouse room like any he'd ever stayed in. Tasteful floral wallpaper, patterned carpet, a washbasin in one corner, a wardrobe in another. A single bed with one locker beside it, and a chair facing them both.

And a reddish-brown cluster on the wall, small pieces of solid matter barely visible from this side of the room.

Ryan took slow steps towards the foot of the bed. Beyond it, a dark pool on the carpet, the vague shape of a folded body scraped in chalk. Powder dusted the surfaces of the windowsill and the bedside locker, ghosts of fingertips scattered through it.

A small suitcase sat open on the floor at the foot of the bed. Ryan crouched down next to it and sorted through the items within. Underwear, socks, three packets of Peter Stuyvesant cigarettes, and a bottle of imported vodka. He stood. A wash bag sat on the edge of the basin, a shaving brush and a razor, a toothbrush and cologne.

He caught sight of his reflection in the mirror above them. Tiredness weighed on his features. He had been jowly since his late twenties. Now aged thirty-six, he sometimes felt he looked like a forlorn bloodhound, especially when fatigue darkened his eyes.

A movement in the reflection startled him.

'Are you the G2 fella?' a voice asked.

Ryan turned. A man wearing a shabby suit and overcoat stood in the doorway. He held up his open wallet.

'Detective Garda Michael Harrington,' he said, returning the wallet to his pocket. 'I was told you'd be visiting us, but I didn't expect you for a day or two yet.'

Ryan extended his hand. 'I wanted to get a head start, see the room before too much time passed.'

Harrington stared at the offered hand for a moment before shaking it. He held a manila folder in the other. 'Fair enough. I've got this report for you. If you want a look at the body, it's over at the Regional Hospital.'

Krauss's naked body lay on the steel table, eyes closed, dry lips slightly pursed and parted as if locked in an eternal whisper. A Y-shaped incision traversed his torso, from the greying cloud of pubic hair to his shoulders. It had been neatly stitched after his organs had been returned to their rightful places. Below his navel was a hole, scorched and puckered.

Another line of stitches started behind one ear, ran across the top of his head, and terminated at the other ear. Ryan pictured the pathologist slicing the scalp, peeling it forward until it covered the eyes like a mask, sawing out a section of the skull, and finally removing the demolished brain.

It had been on Ryan's eighteenth birthday that he first saw the inside of a man's skull. A mist-shrouded field in Holland, some miles north of Nijmegen. Ryan couldn't remember the corporal's name, only that his head had opened like a crushed melon, bone and blood tearing away, the grey within.

He had dropped to the ground, the damp of the mud seeping through his uniform, and crawled to the hedgerow twenty yards ahead, certain beyond all doubt his own brain would be smashed out of his head at any moment. When he reached the others, the sergeant said, 'Wipe your face off, lad.'

Ryan had reached up, felt the wetness and grit there, and vomited on himself.

He was no longer so squeamish.

On a drainer by a large sink, two acrylic glass vials held the deformed bullets. Ryan lifted and examined each in turn.

'We dug one out of the headboard,' Harrington said. 'It went through the intestine and the kidney and out the back. The other was still in his head. The quack fished it out, said the brain was like jelly. He had to ladle it out. I didn't understand that. There's a hole blown out at the other side of his head from where the bullet went in, there was stuff on the wall, but still the quack found that inside him.'

'Gases,' Ryan said. 'They expand inside the head and push outwards. If the killer used a suppressor, the bullet would have lost velocity. That's why it didn't exit the skull, and why the other only got as far as the headboard.'

'Ah,' Harrington said, doing a poor job of feigning interest. 'Well, you live and learn.'

Ryan had read what little information the report contained as Harrington drove him over to the hospital. The only identifiable fingerprints in the room belonged to Krauss. The rest were a faded mishmash of traces left by Mrs Toal and every guest who had stayed in the room in recent weeks. It seemed the killer had touched nothing with bare fingers.

A few possessions lay on a plastic tray. The lighter and cigarette case drew Ryan's attention. He took a pen from his pocket and used it to turn the case, the light picking out the fine lines of the engraving.

Harrington noted Ryan's interest. 'I suppose that's why a G2 fella's looking into this.'

Ryan did not reply.

'There used to be a man rented a farmhouse out towards Boleybeg, a German. He stayed there about six or seven years. There was all sorts of talk about him. I remember when he left, his cleaner told me she'd seen a swastika on his wall, and a painting of Hitler. I didn't believe her.'

Harrington waited as if hoping Ryan would express some surprise. When he didn't, Harrington continued.

'Then there's this Skorzeny, the Austrian, living in Kildare. I saw him in the newspaper, shaking hands with some bigwigs at a party. I'd never support the British, but what them Nazis did wasn't right. I don't like them coming and settling here just because we're soft on them.'

'I've seen enough,' Ryan said.

4

'WHAT ARE YOU DOING LANDING IN ON US THIS LATE?' RYAN'S mother asked.

'I was passing,' Ryan lied. He had pulled over at Athlone and agonised for five long minutes. In the end, he had headed north to Carrickmacree in County Monaghan instead of going straight back to Dublin.

The shopfront stood in darkness when Ryan approached along Main Street. He steered the Vauxhall to the rear of the block and parked behind the small van his father drove when he delivered bread and milk around the town. He let himself into the yard and knocked the door.

'You'd better come in, then,' his mother said. She stood back and allowed him to enter the small hallway.

Ryan's father stood at the top of the stairway, a dressing gown over striped pyjamas, thick socks on his feet.

'Who's that?' he called.

'It's Albert,' Ryan's mother said as she climbed the stairs towards him. Ryan followed.

'At this time?'

'That's what I said.' She looked back over her shoulder. 'If you'd telephoned, I could've had something on for you.'

Ryan never warned his parents in advance of a visit, and he always arrived in darkness. It had been ten years since there'd been any trouble, but still he remained cautious. They had nearly lost the shop after the petrol bombing. Before that, it had been Mahon and his cronies shouting insults in the street, stones thrown at windows, paint slashed across the glass once. Business had dwindled, almost to the point when his father would have to admit defeat and leave the town, but enough of the locals had resisted Mahon's pressure to boycott the shop to keep its doors open.

But the fire had been the worst of it, a last desperate act by a man too bitter and full of hate to let Albert Ryan's transgression go, and he had stayed away for a full year before returning.

On occasion, he wondered if he would have joined up and gone to fight for the British if he had known the cost to his parents. Every time, he dismissed it as foolishness, knowing a boy of seventeen could have no such wisdom even if granted the foresight. He had stolen the money from his father's safe to buy passage from Carrickmacree across the border to Belfast, then made his way to the nearest recruiting office, never once thinking of his mother's tears.

Now he sat at his mother's table with a mug of steaming tea, butter melting on a slab of toast. He hadn't the appetite what with the mortuary's low odours still lurking in his nasal passages, but he ate anyway.

Once the plate was clear, he asked his father how business was.

'Not the best,' his father said.

'Why?'

His father fell silent, staring into his mug. Instead, Ryan's mother answered.

'It's the Trades Association,' she said. 'And that auld bastard Tommy Mahon.'

She covered her mouth, shocked at herself for uttering such coarse language.

'What did they do?'

Ryan's father looked up from his tea. 'Mahon decided he wanted me out of business for good, so he set his son up with a wee cash-and-carry down the way. He got his friends in the Association to have a word with some of my suppliers. Now I can't get milk or bread. The only meat I can get is from old man Harney and his sons. They butcher their own animals out at their farm. The only eggs I can get is what I can buy when I'm out on my rounds.'

'They can't do that,' Ryan said. 'Can they?'

'Of course they can. They can do whatever they want. They call it protectionism. The associations, the unions, all them boys scratching each other's backs. They have this country by the balls, and they're going to run us into the ground.'

'Maurice!' Ryan's mother scolded.

'Well, they do.'

Ryan's mother changed the subject. 'So, are you courting?'

Ryan felt the heat spread from his neck up to his cheeks. 'No, Ma. You know I've no time for that.'

'Och, you're thirty-six,' she said. 'You'll be too old if you wait any longer.'

'Leave him alone,' Ryan's father said. 'He's got time enough for that yet. There's old man Harney's boys are all past thirty, one of them's over forty, and he's no notion of letting them get married yet.'

Ryan's mother snorted. 'Sure, why would he when he's got four big lads working for him and not a penny to pay for it? Our Albert's not a farmer. He should be finding himself a nice wee girl and getting settled.'

'I'm far too busy,' Ryan said. 'Besides, I'm living at the camp. I need a place of my own before I can go chasing after women.'

Ryan's mother sat back in her chair, raised an eyebrow. 'And what would you need a place of your own for? No decent girl would go to a bachelor's home. And any that would, well, she wouldn't be the sort for marrying, would she?'

Ryan slept hard and deep in his old room, tired from the day's driving. The bed creaked and rattled as he stirred with the morning's early light. He borrowed his father's razor to shave at the washbasin in the corner of the cold bedroom, goose pimples sprouting across his body.

Once washed and dressed, Ryan made his way downstairs, creeping to the back door. His mother intercepted him.

'Where are you off to?' she asked.

'Just thought I'd take a quick walk. I haven't seen the town in ages.'

'All right,' his mother said. 'Don't be too long. I'll have some breakfast for you when you get back.'

The sun grazed the rooftops as he strolled along Main Street, a man walking a horse down the centre of the road the only other person he saw. The sound of the animal's hooves echoed from the buildings. The man nodded as he passed. A cool breeze made Ryan button his suit jacket.

He passed shopfronts, businesses generations old, with hand-painted signs above the windows, prices and offers written in white on the glass. A needlecraft shop, a dressmaker, a gentlemen's outfitter.

They all seemed smaller now, as if the wood and bricks and glass had shrunk over the last twenty years. In the farthest parts of his soul, Ryan knew the reasons he seldom returned owed as much to his resentment of these buildings as they did to Tommy Mahon's bullying. As a boy, he had felt a town like this was no place for him, its streets too few and too narrow, the people mired in its quicksand. Even now, he felt the place tug at his ankles, trying to regain its hold on him.

As a teenager, Ryan had wondered at his father's endurance of the town, unable to understand how he did not crave a better life, a bigger life. One day, he asked his father why he took on the family business despite the pittance that it earned, why he had not left and made his own world elsewhere.

'Because you've only got the life you're given,' Ryan's father had said. 'And it's good enough.'

But Ryan knew it would never be good enough. Not then, not now.

He stood outside the shop with the sign saying MAHON'S CASH'N'CARRY. Dark inside. He tried the door, found it locked.

Ryan took another look along the street, saw it was empty, and walked around to the rear of the building. A large car, a Rover, was parked in the alleyway, and a bicycle stood propped against the wall. Ryan heard a voice issuing commands from inside the building. He approached the open doors.

Gerard Mahon, Tommy Mahon's son, stood smoking a cigarette with his back to the alley. A young boy, no more than thirteen or fourteen years old, stacked boxes of washing powder at Mahon's instruction.

'Good morning,' Ryan said.

Mahon turned. He had gained weight since Ryan had last seen him, his face bloating with the onset of middle age. He stared for a moment before recognition softened his expression.

'Albert Ryan? Holy Jesus, I haven't seen you for years. I thought you'd fucked off to England.'

'I'm just visiting my parents.' Ryan stepped into the shadow of the doorway, felt the cold of the building, smelled bleach and tobacco. 'I see you're branching out.'

Mahon smiled and took a drag on the cigarette. 'A new venture. Your auld fella can't have all the business to himself.'

'I suppose he can't.' Ryan took another step inside. 'It's a funny thing, though. I heard he's been having some trouble with his suppliers since your father set you up with this place.'

Mahon's smile became a bitter slash. He wagged a finger in Ryan's direction. 'I set this place up myself. Anyone who says different is a lying bastard.' Mahon turned to the boy, who had stopped stacking boxes to watch the two men. 'Get into the shop. The floor needs mopping. Go on, quick now.'

The boy did as he was told and exited the storeroom.

Mahon turned back, flinched when he found Ryan so close. Ryan stood several inches taller than the other man and he used every one of them.

'I heard someone had a word with the Trades Association and made sure the suppliers stopped dealing with my father.'

Mahon shook his head. 'I don't know what you're talking about. If your auld fella can't stand a bit of competition, he'd best pack up and get out.' Emboldened, Mahon raised himself to his full height. 'He should've got out a long time ago. We could do with a few less of your kind around here, anyway.'

'My kind? What kind is that, exactly?'

Mahon licked his lips, swallowed, sucked on his cigarette. 'Protestants,' he said, exhaling smoke to plume into Ryan's face. 'Especially when they breed Brit lovers like you.'

Ryan slapped the cigarette from his mouth. Mahon stepped back, eyes wide.

'Here, now, you better watch who you're—'

The blow caught Mahon beneath his Adam's apple. He dropped to the floor, his knees cracking on the concrete, his hands going to his throat. Ryan kicked him hard between the navel and groin. Mahon collapsed onto his belly, his face turning from pink to purple.

Ryan undid his belt buckle and stood astride Mahon. The leather came free with one pull, and he crossed his hands to form a loop. He bent down, slipped the loop over Mahon's head and around his neck.

Mahon gave an agonised croak as Ryan hauled him up onto his knees. He brought his fingers to his throat, tried to force them between the belt and his skin. Ryan tightened his hold. Mahon's body jerked and bucked.

Ryan put his lips to Mahon's ear. 'Now listen to me. I will call my father in two days. If he doesn't tell me his suppliers have delivered everything he wants, I will come back for you. Do you understand me?'

He loosened the belt. Mahon choked on air. Ryan pulled again, tighter than before.

'Do you understand me?'

He allowed Mahon to inhale.

Mahon mouthed a word, the only sound the hissing sibilant at its tail. He nodded and coughed, drool spilling from his lips.

Ryan took the belt away, let Mahon crumple to the floor. He walked to the doorway to the alley. Looking back over his shoulder, he said, 'Two days.'

Mahon writhed, his hands up to deflect a blow that would never come.

Albert Ryan returned to his parents' home, enjoyed the cooked breakfast his mother had prepared, and then set off for Dublin.

5

BUSWELLS HOTEL STOOD NEAR THE CORNER OF MOLESWORTH Street and Kildare Street, the white citadel and green gardens of Trinity College to the north, the sprawling open pastures and leafy walkways of St Stephen's Green to the south. The voices of paperboys called the headlines over the grumbling of traffic. The bus strike had ended only a few days before, and the passengers looked happy to no longer have to rely on the substitute transport the army had provided.

The hotel's receptionist handed Ryan a note along with his key as he checked in. He had stopped off at Gormanston on the way to Dublin and gathered a few clothes and wash things into the bag that now lay at his feet. The restaurant jangled and chattered with lunchtime clientele. Ryan recognised a Teachta Dála, an Irish member of parliament, watching a young woman cross the foyer, a key in her hand, heels clicking on the white marble floor. She paused at the foot of the stairs leading to the guest rooms, glanced back over her shoulder at the TD, and climbed. The Oireachtas, the seat of Ireland's government, stood just yards around the corner. Buswells hosted many politicians and their companions, their secretaries, their assistants. The beds above creaked with the secret passions of the country's leaders.

The TD waited a few moments before following the young woman, unaware he was being observed.

Ryan had never stayed at Buswells. It was not the city's most luxurious hotel – the Shelbourne and the Royal Hibernian offered greater decadence – but the room that had been placed at his disposal would certainly be better accommodation than he was used to.

He carried the note and the bag upstairs, found his room on a small landing, at the junction of two flights of carpeted steps. It held a single bed, a wardrobe, a corner washbasin and a radio on a bedside locker. Yellow and brown nicotine stains clouded the ceiling. Through the greying net curtain over the lone window, across the road, he saw the grandeur of the Freemasons' Hall, white stone columns and arches, like a Greek temple transplanted to a city side street. Ryan dropped his bag on the bed, took off his jacket and sat down. He opened the note.

Ryan,

Make sure you go and see my tailor today. I want you looking presentable when you meet our friend in Malahide tomorrow night.

C.J.H.

Ryan fingered the fabric of his jacket. It had been a reasonable suit when it was new – any man would have felt well turned out in it – but it had begun to show its age. He had admired Haughey's attire the previous day, the cut of the cloth, the way it flattered his frame. Even if you hadn't known he was a government minister, you would have recognised a man of wealth and influence. It took more than quality fabric to give such an impression, of course, but it couldn't hurt.

Albert Ryan knew he had a streak of vanity, and of pride,

like a vein of silver running through rock. That part of him smarted when he saw younger men who were better dressed, or who drove shining cars. He did not like this aspect of himself, found it ugly and not in keeping with a man of his upbringing. His parents had taught him the virtue of austerity, the Presbyterian values of modesty and hard work.

But still, the beauty of the clothing on Haughey's back gave Ryan a longing in his soul.

He slipped his jacket on, left the room, and made his way back down to reception with the intention of having lunch. He crossed the high-ceilinged lounge. The maître d' greeted him at the glass doors to the restaurant. Ryan paused and surveyed the room and the diners, the expanse of white linen tablecloths, glittering silverware. His gaze travelled across finely cut lapels, French cuffs, silk ties.

The maître d' said, 'For one, sir?'

Ryan watched the women draped on the men, the jewels and pale skin.

The maître d' leaned closer. 'Sir?'

Ryan coughed. 'Actually, I'm not hungry. Thank you.'

He left the restaurant, exited the building, headed north towards the river, and Capel Street beyond.

'Canali,' Lawrence McClelland said, smoothing the jacket over Ryan's torso. 'From Triuggio in Lombardy, not far from Milan. Much sought after, not many in Dublin. Very, very nice.'

Ryan studied his form in the full length mirror. Even if the trousers were too short, and the jacket too roomy for his midsection, the suit still looked magnificent.

He was the tailor's sole customer, standing among racks of expensive cloth and tables laden with shirts and ties. The dark wooden panels seemed to rob the room of light and sound, a solemn quiet hanging over everything. A chapel of silk, herringbone and leather.

'Have you been to Italy?' McClelland asked.

'Yes,' Ryan said. 'Sicily.'

'Sicily? Oh, I hear it's quite lovely there,' the tailor said as he hunkered down to tug at the trouser hems. 'I'm more familiar with Milan and Rome myself.'

Ryan had spent four days on the south-eastern Sicilian coast in late '45, a stopover on his way to Egypt. He had been billeted with three other men in an apartment in Siracusa, but he spent most of his time wandering the narrow streets of Ortigia, the tiny island connected to the mainland by a few short bridges.

He had rolled his sleeves up as he walked, opened his shirt wide, the sun beating on him like a blacksmith's hammer. In the evenings, the place smelled of sea salt and warm olive oil. He ate in the *trattorias* and *osterias* that clustered in the alleys. Ryan had never before seen, let alone tasted, pasta. He ate platefuls of it, mopping up the sauce with fresh bread. He seldom saw a menu; the choice of food was that of the house, rather than the diner, but he didn't mind. His lifelong diet had been either Irish or army food, the height of culinary sophistication a mixed grill in a swanky hotel, or perhaps a piece of fish on a Friday.

He took four days of pleasure in Sicily before crossing the short stretch of Mediterranean to Egypt and all its torments.

The tailor stood upright and set about Ryan with a measuring tape.

'Hmm.' McClelland placed his forefinger against his lips. 'I might struggle a little to make this work for a man of your stature. A man as deep as you are through the chest will often have a more generous waistband, whereas you're quite a slender fellow.'

He tucked the jacket into Ryan's flanks, pinned the fabric in place. Standing back, he eyed Ryan from head to foot, the travel of his gaze slow and languid. 'Athletic,' McLelland said. 'And long legged. But I think I can let the trouser down enough to suffice. With the right shoe, of course. When do you need the suit for?'

'Tomorrow night,' Ryan said. 'The minister said to put it on his account.'

McClelland's face greyed around a thin smile. 'Yes, the minister does like to take full advantage of our credit service.'

6

AS EVENING LIGHT FADED TO DARKNESS, ALBERT RYAN SPENT an hour at Helmut Krauss's small home on Oliver Plunkett Avenue, close to Dublin's docks. It stood at the middle of a terraced row of identical houses, Victorian or Edwardian, he couldn't be sure. They faced newly built tenement blocks, ugly structures that cast a sullen shadow over the street. A small patch of garden had been laid over with concrete slabs. A brass plaque by the doorbell carried the words HEINRICH KOHL: IMPORT, EXPORT, ESCROW SERVICES. A Garda officer waited on the doorstep to let Ryan in.

Inside the house, the parlour had been converted to a small office with an antique desk surrounded by filing cabinets. A telephone sat on the desk alongside a typewriter, a ledger and a selection of pens. The room contained only two chairs: one for Krauss, and one for a guest. It appeared the German did not employ a secretary.

Ryan opened the ledger at a random page and scanned the entries. Business names, ports of departure, dates, sums of money mostly in pounds. He ran his fingertip down the name column, turning from page to page, looking for anything of significance. The amounts of money were modest, the highest figures in the low thousands, and most only a few hundred. The ports covered northern

Europe, anywhere within easy sailing distance of Dublin or Dundalk.

He closed the book and turned his attention to the filing cabinets. All were unlocked and contained invoices, purchase orders, statements of account, and the occasional letter. Nothing to suggest Krauss had been involved in anything illegal while running his business here.

Ryan left the parlour-turned-office and went to the kitchen at the rear of the house. The cramped room smelled of grease and tobacco. A dresser stood to one side, well stocked with alcohol. Krauss apparently had a taste for vodka. Boxes of bottles sat piled on the floor, emblazoned with Russian text, obviously a perk of his import business.

A tin bath stood propped in the corner, a privy in the backyard. Ryan opened the cupboards, found nothing but stale bread, tinned food and cleaning materials. He made his way upstairs.

Two small bedrooms, one disused, the other filled with neatly arranged personal bric-a-brac. Rolled socks and underwear lay on the unmade bed, the items Krauss had chosen not to take on his trip to Salthill.

An open letter lay on a bedside table. Ryan reached for the lamp beside it, flicked it on so that he could make out the text in the thickening darkness. He sat on the edge of the bed and examined the single sheet of paper. German, handwritten in a neat script. Ryan understood little, but he recognised the name of Johan Hambro, and that of the churchyard near Galway he had been buried at a few days ago.

Given the mild disarray of the room, Ryan guessed that Krauss had left in a hurry, not taking time to tidy away the rejected clothes or make his bed. Krauss seemed to have been a man of order and discipline. Ryan imagined the German would be embarrassed to know a stranger now observed the mess in his home, however minor.

A chest of drawers faced the foot of the bed. Ryan opened the first drawer and searched through the folded shirts with their frayed cuffs and replacement buttons. The second held more socks and underwear, and the third revealed more of the same. But underneath them, a bed of photographs, postcards and letters.

Ryan lifted them out, one by one. The letters were mostly in German, and after a few, he gave up trying to distinguish recognisable names from the tangles of words. Instead, he focused on the photographs.

Many were family portraits, stern mothers and fathers, round-faced children, the occasional horse or dog. A few showed rows of uniformed men, tall men, strong men, peaked caps on their heads, lightning bolts on their collars. Some were formal portraits, the men standing upright or sitting with their hands clamped to their knees, staring hard at the camera. Others showed them eating and drinking, collars loosened, laughter almost audible from the heavy paper.

When Ryan thought of his time on the Continent, back when he was a boy pretending to be a man, these were the scenes he wished he could isolate in his memory. Officers lined up at long tables, mugs of beer, voices raised so high it made his eardrums hurt. But when he tried to focus on such sounds and images, others crept in, the burnt and bloodied things, the howls and screams.

Yet he could not leave that life behind.

The only place that felt like a home was a barracks. The town or country didn't matter, whether he slept in his room at Gormanston Camp, or some tin hut in a foreign field. Ryan might have understood this to be unhealthy had he ever given it thought.

In truth, he wasn't sure if he missed having what most men would consider a home. A wife and children. Walls to contain them all. He had grown accustomed to eating in mess halls, sleeping on thin mattresses, living by the orders of his superiors. Only occasionally did he awake in the night, terrified by the advancing years and what his future life would be when the surrogate family he had chosen had no more use for him.

Ryan leafed through the photographs until he found one, a formal portrait of a young man, his cap worn with pride, his buttons shining in the studio's lights. He recognised the handsome face of Helmut Krauss, twenty years before he lay dissected on a mortuary table. Such confidence, the certainty held in the eyes, the subtle smile on the lips.

You never thought you could lose, Ryan thought. At one time, Helmut Krauss and his kind were sure they would possess the earth and every soul who dwelled upon it. Now Krauss burned in whatever hell had been set aside for him. Ryan searched his soul for pity and found none.

He returned the photographs and letters to the drawer before dropping to his knees and peering underneath the bed. A box lay within arm's reach. A trail through the dust showed that the Guards had already dragged it out and examined its contents. Ryan grabbed the box's edge and pulled, hoisted it up onto the bed, folded back the lid.

The Guards had been instructed to leave everything as they found it. Including the Luger P08 and Walther P38 pistols that lay on top of the red cloth, along with the paper bag of loose nine-millimetre Parabellum rounds and a single leather holster. Ryan lifted the weapons from the box, examining each of them in turn. They appeared well maintained, smelled of fresh oil. He set them side by side on the bed, placed the holster and the bag of rounds next to them, and lifted the red cloth.

It unfolded to a large rectangle, a white circle at its centre, black lines intersecting. Ryan bundled the swastika into a ball and dropped it to the floor.

A manila folder lay at the bottom of the box. Ryan lifted the folder, opened it, revealing loose typewritten letters written in English. He read the first.

To whom it may concern,
This letter is to confirm that the bearer, Helmut Krauss, has been known to me for many years. I can attest to his honesty, integrity and general good character. Should any further reference be required, please write to me at the above address.
Yours sincerely,
Bishop Jean-Luc Prideaux

It listed an address in Brittany. Ryan flipped through the remaining dozen, more letters of reference, all praising Helmut Krauss. The last few were replies from the Department of Justice. Ryan picked out phrases from the text.

This department has no objection . . .
A man of good standing . . .
On condition that Mr Krauss does not . . .

Ryan returned the folder to the box, covered it with the swastika. He looked down at the two pistols, black and glowering on the bedspread. The Luger was much loved by collectors; Ryan had known many soldiers who had taken them home from the front, trophies of their battles on the Continent. But the Walther was also a handsome weapon, similar in performance to the Luger, but a more modern design by thirty or more years.

He tried each of them in the holster, found the Walther a better fit. That decided it. Ryan stripped the case from a pillow, stuffed the Walther, holster and rounds inside, and knotted the opening. He dropped the Luger into the box, which he slid back beneath the bed.

As he left the house, Ryan thanked the Garda officer who had let him in.

'I'm just taking a few items for examination,' he said, showing the weighted pillowcase.

The officer did not object.

7

'HELLO, WHO IS THIS?' A MAN ANSWERED WITH A THICK EASTERN European accent.

'My name is Albert Ryan. I'd like to speak with the rabbi of your congregation.'

Ryan sat on the edge of his bed in Buswells, the telephone to his ear. The skin on his throat stung from shaving. Morning sun warmed his back.

'Well, you are. I am Rabbi Joseph Hempel. How may I help you?'

It took less than fifteen minutes to drive south from the city centre to the synagogue on Rathfarnham Road. The building stood back from the street, separated by a high wall and hedge, with well tended gardens. It was a grey block of a structure, flat roofed, with five windows in the shape of the Star of David above a row of square glass panes. Its sturdy bulk, and the walls around it, gave the synagogue the appearance of a compound under siege.

Ryan pulled into the driveway through the open gates. Rabbi Hempel stood waiting in the doorway. He was a middle-aged man with square-framed spectacles, casually dressed in a knitted vest over an open-collar shirt and a suede kippah on his crown. His beard almost reached the bottom of the V formed by his top button. He extended his hand as Ryan got out of the car and approached.

'Mr Ryan?' he asked.

Ryan shook his hand. 'Thank you for agreeing to speak with me.'

'Not at all. Come to my office.'

Stained-glass windows refracted the morning light inside the synagogue, bathing the rows of seats in a warm peace. The rabbi led Ryan to a room to the rear of the building. It was a modestly appointed office, books lined up on shelves, a sparse desk.

'Please, sit down,' Rabbi Hempel said. Once they were seated, and Ryan had declined any refreshments, the rabbi asked, 'Are you a policeman?'

'No,' Ryan said. 'I work for the Directorate of Intelligence.'

'But you want to talk to me about a crime?'

'Three crimes. Three murders, to be exact.'

The rabbi's lips pursed with concern. 'Oh, dear. I can promise you I know nothing of such crimes.'

Ryan smiled to reassure him. 'I know. But if I explain the nature of the murders you might understand why I've come to you.'

Rabbi Hempel sat back in his chair. 'I'm listening.'

Ryan told him about Renders and Hambro, and Helmut Krauss, and the blood on the floor of the guesthouse in Salthill. He told the rabbi about the note addressed to Skorzeny.

Rabbi Hempel sat in silence for a few seconds, gazing at Ryan across the desk, before he said, 'I am not sure what alarms me more: that these people are permitted to come and live in peace in Ireland, or that your first assumption is that only a Jew could do such a thing.'

'It is not my assumption,' Ryan said.

The rabbi leaned forward. 'And yet here you are.'

'It's a line of inquiry I was instructed to pursue by my superiors.'

'Orders.'

'Yes. Orders.'

Rabbi Hempel smiled. 'So many men have simply followed orders. The men who shot my parents and my elder sister at the edge of a ditch they had just forced them to dig, they were following orders. Does that absolve them?'

'No,' Ryan said. 'But nevertheless, you must see why I have been asked to follow this line.'

'I do indeed see the reason. It's likely a different reason than you believe it to be, but please, go ahead.'

'Thank you. Are you aware of any groups within your community, perhaps younger men, who have strong feelings about the war?'

Ryan realised the stupidity of the question too late, felt heat spread across his face.

'I promise you, Mr Ryan, all in my community have strong feelings about the war.'

'Of course,' Ryan said. 'I apologise.'

The rabbi nodded his acceptance. 'That aside, there are no organised groups that I'm aware of. There are less than two thousand Jewish people left on the whole island of Ireland now, possibly only fifteen hundred. I can barely gather enough for a congregation. Believe me, there are no groups of disaffected young men, hungry for blood.'

'To your knowledge,' Ryan said.

Rabbi Hempel shrugged. 'Who would have the motive? We have suffered comparatively little persecution here. The ugly episode in Limerick at the start of the century, some call it a pogrom, but those who were driven out were in turn welcomed in Cork. The bureaucrats at the Department of Justice did their best to block Jewish refugees entering Ireland before and after the war, but the Department of External Affairs put pressure on de Valera to intervene. Ireland has not always been welcoming, but seldom has it been overtly hostile. These are not the conditions that put hate in young men's hearts.'

Ryan almost laughed, but choked it back. 'There's no shortage of hatred in this country.'

'The Irish have long memories,' Rabbi Hempel said. 'I have lived in Ireland for more than ten years, and this was my first understanding of its people. Were it not so, perhaps Britain might have had another ally against the Germans. Instead, Ireland sat on its hands and watched as Europe burned.'

Ryan thought about letting it go, almost did, but said, 'Ireland had barely found its feet as a state. It had been through the First World War, the War of Independence and the Civil War, all in less than a decade. It couldn't afford to go to war again. It didn't have the strength. Even so, a hundred thousand of us fought.'

The rabbi raised his thick eyebrows. 'You?'

'Yes.'

'And did your neighbours appreciate your fighting for the British?'

'No, not all of them.'

Rabbi Hempel nodded. 'Like I said. Long memories.'

As Ryan eased out of the synagogue's driveway, heading back towards town, he saw the black car parked further down the road. And its two occupants, both men, neither of them watching him.

In his rear-view mirror, he saw the car pull out from the kerb. It kept a distance of thirty yards or so. He glanced as he drove, trying to make out the men's features. All he saw were shapes, shoulders and heads, the impressions of shirts and ties. One of them smoked a cigarette.

As he crossed Terenure Road, another car pulled between them, driven by an elderly lady, forcing the driver of the black car to brake. It edged to the centre of the road, allowing the man at the wheel to keep Ryan in sight.

It stayed there, maintaining its distance, until Ryan reached Harold's Cross, where he pulled to the kerb. He watched in the mirror as the black car slowed then turned off towards the cemetery.

Ryan might have worried about who followed him, which thin finger of the government crept after him, but he had other things on his mind as he pulled away.

He had a suit to collect.

8

CÉLESTIN LAINÉ DOWNED ANOTHER SHOT OF WHISKEY, LET IT bite his throat. Barely seven o'clock, and Paddy Murtagh was already drunk. Before long, he would start to sing. Rebel songs, he called them. The Bold Fenian Men, The Wearing of the Green, Johnson's Motor Car. He would raise his voice, hoarse and tuneless, and would not fall silent until he passed out.

At least Lainé would not have to endure it alone this evening. Elouan Groix, a fellow Breton patriot, also sat at the table in the small cottage. Murtagh's father had given Lainé the use of the two-room dwelling in a remote corner of his farmland, thus the young Murtagh was made welcome out of a sense of obligation.

Lainé and other members of Bezen Perrot, the small but dedicated band that he had led in the fight against the Allies, had fled to Ireland in the aftermath of the war. They had held on longer than many of the Germans they had battled alongside, but in the end there remained no other choice but to run.

As a young man, Lainé had read *La vie de Patrice Pearse* by Louis le Roux. He had been left with a sense of awe, and of duty to those who had been martyred for Ireland in 1916. Like many autonomists, he had felt in his heart that those Irish lives had been sacrificed not just for Ireland, but also for men like him. The struggle to throw the French yoke off Breton shoulders needed the same spirit as had been shown by the Irish if it were to succeed, that shared Celtic fire in the warriors' bellies.

The coming of the Reich had seemed like a kiss from God. A gift, a means to achieve what Bretons lacked the might to do for themselves. So as France fell, Lainé organised and recruited, armed his men with weapons supplied by the Germans, and fought.

Soon, Lainé discovered a talent he had never suspected he possessed. He had trained and worked as a chemical engineer, a useful vocation when manufacturing explosive devices, but a newly unearthed ability shocked everyone, including himself: he found he had an innate expertise in dragging information from prisoners.

On a hot night early in the occupation, Lainé and three comrades captured a Resistance fighter in fields north of Nantes. Two others had got away. Lainé began by asking for the names of the escaped men. The prisoner refused, giving only his own name, Sylvain Depaul. He was not from the area. Lainé would have known him otherwise.

They blindfolded Depaul and brought him to a barn on a sloping hillside. Cattle slept all around, oblivious to the men who crossed their fields. Lainé bound the *résistant* to a pillar. His wrists were slippery with sweat as they were fixed in place, tied tight to the wood. Depaul's own belt was wrapped around his neck and buckled at the rear of the pillar, leaving him pinned and choking.

'Who were the others?' Lainé asked again.

'I've already told you,' Depaul said, the words coughed out from his restricted throat. 'I was alone. I was just out walking.'

'With a Browning pistol?' Lainé stroked Depaul's cheek with the weapon's muzzle.

'For rabbits. I was going to make a fire and cook one.'

Lainé stabbed at Depaul's lips with the muzzle, mashing the flesh against his teeth. Depaul turned his head away as far as the belt would allow, blood spilling from his torn skin.

'I have no patience for this,' Lainé said. 'This is not a game. If you cooperate, you might live. I can't guarantee that, but it remains a possibility. On the other hand, if you lie, if you hold back information, then it is a certainty that you will suffer and die.'

In Lainé's mind, they were only words. He had been interrogated by police officers years ago, after the bombing of the Monument to the Unity of Brittany and France in Rennes. They screamed question after question at him, slapped his face, pulled his hair. Harsh, but hardly torture. He had never experienced such a thing. So he was as surprised as anyone when he set the pistol aside, took an ivory-handled penknife from his pocket, heated the blade in the flame of the oil lamp until its tip glowed, then pressed it against Depaul's cheek.

As the *résistant* howled, and the other men coughed at the smell of scorched meat, Lainé felt a surge of something he did not recognise in his chest. Power? Pride? As Depaul cried, Lainé smiled.

'I'll ask you again,' he said. 'Who were the others who fled when we captured you?'

Depaul growled, spat blood on his own shirt, swallowed his pain. 'There was no one. I was alone.'

Lainé had not expected to be pleased at Depaul's refusal to speak. Nevertheless, there it was: the pleasure of anticipating the next cruel act. He returned the blade to the oil lamp's flame, watched as traces of Depaul's blood and skin bubbled and burned away.

'I was on my own,' Depaul said, his voice liquid, no longer hard and defiant. 'I swear. God help me, I'd tell you if there was anyone else, but there wasn't, I promise.'

Lainé reached behind the pillar, seized the thumb of Depaul's right hand.

'Once more, who were your companions?'

'Please, I was alone. There was—'

Lainé pushed the tip of the blade beneath Depaul's thumb-nail. Depaul screamed. The three Bretons stepped back. One of them ran outside, covering his mouth, vomit dribbling between his fingers.

Keeping the blade in place, Lainé asked, 'Who were your companions?'

Depaul shook his head from side to side, his voice stretching thin as his lungs emptied.

Lainé explored the tenderness beneath the nail. The blade's tip burrowed in, worked the keratin loose from the flesh until it peeled away.

Depaul talked.

He told them the names of his two companions, local men, and the location to which they had been heading. The British were to drop a crate by parachute into a field not even a mile away. When Lainé and his men reached it, they found it contained rifles, ammunition and radio equipment. Within twenty-four hours, Depaul's friends had been rounded up and executed alongside him.

As Lainé developed his newfound talent, his reputation travelled. Soon it only took the mention of the Breton's name to convince a *résistant* to talk. It would have been a lie to deny the pleasure of such notoriety. Power in its purest form. The power of fear. Lainé grew accustomed to it quickly and never suspected he would lose that power.

Now in Ireland, in his mid-fifties, he had nothing. He had lacked the foresight to rob and rape as the Reich crumbled, leaving him to run with empty pockets. Had it not been for the contacts he had made with the IRA – heroes to his mind – he might never have escaped the wrath of the Allies and found his way to Ireland.

Lainé still remembered the crushing disappointment of finally meeting the Irish revolutionaries he had so idolised. In his imagination, they were the noble defenders of the working Celtic man. They were Patrick Pearse, they were James Connolly, they were Michael Collins.

In truth, they were a disjointed network of farmers, socialists and fascists, bigots and blowhards, an army whose war had come and gone decades before. They had sided with the Nazis during the war, even formulating plans to assist the Germans in an invasion of Northern Ireland to oust the British presence there, but they proved themselves incapable of such ambitious schemes.

Fleeing in defeat had been like swallowing thorns for Célestin Lainé. But now, years later, he knew it was better than the hopeless purgatory the fanatics of the IRA wallowed in. They had not quite won their struggle for independence; the northern part of their island remained under the thumb of the British and their Protestant caretakers, while the rest of the nation was ruled by a self-serving government that had turned on the brave warriors whose sacrifice had made its very existence possible.

And now the best the IRA had to offer was ill-educated

louts like Paddy Murtagh and his belligerent father Caoimhín, full of songs about the virtuous struggle of revolution and precious little else.

As Lainé feared, young Murtagh placed his glass back on the table, inhaled a breath that rattled wet and thick at the back of his throat, and sang.

'Come all you warriors and renowned nobles, who once commanded brave warlike bands,' he slurred.

Elouan Groix gave Lainé a weary look. Lainé shrugged, raised a hand to say, what can I do?

Murtagh drew breath and let more of the dirge spill from his mouth. 'Throw down your plumes and your golden trophies, give up your arms with a trembling hand.'

As Murtagh inhaled at the end of the couplet, Lainé heard the dog outside in the yard. It jerked on its chain and let loose a torrent of yelps and barks.

He had found the animal at the side of a road two years ago, no more than a pup, its pelt clinging to its ribs, a waist so thin Lainé could encircle it with one hand. A month of nurture, and he had a healthy and devoted companion he called Hervé, a masculine name, even though the dog was a female. And one could not have wished for a more loyal and fearsome guardian.

Murtagh's voice rose to the next couplet.

Lainé lifted a hand and said, 'Quiet.'

Murtagh let his voice fall to a bubbling exhalation, stared at Lainé with confusion and mild hurt on his face.

'Listen,' Lainé said.

Hervé's cries rose in ferocity. Her chain jangled as she lunged out there in the weakening light.

'What?' Murtagh asked.

Groix placed a hand on the Irishman's wrist, squeezed, silenced him.

The dog's barks melded into a furious stream of noise, the chain jerking and snapping.

Lainé turned his head, peered out the window over the sink. He saw the post to which Hervé was tethered. The chain stretched beyond his vision, somewhere to the side of the cottage. The post leaned under the strain.

'We have a visitor,' Lainé said.

He watched the chain tauten and drop, tauten and drop, threatening to uproot the post. Herve's voice seemed to crack under the strain of her panic, reaching up and up until Lainé was sure it could climb no higher.

Then the dog fell silent, and the chain sagged to the ground.

9

A FULL-LENGTH MIRROR FRONTED THE WARDROBE IN RYAN'S hotel room. He stood before it, his shoulders back, chest forward, stomach in. The grey cloth of the suit clung to his body, accentuated the masculine, flattered his frame. Even, dare he think it, made him appear handsome. Ryan smoothed the tie. The silk whispered on his fingertips. The cufflinks sparked like flints on his wrists.

He did not look like a shopkeeper's son.

'You'll do,' he said.

The Grand Hotel overlooked Malahide estuary, north of Dublin, a broad wedding cake of a building, four storeys high, that had stood for more than a century. A receptionist directed Ryan to the function room. As he approached its doors, he heard a small swing band perform 'How High the Moon'.

Waiters cleared away the remains of the meal that had recently been eaten by the guests. Some government affair, Ryan surmised, diplomats, judges, politicians. Men of power enjoying the spoils. They clustered in groups, girls and their suitors, elder men and their greying wives.

Couples danced, most of them stiff-backed, their bodies apart. A few showed less restraint.

For a moment, Ryan felt an impostor, an interloper. He

didn't belong here, amongst these people with their money and their good taste. His hand went to the silk of his tie. Its texture against his fingertips offered a sliver of reassurance.

'Are you lost?' a velvet voice asked.

Ryan turned, saw her. He opened his mouth, but words betrayed him, his tongue a tripwire. She stood with a young woman Ryan recognised as Charles Haughey's secretary.

'Don't worry,' she said. 'We're all charlatans here. Come on. I'll let you get me a drink.'

She hooked her hand around his elbow, her forearm slender and bare, the skin of her wrist pale and freckled. In her heels, she stood only a few inches shorter than him, the length of her startling, the sleek line of her body drawing his eyes downwards. Deep red hair pinned up, eyes smoky green.

She gave her friend a smile and a wink as she guided Ryan away.

'Who are you with?' she asked.

Ryan gained control of his tongue. 'I have to meet someone.'

'Who?'

'The minister.'

She led him deeper into the room's currents. 'Which minister? We have several.'

'The Minister for Justice.'

She smiled. 'Charlie? I believe he's holding court at the bar. Which is handy, seeing as you're going to get me that drink.'

They walked together from the dimness of one room to the light of another. The music dulled; laughter and chatter swelled.

There was Haughey, perched on a high stool, surrounded by younger men, his face reddened with drink. He fixed Ryan with his hawk's stare, winked, and continued his story.

'You should've seen the fucker,' he said, spittle arcing from his thin lips. 'Galloping like his life depended on it. And it did, I'd have shot the bastard myself if he'd lost. Anyway, he's coming charging up the straight, and wee Turley the jockey, he's barely hanging on, he looks like he's shitting himself. That other fucker, I forget his name, he's looking back over his shoulder, sees my boy coming at him, I swear to God, he near fell off when he seen him.'

The young men laughed the laughter of the beholden.

Ryan felt warm air brush his ear, smelled lipstick. He shivered.

'I'll have a G & T,' she said. 'Lime. Never lemon.'

Ryan reached for his wallet.

Haughey called, 'Hey, hey, hey, get your hand out of your pocket, big fella. It's all taken care of.'

Ryan nodded his thanks and caught the barman's attention. 'Gin and tonic with lime, and a half of Guinness.'

She let her fingers drop from his elbow to join with his, pulled his hand close to her, his knuckles brushing her hip. 'Come on, a real drink.'

Heat bloomed on Ryan's cheeks. He coughed. 'Make that a brandy and ginger.'

'That's more like it,' she said. Her fingers tightened on his before releasing them. She turned, leaned her back and elbows on the bar, the silken fabric of her dress telling tales.

The heat on Ryan's cheeks spread to his neck.

She tilted her head, showing him the smooth place beneath her ear. 'You haven't asked my name.'

Ryan wondered for a moment if he should apologise. Instead, he put his hands in his pockets and feigned confidence. 'All right. What's your name?'

'Celia,' she said, letting the sibilant drip like honey, the vowels thick between her lips. 'What's yours?'

He told her as his assuredness flaked away like weathered paint.

'Well, Mr Ryan, what business do you have with Charles J. Haughey?'

'Private business,' he said, his voice harder than he intended.

She arched a sculpted eyebrow. 'I see.'

The sharp click of glass on marble, the shimmer of ice. Ryan handed Celia the gin and tonic. She held his stare as she sipped. Her tongue sought the glistening droplets on her lips.

Ryan swallowed the brandy's burn, couldn't meet her challenge. He might have seen the corner of her mouth curl in amusement as he looked away.

Haughey broke from his pack, the young men staring after him. He let his gaze crawl the length of Ryan's form, shoe to collar. 'McClelland take care of you all right?'

'Yes, Minister.' Ryan measured carefully the bow of his head, balancing deference and pride, the politician and the woman.

'Good.' Haughey nodded. 'You'll do all right. Won't he, Miss Hume?'

Celia's lips parted in a conspirator's smile. 'Yes he will,' she said.

Ryan couldn't be sure whose conspiracy she was part of, only that he desired it to be his own.

'Come on,' Haughey said. 'The colonel's waiting.'

As the minister turned away, Celia's finger snagged Ryan's.

'Be careful,' she said, her smile lost.

Ryan followed Haughey to a darkened stairwell. The minister lit a cigarette as he walked, didn't offer one to Ryan.

Mounting the steps, Haughey said, 'Watch yourself with Skorzeny. He's smart as a whip. Don't be clever with him. Try it, and he'll rip the shite out of you.'

'Yes, Minister.'

They exited the stairwell onto a carpeted corridor, numbered doors along the hallway. Haughey approached one set apart from the others. He knocked.

The door opened, swallowed Haughey, leaving Ryan alone in the corridor.

He leaned his back against the wall, not thinking of what waited inside the room. Instead, Ryan pictured the woman, remembered her scent, warm and sweet. Time passed, forgotten.

Haughey opened the door, stepped aside to allow two suited men to leave. They eyed Ryan as they passed. Once they had gone, the minister said, 'Come on.'

10

AS RYAN ENTERED THE SUITE, SKORZENY STOOD UP FROM THE leather-upholstered armchair, seeming to fill the room, the breadth and the height of him, the line of his shoulders stretching his pale suit like an oak beam. The scar traced a route from his eyebrow to the corner of his mouth, and onward to his chin, his moustache neat, his gaze bright. His thick greying hair swept back from his forehead.

Haughey stood between them, seemed smaller than he had a few minutes ago, the hawk gone from his eyes.

'Colonel, this is Lieutenant Albert Ryan, G2, Directorate of Intelligence.'

Skorzeny stepped forward, extended a hand so large it swallowed Ryan's whole. Ryan imagined the hard fingers could have crushed his own had the Austrian felt so inclined.

'Lieutenant,' Skorzeny said, the accent sharp and angular. He released his grip. 'The minister tells me you're the best he has. Is this so?'

Ryan's hand tingled deep between the bones. 'I don't think I can answer that, sir.'

'No? Who knows you better than yourself?'

While Ryan searched for a reply, Skorzeny filled two glasses with rich brown liquid from a decanter. He gave one to Haughey, sipped from the other, offered nothing to Ryan.

'Please sit,' he said.

Haughey took the other armchair, leaving Ryan the couch.

'The minister tells me you fought for the British during the war.'

Ryan cleared his throat. 'Yes, sir.'

'Why so?'

'I wanted out of my home town,' Ryan said, opting for honesty. He sensed a lie would not be entertained. 'I knew it was the only way I'd ever get out of Ireland. I didn't want the life my father had. So I crossed the border into the North and joined up.'

'Which regiment?'

'The Royal Ulster Rifles.'

'So you were part of Operation Mallard?'

'Yes, sir.'

Skorzeny took a cigarette case from his pocket, white enamel with the *Reichsadler*, the Nazi eagle perched atop an oak-wreathed swastika, embossed in gold. He opened the case, extended it to Haughey. The minister declined. Skorzeny lit a cigarette for himself. Smoke plumed from his lips and nostrils as he sat down.

'And *Unternehmen Wacht am Rhein*?' he asked.

Haughey looked from one man to the other. 'And what?'

'Operation Watch on the Rhine,' Ryan said. 'The Allies called it the Battle of the Bulge. I was involved to a lesser extent.'

'And after the war?'

'When I came home, I attended Trinity College, studying English.'

Skorzeny smiled. 'Ah, Trinity. So you fenced?'

'Yes, sir.'

'You will come to my home so we can duel.'

'Sir?'

'To Martinstown House. I have fenced since my youth. I earned my *Schmiss* in a university match.' He indicated the scar, his eyes cold and glittery like marbles. 'But I haven't found a reasonable opponent in this country. Perhaps that is you. So tell me, how did you apply this education you received?'

'I didn't. I re-enlisted in the Ulster Rifles and served in Korea as part of the 29th Independent Infantry Brigade. I was selected for special training there.'

'What was this training?'

'Commando tactics,' Ryan said. 'Your tactics.'

Skorzeny gave a slight nod in thanks for the acknowledgement.

'Under control of 3 Commando Brigade, I led small units in raids on enemy positions. We slept in the trenches during daylight and worked at night.'

Skorzeny drew long and deep on his cigarette. 'How many men did you kill?'

Ryan returned the Austrian's stare. 'I don't know,' he said. 'How many did *you* kill?'.

Skorzeny smiled and stood. 'We are soldiers. Only murderers keep count.'

He lifted the decanter and poured a third glass, crossed the room, and placed the drink in Ryan's hand.

'So what do you know of these scoundrels who use dead men for messengers?'

Ryan took a shallow sip of brandy, smoother on his tongue and in his throat than the drink he'd ordered at the bar. 'Very little, sir.'

Skorzeny retook his seat, crossed his long legs. 'Well, a little is more than nothing. Go on.'

'They are efficient, careful, skilled. They left no traces at the guesthouse in Salthill. I wasn't able to visit the scenes of the previous killings, but I can only assume they were as clean.'

Haughey spoke up. 'I've seen the Garda reports. They found nothing useful.' He turned to Ryan. 'What about the Jewish angle?'

'There's nothing to suggest involvement by any group from the Jewish community.'

Haughey sat forward. 'Nothing to suggest it? For Christ's sake, man, there's everything to suggest it.'

'There are no known organised Jewish groups within Ireland,' Ryan said. 'We have a very small Jewish population. It's extremely unlikely that such a group exists. Even if it did, it's less likely that it would have the capability to carry out such actions.'

'Lieutenant Ryan is correct,' Skorzeny said. 'These killings were done by professionals. Trained men.'

'The Israelis, then,' Haughey said. 'The Mossad. Or that Wiesenthal fella, the one who got your friend Eichmann executed last year.'

Skorzeny looked hard at Haughey for a moment, then turned his eyes to Ryan. 'Speculation aside, you are no closer to finding these men than you were forty-eight hours ago.'

Ryan said, 'No, sir.'

'Then what do you suggest we do next? Simply wait for them to kill again? Or come for me?'

'I suggest interviewing everyone who was present at the funeral in Galway. The notes said only the priest who gave the mass was spoken to by the Guards. He said he knew none of the people who attended, didn't speak to any of them, apart from one local man who made the arrangements. And that man has yet to be located.'

'You mean to interrogate the priest?'

'No,' Ryan said. 'I suspect that you know at least some of the people who attended the funeral. You and Johan Hambro must have had mutual acquaintances. Tell me where I can find them, and I will interview them.'

Skorzeny shook his head. 'Out of the question. My friends value their privacy. Even if I could tell you where to find these people, I cannot compel them to talk with you. They would simply refuse.'

'They may have seen something, someone, that could help us,' Ryan said. 'It's the only route I can see.'

'Then you will find another.'

Ryan stood, placed the glass on the coffee table.

'There is no other,' he said. 'I'll study the case notes, review my findings, and write up a report. Without your cooperation, that's all I can do. Good evening.'

Ryan left the suite, closed the door behind him, walked to the stairs. He was halfway down the first flight when Haughey called to him from above.

'Wait there, big fella.'

Ryan stopped, turned.

Haughey descended the steps, thunder on his face.

'Just who in the name of Christ do you think you are? You don't talk to a man like Otto Skorzeny like that. Are you trying to make a cunt of me or what?'

'No, Minister.'

Haughey was nose-to-nose with Ryan despite standing a step higher. 'Then what are you trying to do?'

'The job you assigned me, Minister. For that I need co-operation. Without it, you'll get my report and that's all.'

'I put you in that nice suit, big fella. Now you repay me with back talk. The fucking cheek of you.'

Ryan turned his back on the minister, left him huffing in the stairwell.

11

OTTO SKORZENY CHECKED HIS WRISTWATCH. LATE ENOUGH, SO he poured another glass of brandy.

He found this Irishman Ryan interesting. A soldier who'd spent the majority of his career fighting for another nation, a nation most of his countrymen considered their enemy.

Skorzeny sympathised with the G2 officer's position. All his life he had felt a lack of nationhood. As a younger man and an Austrian, he had sided with the Germans, supported their annexation of his own land. After the war, he had drifted from country to country, Spain to Argentina and back again, then here, to this rainy island.

A nationalist without a nation.

The idea struck Skorzeny as oddly romantic. It was true that many nationalist revolutionaries were not natives of the lands they fought for. Like the Egyptian militant, Yasser Arafat, who stoked the Palestinian flames, urging war against the Zionists. Or Ernesto Guevara, the Argentinian who helped steer the Cuban revolution. Or, indeed, Eamon de Valera, that most ardent Irish nationalist and republican who was in fact only half Irish by parentage, and had barely escaped being executed alongside his comrades of the 1916 uprising by virtue of being born in, and therefore a citizen of, the United States of America.

Truth be told, Skorzeny would have preferred to be back in Madrid, enjoying his friend Francisco Franco's hospitality. These killings might not have been quite so troubling had he been able simply to board a flight to Spain. But an Italian had brought an end to that. At least for the time being.

It had been three months ago, a warm Tarragona evening, on a balcony overlooking the Mediterranean. Franco had invited a score of his closest friends to spend the weekend with him, enjoying the sea air of the Catalan coast, perhaps to take a walking tour of the city's Roman ruins. Skorzeny had flown from Dublin to Paris, then on to Barcelona, before travelling south by train to join Franco at his hotel perched at the end of the Rambla Nova.

A piano chimed inside the crowded hotel suite, mingling with the sound of the surf washing up on the rocks below, as Skorzeny enjoyed a white wine spritzer and a cigarette on the balcony.

'Colonel Skorzeny,' a voice said.

Skorzeny turned from the sea view, fading as the sun set, to see a well dressed man, blond-haired. For a moment, Skorzeny assumed him to be a former *Kamerad*, given his Aryan appearance, but somehow the accent didn't fit.

'*Guten Abend*,' Skorzeny said. 'I don't believe we've met.'

The man smiled, confessed in accented Spanish that his German was poor. Skorzeny switched tongues, he had always been talented in this regard, and repeated his greeting in Spanish.

'We met once, briefly, almost twenty years ago.' The man extended his hand, his slender fingers cool in Skorzeny's grasp. 'My name is Luca Impelliteri. When we met, I was a sergeant in the Carabinieri.'

Skorzeny released his hand. 'You're Italian? I would have taken you for German.'

'My parents were from Genoa.'

'Ah. Northern Italians are of better blood than many of that country. The Sicilians, I believe, are the lowest. Am I correct?'

Impelliteri gave a hard smile. 'I judge a man's worth by his actions, not by his birth.'

'How noble,' Skorzeny said. 'And how do you come to be in Spain?'

'I am adviser to the head of the Generalissimo's personal security team. Tonight, the Generalissimo has graciously allowed me to join his guests for a drink.'

'He must be impressed with you,' Skorzeny said, allowing the slightest note of condescension to enter his voice.

The Italian nodded in a gesture of humility that Skorzeny knew to be as insincere as his own compliment. He regarded the faintness of the lines around Impelliteri's eyes, at the corners of his mouth.

'You must have been a rather young officer when we met.'

'Twenty-one,' Impelliteri said. 'That was in September 1943.'

Skorzeny took another look at the face, searched his memory. 'Oh?'

'To be precise, the twelfth of September.'

Skorzeny lifted his glass from the ledge, took a sip of wine spritzer, waited.

'On Gran Sasso,' the Italian said. 'At Hotel Campo Imperatore.'

'You were one of Mussolini's guards?'

'In truth, I had never set eyes on Il Duce until you brought him out from the hotel, cowering in that ridiculous coat and hat he wore.'

'Did you surrender along with your fellow *carabinieri*?'

'Of course.' Impelliteri smiled. 'Why would I lay down my life to keep a man like Mussolini from the Germans? You were welcome to him.'

Skorzeny returned the smile, raised his glass. 'A wise choice for a young man. I would have crushed any resistance.'

Impelliteri's smile broadened. 'Would you? From where I stood, the only thing in danger of being crushed was the poor officer whose back you stood on to climb that wall.'

Skorzeny felt the smile freeze on his lips.

'But you did very well out of it all, didn't you?' Impelliteri continued. 'They turned you into a hero, the propaganda men. What did they call you? Yes, that's it: Commando Extraordinaire, the daring SS officer who almost single-handedly saved their ally Mussolini from his own traitorous people before they could hand him over to the Americans. It was quite a story they made out of the rescue. I saw that little film they made about it. It did make me laugh.'

Skorzeny returned his glass to the ledge. 'There was no story, only historical record. Do you call me a liar?'

'A liar?' Impelliteri shook his head. 'No. Self-aggrandising, yes. An opportunist, yes. A fraud?'

He left the final question hanging in the warm Spanish air for a moment.

'You know, the Generalissimo, he holds you in the highest regard. He believes every word of your mythology. That's why he welcomes you to his kingdom. It would be a shame if he ever found out the truth of it all.'

Impotent anger churned in Skorzeny's belly. Had there not been a suite full of Franco's guests just feet away, he would have grabbed the Italian by the throat and thrown him over the balcony ledge onto the rocks below. Instead, he held his silence as Impelliteri bade him goodnight and rejoined the party.

In a matter of days, Skorzeny wished he had felt no such reservations and killed the Italian then and there.

Now, he was marooned in Ireland, waiting in a hotel suite for that damned politician to return.

Eventually, a knock on the door, and Haughey entered, breathless and red-faced.

'Colonel,' he said, 'I must apologise for Lieutenant Ryan's behaviour.'

Skorzeny topped up Haughey's glass. 'Not at all, Minister.'

'If you want me to kick him off the job, get someone else, I'll understand.'

Skorzeny handed the glass to the politician. 'No, Minister. I like this Lieutenant Ryan. He has balls. Let's see what he can do.'

12

RYAN STRODE ACROSS THE FOYER, HEADING FOR THE EXIT. MUSIC boomed and moaned from the function room. He paused, listened. 'Autumn Leaves', he thought, picturing the woman, her deep red hair, her slender freckled wrist, her pale skin.

She'd said her name was Celia.

Go or remain?

He stood in a quandary until he remembered the cold empty room back at Buswells Hotel, and the warmth of her breath on his ear. Ryan followed the tide of music back to the function room. He lingered in the doorway, seeking her among the swells of dance and laughter.

There, taller than almost everyone, near the archway that led to the bar, listening with a polite expression as a pudgy man shouted above the music. Ryan kept her in sight as he crossed the room. She saw him approach, held his gaze as he drew near, ignored the man who bellowed at her.

'I saved your drink for you,' she said, lifting the glass from the table beside her.

The man ceased shouting, went to admonish Ryan for the interruption, then thought better of it. The music swallowed up his curses as he walked away, head down.

'Thank you,' Ryan said, taking the glass from her, his skin

tingling where her fingers brushed his. He pulled a chair out from the table and she sat down. He joined her.

'How was the Minister for Justice?' she asked.

'Loud,' Ryan said. 'Coarse. Angry.'

She smiled. 'Sounds like our Charlie. He'll be Taoiseach one day, wait and see. Charles J. Haughey will lead this country. To what, I don't know, but he'll lead it. Some think he's a great man.'

'And what do you think?'

As Ryan asked the question, Haughey entered the room alongside Otto Skorzeny. All eyes turned in their direction. Haughey basked in it while Skorzeny remained impassive. Young men raced to the bar to fetch drinks for them.

Celia stared at the politician. 'I think he's a monster. He wouldn't be the first to lead a nation. What did he whisk you away for? What devilish plans were you and he cooking up with the infamous Otto Skorzeny?'

'No plans,' Ryan said. 'Nothing I can discuss.'

'I see,' she said. 'How intriguing.'

Haughey and Skorzeny advanced through the room, shaking hands, slapping backs. The minister noticed Ryan, his comradely smile freezing on his lips.

Ryan did not look away until Celia tugged at his arm.

'Dance with me,' she said.

Dread and panic sucked the blood from his cheeks. 'No, I don't, I can't, I mean I'm not a very good . . .'

Her fingertips skimmed his jowls. 'Such a saggy face,' she said, her smile crooked. 'Come on. I'll drag you up if I have to.'

'Really, I'd embarrass us both.'

'Nonsense. Don't make me beg.'

Celia grabbed Ryan's hand and hauled. He got to his feet, allowed her to lead him to the dance floor. The band played a mid-tempo tune he did not recognise. She took his left hand in her right, raised it up, brought her body close to his. Her left hand climbed his shoulder, his right found the small of her back. He pressed his palm into the hollow there, felt the suggestion of her shape, the firm and the soft of her.

They danced.

She lent him her grace, her balance, allowed his clumsy feet to follow hers across the floor. The air between them seemed charged, like dark summer clouds, ready to flash and spark. He felt the pressure of her breasts against his torso, did not pull away. She turned within his arms, her hip grazing him. Blood flowed and warmed that part of him. He felt a heaviness there, weight and heat. She felt it also, he knew, they both did. Her lips parted, shining red and pink.

Ryan opened his mouth to speak, but her expression shifted as she watched something over his shoulder. He turned his head to see what had taken her from him.

A middle-aged man spoke in Haughey's ear, the minister's face pale, his brow furrowed. Haughey turned to Skorzeny, repeated whatever he'd been told. Skorzeny's face remained a mask of calm. Only his eyes moved, seeking Ryan out. The music dimmed in Ryan's ears, his feet ceased their awkward shuffling.

'What's the matter, do you think?' Celia asked.

Haughey marched to the dance floor.

'I don't know,' Ryan said.

The minister took Ryan's elbow, led him away from Celia. 'Looks like you've got what you wanted,' Haughey said.

It took a moment for Ryan to understand that the politician did not mean his dancing partner. 'What?' he asked.

'A witness.'

13

RYAN STRUGGLED TO KEEP UP WITH SKORZENY'S MERCEDES-BENZ 300SL as it coursed through the countryside. Its white body disappeared behind hedgerows and reappeared on crests, dazzling in the Vauxhall's headlights. Ryan felt the tyres of his car skitter on the road surface, barely clinging to the bends while the Mercedes seemed to float ahead.

Skorzeny hardly slowed as they passed through Kildare town. Ryan heard the Mercedes roar above the sound of his own engine as it turned up the incline towards Dunmurry. As the town's buildings gave way to farmland, Ryan finally lost sight of the other car. He accelerated, leaning forward, peering through the windscreen for any sign of the Austrian.

Haughey had stayed at the party, thought it best not to get too involved. Yes, Ryan had agreed, keep your distance from the blood.

The road rose for half a mile ahead. Trees and gates whipped by, branches reaching out to skiff and clang against the Vauxhall's doors and wing mirrors. The brow came rushing up, and Ryan's stomach hovered with him as the car lost contact with the tarmac.

Searing red lights filled his vision as the Vauxhall slammed down. He stamped on the brake pedal, his body thrown forward, jamming his foot down again and again. The car groaned and juddered as it slowed, the Mercedes only yards ahead.

Skorzeny pulled away, exhaust bellowing. His hand slipped out of the driver's window, waving: come on, keep up. Ryan cursed as he brought the Vauxhall under control.

He kept the Mercedes within sight until it turned into a lane so narrow Ryan hadn't seen its mouth in the hedgerow. The single track cut through fields for a mile or more, the pocked surface jarring Ryan's spine until the lane ended at a gateway barely wide enough for Skorzeny's car to slip through. Ryan followed and parked alongside the Mercedes as Skorzeny climbed out.

'Who taught you to drive?' the Austrian asked as Ryan walked around the Vauxhall. 'Your mother? You'd have lost me if I hadn't waited.'

Before Ryan could agree or argue, a thin man stepped out from the side of the cottage, an oil lamp hanging from his fingers.

'This way,' he said, his accent thick.

This was Lainé, Ryan thought, the Frenchman. Skorzeny went first, shook the man's hand, old friends.

'Who is this?' Lainé asked.

'Lieutenant Ryan of the Directorate of Intelligence,' Skorzeny said. 'He's helping us get to the bottom of this. He'll want to speak with you.'

Ryan approached, extended his hand. Lainé ignored it and pinched a hand-rolled cigarette between his lips. He held the lamp up, let the tobacco dip into the flame. It flared, revealing the hollows of his face, the sunken eyes.

'Come,' Lainé said.

They followed him to the rear of the cottage. Skorzeny

paused inside the doorway. Ryan reached the threshold and saw why.

A dead man lay on the stone floor, flat on his back. One neat hole in his forehead, another in his knitted pullover, the wool tattered and scorched. A broken shotgun and two unspent shells lay beside him.

Muddy bootprints criss-crossed the floor, circled the body. Ryan noted the damp soil caked on the Frenchman's boots. The dead man's shoes were dirty but dry.

Lainé indicated the corpse. 'This is Murtagh. They kill him first.'

Skorzeny moved further into the cottage. Ryan followed.

Another man sat at the table, his head at an unnatural angle, a flap of scalp peeled back.

'This is Groix,' Lainé said.

The Frenchman walked to the other side of the table, pulled the chair out, and sat down. He shook, coughed, his eyes welling. Mud and what appeared to be blood dappled his cardigan. He set the gas lamp at the centre of the table. It threw yellow light around the room. Lainé's tears sparkled.

'They kill Hervé. She only barks. She never bites. And they kill her.'

Skorzeny rounded the table, placed his large hand on Lainé's bony shoulder. 'Tell us what happened.'

The Frenchman sniffed, dabbed at his eyes with his sleeve, and talked.

Groix had gone to the window, leaned over the sink, peered out. He had craned his neck, explored every part of the small yard within reach of his gaze. The dog's chain hadn't moved for more than a minute.

'I see nothing,' he said in French.

It disappointed Lainé that for all Groix's zeal he had never learned to speak Breton with any degree of competence.

Lainé stood behind him. 'They've come down the hillside, to the back of the cottage. Do you have a weapon?'

'No. Nothing.'

Lainé had a pistol, an old Smith & Wesson that had once belonged to a GI. It lay beneath his pillow.

He turned to Murtagh, said in English, 'There are men come and kill us.' He indicated the shotgun on the table. 'Can you shoot this gun?'

Murtagh stood, his chair rattling across the floor. 'What?'

'Can you shoot this gun?' Lainé repeated.

'Who's coming?'

Lainé decided not to waste any more breath on the young idiot. He moved to the back of the room, as far from the door as he could get, while Groix stood useless at the window.

Murtagh reached for the shotgun, broke it, made a show of checking the shells. He spun around as something slammed into the back door, tearing the bolt from the frame. Two plosive sounds, like balloons popping, and Murtagh fell.

The men entered, one, two, three of them, weapons raised and ready.

Lainé froze. Groix whimpered and raised his hands as fluid trickled over his shoes to puddle on the floor.

The second man who entered said, 'Good evening, Célestin.'

Groix turned his confused face towards Lainé.

The man said, 'I don't know your friend. Who is he?'

'Elouan Groix,' Lainé said.

'Both of you sit.'

Groix obeyed.

'You too,' the man said to Lainé.

Lainé crossed the room, skirted Groix's urine, and sat down.

'Hands flat on the table.'

Lainé and Groix splayed their fingers on the wood.

The three men wore dark overalls, woollen caps rolled down to their eyebrows, leather gloves. Two carried Browning pistols with suppressors. The third carried an automatic rifle. One took up a position at Groix's right, the rifle levelled at his temple. The other came to Lainé's left, aimed his weapon.

The leader pulled up the chair Murtagh had sat in, placed his Browning on the tabletop, one hand resting upon it.

'So here we are,' he said, his accent English.

Tears rolled from Groix's eyes. He sniffed.

'Here we are,' Lainé said. '*Et maintenant?*'

'A quick chat,' the man said.

'I say nothing.'

Groix spoke up, fear in his voice, hope in his wet eyes. 'I will say. You ask. I will say.'

The man lifted the Browning from the table, aimed, squeezed the trigger. Groix's head jerked as if pulled by a marionette string. Bone and skin came away, hair flaming and smoking. He said no more.

The man turned his attention back to Lainé. 'You misunderstand. I'm not looking for any more information. I already know everything I need to know. You don't have to say anything. Not to me. I will talk. You will listen.'

Lainé watched a dark line trace its way around Groix's ear and down his neck towards his collar.

'So talk,' he said.

The man placed the pistol back on the table. Points of red dotted his cheek. 'You will pass a message to Otto Skorzeny.'

Lainé smiled, though it felt more like a grimace on his lips. 'Like Krauss?'

'Not necessarily. I'd prefer you pass the message on in person. I want you to be able to tell Skorzeny how serious we are. How efficient. If you agree to do so, I'll take you at your word and allow you to live. Will you pass on this message?'

Lainé reached for the tobacco pouch and papers, set about making a cigarette. '*D'accord.*'

The man nodded. 'Good. Repeat these words to Skorzeny exactly as I say them. Only three words. Are you listening?'

Lainé leaned into the gas lamp and lit the cigarette. '*Ouais.*'

'Tell him: You will pay.'

Lainé snorted, picked tobacco from his lip. 'This will scare Otto Skorzeny, you think?'

The man raised the Browning, pressed the suppressor to Lainé's cheek. The heat of it made his eyelid flicker.

'Just repeat those words to him. That's all.'

Lainé nodded.

'Good.' The man lifted the Browning and stood.

The other two men backed towards the door.

'Be seeing you.'

They pulled the door closed behind them.

The shaking started then, and Lainé was barely able to bring the cigarette to his lips. Even so, he smoked it until it burned his fingers then dropped it to the floor.

He did not look at Groix's or Murtagh's bodies as he left the cottage. The chain lay loose on the ground. He followed it until he found Hervé lying curled on herself. In the dimness her eyes wavered in their sockets, seeking the source of his scent.

'There, baby,' he said as he crouched down beside her.

Two holes in her flank. He placed his hand there, felt the warm wetness and the faint insistence of her heart. She exhaled, a bubbling deep in her chest. Lainé lay down in the dirt and held her, whispering stories of heaven, until the bubbling ceased and her heart stilled. He kissed her once then got to his feet.

Ten minutes took him across the fields to Caoimhín Murtagh's farmhouse. He rapped the door. Mrs Murtagh answered.

'I need your telephone,' Lainé said.

She looked back over her shoulder, called her husband.

Ryan asked, 'Does Murtagh know what happened here?'

'*Non*. He asks, but I say nothing. When you go, I tell him.'

'Good,' Skorzeny said, squeezing Lainé's shoulder. 'You did well. After you tell him, you will also leave this place. Take everything, leave no trace of yourself. Let this Murtagh deal with the police. Tell him he must not mention you to them. Offer him money if you have to.'

'Where do I go?'

Skorzeny considered for a moment. 'You may take a room at my house.'

'*Merci*.' Lainé's voice turned to a wavering hiss.

'How old was the man with the pistol?' Ryan asked.

'I think forty-five. The others, one was also this age, one was younger.'

'The other men didn't speak?'

'*Non*.'

'So we can't tell if they were British or not.'

'They look, how to say . . .' Lainé waved his open palm across his face. 'Pale, like English men. Not like Spanish or Italian. Not . . .'

'Not Jews,' Skorzeny said.

'*Non.*'

Ryan said, 'The Browning is a British service weapon.'

'You think SAS? MI5?' Skorzeny asked.

'I see no reason why British forces would target you. And if they wanted you dead, you would be.'

Skorzeny smiled, creasing his scar. 'Perhaps. Then tell me, Lieutenant Ryan, who are these men, and what do they want?'

'I don't know who they are. And only you can say what they want. One thing is clear, though.'

'What is this?'

'They must have an informant. If they know so much about you and your . . . friends, then someone must have passed this information to them. May even be working with them.'

Skorzeny went to the window, stared out into the darkness. 'Then I will make enquiries. You will also. If you find this person before I do, you will notify me immediately.'

'And then?'

'Then you will bring him to me.'

14

CHARLES J. HAUGHEY SAT AT HIS DESK, A CUP OF COFFEE AND a glass of fizzing Alka-Seltzer in front of him. Ryan sat opposite.

'So what do you need?' Haughey asked.

'I need the names and locations of all the foreign nationals who were Nazis or collaborators and are now resident in Ireland.'

'No,' Haughey said.

'Minister, I need this information if I'm going to find whoever has been working with these men.'

Haughey took a swig of the Alka-Seltzer, belched, and said, 'There are currently well over a hundred such people resident in Ireland. That we know of. There are very likely others that have sneaked in through some back door. I can't go handing that kind of information out, even if I had it to hand. Besides, how many of them do you think know Colonel Skorzeny?'

'All right,' Ryan said. 'Compile a list of those who have direct contact with Skorzeny. I can start there.'

Haughey leaned forward, his forearms nudging the coffee cup, making it rattle in its saucer. 'What am I, your fucking secretary?'

'Minister, it is vital I find the informant before Skorzeny does.'

'Why?' Haughey asked. 'Why can't you just let him deal with it?'

'Because if Skorzeny finds the informant, I believe he will torture him. Then I believe he will kill him.'

Haughey's secretary smiled as Ryan passed through the outer office. He paused at the door, turned, came back to her.

'Excuse me,' he said. 'Last night, I saw you speaking with a woman. Her name was Celia Hume.'

The secretary's lips curled in a smirk. She let her gaze travel the length of Ryan, took her time about it. 'Yes, I know Celia.'

Sweat chilled Ryan's brow and back as his cheeks smouldered. 'Do you know where I could contact her?'

The secretary's smirk blossomed into a crooked grin. 'And what would a nice man like you want with our Celia?'

A small but bright flash of anger at the girl's intrusion. He quelled it, returned her smile. 'Just to say hello.'

'I see.' She scribbled a telephone number on a pad, tore off the sheet, handed it to him. 'If she doesn't want to say hello back, you can always give me a try.'

Ryan took the paper from her fingers, held her gaze despite how it burned his skin.

Late in the afternoon, a messenger boy brought a thick manila envelope to Ryan's hotel room. A note inside said: *Here's your list of names. Be careful with them and destroy it when you're finished.*

It was signed, C.J.H.

Ryan pulled three sheets of paper from the envelope and spread them out on the bed. A dozen typewritten names in total, addresses, some of them only townlands. Ryan pictured those places, low cottages or grand houses at the end of single track lanes, roads without names, places known only to the postmen who delivered to them.

One name seemed familiar to Ryan: Luykx who had made his fortune with restaurants and bars. Beside that name, a scribbled note: *Don't go near Albert Luykx. He's a personal friend of mine. I don't want him bothered.*

Haughey had written elsewhere on the paper. Nationalities, organisations, ranks, relationships, professions. Some were businessmen, one of them a writer, one a schoolmaster, two doctors; more of them wealthy than not.

Ryan paid attention to those who were not.

Catherine Beauchamp, a novelist, a Breton nationalist like Lainé. She worked for a charity, a normal salaried job. But a decent job, nonetheless. She made a living. Would she crave more? Enough to turn on her friends?

And here was Hakon Foss. A Norwegian nationalist who had found work as a gardener and handyman, much of that work for Skorzeny and his associates. He would be in a position to see much of their comings and goings, perhaps enough to foster jealousy and rage at what they possessed and he did not.

Ryan scanned the list once more. The businessmen had all prospered in Ireland. Property, hospitality, a printing business, one of them a breeder of racehorses.

All endeavours that required capital, money, and plenty of it. These men fled the Continent with enough cash, or access to it, to establish comfortable lives. Why would they risk what they'd built for themselves? He thought once more about Catherine Beauchamp and Hakon Foss.

He would start with them.

Ryan checked his watch. Almost six. He took the folded

sheet of notepaper from his pocket. The name Celia written in a fluid script, and the numbers.

He sat on the edge of the bed, lifted the receiver, dialled an outside line, then turned the wheel of numbers, heard the whirr of the mechanism as it returned to zero after each one.

The dial tone repeated in his ear five times before a gravel-voiced woman answered.

'I'd like to speak with Celia Hume,' Ryan said.

'She's not here,' the woman said. 'If you want to leave a message, I'll make sure she gets it.'

'Please tell her Albert Ryan called.' He gave the hotel's number, and his room, and she promised to pass the message on.

Ryan sat silent and alone for thirty minutes before the telephone rang.

15

OTTO SKORZENY COUNTED THE MONEY AS PIETER MENTEN sipped coffee. Five thousand in American dollars, ten thousand in British pounds, and a further thirty thousand in Irish currency laid out on the desk in Skorzeny's study. Menten had travelled by ferry and train, carrying the suitcase of money from Rotterdam to Harwich in England, then from the Welsh port of Holyhead across to Dun Laoghaire where Skorzeny collected him in his Mercedes.

The Dutchman had aged well, the years since the war having been kind to him. His long nose and high cheekbones gave him an aristocratic appearance, as if wealth were his by birthright, not labour.

The money had been delivered to Rotterdam by an Arab courier who retrieved the funds from a bank in Switzerland in return for a five per cent commission. Skorzeny had been told by more than one source that the Arab was actually an Algerian of Berber descent, but he had never been able to confirm the speculation. Regardless of origin, the Arab travelled with two bodyguards, both hulking dark-skinned men also of uncertain nationality. Only a very brave or very foolish man would think of robbing him.

The Arab always took his percentage in dollars. Skorzeny

had heard that he spent most of it in Rotterdam's brothels, but again, he had no proof of this claim.

Satisfied, Skorzeny peeled off one thousand Irish pounds and handed them to Menten. He transferred the rest to the safe mounted in the wall behind his desk, shielded the combination with his broad body as he locked the door. He returned the landscape painting to its hook.

Menten lifted the cloth-wrapped rectangle that sat at his feet. 'A small token,' he said in English.

Skorzeny took the package, unwrapped the cloth, revealing a small, simply framed portrait of a young woman dressed in black. A bird perched on her hand.

'By Hans Holbein the Younger,' Menten said. 'Painted on his return to Basel *circa* 1530. Exquisite, don't you think?'

'Quite beautiful,' Skorzeny said, taking his seat across the desk from Menten. 'And very much appreciated, *mein Kamerad*. Is it from your own collection?'

Pieter Menten's personal art collection had once been so large he had required his own private train in order to transport it.

'No, it is newly acquired. From an old *Kamerad*, Dominik Foerster. Do you remember him?'

Skorzeny thought back, remembered a thin bespectacled man he had met once in Berlin. 'I believe so.'

'I chanced upon him while spending a weekend in Noordwijk, on the Dutch coast. He was staying in a small boarding house under an assumed name. He was in rather a state of distress, living in constant fear of discovery by some fanatic or another. I told him he might be able to find sanctuary in Ireland, and perhaps travel on to South America if he had sufficient funds. Wisely, most of his assets are tied up in art he liberated from the Jews.'

Skorzeny held the painting at arm's length, admiring the detail in the girl's clothing, the glistening of her eyes.

'Yes, very wise,' he said. 'Tell him to contact Abbot Verlinden at Priorij Onze-Lieve-Vrouw van Gent. I will send a letter of introduction on his behalf. Abbot Verlinden will in turn make introductions to the appropriate institutions in Ireland and help our *Kamerad* make travel arrangements. Whatever costs he cannot meet personally can be funded from our account in Zurich.'

Menten smiled. 'Thank you. Dominik will be most relieved. I will contact him on my return to Rotterdam in a few days. Before that, I have property to view in Waterford.'

'Waterford?' Skorzeny asked. 'It's beautiful country there. Have the Irish authorities been accommodating?'

Menten nodded. 'As much as one could hope for. But my contact in the Department of Justice has advised me to take another name.'

Skorzeny had been fortunate to be denazified by the German authorities. It had taken a considerable sum of money, but the ability to live in freedom under his own name had been worth the cost of the bribes.

'You would be wise to take his advice.'

'I intend to.' Menten gave a nod, a look of regret on his round face.

'Good. Frau Tiernan will serve dinner in an hour or so. You will stay, of course.'

'Yes, thank you.' Menten leaned forward. 'What of the killings? I heard about *Kamerad* Krauss before I sailed from Rotterdam.'

'There has been another,' Skorzeny said.

'My God. Who?'

'A Breton. No one important. An Irishman also. They caused me a late night, but my friend the Minister for Justice has put his best man on it.'

Skorzeny did not blush at the lie. He did not consider the minister a friend. More a useful acquaintance. He knew full well that the likes of Haughey were drawn to his notoriety, desired his company so that they could bask in reflected glamour.

Fools, all of them.

'I'm glad to hear this,' Menten said. 'Helmut Krauss was a good man. He didn't deserve such a fate.'

'Helmut Krauss was a drunkard and a womaniser. We each meet the fate that awaits us, whether we deserve it or not.'

Menten withered under his stare, visibly struggling with the desire to dispute Skorzeny's opinion of his old friend. Eventually, he moistened his lips and said, 'Naturally, they will suspect Jewish extremists. Or the Mossad, perhaps.'

Skorzeny considered telling Menten the truth, but realised it would be easier to allow him the comfort of his hate. 'Of course,' he said.

Skorzeny had spent the following day in the fields, watching as his farmhands herded the sheep from one paddock to another. He admired the dogs and the way their master, a long red-faced rope of a man called Tiernan, controlled them with whistles and yips.

Skorzeny had observed from the top of the slope as the dogs arced out across the grass, and he was reminded of fighter planes flying in attack formation. Tiernan's whistle gave a short pip, and the dogs halted, crouched low to the ground, their concentration absolute. One was the sire to the other, Tiernan had said, and the youngster took hardly any training at all, he simply watched what his father did and copied him.

Another blast of the whistle and the dogs sprang forward, working in tandem, circling the flock, gathering the sheep up like hands scooping earth. Within minutes, the flock had streamed into the next field and one of the farmhands had swung the gate closed behind them.

Their task complete, the dogs ran to their master and lay at his feet. Tiernan reached down and scratched each of them behind the ears with his knotty hands.

Not for the first time, Otto Skorzeny wondered at the difference between what brought him happiness now and twenty years before. As a younger man, it had been the smell of cordite, air burned by gunpowder, the thunder and screech of battle. And boys, strong beautiful brave boys, charging into death's maw, all at his command.

Now his belly had grown and his hips and knees sometimes rebelled; now the inclines of his fields often robbed his lungs of breath as his thighs ached with the climb. But age did not concern Skorzeny to any great degree. Despite the signals of his deterioration, he remained in good health. He could count on another ten or fifteen years of good living, maybe a further ten of tolerable existence, before his heart gave out.

He would fill that time as he had this day, walking in his fields, admiring the work of the men who tended them, watching the dogs perform their duties with the dedication only a simple mind can summon.

And of course that made for good soldiers. For Skorzeny, the best infantrymen came from the working classes. Men used to spending their days toiling in factories or fields, their minds concerned only with the tasks before them. Give such men rifles and an enemy to shoot at, and one could see the natural order of life played out in gunfire and blood.

A good commando was a different beast entirely. That required a higher mind, and more than a little cunning, an intelligence matched to a hardness of the heart.

Someone like Lieutenant Ryan.

Skorzeny had seen it on the Irishman when he first entered the suite at the Grand Hotel in Malahide. Ryan had not flinched when he saw the bodies at the cottage, even at the gaping hole in Groix's temple, the burnt hair, the torn scalp. Ryan had that flint at his centre, just as Skorzeny himself had.

And Ryan was smart. Not like Haughey, whose intelligence and guile served only his greed. Ryan possessed an acumen earned in the barren and bloody places of the world. Skorzeny had no doubt that he could find the traitor. But would the Irishman bring the traitor here to him? Ryan would surely know what awaited the informant. Would he have the mettle to knowingly deliver a prisoner to such a fate?

Skorzeny could not be sure.

When he returned to his house, he washed and changed, then went to his study. He had intended to summon Lainé but found him already waiting there, smoking one of those stinking cigarettes he rolled himself.

The thin Frenchman sat hunched in the chair, arms and legs crossed, making him appear crippled. Skorzeny sat opposite and took a cigarette from the case on his desk. He quietly wished Lainé had stolen one of these instead of filling the office with his own bitter smoke.

Lainé asked, '*Qui est l'Irlandais?*'

Skorzeny had spoken French fluently since a young age. 'I

told you. Lieutenant Albert Ryan, G2, Directorate of Intelligence.'

'I don't like him. I don't trust him.'

'You don't have to trust him,' Skorzeny said. 'Just let him do his job. I have faith in his ability. He's a soldier. Like me.'

Lainé inclined his head to show he hadn't missed Skorzeny's veiled insult. 'What was I, a washerwoman?'

Skorzeny chose not to answer the question. Instead, he said, 'I would appreciate it if you stayed in your room this evening. I have important guests coming to dinner.'

Lainé's tongue licked tobacco flakes from his lips. He spat them out, *pfft*. 'What guests?'

Skorzeny looked at the damp flakes that had landed on the leather of his desktop. 'Political guests. Esteban will bring you a tray and a bottle from the cellar.'

Lainé's eyes brightened. 'You have a cellar?'

'Frau Tiernan is cooking lamb, so I suggest the '55 Penfolds Grange Hermitage. It's Australian, but excellent.'

Lainé's lip curled at the wine's origin, then he shrugged and nodded. 'All right. But I tell you, I don't like the Irishman. How do you know he won't betray us?'

Skorzeny shook his head. 'He is a soldier. A good one. He will follow orders. Besides, I have placed someone close to him. Someone to keep watch for us.'

16

THE LANDLADY SHOWED RYAN TO THE PARLOUR WITH ITS stiff-cushioned chairs and dark wallpaper. Two young women had peeked down at him from the landing above when he entered the boarding house. They had ducked back beyond the banister, giggling, when he looked up at them.

Mrs Highland left Ryan alone to fidget on the settee. She returned a few minutes later, said Celia would be down presently.

'What are your plans for the evening?' she asked, hovering by the door as if standing sentry, her hair pulled back hard into a bun, her smile polite and tight-lipped.

'The pictures,' Ryan said.

'Oh? What's playing?'

'The James Bond film. *Dr No*. It's based on a book by Ian Fleming.'

Her smile turned to a scowl. 'I hear those books are really quite vulgar.'

Sweat gathered at the small of Ryan's back. 'I haven't read any of them.'

'Hmm. As I'm sure you can see, I run a respectable house. I regard my girls not just as lodgers, but as wards in my care. I know some of their parents personally. I won't insist, but I would be grateful if you brought Miss Hume back before eleven o'clock.'

Ryan smiled and nodded.

The door opened, and Celia entered. Her red hair gathered loose above her shoulders, the short-sleeved green dress simple and snug, an emerald brooch the only embellishment. Mrs Highland stood back, her frowning at the sight of Celia's freckled skin. Celia ignored her.

'Albert,' she said.

Ryan stood. 'Celia.'

They stood in silence save for the ticking of the carriage clock on the mantelpiece until Celia said, 'Thank you, Mrs Highland.'

The landlady looked at them each in turn, cleared her throat. 'Well, I'll leave you two to make your plans. Good evening, Mr Ryan.'

He bowed his head. 'Good evening.'

Mrs Highland left them, closed the door behind her. Ryan heard her scold the girls on the stairs.

Celia's green-eyed gaze caused Ryan's mouth to dry and his lips to seal shut.

When he thought he could bear the silence no longer, she said, 'Mrs Highland does like to fuss over her girls.'

Ryan's laugh burst from him like a greyhound from a trap. He blushed, and Celia smiled.

'Shall we go?' she asked.

They sat in the flickering dark, still and silent. Other couples leaned close, touched, the silhouettes of their heads sometimes joining together. Everyone in the room *oohed* in soft unison as Ursula Andress emerged tanned and shining from the sea.

The girl next to Celia looked up for a moment before turning her lips back to the boy whose hand had slipped inside her blouse. Ryan watched the shapes of the boy's fingers move beneath the fabric. When he raised his eyes, he saw Celia looking back at him, a sly smile, her eyes glistening in the dimness.

They walked south along D'Olier Street towards the northerly buildings of Trinity College, Celia's arm hooked in Ryan's. A rain shower had slicked the pavement while they'd been in the cinema, street lights reflected in the sheen. The windows of the *Irish Times* building glowed across the way.

'He's ever so handsome,' she said.

'Sean Connery?'

'Yes. I met him once, at a party in London. Well, I didn't meet him exactly, he was in the room. It was last year, just before *Dr No* came out in England. You could tell to look at him he'd be a star. He had a grace about him, like an animal, a tiger or a leopard, something dangerous and beautiful.'

She spoke the words as if they were the most savoury ingredients of an exotic recipe.

'I don't suppose it's really like that, is it? Being a secret agent.'

Ryan smiled. 'I'm not a secret agent.'

'Well, you're G2. It's the nearest thing we have to a secret agent in our little country.'

'Maybe so, but it's nothing like that film.'

'No?' She forced an exaggerated frown of disappointment. 'No lithe beauties coming ashore and throwing themselves at you?'

They reached the end of the street, the elaborate facade of D'Olier Chambers rising above them. Celia indicated the pub tucked away on Fleet Street, opposite.

'Buy me a drink,' she said.

Inside, thick curtains of tobacco smoke hung in the air. Ryan went to the bar while Celia found a snug at the rear. The barman stared in confusion when he asked for lime in the gin and tonic, so lemon had to do.

Suited men, red faced with shirt collars unbuttoned, guffawed and shouted. Journalists, Ryan guessed, writers for the *Irish Times*, downing whiskeys and pints of stout, exchanging stories. They had watched Celia as she entered on Ryan's arm, their eyes following the flow of her through the room. Ryan had taken no offence at their covetous stares. Instead he had felt pride, his vanity glowing like a filament in his chest.

Many would have thought it scandalous for a young woman to enter a pub like this, but that didn't seem to bother Celia. But the lack of lime in her drink did.

'Rum and Coca-Cola would be fine next time,' she said, her smile polite but scolding.

Ryan wondered if he should apologise. Instead, he sipped his half of Guinness. Celia's gaze settled somewhere beneath his chin.

'Isn't that the same tie you wore in Malahide?' she asked.

His fingers went to the silk before he could stop them. 'Is it? I don't know. I don't pay much attention to fashion.'

'Really? It's a very nice suit. What is it?'

She reached across the table, lifted his lapel and read the label on the inside pocket.

'Canali. Italian. You dress well for a man who doesn't follow fashion. Better than most of the men in Dublin, anyway. Have you ever been to Paris?'

'I've passed through,' he said.

She told him about her time there, stationed in the Irish embassy. How she walked around Montmartre, and how once, entirely out of the blue, a man came right up to her and asked her to model for him.

'And did you agree to it?' Ryan asked.

'Almost,' she said. She leaned close, shielded her mouth with her hand, and whispered, 'Until he said it was to be a nude.'

She said her father was a High Court judge, now retired, a fussy old man, stiff with snobbery, but she loved him all the more for it. He told her about his father and his small grocery store where he had toiled for year upon year, just like his father before him, with little to show for it.

Celia told him about the garden party for President Kennedy that was scheduled for the Áras, President de Valera's official residence. She had been promised an invitation, and confessed that the idea of being in the company of, perhaps even meeting, Kennedy and his beautiful wife made her as giddy as the schoolgirl she had been at Mount Anville, the private convent where she had received her education.

They talked about the places they had been in the line of their work, he as a soldier, she as Third Secretary to one diplomatic mission or another. Ryan talked about the cold Dutch fields and the warm Sicilian streets, the days dug into gritty ditches in Egypt, the stifling wet heat of the Korean summer followed by the hard bite of its winter. Celia spoke of days typing letters, fetching coffee, collecting dry cleaning, the tedium made worthwhile by parties in hotel suites with cocktail bars and gilded furniture. Months spent in one city or another, weekends on yachts, banquets in palaces.

At twenty-six she had seen more of life than almost any

man, and certainly any woman, Ryan had ever known. So different from the girls he had shared coy exchanges with as a boy and a young man, so confident in her words and her gestures. Her hands did not lie curled in her lap. Instead they moved with her speech, bold and free. She did not wait her turn to speak, in deference to his masculinity. She laughed from her belly, out loud, didn't titter politely as if she sat in a church pew. She knew the world.

But not the barren places, the dark corners, the bleeding crevices. He measured his words, allowed her a glimpse of the harsh terrains he knew, but no more. Men came back damaged from such places, their souls scooped out of them. He did not wish her to think he was one of them, even if he sometimes feared he was.

Ryan neared the bottom of his second glass of Guinness – a pint this time – while Celia stirred her second rum and Coca-Cola.

'It's good to meet a man who's travelled,' she said. 'This country is so self-absorbed, our tiny little island. It's as if we're surrounded by a wall or a fence, like that one they've put up in Berlin, except it's been built all the way around the coast. The only reason anyone gets on an aeroplane or a boat is to emigrate, and then the only places they can think to go to are England or America.'

'It's expensive to travel,' Ryan said. 'Who can afford it, unless they do it for a living?'

Celia leaned forward, pointed a finger, her eyes wide with an idea. 'Then everyone should be a soldier or a Third Secretary.'

Ryan raised his own finger. 'Then who would stay at home to tend the fields? Or go to church? We can't leave all those priests with no one to preach to. Whose confession would they take?'

Her brow creased. 'Clearly, I haven't thought this through.'

'Why did you talk to me?'

Her smile faltered. The question had preyed on him since the night they danced, but he hadn't meant to ask it aloud.

'In Malahide, I mean. Why did you come over to me?'

'That is an improper question, Albert Ryan.'

She brought her glass to her lips.

'But I'd like to know,' Ryan said.

Celia returned the glass to the table, watched the bubbles scale its walls and cling to the melting ice.

'I saw you walk in,' she said. 'I saw the way you carried yourself. I thought: this man is not like the others. All those little boys and old men, politicians, civil servants, chinless pencil pushers and clock watchers. You were clearly not one of them. You were clearly something . . . else.' She looked up from the glass. 'And also a little bit sad.'

Ryan felt naked, as if her eyes picked over the skin beneath his shirt. He couldn't have borne it a moment longer if she hadn't tripped him with a sudden smile.

'And then you opened your mouth, and you were like a schoolboy at his first dance in the Parochial Hall. I could almost imagine your mother spitting on her hankie and wiping your face before she let you out the door.'

'It's a long time since my mother cleaned my face,' Ryan said. 'Almost a month, in fact.'

Her chiming laughter and a hand on his knee caused a fluttering in Ryan's belly. He excused himself and went looking for the WC. He found it at the rear of the room, the door hidden in a darkened corner, the mixed smell of disinfectant and human waste meeting him as he entered.

Ryan went to the toilet stall rather than the trough that served as a urinal. He preferred the privacy of the enclosed space over the vulnerability of standing exposed. When he was done, he pulled the chain and heard the roar of the flush.

He stepped out of the cubicle and saw a man at the wash-basin, running water over the teeth of a comb. In the mirror above the basin, the man watched the reflection of the wet comb as it smoothed his thick dark hair to his scalp.

Ryan knew this man was not local, his charcoal-coloured suit too well cut, his skin too tanned. The man stepped aside to allow Ryan to wash his hands, but he lingered, taking his time over his grooming, watching himself over Ryan's shoulder.

The man asked, 'Did you enjoy the picture?'

Ryan took his hands from the water. 'Excuse me?'

'The picture,' the man said, putting his comb in his pocket. 'Did you enjoy it?'

His accent was American, seasoned by something else. It had that nasal twang, but a depth to the vowels that was more European. His facial expression might have passed for friendly if not for his eyes.

Ryan shut off the tap and lifted paper towels from the stack above the basin. 'I'm sorry, do I know you?'

The man smiled. He had good teeth. 'No, you don't. I saw you in the movie house.'

Ryan estimated the man's age at forty to forty-five. He had small scars on his hands and what might have been an old burn on the skin of his neck, not quite concealed by his collar.

'It wasn't bad,' Ryan said, dropping the paper towels into the bin. 'A bit silly. But I enjoyed it.'

'Silly.' The man weighed the word. 'Yes, that's a good way to describe it. Entertaining, but hardly realistic, don't you think?'

Ryan stepped away from the basin, towards the door. 'I wouldn't know. Goodnight.'

'She's very pretty.'

Ryan stopped, his fingers on the handle. He turned to see the man incline his head towards the door, and the unseen room beyond.

'The girl. Your date. She's very pretty.'

Ryan let his hands drop to his sides, found his balance. 'Yes, she is.'

'You're punching above your weight a little, though, aren't you?'

Ryan did not answer.

'I mean, you're getting a little out of your league.'

'Who are you?'

The man's smile broadened. 'You don't want to be out of your league, do you? If you get in over your head, who knows what might happen?'

Ryan shifted his weight forward on the ball of his right foot. The man braced.

'Who sent you?' Ryan asked.

'I'm sure I don't know what you—'

Ryan moved, one hand going in low, the other high, ready to seize the man, turn him, pin him against the tiled wall. Ryan was quick, but the man was quicker. A hard hand on his wrist, pulling, stealing his momentum, using it against him. The man turned and ducked within Ryan's reach, nimble like a dancer, the sharp point of his elbow jutting into Ryan's groin, robbing him of air.

The tiles slammed into Ryan's cheek. He tried to push himself away from the wall, but the man kicked at the backs of his knees, taking his legs from under him. Ryan's kneecaps cracked on the cold wet floor. He felt the other man's knee press hard between his shoulder blades, pinning his chest to the wall. A hand gripped his hair, pulled his head back.

Ryan heard a metallic click, saw the tip of a blade close to his right eye, felt it brush his eyelashes, the chill of it against his cheek.

'Be still, my friend.'

Ryan put his palms on the tiles, fought the heaving in his chest.

'I only asked if you enjoyed the picture,' the man said, his voice calm and even. 'That's all. Nothing to get worked up about, is it? Just a friendly question, right?'

The man released Ryan's hair, took the knee from his back, the knife from his vision, and stepped away.

'I'll see you around, Lieutenant Ryan.'

The door creaked, the chatter of drinkers swelling for a moment then receding. Ryan looked over his shoulder. Alone, he rested his forehead on the coolness of the tiles for a few seconds before dragging himself to his feet.

He went to the mirror over the basin, checked for any mark from the blade, saw none. His knees carried damp stains from the moisture on the floor, and his tie hung crooked. He straightened it, wiped at his knees with paper towels. When his breathing steadied, he left the WC.

Celia looked up as he approached. 'Are you all right?' she asked.

'I'm fine,' Ryan said. 'I promised Mrs Highland I'd have you back by eleven. We'd better be going.'

Celia scoffed. 'Oh, Mrs Highland can wait up. That dried-up old bag should step out herself now and then. It'd do her the world of good to blow the cobwebs from her knickers.'

She giggled, brought her fingertips to her mouth. 'I'm sorry, that was quite coarse of me, wasn't it? Perhaps I've had one drink too many. You're right, we should go.'

Ryan offered her his arm, and they made their way through the smoke and the red-faced men. He watched for dark hair and a well-cut suit, knowing eyes set in a tanned face, and saw no one but the drunken newspapermen.

The drawing room curtains twitched as they reached the doorstep. Celia rested her hand on his chest.

'I'd invite you in, but I'm afraid we'd have Mrs Highland for company. Unless you want to watch her knitting, we'll have to say goodnight here.'

'Here is fine,' Ryan said. Once more, he found himself short of words. He stood with his arms by his sides, the agony of silence between them. Celia broke it with a smile.

'I had a very nice time,' she said. 'I hope you'll call me again.'

'I will. Absolutely.'

'The restaurant at the Shelbourne isn't too bad.'

'Then I'll take you.'

Ryan couldn't help feeling they were negotiating a contract, making promises, reaching accords. He didn't care, as long as he saw her again.

'Good,' she said.

She leaned in, raised herself slightly on her toes, and kissed him. Warm, moist, fragrant lipstick. The tip of her tongue grazed his upper lip. When she moved away, he still felt her there, the heat of her.

'For God's sake, Albert, don't just stand there looking like you've seen the Blessed Virgin.'

He half coughed, half laughed. 'I'm sorry. I didn't expect . . . I didn't know . . .'

She raised her fingertips to his cheek. 'Such a saggy face. Goodnight, Albert.'

Ryan left her there and went to the car. The drive from Rathgar into town took less than fifteen minutes, and he spent it trying to think of the dark-haired man who bested him in the toilets, and not the feeling of Celia's lips against his.

He did not succeed.

17

SKORZENY LEFT HIS BRANDY AND HIS GUESTS IN THE DRAWING room. He followed Esteban to the darkened study and picked up the telephone receiver. The boy flicked on the lamp, casting a pool of soft light over the desk.

'Who is this?' Skorzeny asked.

'Celia Hume.'

Skorzeny took a cigarette from the case on the desk. 'Well?'

'We had a very pleasant evening. We went to the pictures, then afterwards, a drink.'

Skorzeny noted the softness of the consonants, the way she enunciated the words with care so as to hide the effects of those drinks.

Esteban lifted the desk lighter, struck a flame, and held it out. Skorzeny tasted petrol and tobacco, carried to his throat by the heat. He waved Esteban away. The boy left the room, closed the door behind him.

'Were any sensitive matters discussed?' he asked.

'No. At least, none that concerned you or the work Lieutenant Ryan is doing for you.'

'And what were your impressions of him?'

The girl paused, then said, 'He is very sweet. Like a child, in some ways. But there's something else to him, something I can't quite describe. I know he's a soldier, but it's more than that. Something in his eyes, in the way he holds himself, the way he speaks. But not what he says. Something that frightens me, just a little.'

Had he felt so inclined, Skorzeny could have put it into words for her. Ryan carried the souls of the dead with him, just as every killer does. However gentlemanly the exterior, no matter how kind the man might appear, those souls will watch from behind his eyes.

'When will you see him again?'

'I don't know,' she said. 'Soon, I think. He promised to call.'

'Good. Bring him close to you. As close as he desires to be.'

Silence for a moment, then, 'What do you mean?'

Skorzeny flicked the cigarette against the crystal ashtray. 'Do I not pay you well for this service?'

'Colonel Skorzeny, I am not a prostitute.'

'Of course not,' he said. 'Goodnight, Miss Hume.'

He hung up and returned to his guests, picking up the story he'd been telling. The one about rescuing Mussolini from the hotel on Gran Sasso that served as the dictator's prison. Skorzeny's political guests always enjoyed that one.

He had told the tale so many times, at so many parties and dinners and banquets, that he occasionally struggled to separate truth from fiction. In moments of doubt, he would remind himself that he was not a historian. If the people he met desired to be enthralled by stories of his adventures, who was Otto Skorzeny to deny them their pleasure?

Luca Impelliteri would deny them, given the chance.

The morning after the Italian had goaded him on that balcony in Tarragona, he had a message delivered to

Skorzeny's room inviting him to coffee. At noon, Skorzeny found Impelliteri waiting at a table outside a cafe on the Rambla Nova. He wore an open-necked shirt and sunglasses. He clicked his fingers to attract a waiter as Skorzeny approached.

'Please sit,' he said.

Skorzeny obliged. 'What do you want?'

'Just a chat,' Impelliteri said, keeping his demeanour friendly. The sunglasses hid his eyes. 'Coffee?'

Skorzeny nodded.

Impelliteri addressed the waiter. 'Two coffees, and bring us a plate of pastries, whatever you recommend.'

'Not for me,' Skorzeny said.

'Oh, please, you must. The pastries here are the best I've tasted outside Italy.'

The waiter went to fetch the order.

'You wanted to talk,' Skorzeny said. 'So get to it.'

'Colonel Skorzeny, you're an impatient man.'

'Amongst other things. Do not test me.'

The Italian smiled. 'Well, then let's not keep you any longer than necessary. As we discussed last night, I was there on Gran Sasso when you snatched Il Duce. I watched you run around the hotel, trying to find a way in. I saw you scamper away from the guard dogs – lucky for you, they were chained up – and I watched when you couldn't climb a wall no higher than a metre and a half. You had to use one of your men as a platform to stand on. It was almost comical.'

The waiter returned, placed a coffee in front of each man, and a plate of pastries at the centre of the table. The confections glistened in the sunlight, red jam and yellow custard set in pastry cases that looked like they might blow away on the breeze. Impelliteri lifted the plate, presented it to Skorzeny.

'No,' he said.

Impelliteri shrugged and took one for himself, mimed ecstasy as he ate.

Skorzeny knocked the table with a knuckle to regain the Italian's attention. 'So you dispute the historical record of Operation Oak, you claim I and many of my *Kameraden* are liars, that you know better. Why should I care what you believe?'

Impelliteri dabbed pastry crumbs from his lips with a napkin. 'You shouldn't care what I believe. After all, who am I? But I think you might care what the Generalissimo believes. After all, you are a guest in Spain at his indulgence. If he were to discover you to be a fraud, that you had taken his friendship by deceit, then perhaps his indulgence might not stretch so far. Perhaps you would not find this beautiful country so welcoming. Please do try one of these pastries, they're quite lovely.'

He held the plate up once more, and Skorzeny pushed it away.

'My friend Francisco will not believe such fantasies. He will take the historical record for the truth it is.'

'Historical record,' Impelliteri echoed. 'You keep saying these words as if repeating them will make them real. There is no historical record. There is only SS propaganda, and your own bluster.'

Skorzeny stood, his chair screeching on the pavement as it slid back. 'I've heard enough of this. Do not bother me again.'

He marched towards the hotel, the Mediterranean blue and glassy beyond.

Impelliteri's voice called after him. 'Wait, Colonel Skorzeny. I haven't told you what I want, yet.'

Skorzeny stopped and turned, already sure in his gut what the Italian wanted.

18

RYAN SLEPT LITTLE, THE HOTEL BED FEELING TOO NARROW FOR his frame, too short for his legs. If he wasn't thinking about Celia and the feel of her lips on his, he was brooding on the dark-haired man and his blade.

He played out scenarios in his mind.

In one, the man did not get the better of him, did not have him on his knees on the piss-soaked floor. Instead, Ryan outmanoeuvred the man, disarmed him, had him quaking and talking, telling Ryan everything he wanted to know.

In another, Celia brought Ryan to the parlour of her boarding house, dismissed Mrs Highland as if she were a housemaid. And there, on the hard cushions of the settee, Celia kissed him again, this time letting her tongue linger, explore, quick and nimble. And she guided his hands over her body, finding the secret places, warm to his touch.

When he did sleep, he dreamed of her open mouth and the taste of her lipstick, the tobacco and alcohol on her breath. And as he moved against her, she became one of the whores the boys had brought him to visit in Sicily and Egypt, plump and eager, smelling of sweat and strong soap.

And the man watched from the corner, his knife held in his hand.

'She's very pretty,' he said, the blade held out from his groin, shining and obscene.

Ryan awoke in the greyness of the dawn, the blankets twisted around his ankles. He freed himself and sat up on the edge of the bed, lifted his watch from the bedside locker. Just gone five. He rubbed the sleep from his eyes, yawned, tasted the Guinness from the night before.

His stomach grumbled. An hour and a half before they served breakfast. Ninety minutes with nothing but his own thoughts. Exercise was the only answer.

Wearing just his underwear, he stood upright and stretched his arms towards the ceiling, feeling the movement work the muscles of his back. Then he bent forward, his legs straight, dropping his fingertips towards the floor, down, down, until they touched the carpet's vulgar pattern.

Ryan lay on the floor, wedged his feet beneath the bed, twined his fingers behind his head, and started counting sit-ups.

The effort cleared the jumble from his mind.

He thought about Otto Skorzeny, once called the most dangerous man in Europe. Now a gentleman farmer. Had the eighteen years between now and the end of the war washed away his sins? True, the respect and admiration other soldiers held him in was deserved to an extent. He was a master tactician, a revolutionary of battle, had changed the way men thought about warfare. But he was also a Nazi. And not some poor man conscripted to that cause by accident of birth. No, he had been a member of the party long before the war, and had volunteered to fight for the Reich, had not been forced into service.

Whatever these killers wanted from Skorzeny, whatever fate awaited him, many would say he had it coming.

Many, but not all.

Ryan remembered the discussions in his father's shop. As a boy, stacking shelves and sweeping floors for the odd penny his father would allow him, he listened to the men discuss the goings-on in Europe. They talked about Chancellor Hitler. Would de Valera – still Taoiseach then, still riding on the back of the revolution – side with Chamberlain? If it came to it, would he ask his fellow Irishmen to fight alongside the British?

Unthinkable, some would say. Old Dev would never sell his people out to the Brits.

But that Hitler, others would say, he's bad news. No good could come of his shouting and blustering. Someone needs to put some manners on him.

But he's just a good nationalist, like us, looking out for his own people. Just like old Dev did, like Pearse and Connolly did in 1916.

Not the same, no, not at all. Dev and the rest fought for freedom. That Hitler's a dictator, pure and simple, and he's a fascist.

And so the arguments would go on as young Albert Ryan swept the floors and cleaned the windows, and Ryan's father would keep his counter tidy and say little. Sure, it's nothing to do with me, he'd say, let them fight it out if they want, just so long as they leave me and mine out of it.

In the end, Ryan's father had been right. Ireland stayed out of it, after a fashion.

But Ryan did not. He saw what the Nazis had done, the charred remains of the continent they had raped and mutilated. The men, women and children, the human beings, left to wander the roads, everything they owned clutched in their hands or tied to their backs. They spoke of what they'd left behind. Not the possessions, but the bodies. The bodies of those they loved, abandoned to the dogs and the insects.

Ryan still dreamed of them. Not as often as he used to, but sometimes. He thanked God he had not entered the camps. The stories travelled across Europe's wastelands, about the living skeletons, the mass graves, the bodies stacked high, half burned, half buried.

Men like Skorzeny had done that. Willingly.

And now Ryan was protecting them.

He stopped, his chest pressed to his knees, his breath held tight in his lungs. He had stopped counting, had no idea how many he'd done. No matter. He turned over, his body straight, his hands flat on the floor, and pushed.

Who were the predators who stalked Skorzeny? The man who had humiliated Ryan the night before, was he one of them? Or something other?

The floor rose and fell beneath Ryan, drops of sweat darkening the carpet's fibres. He relished the sensation of the muscles of his shoulders and flanks taking the strain, the clarity of it. He worked until his body burned, his lungs straining, his mind flitting between a dark-haired man and a red-haired woman, uncertain of whom he feared more.

With his mind focused by the exertion, he returned to the file Haughey had supplied. He read and reread the minister's notes, and his own. The same two names snagged his suspicions however hard he tried to broaden his gaze.

Hakon Foss and Catherine Beauchamp.

He repeated the woman's address in his mind and went to the map that lay on the desk.

* * *

Ryan had washed, shaved and dressed in his old suit, and was about to go for breakfast when the telephone rang. The receptionist asked if he could put a call through. The caller had declined to identify himself. A foreign gentleman, the receptionist said.

'Yes,' Ryan said, knowing.

'Good morning, Lieutenant Ryan,' Otto Skorzeny said.

'Good morning, sir.'

'What have you to report?'

Ryan told him he had two names he wanted to investigate further, people close to Skorzeny.

'Who are they?'

Ryan paused, said, 'I'd rather not say.'

'No?'

'No.'

'And if I insist?'

'I will refuse,' Ryan said.

Skorzeny remained silent for some time before he said, 'Very well.'

Ryan considered whether he should tell the Austrian about the dark-haired man. He saw no advantage in keeping the information secret, but neither could he see a way to impart the information without revealing to Skorzeny that Ryan had been left on his knees in the toilet of a public house. He knew by instinct and experience that to show such weakness to a man like Otto Skorzeny could be fatal. Should he take that risk?

Before he could decide, Skorzeny said, 'I would like to extend an invitation.'

Ryan blinked. 'Oh?'

'To my home. I'm hosting a small gathering tomorrow

evening. You will know some of the people. Our friend the minister, for one. Tell me, do you have a sweetheart?'

Ryan hesitated. 'I know a young lady,' he said eventually, then cursed himself for the way it sounded. He could hear the smirk in Skorzeny's reply.

'Then, please, bring along this young lady whom you know.'

'Thank you, sir.'

'And one more thing. Be ready for a match.'

'Sir?'

'We shall fence. I told you I've been seeking a reasonable opponent. You might be that man. I'll see you tomorrow evening.'

The telephone clicked and died.

Ryan enjoyed a substantial breakfast before dropping his good suit off at a cleaner's, then walked to Capel Street where McClelland's Tailors had just opened. Lawrence McClelland stood arranging shirt boxes on a shelf when Ryan entered. He turned to see the visitor, his face blank for a moment before recognition burst upon it.

'Ah, sir, how is the Canali doing for you?'

'Very well,' Ryan said.

McClelland circled the table stacked with garments and fabrics. 'And what can I help you with this morning?'

'I'd like to see some ties,' Ryan said. 'And maybe a couple of shirts.'

McClelland nodded, his chest deflating. 'And should these also be added to Mr Haughey's account?'

Ryan did not hesitate.

'Yes, please,' he said.

19

RYAN DROVE NORTH OUT OF DUBLIN, HEADING FOR SWORDS. The city thinned and gave way to green fields. Within a few minutes, the white hulk of the airport terminal came into view, an Aer Lingus craft leaping skyward from the near horizon. The airport had expanded apace since the terminal had been built in the early forties, routes to almost anywhere you could imagine.

The map lay open on the passenger seat next to Ryan, a circle drawn in pencil where he believed the home of Catherine Beauchamp to be.

He passed through Swords and its quiet Main Street, then the council housing of Seatown. Dirty-faced boys paused their soccer games to watch him pass. A gang of dogs chased the car, barking. They let him go after a hundred yards or so, satisfied they had protected their domain.

Ryan held the map across the steering wheel, his attention flitting between it and the way ahead. The road narrowed to a short bridge that crossed the river. On the other side he turned right, the trail barely wide enough for the Vauxhall. Branches clanged on the metalwork.

He followed the road, hedgerows and trees to his left, water to his right. The spindle of a river broadened as he drove, at first only half a dozen yards wide, then a dozen, then fifty, then a hundred, until it swelled into the estuary.

Swans gathered in the reeds and wandered onto the road, blocking Ryan's path. Fearless, they ignored the car as he inched towards them. He half-clutched, nudging forward, the swans merely waddling a few inches further along the track, no notion of making way for him.

Ryan got out of the car and tried to shoo them away. They hissed at him, then resumed their loitering. Ryan opened his jacket wide, like wings, and flapped at them, made himself as big as he could. At last the swans were sufficiently annoyed to return to the water. He got back into the car and set off again.

Up ahead, the road arced out towards the water where the land formed a miniature peninsula. Water lapped onto the track, and the Vauxhall's tyres whooshed through it. As the wheels once more found a dry surface, a wall seemed to grow out of the hedgerow. Within it, set into an archway, a gate. Ryan slowed as he checked the map.

Yes, this must be it, the small nub of land stretching away to the estuary opposite the gate.

He pulled the car onto the coarse grass between the road and the shore, applied the handbrake, and took the key from the ignition. A sharp wind blew in from the open expanse of water. Across the estuary, hazed in the distance, he could see Malahide.

Ryan walked back to the gate, found it locked. He peered through the bars, saw a low cottage beyond a beautifully tended garden and a gravel path and, off to the side, a barn that served as a stable.

A slender woman, a bucket of feed in her hands, stared

back at him from the barn door. A horse ate from the bucket, its long neck reaching over a gate that had been cobbled together from wood and corrugated metal sheets.

'Catherine Beauchamp?' Ryan asked.

The woman put the bucket down, slipped her hands into her trouser pockets, and walked towards him.

'Who are you?' she asked, her French accent delicate as a petal.

'My name is Albert Ryan. I work for the Directorate of Intelligence.' He held up his identification. She stopped halfway across the garden, too far away to see the card. 'I'd like to speak with you,' he said.

'I'm not sure I wish to speak with you,' she said, her English perfect, a layer of grit in her voice. She wore her greying hair in a bob, held back with clips. Ryan could make out her fine features, now turning jagged with age, and the heavy smoker's lines on her upper lip.

'I'm working for Otto Skorzeny.' It was barely a lie, and worth the telling, because her expression shifted when she heard the name. 'I'm investigating the killings of Alex Renders, Johan Hambro and Helmut Krauss. And Elouan Groix.'

She flinched. Hadn't she known of the Breton's death?

'I don't know anything about that,' she said, keeping her distance, a waver creeping into her voice. 'I'm afraid you've wasted a journey.'

'Even so, I'd like to speak with you. It won't take long.' He considered a gamble, decided to risk it. 'I'd rather not tell Colonel Skorzeny you refused to cooperate.'

Her face hardened. She marched towards the gate.

'Threats might gain you some advantage in the short term,

but they will cost you more in the long run, Mr . . . what did you say?'

'Ryan. Lieutenant Albert Ryan.'

She fished a key from her pocket and unlocked the gate.

Beauchamp heated coffee in a pot over the fire and poured two cups. She placed one on the table in front of Ryan. It tasted stale and bitter, but he did not grimace.

The interior of the cottage was not dissimilar to the one in which Elouan Groix had died, the home Célestin Lainé had abandoned. The kitchen served as a living area with its sink and fireplace. One of the two doors stood ajar, and Ryan saw a neatly made bed, and shelves stacked with books. The kitchen too housed full bookcases, four of them. On the table were several notebooks, jotters, loose sheets of paper. They carried looping scripts, arranged in rows, verses in a language Ryan did not recognise.

'I still write,' Beauchamp said, taking a chair opposite Ryan. 'No one wants to publish me these days, but still I write because I must.'

'Poetry?' Ryan asked.

'Yes, mostly, and essays, and stories. I used to write novels, but I don't have the will any more.'

'In Breton?'

'*Ouais*,' she said, lapsing into French. 'It's a beautiful language, lyrical, like music. My work does not translate well into English. It doesn't have the rhythm, the melody of Breton. Breton is more like the Cornish language, and shares much with your Irish. Tell me, how is your Irish?'

'I only remember a few words from school,' Ryan said.

She gave a sad smile and lit a cigarette. 'You don't speak

your own language? You prefer to speak the words of your oppressor? Don't you see the tragedy of this?'

'I never had the desire to learn.'

She let out a lungful of air and smoke, disappointment wheezing from her. 'So go on and ask your questions. I will answer if I can.'

'How close are you to Otto Skorzeny?'

'Not very. He assisted me in finding my way to Ireland, along with some other Bretons. Célestin knows him better.'

'Célestin Lainé is a friend of yours?'

Again, that sad smile on her lips. She pulled one knee up almost to her chin, her heel perched on the edge of her seat. 'Yes. More than that. Many years ago, we were lovers. Now, I don't know.'

'Elouan Groix died at Lainé's home.'

She stared at some distant point, far away from her cottage. 'Poor Elouan. He was a good man. But not a strong man. Not a fighter. How is Célestin? Was he hurt?'

'No,' Ryan said. 'Mr Lainé is staying with Colonel Skorzeny, as far as I know. You knew him in France?'

'Yes. We carried out actions together, back in the Thirties.'

'And during the war?'

'He fought. I wrote. Propaganda. Essays, articles, that kind of thing. We distributed pamphlets in the towns and villages.'

'You were a collaborator.'

She turned her gaze on Ryan, her eyes like needles piercing his skin. 'Call me that if you must. I considered myself a patriot and a socialist. The Germans promised us our independence, our own state, our own government. We believed them. Perhaps that was naive, but isn't that the prerogative of the young?'

Beauchamp drew deep on the cigarette, its tip flaring red in the dim cottage. She held the smoke in her chest for a while before letting it leak from her nostrils. Then a cough burst from her. She took a tissue from her pocket, spat in it.

'Tell me,' she said. 'Do you know the term: Dweller on the Threshold?'

Ryan shook his head. 'No, I don't.'

'It's a spiritualist idea. Or occultist, depending on your point of view. It has different meanings to different people. Some consider the Dweller a malevolent spirit that attaches itself to a living person. Others describe it as a past evil, a dark reflection of oneself from a former life. We all have this thing. Something that hides in our shadow, something that shames us.'

She studied the swirling blue patterns of the smoke that hung between them.

'I don't understand,' Ryan said.

'What I did during the war, the people I allowed to attach themselves to me, the things I wrote. What I allowed myself to be in that life. All these, they are my Dweller on the Threshold.'

'You mean guilt.'

'Perhaps,' she said. 'If I had known the truth of it, the Germans who promised us so much, if I'd known what they were doing to those people, the Jews, the Roma, the homosexuals, I would have made a different choice. Do you believe me?'

Ryan did not answer the question. Instead, he asked, 'Do you resent Otto Skorzeny?'

'In what way?'

'Any way.'

She laughed. 'I resent that he has grown rich and fat. I resent that his love of money and power has drowned the love of his country. I resent that he allows himself to be a show pony for the Irish bourgeoisie. Are those enough ways?'

Ryan leaned forward, his forearms on the table. Pages of poetry rustled beneath his elbows.

'Has anyone ever come to you and asked about Colonel Skorzeny or any of the other people like you?'

She tried to hide it, but there it was, a flicker. Then it was gone.

'People like me?'

'Foreign nationals. Refugees from Europe.'

'You mean Nazis,' she said. 'Collaborators.'

'Yes.'

She stubbed out the cigarette. Glowing tobacco embers floated up from the ashtray. 'Why do you ask me this?'

'Whoever has been targeting Skorzeny's associates, your friends—'

'My friends? They are not my—'

'Whatever they are to you, a well-trained and organised team of killers has been targeting them. And they have an informant. Someone with access to Skorzeny's circle. Someone who has reason to turn against their friends. Someone like you.'

She shook her head, her eyes distant. 'This is nonsense. Where do you get this idea? Nonsense.'

Ryan kept his silence, watched her as she turned her gaze to the window overlooking her garden and held it there. He counted the seconds until she said, 'I would like you to leave now.'

'Listen to me,' Ryan said. 'If you have betrayed Colonel

Skorzeny, your only hope is to tell me now. If you have passed on information to others, tell me who they are, and what you told them.'

She opened her mouth, closed it, opened it again. 'I . . . I didn't . . . not me.'

Ryan reached for her, touched her forearm. She recoiled.

'You know what Skorzeny will do to you. Talk to me and I'll protect you.'

She shook her head and smiled. 'Oh, you are a child, aren't you?'

'On my life, I will—'

Papers scattered as she slapped the tabletop with her palm. 'If Otto Skorzeny desires a man's death, or a woman's, then death will come. Don't you know this? He plucked Mussolini from a mountaintop. He fucked Evita right under Perón's nose. Then he robbed the fascist bastard blind and was thanked for it. This is his power. Not an office, not a title. No law will stop him.'

Beauchamp stood, went to the sink, gripped its edge.

Ryan got to his feet. 'Please, you know the alternative. You know what Skorzeny will do to you if he gets to you first. Either you talk to me, or you—'

Her hand dipped behind the gingham curtain that hung below the sink. She turned, a small semi-automatic pistol aimed at Ryan's chest. A .25 ACP, he thought. Her hand quivered, the pistol jittering in her grasp. The other hand gripped the slide assembly, pulled it back.

Ryan raised his hands as high as his shoulders.

'Does he know about me?' she asked.

'I didn't give him your name,' Ryan said. 'But he knows there's an informant. I found you without any trouble. He can do the same. And he will. Please, let me protect you.'

Tears sprang from Beauchamp's wide eyes, darkening her blouse where they fell from her cheeks. Her breathing quickened with fear, her chest heaving. She wiped at her cheeks, sniffed hard. 'They told me I would be safe. They promised me. It was my penance. I told them what they wanted to know so God would forgive me. Has God forgiven me?'

'I don't know. Who were they?'

'They showed me photographs. The children.' Her free hand went to her belly, clutched at the flesh over her womb. 'The dead children. The bones. Their dead eyes. Their mouths open. Flies on their lips.'

'You didn't do that to them,' Ryan said. He stepped around the table. 'Like you said, you didn't know. Please, put the gun down.'

'Will God forgive me?'

'I don't know. Catherine, please, put the gun down. Talk to me. We can work something out. You can run, get out of the country.'

She asked again, her voice firm and final. 'Will God forgive me?'

Ryan lowered his hands. 'Yes. He will.'

Catherine Beauchamp smiled. She opened her mouth wide, brought the pistol up, put the muzzle between her teeth and closed her eyes.

Ryan said, 'No,' but it was done before he could take a single step.

20

CÉLESTIN LAINÉ HAD ENJOYED THE PENFOLDS GRANGE HERMITAGE so much the night before that he had crept down to the cellar in search of a second bottle. He had descended the wooden steps, feeling the chill of the damp air crawl beneath his clothing, and gasped as his feet touched the concrete floor. Row after row of bottles from all over the world, some shining, some dusted with age. He had wandered between the racks, his tongue squirming behind his teeth, anticipating the delights ahead. It took several minutes to find the second Shiraz.

Now, in daylight, his brain seemed to grind against the inside of his skull. Of course, the only answer was more wine. He returned to the cellar hoping to find another Penfolds, but there was none. Instead, he settled for an Italian white. It might have benefited from an hour on ice, but it was more than tolerable.

He wandered the grounds of Martinstown House, the uncorked bottle in one hand, the other holding his jacket closed. Skorzeny's homestead was certainly impressive. Lainé had never been one for ostentation, displays of wealth – he'd never had the money – but still he had to admire the house with its sprawling wings, its arched windows, the gardens it nestled in. He stood back, surveyed the property.

Yes, Skorzeny had done well. Perhaps if Lainé had possessed a similar ambition, he could have attained such wealth. But then he'd only have spent it on drink.

He took a slug from the bottle. The wine cloyed in his throat, treacly sweet.

One of Skorzeny's guards ambled past, patrolling the grounds, no attempt to conceal the Kalashnikov automatic rifle. Lainé nodded. The guard grunted some reply in German. A group of five men, refugees from East Germany who had been smuggled into Ireland, shared two rooms in one of the outbuildings.

Hakon Foss trudged across the front of the house, dressed in mud-caked overalls, a watering can in his hand. Lainé waved. Foss waved back.

The Norwegian knelt by one of the planters that lined up along the wall, spring flowers bursting like fireworks from the compost. He began plucking weeds from amongst them, dropping the scraps on the gravel beside him.

Lainé crossed the path.

Foss looked up from his work. 'Hallo,' he said.

Lainé smiled. 'You work hard?'

The Norwegian shrugged. 'Not hard. I do this work two days ago. The Colonel, he calls, says come, do this work some more. What for?'

Lainé extended the bottle to him. Foss smiled, took the wine from Lainé's hand, and drank. His Adam's apple bobbed as he swallowed. He handed the bottle back and wiped his mouth.

'You don't want this work?' Lainé asked. 'You don't want the money?'

Foss returned his stubby fingers to the compost. 'Oh, yes, I want work. I want money. Always I want money.'

Lainé raised the bottle to his lips, swallowed. 'To have money is good.'

Foss laughed, shrugged, nodded. 'Yes. Yes. Money is good. And to eat. And a place for sleeping. Money is good for these things.'

Lainé smiled, patted Foss's back, and said goodbye. He strolled away from the house, out of the gardens, towards the outbuildings. Chickens roamed and pecked at the earth. He nudged them aside with the toe of his boot.

He found Tiernan in an open barn, fussing over a roiling mass of fur, cursing. The red-faced man looked up as Lainé entered.

'How're ya,' he said, giving a deferential nod.

One of Tiernan's collies, a bitch, lay in a bundle of blankets. Half a dozen pups wrestled and ran around her, hemmed in by a makeshift pen of wooden boards.

'How old?' Lainé asked.

'Seven weeks,' Tiernan said. 'Some stray fucker got to her. Six bloody mongrels, no use to anyone. I should've drowned the wee bastards by now, but I didn't have the heart. They're just about weaned now, so there's no avoiding it. It'll be the sack and the river for them as soon as I gather the nerve to do it.'

The old man reached out a hand, all sinew and knuckles, and scratched one of the pups behind the ear. It batted at his bony fingers with its paws, nipped his hard skin with needle teeth. Its siblings joined in the game.

'I will take one,' Lainé said. He hunkered down, placed the bottle by his side, looked from one pup to the next. All but one of them mobbed Tiernan's hand, a black and brown male, smaller than the others. Lainé dipped his fingers towards it. The pup hesitated, sniffed at his skin, then its tiny tongue lapped at him.

'This one,' he said.

'All right, so,' Tiernan said. 'But don't let the missus see it in the house. She'll have a blue fit.'

Tiernan's wife served as Skorzeny's housekeeper. A German woman, stout and fierce, she had come to Ireland before the war and married the Irishman. She had already scolded Lainé for walking mud into the house.

'I will hide it from her,' Lainé said.

He reached down, plucked the pup from the pen, and thanked Tiernan. It squirmed in his hands. He tucked it under his arm, took the wine in his free hand, and set off for the house.

When he entered through the kitchen, Mrs Tiernan stood arguing with the chef who had arrived that morning from the Horcher restaurant in Madrid, Skorzeny's favourite eatery in Europe. The Spaniard had been flown over to prepare the feast for the following evening. Half a dozen pheasants lay in two rows on the kitchen table. Evidently Mrs Tiernan and the chef disagreed on how best to prepare the birds, each speaking in their own language, miming their points with their hands, their voices rising.

Lainé slipped past unnoticed.

He made his way to the stairs, was halfway up when a voice called, 'Célestin.'

Lainé stopped, turned, saw Skorzeny.

'Yes?'

'What have you got there?'

'A pup,' Lainé said. He held the mite up, its little legs thrashing at the air.

'Don't let Frau Tiernan find it in your room.'

'I won't.'

Skorzeny pointed. 'And that?'

Lainé's fingers tightened on the bottle of wine. 'I was thirsty.'

'No more,' Skorzeny said. 'I want to begin questioning Hakon Foss tonight. You must be sober. Understood?'

'Yes.'

'Good.'

Lainé went to his room, placed the wine on the bedside locker and the puppy on the bed. It explored the blanket, sniffing, whimpering. Lainé rolled it on its back, scratched its belly. It boxed his hand with its paws.

Alongside the puppy, on the bed, sat a worn leather satchel, not unlike the kind of bag a doctor might carry. It contained no medicines, no pills; only tools. Sharp things. Jagged things.

From outside, below his window, Lainé heard whistling. Foss, cheerful in his labour, even if he believed his services were not truly required today. And he was right, the work was not needed. Skorzeny simply wanted the Norwegian here, on the grounds. At the end of the working day, he would be asked to stay for supper. Perhaps he would protest, say that he should leave for home, but Skorzeny would insist. Foss would eat well, perhaps have some wine.

Then Foss would be escorted to one of the outbuildings,

and Lainé would bring his bag, and all his shining tools. Lainé and Foss would talk long into the night.

The puppy's teeth closed on Lainé's forefinger, causing a bright point of pain. Lainé pulled his hand away, scolded the little dog. He sucked the blood from his finger, tasted salt.

21

RYAN FLED, LEFT HER THERE.

He drove for an hour or more, main roads, country lanes, paying no attention to where he was heading as the sun dipped towards the hills. The scene played out in his mind, over and over. The muffled pop of the pistol, the shocked look in her eyes. Her body falling.

The fuel gauge slipped into the red. He took note of road signs and navigated his way towards a village. A petrol station stood at the middle of its one street. He pulled in and told the attendant to fill the tank.

A phone box stood on the other side of the road.

Ryan crossed to it. He told the operator what he wanted. The operator hesitated, and Ryan told her to just fucking do it.

Two more transfers, and he was through to Haughey's secretary.

Three minutes later, he had what he wanted, and the secretary was in tears.

Ryan pulled in to the kerb outside the Royal Hibernian Hotel, its four storeys looming white over Dawson Street. He got out of the car, took the steps up to the hotel entrance two at a time, ignored the doorman beneath the awning.

Inside, porters and receptionists eyed him with suspicion. A man with a thin moustache asked, 'Can I help you, sir?'

They knew Ryan didn't belong here, and so did he. The clientele of this place dressed well, lived well, and ate well in its restaurant and tea rooms. They came from the country estates outside Dublin, or the grand city houses with archways leading to stable blocks. They rode horses through Phoenix Park, they went to the races, they took holidays abroad and gave generously to charities.

Ryan ignored the man with the thin moustache and strode through the foyer to the restaurant. The maître d' blocked his path. Ryan shoved him aside.

Charles J. Haughey looked up from his soup. A young woman, who Ryan guessed was not the minister's wife, followed his gaze, turned back to Haughey, said something.

Ryan crossed the room.

Haughey pulled the napkin from his collar, dropped it on the tablecloth.

'What do you think you're doing, Ryan?'

The restaurant's patrons craned their necks to see the intruder.

Ryan straightened his jacket, smoothed his tie. 'A word, Minister.'

Haughey smiled at his companion. 'You might have called my secretary and made an appointment.'

'A word. Now.'

Haughey's smile slipped away, the hawk's glare hard on Ryan. 'You might also keep a civil tongue when you talk to me, big fella. Come by my office in the morning if you need to discuss something. Until then, fuck off and leave me in peace. Understood?'

The maître d' appeared at Ryan's side, addressed the minister. 'Sir, is there a problem?'

'No problem,' Haughey said. 'This gentleman was just leaving.'

The maître d' took Ryan's elbow, tried to guide him away. Ryan shook him off, kept his gaze on Haughey. 'Shall we discuss it here in the restaurant? Or somewhere else?'

The maître d' turned his pleading eyes back to the minister. 'Sir, really, I must ask you to—'

'All right, for fuck's sake.' Haughey stood, pushing his chair back to collide with the diner behind him. 'Come on, then.'

Ryan followed him out of the restaurant. In the foyer, Haughey spotted the cloakroom, steered Ryan towards it.

The coat-check girl said, 'Tickets, please.'

Haughey pulled a ten shilling note from his pocket, pushed it into the girl's hand, said, 'Piss off, love, go and have yourself a cigarette or something.'

She stood open-mouthed for a moment, then looked at the note in her hand, grinned. 'Very good, sir.'

Haughey grabbed Ryan's sleeve, shoved him into the cloakroom, slammed the door behind them.

'Right, now what in the name of holy God do you want, you ignorant shite?'

Ryan prised Haughey's fingers from his sleeve. 'I want off this assignment.'

'What? You dragged me away from dinner to tell me that? No. No fucking way. You were given a job, now you bloody well do it, do you hear me?'

'I don't want your job,' Ryan said. 'I won't do it.'

Haughey placed the fingertips of his left hand at the centre of

Ryan's chest, raised the forefinger of his right. 'Yes you will. You'll do what you're told, big fella, or mark my words, I will destroy you. Ask anyone about Charlie Haughey. They'll all tell you the same. I take shite from no man, least of all a fucking jumped up squaddie like you. Believe me, boy, I'll make you wish your father had pulled out of your mother, you hear me?'

'I won't do—'

Haughey shoved Ryan back against the coat rail. 'You hear me, big fella?'

Ryan launched his body forward, grabbed Haughey's tie with one hand, gripped his neck with the other, pinching the windpipe. Haughey fell back into the coats, fur and tweed flapping around him, his eyes bulging.

'I watched a woman commit suicide today,' Ryan said.

Haughey's throat made clicking sounds as his mouth opened and closed.

'She put the barrel of a pistol in her mouth and pulled the trigger. She did that because she knew what your friend Skorzeny would do to her. I will not protect a man like him. I watched too many good men die fighting his kind. I won't take orders from scum like that.'

Haughey dug at Ryan's fingers with his own. Ryan eased the pressure, let him breathe.

'I won't do it,' Ryan said.

Haughey squirmed in his grasp, choking for air.

'Get your . . . fucking . . . hands off me.'

Ryan let him go, stepped back.

Haughey bent over, hands on his knees, coughed, spat on the cloakroom floor. He gulped and swallowed.

'Jesus Christ, man. What woman? What are you talking about?'

'Catherine Beauchamp. She was the informant. She told me before she died.'

Haughey made the sign of the cross, his chest heaving. 'Mother of God. Have you told Skorzeny?'

'No.'

'All right, I'll tell him. Did she give you anything?'

'Nothing,' Ryan said. He would not mention the pictures of the children, or the flies on their dead lips.

Haughey shook his head. 'This is getting out of hand. It needs to stop. You can't quit now. I won't allow it.'

'You have no authority to—'

'The director put you at my disposal. That means you do whatever the fuck I tell you to do. I know you don't like it. Neither do I. But I'm the Minister for Justice. Justice, you hear me? Do you understand what that means? You might think Otto Skorzeny is a piece of shit, him and his whole bloody crew, and for all you know I might think the same. You can think what you like, but murder is murder. I won't have it. Not in my country. It's my job to put a stop to it, and that's what I'll bloody well do. You have a problem with that, then you can talk to the director.'

Haughey straightened his tie, smoothed his hair, and went to the door. He turned back to Ryan.

'This is your country too, you know. You might have been a lickspittle to the Brits at one time, but this is still your country. You remember that.'

He exited, left Ryan alone with his anger.

Ryan left the cloakroom, marched across the foyer, and down to the street beyond. Darkness had fallen on the city, bringing with it a sickly drizzle. He buttoned his jacket, shoved his hands down into his pockets.

The western end of Molesworth Street faced the Royal Hibernian's entrance. He decided to leave the car where he'd parked it and walk the two hundred yards or so to Buswells, at the eastern end.

Ryan kept his head down as he walked. The street was almost empty, but even so, he didn't want to risk anyone seeing the rage that burned in him.

He paid no attention to the unmarked van as he passed it. Not until the dark-haired man in the good suit stepped out from in front of it to block his path.

'Good evening, Lieutenant Ryan,' he said in his not-quite-American accent.

Ryan stopped, his hands ready. 'What do you—'

The blow came from behind, hard to the base of his skull. His knees gave way and he sprawled on the wet pavement. Before he could recover, someone straddled his back, and a hand pressed a rag to his nose and mouth.

Cold sweetness swamped Ryan's skull. He tried to roll, throw his weight to the side, but the man astride his back grew so heavy, and Ryan was so warm here on the ground, and it was so soft.

Through flickering eyelids, he saw the dark-haired man hunker down in front of him, a smile on his lips.

Ryan wanted to say something, ask the man something, he couldn't remember what, but anyway, it was too late.

The world had already disappeared.

II

RÉSISTANT

22

SKORZENY WATCHED HAKON FOSS EAT THE PORK SCHNITZEL with a side of potatoes in a cheese sauce. Frau Tiernan had prepared the meal before Skorzeny sent her home with her husband.

Lainé picked at his food. He had smelled of wine and tobacco when he came down to supper. Skorzeny made a point of placing a glass of water in front of him, alongside the glass of beer the Breton poured for himself from the pitcher at the centre of the table.

The dining room with its patio doors overlooking the gardens seemed far too large for the three men who ate there, Skorzeny at the head of the table, Lainé at the far end, the Norwegian midway between them. Foss downed another swallow of beer, mopped up cheese sauce with a chunk of bread.

Lainé cut off a slice of schnitzel, wrapped it in a napkin, and stuffed it into his pocket. He noticed Skorzeny's attention on him.

'For the puppy,' he said.

Skorzeny gave him a hard stare, then turned his gaze to Foss. 'Did you enjoy your meal?'

Foss nodded, his mouth full of bread, cheese sauce dripping from his lip. He sat in his socks. Frau Tiernan had insisted he remove his boots before she would permit him entry to the house.

'Perhaps you would join me for my evening walk. I like to stroll around the gardens after dinner.'

Foss looked towards the patio doors. 'It's raining.'

'Come, a little rain won't hurt you.'

Foss shrugged.

'Good,' Skorzeny said. He reached for the hand bell, rang it.

Esteban appeared from the hall.

'My coat,' Skorzeny said. 'And Mr Foss's shoes.'

Esteban fetched them, opened the patio doors, placed Foss's boots outside, and brought Skorzeny's coat to him.

As Foss tied his bootlaces, the telephone rang. Esteban left to answer it. He returned a few moments later.

'Is Mr Haughey,' the boy said. He pronounced it *hoy*.

Skorzeny buttoned his coat. 'Tell the minister I'm unavailable, and I'll return his call in the morning.'

Esteban bowed and left the room.

Skorzeny nodded to Lainé and followed Foss out into the drizzle and the dark.

Gravel crunched under their shoes as they walked along the path towards the outbuildings. The rain, fine and cold, caused Skorzeny to blink as the drops wet his eyelids. In the corners of his vision, he saw a guard on either side, keeping to the black pools of darkness, shrouded by trees. They kept pace, watching.

Skorzeny asked, 'Are you a happy man, Hakon?'

Foss grunted as he pulled up the collar of his overalls. 'Yes, I am happy. Sometimes, I miss home. I miss Norge. I want snow, not rain. But here is not bad. Here, they won't put me in jail. In Norge, they jail me. I don't want to go to jail.'

They passed the boundary of the garden, the barns and sheds visible ahead, the light from a powerful halogen lamp bleaching the grounds to whites and greys. Rain slashed lines through the light, like comet trails falling to earth. The guards stayed beyond its reach.

Skorzeny asked, 'Would you ever betray me?'

Foss stopped walking. Skorzeny turned to regard him and the small quick movements of his eyes. Foss shifted his weight between his feet, soles scraping on the loose earth and stones.

'Why do you ask this?'

Skorzeny smiled, patted Foss's shoulder. 'No reason. You're a good man. Of course you wouldn't betray me.'

'No,' Foss said, his shuffling intensifying. 'I need for . . .'

He pointed to his groin. Skorzeny said, 'Very well,' and turned his back.

The rustling of clothing, a guttural sigh, then water pouring on the ground. Skorzeny smelled the sour-sweet odour.

'Have men ever come to you, asked you questions? About me, or any of our friends?'

The flow stuttered along with Foss's breathing.

'What men?'

Skorzeny turned his head, saw Foss's back, the rise and fall of his shoulders, the splashing on the ground. 'Perhaps they offered you money.'

'No,' Foss said. Even though he hadn't finished, he tucked himself away, urine spilling over his thick fingers.

'Perhaps they said to you, tell us these things, and we will pay you. Did that happen?'

Foss stood for a moment, hands by his sides, liquid dripping from his fingertips.

Then he ran.

Skorzeny watched him barrel into the darkness, whimpering, arms flailing. He could barely make out the shape of a guard stepping into the Norwegian's path, knocking him to the ground. Foss grunted as he landed and struggled back to his feet. He made off again, but the guard fired a warning shot into the treetops.

Foss threw himself down, his hands over his head. The trees rustled with startled night creatures. Somewhere in the outbuildings, Tiernan's dogs barked.

The guard grabbed Foss's collar and pulled him upright, led him back to the light and Skorzeny.

Lainé approached from the house, bag in hand. Foss closed his eyes and muttered a prayer to whichever God he worshipped.

Skorzeny said, 'Let's begin.'

23

RYAN LISTENED.

His consciousness had ebbed and flowed for time immeasurable, but now, at last, he could remain awake. A sickening ache still swelled inside his skull, pressing at the back of his eyes, and that cold sweetness lingered in his throat and nasal passages. He knew what chloroform felt like, had recognised it as the rag was pressed to his nose and mouth, but had been unable to fight it.

The climb to wakefulness had been arduous, the unending struggle against the warm pit of sleep. And when he first opened his eyes, he saw nothing, felt his eyelids rub on fabric. He moved his wrists, found them bound, a metallic clanking as he pulled the cuffs tight. His ankles also.

Ryan took stock. He rolled his shoulders, felt the cotton of his shirt against his skin. Whoever had taken him had not removed his clothing. He shifted his limbs as best he could, wriggled each toe and finger in turn and none reported injury, other than a tenderness on his palms, that hot sting of grazing one's skin on the ground.

He moved his head, and it met something solid, he guessed the high back of a chair. His scalp stung where it touched. The blow before he fell.

His tongue moved freely behind his teeth. He opened his mouth. No gag. He swallowed. His throat gritty from thirst.

Should he speak? He decided against it.

He heard a constant soft hiss from his left, felt warmth against his shoulder and thigh. A gas heater, burning.

Water dripped, a steady rhythm, each plink reverberating in an empty space. He raised the toe of his shoe off the ground, brought his foot down, a sharp tap of the sole on hard floor. Not a large room, but high ceilinged.

He strained to hear. Muffled voices in another room. Men's voices, he couldn't tell how many.

The voices ceased. A door opened.

Footsteps, two pairs of feet, approaching across the hard surface.

Something tugged at his head, the blindfold lifted away. Light speared his vision. He closed his eyes against it, turned his head.

'Easy now,' a man said.

Ryan knew the voice.

He heard the squeak of a tap turning, water running for a few seconds. Footsteps came near.

'Here, drink this.'

The hard edge of a cup pressed against Ryan's lips. He opened his mouth, allowed the water in, swallowed, coughed. The ache in his head shifted, burrowed its way from the base of his skull to his crown.

Ryan let his eyes open to a squint. The man from the pub toilet, his dark hair combed flat and sleek to his head, his jacket and tie removed, shirtsleeves rolled up. He returned the cup to the sink in the corner. Another man beside the sink, shorter, heavier set, casually dressed. A pistol gripped in his right hand.

'How do you feel?' the man from the bathroom asked. 'Your head hurts, right? Chloroform will do that to you. Please accept my apology. I hope you understand it was the only safe way to transport you here.'

Ryan craned his neck to take in as much of his surroundings as he could. Cement block walls, concrete floor, oil stains, a pit large enough for a man to stand upright. A tall and wide roller door at one end. A windowed office at the other.

'I'm guessing you want to know where you are,' the man said. 'Of course, I can't tell you our exact location, but a car mechanic owned this place. He went out of business, so we're making temporary use of it.'

The man took a chair from the corner, placed it in front of Ryan, and sat down. He crossed his legs, twined his fingers in his lap.

'Who are you?' Ryan asked, his voice rasping in his throat.

'My name is Goren Weiss. Major, as it happens, back in my army days.'

'Mossad?' Ryan asked.

'Of course.' Weiss indicated the man with the pistol. 'Though my colleague Captain Remak here is actually Aman, Directorate of Military Intelligence, not unlike the Irish G2, of which I believe you are a member. Unlike mine, his rank actually means something.'

Weiss's smile, his tone, would have made him seem friendly if not for the handcuffs that held Ryan's wrists to the chair.

'What do you want?'

'A chat, that's all.'

'What if I don't want to chat?'

Weiss held his hands up. 'Please, let's not be confrontational. I really don't see any need for this conversation to be hostile, so let's not begin that way. Don't assume I'm your enemy, Albert. May I call you Albert?'

Ryan rattled the handcuffs. 'You look like an enemy from here.'

Weiss shrugged. 'Given the company you've been keeping, I think your character judgement might be a little, shall we say, flawed.'

'The company I keep is none of your business.'

'Well, actually, it is.' Weiss leaned forward, his forearms on his knees. 'You see, our professional interests somewhat overlap.'

'In what way?'

'In several ways. Primarily, our interest in foreign nationals currently residing in Ireland. Helmut Krauss was one of them, another was Johan Hambro. Do I need to go on?'

'No,' Ryan said.

'And of course there's Colonel Skorzeny. A remarkable man, wouldn't you say?'

Ryan did not reply.

'Remarkable for many reasons. His military innovations, his amazing feats of daring in the war – sorry, the Emergency, as you folks call it – and his quite extraordinary ability to influence those around him. But do you know what I find most remarkable about him?'

'No,' Ryan said.

Weiss grinned. 'What I find most remarkable about Otto Skorzeny is that he came to be a fucking sheep farmer in the rolling green hills of this fair land.' His smile faded. He raised a finger. 'But we'll come back to that. First, if you don't mind, I'd like to talk about Catherine Beauchamp.'

Ryan moistened his lips. 'She's dead.'

'Oh, I know she is, Albert. I know she is. Just this afternoon, I saw her lying on the floor in her cottage, a neat little hole in the roof of her mouth. I found her just the way you left her.'

'I didn't kill her. She committed suicide.'

'Is that so? I guess we'll just have to take your word for that, won't we? We've been keeping an eye on you, Albert. Not constant surveillance, a two man team couldn't do that, but enough to know what you've been up to. When Captain Remak saw you were heading for the estuary today, he got in touch with me. We thought we'd better check in on Catherine once you'd left. I have to say, it was a shock to find her like that. I was most upset.'

'Upset?' Ryan couldn't keep the sneer from his lips. 'You seemed happy enough to kill three of her friends.'

Weiss raised his eyebrows, laughed. 'You mean Krauss and the rest? Oh no, Albert, you misunderstand. We didn't kill them.'

'I don't believe you.'

'You believe what you like, Albert, but I tell you with all honesty, we did not harm those men.'

Ryan shook his head. 'The woman, she told me she was your informant. The one I was looking for.'

'Yes, Catherine was working for us, passing on information about her associates, but we didn't use that information to target anyone for termination.'

'Then what did you want the information for?'

Weiss stood up, put his hands in his pockets. 'Let me tell you a little about Catherine Beauchamp. She was a nationalist. She was a socialist. But she was not a Nazi. She made some bad judgements in her youth, aligned herself with people she perhaps shouldn't have, but she was not of the same ideology as others in the Bezen Perrot. You spoke with her. You must have seen that she was a sensitive and intelligent woman.'

'She was terrified,' Ryan said. 'She killed herself out of fear.'

'Not of us,' Weiss said. 'She understood the wrong she'd done. So when I first approached her, she had no reservations about talking to me, giving me information.'

'She told me you showed her photographs. Dead children. You manipulated her.'

'Look at it that way if you want. I think of it as showing her the truth. If truth is manipulation, then so be it.'

'What did you want from her?'

Weiss paced. 'We wanted information on Skorzeny. Who his friends were, who he associated with, who visited him at that big country house of his.'

Ryan watched Weiss stroll the length of the room and back again. 'So you could target him and his people. Kill them.'

Weiss stopped. 'Oh come, Albert, I thought you were smarter than that.'

'I don't have to be that smart to see three men have been killed.'

Weiss leaned over Ryan like a patient schoolteacher. 'But not by us. I told you already. No, we don't want Otto Skorzeny dead. He's no use to us dead.'

'Then what?'

'Doesn't it strike you as odd that a Lieutenant Colonel of the SS should have sufficient funds to live the way Skorzeny does? He is, by any measure, a very wealthy man, wouldn't you say? How does a man escape from custody less than fifteen years ago, nothing to his name, then turn up just a few years later a multimillionaire? How does that work?'

'I don't know.'

Weiss put a hand on Ryan's shoulder. 'You seem like a calm and rational man, Albert. I think if I take those cuffs off your wrists and ankles, you won't try anything stupid. Am I right?'

Ryan stayed silent.

Weiss took a set of keys from his pocket and unfastened each of Ryan's limbs in turn.

'Go on,' Weiss said. 'Stand up if you want. Stretch your legs.'

Ryan gripped the chair's armrests, pushed himself up. His knees buckled, and Weiss seized him in a bear hug.

'Easy, my friend. Put your hand on my shoulder. There you go.'

Ryan stood quite still for a time, breathing hard, before lowering himself back into the chair. Weiss took his own seat once more.

'So, we were talking about Colonel Skorzeny's money. The story is he set up a concrete business in Buenos Aires and got rich. Now, call me an old cynic, but I don't buy that explanation for one second. If you scrape around in the dirt a little, you dig up all sorts of stories. We know, for example, that Martin Bormann siphoned off a huge fortune right out of Hitler's pockets. In 1945, when the end came, as far as we know, Bormann never made it out of Berlin. But the money did. Eight hundred million dollars wound up in Eva Perón's bank account, not to mention the gold bullion and the diamonds. We're talking enough money to run a small country. And who do you think was right there, whispering sweet nothings to Evita?'

Ryan remembered what Catherine Beauchamp had told him. 'Skorzeny.'

'That's right. And that's just the start. Cash, precious metals, diamonds and every other kind of stone, paintings and sculptures. Every damn thing he and his friends could steal and smuggle out of Europe. Given what we know of the funds Otto Skorzeny has access to, it's a wonder he lives as modestly as he does.'

'So what do you want from him?'

'Well, it's how he uses this money that concerns us. We wouldn't mind so much if he blew it on racehorses and sports cars and women, all the stuff the average ageing millionaire entertains himself with. But that isn't what Skorzeny does. You see, strictly speaking, the money isn't his. He's more of a caretaker, a trustee if you like. Have you heard of ratlines?'

'No,' Ryan said.

'Most people haven't. See, right at the end of the war, some Nazis, guys like Skorzeny and Bormann, they saw it coming. They knew that even if they escaped, hundreds of others wouldn't. They needed to set up routes, channels, ways out for their friends. Ratlines. You know what Europe was like in the couple years after the war. A passport was worth shit. The borders were meaningless. Hundreds of thousands, maybe millions of displaced people wandering around with no place to go, and no way to prove their nationality. And Skorzeny's kind exploited that. They'd just swap their uniforms for pants and a shirt, walk up to some GI and say, "Hey, I'm Hans, and my town got burned to the ground. Show me where to go." And they're home free. Except once they find a place to settle, they need money.'

'Skorzeny's money,' Ryan said.

'That's right.' Weiss leaned over and patted Ryan's thigh. 'Well, the money he looks after, at any rate. I could tell you a dozen German and Austrian companies, million-dollar international enterprises that were bankrolled by the funds Skorzeny controls. Companies you've heard of, companies whose products you've bought, household names. Of course, the free-for-all couldn't last for ever. Once the borders firmed up, once the European nations got the passport problem under control, then those routes, those ratlines needed to come into play. A lot of times through the church, or some government official or other. A letter of introduction, a little currency to ease the way, cash to set up a new life. Again, Skorzeny's money.

'Since the end of the war, Otto Skorzeny and that fund have helped hundreds of murdering bastards escape Europe. And they aren't all glorified office boys like Helmut Krauss. We're talking about Adolf Eichmann, Josef Mengele, the worst pieces of filth who ever walked this earth. Now, do you see why Otto Skorzeny is of so much interest to me?'

Ryan held his gaze. 'Then why didn't you go after him instead of those others? How did killing Helmut Krauss help you?'

'Albert, I've told you twice already, but let me tell you again. We did not kill Helmut Krauss, Johan Hambro or Alex Renders. Their deaths have rather compromised us, in fact. This business has spooked Skorzeny. If he wasn't such a stubborn bastard, he'd have cleared out by now, gone back to Madrid and his buddy Franco. And our mission would be over. A failure.'

'So what is your mission?'

'We want those ratlines.'

Ryan smiled. 'It seems to me the quickest way to close them down would be to kill Skorzeny.'

Weiss cringed. 'You disappoint me, Albert. If Skorzeny died, control of the money and the ratlines would simply pass to someone else. No, I didn't say we wanted to close down the ratlines. We want control of them. We want Skorzeny under our thumb, and we want to know every single person who tries to escape through the network, and everyone who got through in the past. We can let most of them go, the nobodies, but we can grab the big fish. We want them on trial. Failing that, we want them dead. Either way, we want justice to be done.'

'Why would Skorzeny ever give them up? You've got nothing to threaten him with.'

'Ah, but I do.' Weiss's grin spread so wide it seemed to glow. 'Skorzeny lives damn well on what he draws from the fund for himself. His friends gave him a pretty good allowance, plus he earned some on the side, running those mercenary training courses in Spain and so on. A CIA friend of mine attended one, said he learned a lot.

'But Skorzeny got greedy. We acquired some paperwork from Heidegger Bank, a little family-run institution just outside of Zurich. Some statements that were mislaid and found their way to me. You see, about seven or eight years ago, Skorzeny started channelling a little of his *Kameraden*'s money away. Not much at any one time, a few thousand from an interest dividend here, a hundred thousand from a lodgement there. Pretty soon, he's got a few million stacking up in a little side account that his buddies don't know about. He's been skimming off the top, as they call it in Las Vegas.'

'You're going to blackmail him?'

'Exactly. Now, we've spent a lot of time and resources on this mission, and we don't want it destroyed by some hotheads with a grudge. Is that unreasonable?'

'No,' Ryan said.

'No, indeed. Some gang of rogues comes along and starts picking off Skorzeny's friends. Skorzeny gets worried, involves the government, and here you are. Right in the middle of it all.'

'So what do you want from me?'

'The same thing your friend the Minister for Justice wants. I want it stopped.'

24

CÉLESTIN LAINÉ KNEW HAKON FOSS WAS STRONG, BUT STILL, HE was shocked at the Norwegian's resilience.

The guards had brought Foss to the barn and sat him down at an old wooden table, holes drilled in its top to allow the leather straps to be passed through and hold his wrists in place, fingers splayed on the surface. Skorzeny had sat opposite and talked to Foss in his calmest, softest voice while Lainé readied the kerosene blowtorch.

'Please speak honestly,' Skorzeny said. He enunciated slowly, clearly. 'It would be best for all of us, but most especially for you. We can avoid any unpleasantness if you answer my questions truthfully.'

Foss's fingers twitched on the tabletop. He watched as Lainé lit the small reserve of fuel in the blowtorch's drip pan.

'What do you want?' he asked.

Lainé left the torch to heat and began arranging his tools on the table. A sturdy penknife, a pair of sharpened secateurs, a scalpel, a set of dental pliers.

The pliers were mostly for effect, to frighten the subject under interrogation. Lainé had only resorted to using them on a subject's teeth on a handful of occasions. It was far too difficult to hold the head in place, and the jaw open, to make an extraction worthwhile under all but the most extreme circumstances.

Often, and to Lainé's disappointment, the subject would offer up the required information the moment he or she saw the tools and the blowtorch. The anticipation of pain is a far greater torment than pain itself. All skilled interrogators know this.

Skorzeny said, 'I want to know who you have been talking to.'

Foss shook his head. 'I talk to no one. Who says I talk?'

Lainé opened the blowtorch's fuel valve. The blue flame burst to life with a pop and a hiss. Foss jumped in his seat, a high yelp escaping him. Lainé lifted his penknife, opened its blade, and held the steel to the flame.

'How long?' Skorzeny asked.

'A minute, no more,' Lainé said.

Skorzeny turned his attention back to Foss. 'A minute. You have this time to tell me the truth, Hakon. Who have you talked to about me?'

The Norwegian's face creased with fear. 'No one. I talk to no one. Why do you ask this?'

'I ask this because I know someone close has betrayed me. I know someone has passed on information to others. Information about me, about my associates. My friends, Hakon. Your friends.'

'Not me,' Hakon said. 'I talk to no one.'

'If you have not talked to anyone, then why did you run?'

Foss had no other response to offer than an open mouth, the corners turned down, the rapid blinks of his glistening eyes.

'I will ask you once more. If you do not answer truthfully, Célestin will cause you great pain.'

'I talk to no—'

'Who have you talked to about me?'

'No one. I talk to no one.'

Skorzeny gave a small nod, and Lainé seized Foss's thumb. He took the glowing blade from the flame and began his work.

25

WEISS HANDED RYAN TWO PHOTOGRAPHS. ONE WAS A GRAINY head-and-shoulders image of a man, mid to late twenties, a beret on his head, the collar of his combat uniform open. He had the hard-jawed expression of a man uncomfortable with having his portrait taken. Ryan looked at the second photograph. A group picture, a dozen uniformed men, one of them circled: the same image, blown up.

'Who is this?' Ryan asked.

'This is Captain John Carter,' Weiss said. 'He wasn't a captain at the time that photograph was taken, but he was by the time he left the British Army.'

Ryan studied the group picture. The men lined up against a rough wall, short sleeves and trousers, some with handkerchiefs held in place by their hats to protect their necks from the sun. Sand dusted their boots.

'Special Air Services,' Weiss said, completing Ryan's thought for him. 'Deployed in North Africa. Covert operations, behind enemy lines. The dirty stuff.'

Ryan looked again at the blown-up photograph of Carter, the hard features, the cold stare.

'Is he . . . ?'

Weiss nodded. 'Yes, I believe he leads the band of merry men who've been dealing with Ireland's Nazi problem.'

'How do you know this?'

'A South African information broker. He let me know that a certain Captain John Carter, quite by coincidence, had been showing an interest in Otto Skorzeny. He had procured some small arms through a mutual contact in the Netherlands. At the same time, Carter let it be known that he had a spot to fill on a small team of former comrades he had gathered. He wouldn't be drawn on the nature of the team's work, other than it would be most interesting.'

Ryan traced a fingertip across the image. 'It has to be him.'

'Of course. I couldn't expose my own mission by going to either the British or Irish intelligence services about this. Thus the rather elaborate means of getting you here.'

'Well, you got me here. What now?'

'Now we each set about finding Captain Carter and his men. We'll continue to keep an eye on you. If you want to make contact, place a copy of the *Irish Times* on the dashboard of your car wherever you have it parked. I'd appreciate it if you share anything you discover. I will do likewise. But one thing.'

'What?'

'Don't let Skorzeny know about me, or what I've told you. Don't let him know about Carter, or anything we've discussed here. If you tell him, he'll want to know how you found out. If he suspects you're holding anything back, then believe me, the discussion you have with him will not be as cordial as this one.'

'And what if I don't want to cooperate with you? What if I tell Skorzeny everything?'

Weiss leaned forward, the broad grin returning to his lips. 'Then I'll kill you and everyone you love.'

26

FOSS WOULD NOT BREAK.

Even as his second thumbnail peeled away, he resisted. He cried, babbling in his native tongue, the dogs across the yard replying with their own howls. He bucked and writhed until the guards had to hold him down. But still he would say nothing. Always the same denial.

Two more fingernails, more screaming, more writhing, and no confession.

'This is going nowhere,' Skorzeny said. 'Take a finger.'

Lainé suppressed a smile and placed the penknife back on the table. He lifted the secateurs, gripped the little finger of Foss's left hand between the blades, just below the knuckle, and squeezed the handle.

Foss opened his mouth, a high whine from his throat, as the blades closed on bone. Lainé applied more pressure until the bone gave way. The amputated finger rolled away from the spray of blood.

Lainé returned the penknife's blade to the jet of the blowtorch. When it glowed, he pressed it to the stump on Foss's hand, ignored the smell as it cauterised the wound.

Foss's head sagged back, his shoulders slumped.

'Have we lost him?' Skorzeny asked.

'I don't know,' Lainé said. 'He is strong, but he is tired. Let me see.'

He rummaged in his bag until he found a small brown glass vial. The ammonia stench made him recoil as he undid the stopper. He held the vial under Foss's nose.

The Norwegian's head jerked away from the smelling salts. He gasped, snorted, coughed. A thin stream of bile spilled from his lips, beer and undigested cheese sauce.

Skorzeny stood and walked away from the table, the corners of his mouth downturned in abhorrence.

'Enough,' he said. 'We will continue tomorrow. Give him the night to think about his fate.' He addressed the guards. 'Don't let him leave this room. If he tries anything, wound him, but keep him alive.'

The guards nodded their acknowledgement, and Skorzeny marched to the door. Outside, Lainé caught up with him.

'Are you sure it's him?'

'Of course,' Skorzeny said. 'He pissed on himself and ran. He is guilty. And you will make him talk.'

'I'll try,' Lainé said. 'But he's strong.'

'Even the strongest man has a breaking point. You will find that point. Goodnight.'

Lainé watched Skorzeny stride towards the house, the Austrian's head held high, his shoulders back, his coat tails billowing behind him. Lainé hated and admired his arrogance in equal measure.

He went back to the outbuilding and found one of the guards giving Foss water. The Norwegian pulled his head away from the cup.

'Célestin,' he said. 'Please, Célestin.'

Lainé ignored him as he washed the penknife in the bucket

of water that sat on the ground. He scraped the blade on the bucket's lip, charred flesh falling away.

'Célestin, help. Help. My friend. Help.'

Lainé rinsed the secateurs clean of Foss's blood. He gathered the tools and returned them to the leather bag, then extinguished the blowtorch's flame.

'Help, Célestin. I talk to no one. Tell him. Célestin.'

Lainé set the blowtorch on a shelf and carried his bag to the door.

'Célestin, please.'

He walked from the light to the darkness, back to the house. The kitchen stood dark and empty. He lifted a small plate from the drainer on his way to the cellar. Lainé emerged a few minutes later with a 1950 Charmes-Chambertin under his arm. He carried the wine, the plate and his bag upstairs to his small room.

The puppy pawed at Lainé's shins when he entered. It had messed in the corner, but he didn't mind the smell. It would do until morning. He set the plate on the floor, then placed the piece of schnitzel he had saved from dinner upon it. The puppy sniffed and licked the meat.

Lainé used the corkscrew he kept in the top drawer of his bedside locker to open the bottle. Perhaps he should have let it breathe, but thirst insisted that he drink now. As he did so, he noticed the puppy struggling with the pork, the piece too large for it.

He reached down, lifted the schnitzel, bit off a piece of grey meat and breadcrumb, and chewed. When the meat had turned to a warm mush, he spat it onto his fingers and lowered it to the puppy.

Lainé smiled as it ate.

He hardly thought of Hakon Foss at all.

27

RYAN CHECKED THE TIME AS HE ENTERED HIS HOTEL ROOM. Half past one in the morning. He didn't undress, just removed his tie and lay down on the bed.

Weiss had reapplied the blindfold, guided Ryan outside and into the van. They had driven for at least forty minutes, but Ryan had felt his weight shift from side to side with constant turns, so he guessed the garage to which they'd brought him was not far from the city centre.

When the van stopped, the blindfold was removed. Weiss crouched beside Ryan.

'Remember what we agreed, Albert. You help me, I'll help you.'

Ryan did not reply. They left him in an alley off Grafton Street, a few minutes' walk from Buswells.

The night porter opened the locked doors of the hotel for him. Ryan gave him the room number, and the porter fetched the key from behind the desk.

'Rough night, was it?' the porter asked.

Now Ryan lay in the dark, his head throbbing, the room swaying around him in sickly waves. He tried to think only of Celia, but sleep crept up on him like a thief, and he dreamed of children and the flies on their dead lips.

* * *

Bathed and shaved, but weary – he had been woken by the light from his window not long after seven – Ryan walked the paths of St Stephen's Green, thinking. He found a quiet spot, a bench shaded by trees, overlooking the pond and the ducks swimming there.

Weiss had let him keep the photographs. He studied them now. The men in the group portrait – were any of them part of Captain John Carter's team? Ryan looked at each man in turn, committing their faces to his memory. The photograph was marked June 1943 on the back. Carter, all of them, would be twenty years older than in this picture.

He had spent the morning turning it over in his mind. How to find one man who could be hiding anywhere in the entire country?

Carter had left the military two years ago, Weiss said. He had married a woman from Liverpool, fathered a boy, but the mother and child had perished in a car accident. The last twenty years of his duty had been spent as a member of the Special Air Service, the most secretive branch of the British Army. Any attempt to trace him through his service record would be futile.

But Weiss had dropped a thread for Ryan to tug at. The Israeli had made it appear incidental, a throwaway comment, so that it would plant a seed in Ryan's mind. But Ryan knew it had been deliberate. When he drove to Otto Skorzeny's country home this evening, he would see whether or not the thread led to the destination he imagined.

'Albert.'

Celia's voice startled him, first in the fright it lit in him, then the pleasure it brought. He looked up, saw her approach from the western end of the park, dressed in a manner that would have seemed businesslike on any other woman. She had been placed in one of the nearby government offices while she awaited a new foreign posting. Practically a secretary, she'd said, and deathly dull.

Ryan tucked the photographs into his pocket and got to his feet. Celia stood on tiptoe to kiss his cheek, her hand on his arm for balance, warm and delicate.

'You were looking terribly thoughtful,' she said.

'Was I?'

'What were you thinking about?'

Ryan smiled. 'You.'

Celia blushed.

She ordered Eggs Benedict. When the waiter reminded her that the Shelbourne Hotel's breakfast service ended at ten o'clock, Celia pouted.

The waiter crumbled. 'I'll see what I can do,' he said. 'And for sir?'

Ryan ordered the salmon, and the waiter left.

She sipped her gin and tonic. He took a mouthful of Guinness.

Celia asked, 'Really, what were you thinking about in the park?'

'Nothing,' he said. 'Work, that's all.'

'You looked troubled.'

Ryan couldn't hold her gaze. He studied the fibres of the tablecloth.

'Tell me,' she said.

'I don't like the job I'm doing.'

She laughed. 'Nobody likes their job. Apart from me, but I'm an exception. Everybody hates getting up in the morning and going to work.'

'I don't mean it that way,' Ryan said. 'I can't talk about it.'

'Not even to me?'

'The job I've been ordered to do. It's wrong.'

'How?'

'I can't say any more.'

She reached out and placed her hand on top of his. The slenderness of her fingers made them appear brittle, fragile things. He turned his palm upwards, let her fingers slip between his.

'If it's in service of your country, how can it be wrong?' she asked.

Ryan met her eyes. 'You're not that naive.'

'No, I suppose not. If you really can't bear it, then tell them no, you won't do it.'

'I have no choice. Not now. It's gone too far.'

'Albert, stop talking in riddles.'

He ran his thumb across her fingernails, felt the smooth polish, the sharp edges.

'Yesterday, I watched a woman commit suicide.'

Celia's fingers left his. Her hands retreated to her lap. She sat back.

'Where?'

'The other side of Swords,' Ryan said. 'In her home. She did it out of fear.'

'Fear of who? You?'

'I tell myself no, not of me but the people I'm working for. But then I remember, if I work for them, I am one of them.'

Celia shook her head. Her eyes stayed on him, but her gaze elsewhere. 'No. That's not true. We do things for people. It doesn't mean we like it. It doesn't make us the same as them.'

Ryan watched as she returned to herself. 'Even if you know it's wrong?'

Celia turned away, looked towards the kitchen. 'I wonder where the food is.'

'We only just ordered. What's the matter?'

She turned back to him. 'Nothing. Albert, I shan't be able to come to the dinner party tonight.'

Ryan felt something fall away inside him. 'Why not?'

'Mrs Highland needs help around the house. I promised I'd do it for her.'

'When did you promise her?'

'Last week. I forgot. I'm sorry.'

'All right. Maybe we can do something tomorrow evening instead.'

'Maybe,' she said with a flicker of a smile.

28

SKORZENY WAS EATING ALONE IN THE DINING ROOM WHEN HE heard the telephone ring, followed by Esteban's soft knock at the door.

'Enter,' Skorzeny said.

'Is Miss Hume,' Esteban said. He pronounced it *joom*.

Skorzeny wiped his lips with a napkin, then followed the boy out to the hallway where the telephone waited. He lifted the receiver. He heard the distorted noise of a street.

'Miss Hume?'

'Sir, I need to speak with you.'

Her voice resonated in the telephone box.

'Go on,' he said.

'I no longer wish to carry out the assignment you gave me.'

'Why not?'

'I met with Albert Ryan for lunch today. He told me someone has died because of what he's doing for you. I don't want to be a part of that.'

Skorzeny lowered himself into the chair beside the telephone table. 'Who died?'

'A woman. Near Swords, he said. She committed suicide.'

Skorzeny thought of Catherine Beauchamp, her fine and delicate features, the hard intelligence of her eyes.

'What else did Lieutenant Ryan tell you?'

'Nothing. Only that he's unhappy doing whatever work it is he's doing for you. He feels it's wrong.'

'Lieutenant Ryan is confused. He is protecting people in his work. Saving lives. Perhaps you could remind him of that.'

'No. I won't see him again.'

'But you must. There's the dinner tonight.'

'I told him I wasn't able to come.'

Skorzeny kept his voice even. 'That was foolish.'

'I only took this assignment as a favour for Mr Waugh. I've let men take me to dinner before, drinks and such, to find out things about them. But they were diplomats or businessmen; all they talked about were negotiations and deals. Never anything like this. I won't be a part of it.'

'My dear, you are a part of it whether you wish to be or not. You will carry out the orders you were given.'

'No. You'll have to find some—'

'Young lady, you misunderstand. You will accompany Lieutenant Ryan to my home this evening. You will continue to see him and report his conversations to me. Do I make myself clear?'

'Sir, you are not my employer. You have no right to—'

'What right do you think I need? What authority?'

'You can't—'

'Yes, I can. Now listen to me very carefully. You will do as I have instructed or the consequences will be most serious.'

She paused. 'In what way?'

'In any way you can imagine.'

Silence for a time, then, 'Sir, are you threatening me?'

'Yes.'

A click, and she was gone.

Skorzeny stood, replaced the handset, and became aware of

a presence above him. He turned, saw Lainé sitting on the stairs, watching. The pup in his lap, on its back, wriggling as he scratched its belly.

'There is trouble?' Lainé asked.

Skorzeny walked to the foot of the stairs. 'No trouble. But there is news you should know. The girl I placed with Ryan. He told her he'd seen a woman commit suicide. A woman near Swords.'

Lainé's fingers ceased their scratching. 'Catherine?'

'I believe so.'

Lainé got to his feet, the pup held close to his chest, turned to go.

Skorzeny said, 'Ryan must have suspected she was the informant.'

'No.' Lainé shook his head. 'Not Catherine.'

'Foss still denies it. It's possible I was mistaken.'

Lainé looked back over his shoulder. 'No. It is Foss. He will talk. I will make him talk.'

The Breton climbed from Skorzeny's view.

29

RYAN SLEPT HARD, STRETCHES OF BLACK PUNCTUATED BY RAGGED and bloody dreams. The telephone kicked him awake, consciousness flooding in, nausea in its wake. He rolled across the bed, lifted the receiver.

'Hello?'

'A call from a Miss Hume. Shall I put her through?'

Ryan sat up, rubbed his face, fresh stubble scratching his palm. 'Yes.'

'Albert?' she said.

'Celia. What's wrong?'

'I was thinking,' she said, a waver in her voice. 'I'd very much like to go with you to that dinner this evening.'

In his heart, Ryan rejoiced.

Celia held the map on her knees, navigating. She offered little conversation other than the directions. As they passed through Naas, Ryan asked if everything was all right.

She turned to him, her smile prim and polite, and said, 'Yes, everything's fine.'

He did not believe her.

'It's not too late to turn around,' he said. 'I can bring you back to Dublin.'

Celia turned her eyes back to the map. 'No. I want to go. Really.'

'If you're sure.'

'I am.'

Time and silence lay thick upon them until she spoke again.

'Up here, I think.' She pointed to the curve ahead, and the stone wall, the map held in her other hand. A gateway came into view. 'There.'

Ryan slowed and steered the Vauxhall towards the gateway. Two broad-shouldered men blocked his way. Ryan braked and halted.

One of the men approached the driver's window. Ryan wound it down.

'Your names,' the man said, his accent thick.

Ryan told him. The man nodded to his colleague, who stepped back. Ryan put the car in gear and moved off, through the gates to a long driveway lined by trees. Among them, he saw another man. Watching from his dark cover, he made no attempt to conceal his weapon.

From the corner of his eye, Ryan saw Celia turn her head to look at the man as they passed. She touched the fingertips of her left hand to her lips, clenched the right into a fist in her lap.

Ryan realised with a hard certainty that he should not have brought her here. He tried to push the feeling away, dismiss it as a fretful notion, but it lingered in his stomach.

The house rose up ahead, the pitched roofs of its wings, its arched windows, the gardens all around. Other cars lined up beside Skorzeny's white Mercedes. Two Rovers, a Jaguar, a Bentley. Ryan pulled the Vauxhall alongside them, the other vehicles dwarfing his.

He got out, opened Celia's door, guided her towards the house. A young olive-skinned boy waiting for them in the open doorway took Celia's coat and showed them to the drawing room.

The four couples who stood there, drinks in hand, turned to watch them enter. Ryan recognised one of the men as a prominent solicitor, another as a senior civil servant, something in the Department of Finance, and yet another as the owner of a department store. And there, watching, Charles J. Haughey with the girl who'd been his companion at the restaurant, the girl who was not his wife. In fact, none of the men here looked well matched in age to their partners. The women eyed Celia with dagger glares.

Celia seemed to shrink from their gaze, her shoulders hunched. She gripped Ryan's forearm tight as she smiled back at them.

'There's the man,' Haughey said.

Ryan nodded. 'Good evening, Minister.'

The politician crossed the room to him, studied Ryan from head to foot, the hawk eyes picking over his clothing.

Haughey cleared his throat and winked, said, 'Nice tie.'

They were seated around the dining table when Skorzeny appeared. All stood, Ryan and Celia following their lead. The Austrian circled the room, shaking hands, accepting chaste kisses on his scarred cheek. Haughey gripped Skorzeny's hand the hardest, shook it with the most vigour, slapped the big man's shoulder.

Ryan said nothing as Skorzeny took his hand, did not wince as the Austrian squeezed it tight. Skorzeny leaned in to Celia, offered his cheek to her. She closed her eyes, obliged him, left a faint red circle on the scar. Ryan saw something move across her face, fear or disgust, he could not be sure.

Skorzeny went to the head of the table. He rested his hands on the chair back.

'Welcome, my friends,' he said. 'My home is yours. I offer you my hospitality as your noble nation has offered me its hospitality. Please sit. Eat. Enjoy.'

The guests took their seats, laughter and good cheer between them all.

Ryan turned his attention to Celia, saw a tear escape her eye. She caught it, wiped it on her cheek, and then he wasn't sure if he'd seen it at all.

30

CÉLESTIN LAINÉ SAT ON THE EDGE OF THE BED, A TRAY ON HIS lap, eating pheasant and roast vegetables with a red wine reduction. Esteban had also delivered a bottle of red wine, a 1960 Pontet-Canet, along with a note from Skorzeny requesting that Lainé remain in his room for the duration of the evening.

The puppy circled his feet, sometimes resting its front paws on his shins as it sniffed at the tray. Lainé tore off occasional scraps of meat, dipped them in the reduction, held them out for the puppy. Already it had learned to sit in anticipation of a treat.

Lainé tried not to think of Catherine Beauchamp, or what fear had driven her to suicide. He tried not to think of the last time he'd seen her, when they'd met in a small hotel in Skerries, overlooking the harbour.

Weariness had drawn her features, sharpening them, deepening the hollows. They had drunk the piss they served for coffee in Ireland and talked about home and how they could never return.

Fishing boats lay stranded on the sand flats beyond the harbour wall. Wind threw spray and rain against the windowpanes, and cold draughts snaked beneath the tables and chairs, chilling Lainé's ankles despite the peat fire that glowed red and orange in the corner.

Their passion had died years ago, back when she softened in her heart, turned her back on the actions they had undertaken together. She might hate him now. He thought it likely, but still they met to speak to each other in the language of their land, to listen to the melody and rhythm of it. It was the only time either of them heard Breton spoken beyond the walls of their own minds.

'Do you sleep at night?' Catherine asked.

Lainé shrugged. 'Depends where I am. Give me a comfortable bed, and I'll sleep sound as a baby.'

'I don't.' She took two cigarettes from the packet of Gitanes on the table, offered him one. He accepted. 'If I can keep my eyes closed for a couple of hours, I consider myself lucky.'

'You did nothing wrong. There's no reason for you to lose sleep over someone else's sins.'

She smiled. 'You see, that's where we differ. You think what they did, the Nazis, had nothing to do with you. But it did. Once you took arms at their side, you became one of them. So did I.'

'No. We had a common enemy. The French oppressor. It didn't make me a Jew killer.'

'You would have killed anyone they asked you to. Jews, Frenchmen, women, children.'

Now Lainé smiled. 'If you despise me so much, why don't you leave?'

'Who else could I speak my own language with?'

Lainé believed he loved her then, and he still believed it now. He watched drops of water splash on the tray and plate for long seconds before he realised they were his own tears. He sniffed and wiped them away.

His appetite gone, he set the tray aside and took a swallow

of wine from the bottle. He lifted the puppy, set it in his lap, turned it on its back, scratched its pink belly.

From downstairs he heard the laughter of the guests. Bourgeoisie, Catherine would have called them. And she'd have been right. Politicians, bureaucrats, businessmen, men of wealth and influence. All while Lainé was banished to this small room like a deformed child the parents kept secret from their neighbours.

And Ryan was among them. Ryan, who had watched Catherine Beauchamp die the day before, now ate pheasant and drank good wine with Skorzeny and the rest.

Lainé decided that before the evening was done, he would have a private discussion with Lieutenant Albert Ryan.

31

A DESSERT OF *ROTE GRÜTZE* WITH CUSTARD FINISHED THE MEAL, a gelatinous stew of berries, tangy and bitter on the tongue.

Skorzeny held the guests enraptured with stories of daring and danger. He told them of Operation Greif, how he commanded Panzerbrigade 150 as its men donned American uniforms, moved behind enemy lines and spread misinformation, including a fabricated plan to kidnap Eisenhower and his staff. The punchline of the General's unhappiness at being forced to remain indoors for the duration of Christmas 1944 caused a ripple of approving laughter to roll through the room.

Neither Lieutenant Ryan nor his companion joined in the laughter. The young woman raised a polite smile, but no more, and Ryan could not allow even that much.

Skorzeny fixed Ryan with a stare. 'Come, Lieutenant, don't you enjoy stories of my exploits? Perhaps you have your own tales to tell.'

Haughey chimed in. 'Come on, big fella. What did you get up to?'

Ryan looked from the minister to Skorzeny. 'I don't like to talk about my time in service.'

Haughey smiled his lizard smile. 'In service to the Brits.'

The men chuckled. Ryan said nothing. The young woman

Celia blushed, redness creeping down to the fair skin of her chest, glowing above the line of her dress.

'Minister,' Skorzeny said, 'we don't always fight for the nation of our birth. That isn't always where one's heart lies. After all, I am an Austrian, as was the Führer. Yet I took part in the *Anschluss*. I gave my country to the Germans, because at heart, I am German.'

'Is that you, Ryan?' Haughey asked. 'Are you a Brit at heart?'

Ryan dropped his spoon into his bowl with a loud clank that made Celia flinch. 'No, Minister. I'm no less an Irishman than you.'

'What about you, Minister?'

Haughey turned to face Skorzeny's question, his smile faltering.

'If we had invaded Ireland, would you have resisted? Or would you have welcomed us like the IRA promised to? Would Britain's enemy have been your friend?'

Haughey waved a finger. 'I would've fought on one side, and one side only: Ireland's side.'

'And yet the story persists about you leading a march on Trinity College on VE Day, carrying swastikas and burning the Union Jack on the college gates.'

Haughey's face reddened. 'Now look here, that lie has gone on long enough. I never saw a swastika that day. Some yahoos might have been flying them, but my hand never touched one, I'll tell you that for nothing. Those Prod bastards in Trinity were flying a Union Jack on the roof. The nerve of them, bloody drunken Orangemen. Then they had the gall to set light to a Tricolour. So I burned a Union Jack on the gates, I did that all right, just to show them you can't disrespect our flag, not while Charlie Haughey's around.'

'Prod bastards?' Skorzeny asked. 'You mean Protestants?'

Haughey nodded, his cheeks florid with anger. 'That's right, Protestants. Orange bastards, the lot of them.'

'Like Lieutenant Ryan here?'

Haughey paled, glanced at Ryan, then cleared his throat. 'Well, I suppose I can't tar everyone with the same brush. Wouldn't be fair. No offence, Ryan.'

'None taken, Minister,' Ryan said, his eyes hard.

As Esteban and Frau Tiernan began clearing plates from the table, Skorzeny watched Haughey lift a glass, drink from it, his anger choked by the wine. He considered taunting the politician some more, but thought better of it.

The guests made their way to the drawing room for coffee and brandy. In the hall, Ryan approached Skorzeny.

'I hoped I might have a word with Célestin Lainé tonight.'

'Not at the moment,' Skorzeny said.

'He's still here, isn't he? I haven't had a chance to speak with him alone yet.'

'Yes, he's here, but you may not speak with him. I've asked him to stay in his room while my guests are here. Perhaps later.'

Skorzeny guided Ryan towards the drawing room, where cigar smoke and coffee aroma mingled in the air. The guests played the roles that were expected of them, the men telling lewd jokes, the women gossiping and comparing dresses.

Skorzeny didn't know how long had passed before he realised Ryan and his companion were missing.

32

CELIA HAD LEFT FIRST, NOT A WORD AS SHE EDGED TOWARDS the open patio doors and slipped out. Ryan found her standing in the shadows beneath the eaves of the house, shivering.

'What's wrong? Why did you sneak out here?'

In the blue darkness, he saw her diaphanous smile. 'It was too smoky for me, that's all. I wanted a little fresh air.'

'You don't want to be here, do you? I could hear it in your voice when you called. I could see it on you in the car. Tell me what the matter is.'

'Nothing,' she said, but her exhalation turned to a sob. She brought her hand to her lips, sealed her mouth tight.

Ryan stood with his hands at his sides, awkward, useless, an infant in a world of men. Then he raised his hands up to her shoulders, gripped them.

'Tell me.'

He felt her tremble.

She sniffed back tears. 'I can't.'

'Why not?'

'I'm afraid.'

He slipped his arms around her, brought her close. Her breath warmed his throat.

'You've nothing to be afraid of. Not when I'm here.'

She said, 'Oh God,' and pressed her eyes against the side

of his neck. He felt the movements and the heat of her eyelids, the lashes prickling his skin, the wetness.

'Please tell me.'

Celia pulled her head away from him and sniffed, her shoulders hardening in his arms.

'He sent me to you,' she said.

'Who?' Ryan asked, but he already knew. 'Skorzeny.'

'He wanted me to make friends with you, talk with you, tell him if you said anything about the job, to tell him what you were thinking, to make sure he could trust you.'

Ryan's hands slipped away from her. He stepped back. His heart raced. He leaned against the wall for balance.

'I'm sorry.' She found a tissue and wiped at her cheeks, cutting through the mascara smears. 'Please don't tell him I told you. He'll . . .'

'He'll what?'

'I don't know. He didn't say exactly.'

The storm at Ryan's core intensified. 'You mean he threatened you?'

She turned away as if it shamed her. 'Yes. I think so. I mean, I'm not sure. But yes. It was never like this before.' Celia told him of the men she'd accompanied to dinner, how she'd acted impressed with them, encouraged them to tell their banal secrets.

'I don't belong here. Can we leave?'

Ryan took her in his arms once more. 'Of course we can. We'll go right now. And don't worry, I won't say anything. I won't let anything happen to you.'

He guided her back to the patio doors and the laughter and smoke within.

Skorzeny blocked their path.

‘Are the young lovers seeking the shadows?’ he asked.

‘Celia wanted some air,’ Ryan said, an arm around her waist, keeping her close.

Skorzeny eyed her from head to toe, letting his gaze linger where it shouldn’t. ‘Aren’t you feeling well, my dear?’

Celia gave him a weak smile. ‘The food was a little rich for me, I think. And the smoke.’

Skorzeny nodded, his eyes wary. ‘I see. I’ll have Esteban fetch you some water.’

‘Actually,’ Ryan said, ‘I was about to bring Celia home. But thank you for your hospitality.’

‘Leave? Now? Absolutely not. Have you forgotten, Lieutenant Ryan?’

‘Forgotten what?’

Skorzeny smiled.

33

THE DINING ROOM TABLE HAD BEEN PUSHED TO THE WALL, THE rug rolled up, leaving the polished wooden floorboards. A selection of swords lay on the tabletop along with two jackets, one white, one black. The chairs had been lined up along the opposite wall. The men and women took their seats, drinks in their hands.

'You're not serious,' Ryan said.

Skorzeny grinned, his eyes flashing. 'Of course I am. Épée or sabre? Foil is for women and little boys.'

Celia stood in the corner, biting her nail.

Ryan felt the gaze of the room on him. 'Neither. I won't do this.'

Haughey laughed. 'What's the matter, Ryan? Where's your fighting spirit?'

Ryan gave him a hard stare. 'Would you like to take my place?'

Haughey choked on his brandy, guffawed. 'Holy Christ, big fella, do I look like a fighter?'

'No, Minister. You don't.'

Haughey's smile dimmed, his eyes narrowed.

'Choose,' Skorzeny said. 'Épée or sabre?'

Ryan looked at the swords on the table. The two sabres had French grips, the épées had pistol grips. He lifted one of each, tested their weight, their balance. The épées were old-fashioned pieces, large cupped hand guards, three-pronged tips rather than the buttons used for modern electronic scoring. Ryan chose.

'Épée,' he said.

Skorzeny lifted the black long-sleeved jacket, the master's colour. 'Good. Five touches. Agreed?'

'Agreed.' Ryan lifted the white jacket. 'Where are the masks?'

'No masks.' Skorzeny took the other sword for himself. 'We are not children.'

Ryan slipped his arms into the thick cotton sleeves and fastened the jacket at his side, shortening the straps until the fabric gripped him tight around the midsection. He reached between and behind his legs, fastened the groin strap to the small of his back.

Skorzeny moved to one end of the cleared area of floor, his jacket snug on his barrel torso, his sword ready. 'You will keep score, Minister.'

'Right you are,' Haughey said.

Ryan took up his position facing Skorzeny. Each adopted the *en garde* stance, swords raised, knees bent, feet aligned.

The room hushed.

Skorzeny nodded. Ryan mirrored the gesture.

They began, small movements, the épée tips circling inches apart. Skorzeny advanced, testing Ryan's reflexes with threatened lunges. Ryan responded with his own lunge, committed to the move, but Skorzeny tapped his blade against the other, a beat to throw its aim, and followed through with a jab to Ryan's hip. The pronged tip tugged on his jacket. He felt the sharp points through the thick fabric.

'Touch,' Ryan said.

They resumed their positions.

'Fifty on Colonel Skorzeny,' Haughey said.

'I'll take that,' the man from Finance said.

Again Skorzeny came on the offensive, beating and parrying, until Ryan took the blade, circling it, and connected with Skorzeny's chest.

'Touch,' Skorzeny said.

'A hundred on Ryan,' the store owner said.

This time Ryan led, pushing Skorzeny back, forcing the Austrian to parry until Ryan found an opening. He took it, the tip of his blade landing on Skorzeny's shoulder.

Skorzeny's eyes darkened. 'Touch.'

He came back hard, one lunge after another, Ryan blocking each, but unable to riposte. Finally, Skorzeny made a violent downward beat, followed through, and the tip of his blade caught the inside of Ryan's thigh, the prongs piercing the flesh beneath his trousers. He cried out.

Skorzeny stepped back. 'Touch, I assume?'

'Yes,' Ryan said.

Heat trickled down his thigh. He took his position, waited for Skorzeny to do the same, then he advanced. Skorzeny met each attack with a parry, three, four, five, then a riposte, coming in at Ryan's flank, but Ryan sidestepped and caught him beneath the arm.

'Touch,' Skorzeny said.

Now Ryan retreated, Skorzeny pressing hard, allowing him no room to form an attack. Ryan planted his feet firm on the ground, forcing his opponent to come in close. Skorzeny's forearm slammed into Ryan's chest, sending him staggering back. Before Ryan could recover, Skorzeny jabbed at the centre of his stomach, the blade twisting.

The prongs scraped at skin beneath the cotton. Ryan hissed through his teeth, said, 'Touch.'

'Here now,' Haughey said, standing. 'Is that allowed?'

'Épée allows for body contact.' Skorzeny smiled. 'That makes three points each, I think.'

'That's right,' Haughey said as he lowered himself back into his seat.

Ryan looked to Celia. She could not return his gaze. He turned his attention back to Skorzeny.

The Austrian came at him fast and low, using his bulk to power through the attack. Ryan feinted a sidestep. When Skorzeny's blade followed, Ryan turned his body, and his blade made contact high on Skorzeny's chest.

'*Schwein!* Touch.'

Skorzeny rubbed at the spot the blade had caught.

'That's four to Ryan,' Haughey said. 'One more and he wins.'

Skorzeny glared at the minister, then retook his position.

Both men inched forward, blades touching, scraping. Skorzeny swept his downward, taking Ryan's with it, tried to come back up with an attack, but Ryan was ready, blocked it, responded with his own lunge. It missed its target, and Skorzeny jabbed forward.

Ryan felt pressure then heat beneath his ear.

The women gasped. The men swore.

Celia said, 'Oh, Albert.'

Skorzeny smiled and backed away.

Ryan put his left hand to his neck, felt the slick skin, the sting as his fingertips brushed the cut.

'Touch,' he said.

'Do you wish to concede?' Skorzeny asked.

Celia took a step forward. 'Albert, please.'

'No,' Ryan said, taking his position. 'I don't.'

Skorzeny mirrored Ryan's stance, a smirk on his lips, his eyes blazing.

Ryan wondered for a moment if the Austrian had that same smirk when he had threatened Celia earlier that day. Then he attacked.

Skorzeny parried, tried to take the blade with a circular sweep, but Ryan countered, beating Skorzeny's blade down before lunging at the big man's thigh. He missed, his body carrying too much momentum to halt his forward movement. Their swords crossed between them, they came chest to chest.

Skorzeny pushed. Ryan pushed back. Skorzeny rammed his elbow into Ryan's ribs. Ryan slammed his knee into Skorzeny's thigh.

They stayed like that, a jerking, jarring dance, their blades locked, until Ryan heaved once more, throwing Skorzeny's balance. Ryan brought his blade down, aiming for Skorzeny's belly, but he saw the Austrian's left hand rising up to him, clenched in a fist.

His head rocked with the blow, and his legs buckled. He sprawled on the floorboards, the épée clattering away to stop at Haughey's feet.

Skorzeny stabbed hard at Ryan's chest with his sword. Ryan felt bright points of pain above his heart as the prongs speared through the cotton.

'I believe that makes five,' Skorzeny said.

34

RYAN WATCHED HIS REFLECTION IN THE BATHROOM MIRROR AS he dabbed at his reddened lip. The graze on his neck still bled, but the one on his thigh had stopped.

He hadn't been able to look Celia – or anyone else – in the eye as he left the dining room. He had crept upstairs alone and tried doors until he found this room.

Red swirls circled the plughole. He spat more discoloured sputum into the water and pressed the facecloth to the wound on his neck. The shirt collar bore a dark stain. Ryan wondered if it could be cleaned.

No matter. He hadn't paid for it.

A small hole had been torn in the trousers, another dark stain spreading from the loose threads. The sad ache this caused in his heart surprised Ryan. It was only a garment, albeit more expensive than any he'd owned before. Money had never mattered a great deal to him, yet he mourned the loss of this sign of wealth, even if it was someone else's.

Ryan checked the cut on his neck once more. Still a trickle of red. He pressed the facecloth harder against the wound and let himself out of the bathroom.

Célestin Lainé waited in the hallway, leaning against the wall, an almost empty wine bottle clutched to his chest.

'Monsieur Ryan,' he said. 'Albert.'

'Célestin.'

'What happen?' Lainé waved his fingers in front of his face. The wine seemed to have blunted his English.

'Colonel Skorzeny challenged me to a duel.'

Lainé smiled. 'He beat you?'

'Yes,' Ryan said.

Lainé's laughter resonated in the hallway as it rose in pitch. It died away as suddenly as it had erupted.

'You see Catherine die.'

'I was there, yes.'

'You did not stop her.'

'I couldn't. She moved too quickly.'

Lainé raised a finger, pointed it at Ryan. 'She do it because of you.'

Ryan resisted the urge to slap Lainé's hand aside. 'No. She did it because she was afraid of Skorzeny.'

'She had not to fear from him.'

'She was suspected as an informant. Skorzeny would have questioned her if I hadn't.'

Lainé dropped the bottle, lurched forward, shoved Ryan against the wall. The facecloth fluttered to the floor. 'Catherine was not informant.'

Ryan did not react. 'I know that now.'

'But still she is dead,' Lainé said, his breath sour with wine. 'For nothing.'

'I know who the informant is.'

Lainé's face slackened. 'Is Hakon Foss. I question him. He does not confess, but he will.'

'No,' Ryan said. 'The informant is you.'

Weiss had first put it in Ryan's mind. In that workshop, the smell of oil and sweat and chloroform clinging to Ryan's nostrils, Weiss had dismissed Ryan's suspicions of Hakon Foss.

'He's a gardener,' Weiss had said. 'He's a handyman. He trims hedges and repairs broken windows. What kind of information do you think he can give to anybody?'

'There's no one else so close to them,' Ryan had said. 'No one with a reason to turn on them.'

'Yes there is, Albert. Don't you see?'

'Who?'

'Think, Albert. He's as close to Skorzeny as anyone right now.'

Ryan's mouth struggled to keep up with his thoughts. 'You mean . . . Lainé?'

Weiss held his hands up, palms towards the ceiling.

Ryan shook his head. 'But he was there when they killed Groix and Murtagh.'

'And yet he lives.'

'He told us what happened. They wanted him to deliver the message.'

'Célestin Lainé has tortured and killed many, many people. What makes you think he's above telling a lie?'

The logic had grown in Ryan's mind in the hours since then until he couldn't avoid its glare. Now Lainé's eyes widened, his mouth opened, and Ryan knew it was the truth even as he denied it.

'*Non*,' Lainé said, backing away.

Ryan locked his gaze on him. 'I know, Célestin. You're the informant. What did they pay you?'

Lainé slapped Ryan hard across the cheek. 'You lie.'

Ryan closed his eyes, savoured the heat and the sting. 'You hate Skorzeny and everything he has. His money, his car, this house. You hate him for it. So you sold him out.'

Lainé's hand lashed out again. Ryan's head lightened.

'How much, Célestin? Hundreds? Thousands?'

Once more, Lainé's hand slashed at Ryan's face, but this time Ryan blocked it, grabbed Lainé's throat, pushed him back towards the far wall. Lainé croaked as Ryan applied pressure to his windpipe.

'You know what Skorzeny will do to you when he finds out.'

Lainé struggled in Ryan's grip, tried to throw him off. Ryan increased the pressure on Lainé's throat until he stilled.

'You know what he'll do. He'll tear you to pieces. That's why Catherine killed herself, because she knew he'd torture her. He'll do the same to you.'

Once more, Lainé bucked in Ryan's grasp. He tried to spit in Ryan's face, but the saliva only dribbled down his chin.

Ryan pushed him again, harder against the wall. 'Listen to me. Skorzeny doesn't have to know.'

Lainé's body softened.

'You do as I say, Skorzeny will never find out you betrayed him. Do you understand?'

Ryan loosened his grip on the Breton's throat enough for him to take a breath.

'How do I believe you?'

'You have no choice,' Ryan said. 'Either you tell me what I want to know, or I go to Skorzeny with the truth. And you will suffer.'

'I do not trust you.'

'All right, I'll give you something. I'll tell you something Skorzeny doesn't know. Their leader is Captain John Carter.'

Lainé's eyes widened.

Voices came from downstairs, the guests milling in the hall.

Ryan stepped back, releasing his hold on Lainé.

'I want to know where they are. And what they want.'

The sound of laughter just below, a door opening, a cool draught.

'I'll give you the night to think about it. I'm staying at Buswells Hotel. Call me there tomorrow or Skorzeny will know everything. Understood?'

Lainé's teeth glittered as he smiled. 'Why should I not kill you?'

Ryan returned the smile. 'Because then you'll never know why I didn't hand you over to Skorzeny.'

Ryan descended the stairs to find Haughey and his companion standing with Celia and Skorzeny by the open door.

'My guests are saying goodnight,' Skorzeny said, 'but you will stay. We have business to discuss.'

Ryan looked to Celia. 'I need to drive Celia home.'

'The minister will take care of your friend.'

A shadow of fear crossed her face.

'I'll take her,' Haughey said. 'Come on, sweetheart.'

Haughey draped Celia's coat around her shoulders.

'I'll call you tomorrow,' Ryan said.

Celia gave him a resigned smile and allowed Haughey to lead her outside. Ryan and Skorzeny watched from the doorway as the three of them climbed into Haughey's Jaguar, Celia in the back, his companion in the front, and drove away into the darkness.

Skorzeny handed Ryan his jacket and tie. Ryan pulled the jacket on and stuffed the tie into his pocket.

'You gave a good match,' Skorzeny said. 'The best I've had in this country.'

Ryan said, 'What do you want to discuss?'

'Our informant.' Skorzeny turned to the boy who stood half sleeping against the wall. 'Esteban, go upstairs and fetch Monsieur Lainé.'

The boy stirred, nodded, and ran up the staircase. He returned two minutes later, Lainé coming behind, buttoning his overcoat. His eyes met Ryan's as he reached the hallway.

'Come,' Skorzeny said, and led them out into the night.

Ryan and Lainé followed in silence, across the gardens towards the outbuildings and the halogen lamp that burned there.

As they walked, something tugged at Ryan's mind. He looked at the trees around them, searching the pools of darkness.

'Colonel,' he said.

Skorzeny halted, looked back to him.

Ryan asked, 'Where are your guards?'

35

OTTO SKORZENY HAD NEVER SUBMITTED TO FEAR OR THREAT. Not as a boy, and certainly not as a man. Even as a student, duelling with sabres at the University of Vienna, his padded tunic stained deep red, he had fought on long after others had conceded. He recalled a photograph, his smile broad and bloodied alongside those of his brethren, a tankard of beer in his hand, all of them toasting yet another brutal tournament.

So when Luca Impelliteri made his threat, Skorzeny did not retreat.

Standing over the table outside a Tarragona cafe, he had held his ground, listened, his face expressionless.

'I will tell the Generalissimo everything,' Impelliteri had said, smiling up at him. 'I will tell him you are a liar and a fraud, that your fearsome reputation is built on a propagandist's story, and that he should not court your company.'

'And why should he believe you?'

'Francisco Franco is a careful man. He is always suspicious. He has not held his position for decades by being reckless. If there is doubt, he will remove you from his circle of friends rather than risk being made to appear foolish. Don't you agree?'

'I do not,' Skorzeny said.

Impelliteri shrugged. 'Even so, that's how I see things. Of

course, the Generalissimo need never know any of this. I am open to persuasion.'

Skorzeny waited for a moment, then said, 'How much?'

'Fifty thousand American dollars to start with. After that, well, we'll see.'

Skorzeny did not reply. He turned his back on the Italian and walked to the hotel. Once inside his room, he lifted the telephone receiver and asked for an international line. Within thirty minutes, he had made all the necessary arrangements.

Now this new threat, these murderous barbarians seeking to frighten him with the corpses of men he barely considered acquaintances. Whatever they sought, they would not take it from him by fear.

The absence of his guardsmen on this dark night did, however, cause him a moment of concern.

Skorzeny turned in a circle, scanning the treeline. He kept his expression calm, his voice flat. He said, 'They're patrolling the grounds, probably. Come.'

He set off for the outbuildings again, unease slithering around his stomach with the pheasant and the *Rote Grütze*. The others followed.

He had seen the look Lainé and Ryan had exchanged. The G2 officer had been gone for some time. Had he and Lainé spoken while he was upstairs? Lainé had made his dislike of Ryan clear to Skorzeny. Had they had some sort of confrontation?

No matter, there were more immediate concerns.

Such as why no one guarded the building that held Hakon Foss.

As he drew closer, Skorzeny saw that the door stood ajar,

a slash of light from within. And the toe of a boot lying inside the gap. He quickened his step.

'What's that?' Ryan asked.

Skorzeny reached the door, pushed, found it blocked. He pushed harder, and again, forcing the dead man's legs away from the opening.

'*Merde*,' Lainé said.

One of the guards, a neat hole at the centre of his forehead, two more in his chest. Skorzeny stepped over his body, avoiding the blood that pooled around him.

The rage in Skorzeny's belly threatened to rise up like a dragon, burn all reason from his mind. He quelled it.

Hakon Foss remained in his seat, hands still strapped to the table, feet awash in his own urine. He reeked of faeces and sweat. But he was alive.

Skorzeny approached the table, mindful of the foulness on the floor.

'What happened here?'

Foss cried. 'Men came. They shoot.'

Skorzeny leaned on the table. Ryan and Lainé kept their distance.

'Who?'

Foss shook his head, mucus dribbling from his nose and lips. 'I don't know. I ask them to let me go. They don't answer.'

Skorzeny slammed his fist down on Foss's splayed right hand, felt the metacarpals give under the force.

Foss screamed.

'Who were they?'

Foss swung his head from side to side, saliva and mucus spilling from him.

Skorzeny brought his fist down again. Foss's voice cracked, turned from a scream to a whine.

'Tell me who they were.'

Foss's lips moved, mouthing words no one would ever hear.

Skorzeny reached down, grabbed Foss's devastated hand in his own, squeezed, felt the bones grind within the flesh.

Foss's eyes fluttered, his consciousness failing. Lainé appeared at his side, a knife in his hand. He plunged it into Foss's neck, tore it across his throat.

Skorzeny stepped back as the deep red fountain burst from the Norwegian, splashing across the table. 'What are you doing?' he asked.

Lainé tossed the knife onto the table. It skittered through the red. 'He should die.'

Foss choked, his eyes dimming.

Skorzeny's rage bubbled up. 'Not before he told me what he knew.'

'He would not talk.' Lainé wiped his hands on his coat. 'He was more strong than that.'

Ryan's voice from behind. 'He knew almost nothing, anyway.'

Skorzeny turned to the Irishman. 'What do you mean?'

'He was the informant,' Ryan said, a new hollowness in his eyes. 'Catherine Beauchamp told me before she died. He knew nothing about them. He never saw their faces. They gave him money. He gave them information. That was all.'

'Why didn't you tell me this before?'

Ryan put his hands in his pockets. 'I would have if you'd given me the chance. Besides, don't you have bigger things to worry about right now?'

Skorzeny looked at the body on the floor. He pushed past Ryan, stepped over the corpse, and kicked the door aside.

The light from the halogen lamp scorched everything within its reach. Fire all around him. The rage rising up like a shark from the deep.

'Come!' His mighty voice echoed through the trees. 'Come for me now! If you have the courage, come for me now! If you are men, come and face me!'

He roared at the night until his voice could bear the force of his anger no more.

36

THE SKY EDGED FROM BLACK TO DEEP BLUE AS RYAN FOUND himself outside Buswells Hotel. A bristling hush hung over the city, like a breath before a word, the streets about to wake.

The night porter opened the door. Ryan told him the room number and waited for his key. As the porter handed it over, he gave Ryan a sly smile and a wink. Had it not been for the fatigue, Ryan might have wondered why.

He climbed the stairs, each step dragging at his feet, his body getting heavier as he rose. It seemed an age between the key settling in his palm and slotting into the hole in his door. He turned it, let the door swing inward, saw the warm light the bedside lamp cast around the room.

Seconds passed before he made sense of the shape curled on the bed.

'Celia?'

She jerked awake, fear and surprise followed by recognition. 'Albert. What time is it?'

Celia turned to the window, saw the creeping dawn. She had used her coat for a blanket. It fell away, revealing bare, freckled shoulders. The pale smooth skin, the lamplight reflected like a halo.

'It's early.' Ryan closed the door. 'What are you doing here?'

She propped herself up on her elbow and rubbed mascara

across her cheeks. 'I wanted to see you. The night porter let me in.'

Ryan wanted to cross the room to her, but his feet seemed locked in place.

'Won't Mrs Highland be worried?'

Celia smiled, lazy creases on her face. 'She'll be having kittens. I didn't think you'd be so long.'

'There were . . . problems.'

'I don't want to know,' she said. 'Come and sit.'

Ryan hesitated, then walked to the bed, sat down. Her body swayed with his weight. He saw the shape of her as the dress stretched across her breasts, indecent and beautiful. Her faded perfume laced with her own scent, flowers and spices and the faint warm tang of woman.

She turned her eyes to the window. 'I don't know what you must think of me.'

A dozen answers flitted through Ryan's mind, not one he could utter without shaming himself. Instead, he kept his silence.

'I was never a pretty girl,' she said.

He swallowed, a loud click in his throat. 'That's not true.'

'Oh, it is,' she said, the seriousness of her expression denying any other notion. 'I was skinny and awkward and gangly, and this frightful ginger hair. Like a lanky boy. Then one day, all of a sudden, I was different. And men noticed me, like I'd been hiding in plain sight. My father's friends, their sons, all saying, my, how you've grown, and aren't you blossoming. But when I looked in the mirror I still saw the same gangly girl, all elbows and knees and buck teeth.

'I told you about Paris, and that artist coming up and asking me to model. I acted offended when I told him no, but I went back to the little apartment I shared with the other girls, and I looked at myself in the mirror, and I asked, am I pretty?

'That very same week, a man came to see me in the consulate and asked if I would do something very special. He asked if I would go to a party and strike up a conversation with a particular gentleman. An attaché at the British embassy. See if I could get him to ask me to dinner. And he did. And he was dreadfully dull, talking about trade missions, and policies, and which countries had the most to invest, and I thought I'd fall asleep in my soup.

'But the man came back to the consulate – Mr Waugh, his name was – and I told him what had been said, and he was very pleased, and I got a weekend in a very swanky hotel in Nice and a very, very generous bonus. And so it went. A clerk, a diplomat, a businessman. Sometimes even an Irishman. No one got hurt, the gentlemen had a pleasant time, and I was terribly well paid. Mr Waugh always took care of things.'

Celia sat up, put a hand on Ryan's shoulder.

'What I'm trying to tell you is, I thought this would be the same. We'd have a nice time, we'd talk, and I'd tell Skorzeny what you'd said. I never thought there would be anything more to it than that. Anything . . . bad.'

Ryan was certain he should be angry at her. He couldn't be sure if it was the fatigue or the low heat in his belly that prevented it. His mind should have seized on the betrayal, but instead it dwelled on the pressure of her fingers against his arm.

'Who asked you to do the job?' he asked.

'Charlie Haughey by way of Mr Waugh.'

'You should contact this Mr Waugh as soon as you can. Tell him you can't continue this assignment. It's too dangerous.'

Her eyes hardened, told him not to lie. 'How dangerous?'

'Dangerous,' Ryan said. 'Six men died tonight.'

Skorzeny had barrelled into the trees, his voice torn up by anger. Ryan had followed, leaving Lainé in the harsh glow of the halogen lamp.

The curses in the dark made waypoints for Ryan to navigate by, roots snagging his toes, bushes grabbing at his thighs.

'Here!'

Skorzeny's voice cut through the night. Ryan headed towards it.

He found the Austrian in a clearing, crouched, his cigarette lighter in one hand, the other cupping the flame. A man lay dead in the moss and rotten leaves, an AK-47 at his side. The flickering of the lighter seemed to animate his face, the expression turning from surprise to terror and back again.

Skorzeny hauled himself to his feet and set off again. Ryan tailed him, following the sounds of his crashing through the trees. They rounded the house, circled clearings and thickets. Time stretched, the sound of Skorzeny's breath a metronome, a rhythm to trace in the dark.

Ryan tripped on something heavy and pliant. He landed on the moist cold earth, his feet tangling in something he knew to be human.

'Over here,' he called.

The answer from a dozen yards away. 'Where? Talk. I'll find you.'

Ryan spoke to the darkness, words of no meaning, sounds to guide Skorzeny in.

He knelt down beside Ryan and flicked the lighter. The

flame stuttered and caught. The dead man stared at the sky, a piece of his cheek gone.

They stumbled down to the gateway that opened on to the road. A few minutes' searching found the bodies, dragged from the driveway to the black places behind the wall.

Skorzeny stood panting like a beaten dog, smaller than he'd been before.

'What do they want?' he asked.

Ryan knew the question was not for him. He answered it anyway. 'You.'

Skorzeny grabbed Ryan's shirt front. The fabric stung him where the sword's tip had pierced his skin. 'Then why don't they come for me? Why this?'

'Because they want you afraid.'

Skorzeny released his grip. 'Never.'

Ryan thought of Weiss and his mission. Only one logical thought would stay in his mind, and he knew Weiss would kill him for it.

'You should leave,' Ryan said.

'What?'

'Get out of here. You have friends in Spain. You'll be safe there.'

Skorzeny's laugh echoed through the trees. 'Run?'

'I don't see any other choice.'

'Never.' Skorzeny pushed Ryan hard, sending him sprawling in the weeds. 'I have never run from anyone. Do you take me for a coward?'

Ryan got to his feet, dusted off his trousers, careful of the wound on his thigh. 'No, I don't.'

Skorzeny came close. Ryan smelled brandy on his breath. 'Would *you* run? Would you show them your tail as you fled?'

Ryan stepped back. 'I don't know.'

'Are you a coward?'

'No, sir.'

'Then why do you talk like one? You talk of running. Like a woman. Like a child. Where are your balls?'

'Sir, I—'

'And why haven't you fucked that red-headed girl?'

Ryan turned his back on Skorzeny, walked towards the gravel of the driveway, ignored the taunts.

'Why not? She's there for you, a gift. And you haven't the balls to take her. What kind of man are you?'

Ryan left him ranting in the darkness.

Celia's fingertip brushed the graze on Ryan's neck, already dry and scabbing.

'Does it hurt?' she asked.

'No,' he said.

She rested her chin on his shoulder. Her breath on his skin.

'You're a strange man, Albert Ryan.' She touched his cheek, skimmed his jowl with the backs of her fingers. 'Such a saggy face. If I saw you on the street, I'd think, there's a nice man. A quiet man. He's got a job in a bank, or maybe a department store, and he's going home to kiss his wife and play with his children.'

Her words caught like splinters.

'And here you are, bleeding, telling me about all the dead men and how they died.'

Ryan turned his face to her, every intention to speak, but she silenced him with her lips.

Soft and warm on his, her fingers woven in his hair, her

body pressed against his shoulder. No air, he pushed her away, gasped, fell on her, hands hungry and seeking.

She guided them away from her breasts, said, 'No,' and he obeyed. The bed seemed too small for them both. Her body moved beneath his, her thigh between his legs, shying from the hardness it found there, her teeth grazing his lips.

'God,' she said. 'Sweet Jesus.'

She pushed him away.

Ryan leaned back on his knees, breathless, confused.

She shook her head. 'I want to. But I won't. I'm . . .'

He understood. 'I know.'

Celia took his hand, brought him down to her. She turned on her side, her back to him, and he nestled there, his mouth against the heat of her neck, his chest against her bare shoulder blades, his arm wrapped around her.

She did not pull away from the hardness of him now, allowed him to press against her. Her foot hooked around his ankle.

They lay there, knotted and breathless. Ryan felt her ribcage expand and contract, the rhythm steadying, her body loosening. He closed his eyes.

When he opened them again, it was light, and she was gone.

37

LAINÉ DID NOT SLEEP. WHEN RYAN AND SKORZENY HAD disappeared into the trees, he had gone back to the house, taken another bottle from the cellar, and climbed the stairs to his room.

He listened to the hoarse shouting in the distance, then the sound of Ryan's car starting and pulling away, and finally Skorzeny entering the house and barking orders into the telephone downstairs. An hour later, perhaps more, the sound of two engines approaching and stopping outside. Big, coarse engines, like Land Rovers, farmers' vehicles, built for carrying their loads across fields and streams. The voices of men issuing instructions, accepting commands.

IRA men, probably, tasked with cleaning up whatever mess had been left among the trees surrounding Skorzeny's property.

Lainé lay on his bed, taking the last swallows from the bottle, the puppy dozing at his feet. He pictured the dead being ferried away into the night, buried in the corner of some barren field, or in the dark channels of a forest, or weighed down in the deepest part of a cold lake.

Among them Hakon Foss, poor innocent idiot, now to be fed upon by foxes or fish.

The wine turned sour like vinegar in Lainé's mouth, but he finished it anyway, dropped the empty bottle on the carpet.

The puppy woke, stirred by the noise, and came up to nestle in the V between Lainé's body and arm.

He thought of Catherine Beauchamp. Had anyone gone to a telephone box, placed a call to the police, told them she waited on the floor of her cottage? Had anyone come to investigate the distressed whinnying of her horse, alone, hungry and afraid in its stable?

Ryan had lied about what she'd said, putting the blame on Foss, and Lainé knew why: to take his trust, to thieve it by deception, to let him think Ryan was on his side. Lainé was smarter than that, and he believed Ryan knew it, but he would play the Irishman's game. He had no other choice.

No, that was untrue. Had never been true. Back when he had taken up arms alongside the occupying Nazis, he'd had a choice, just as he did now, and he chose to follow Ryan's path.

If he had dared to wonder why, his conscience would have told him it was because he had grown to hate Skorzeny. His greed for money and power and influence. His vanity, his desire to be admired and feared. At one time, Lainé had seen the Nazis' ideals as being in line with his own: the assertion of nationhood. But ideals wither in the glare of money and power, until greed is all that survives.

And why shouldn't he, Célestin Lainé, share in that greed?

So when those men came to him, pressed that thick, greasy paper into his hand in return for his tongue, he offered it gladly. They had promised more, a fortune he'd never thought he could possess, and he had believed them.

But when he had told them all he knew, the money ceased to fill his palm and he realised they had used him, just like the Nazis had. Made him a traitor to himself with no reward but the guilt that lay rotting in his breast.

Yes, they had made Célestin Lainé a traitor, and a traitor he would be.

He lay silent and still as the hours to daylight passed, leaving his room only to take the puppy outside for its toilet. Later still, as the morning lengthened, he heard the noise of the big Mercedes engine coughing into life and roaring as Skorzeny sped away.

Lainé went downstairs, quiet and secret, and took his bicycle from under the tarpaulin at the back of the house. He rode the few miles to the tiny village of Cut Bush. There a telephone box stood outside a small public house. Breathless, he propped the bicycle against the wall and went inside for a whiskey while he recovered from the effort. When his chest and his heart stopped their heaving and battering, he finished the drink and went to the bar to ask for change.

A light drizzle made dark spots on the road outside. Lainé stepped inside the telephone box. He asked the operator for Buswells Hotel, Dublin, inserted coins, pushed the button when instructed, and waited. The hotel's receptionist asked him to hold, and he listened to clicks and hissing.

'Yes?'

'Ryan. It is me. Célestin.'

A pause, then, 'Tell me about Captain John Carter.'

Lainé talked.

38

WITHIN THIRTY MINUTES OF RYAN LEAVING A COPY OF THE *Irish Times* on the dashboard of the Vauxhall, the telephone in his hotel room jangled.

'The University Church, southern end of St Stephen's Green,' Weiss said. 'I'll wait inside.'

Ten minutes later, Ryan approached the church's ornate facade, red brick and short stone columns, a belfry above, seemingly suspended in mid-air. It stood sandwiched between taller buildings, creating the illusion of a chapel in miniature, but stepping through its double doors revealed the truth. A small porch opened into the atrium beyond. A tall vaulted ceiling, high white walls decorated with granite plaques dedicated to scholars and philanthropists. The chill on the air crept beneath Ryan's clothing. A short flight of stone steps led down to the floor where Goren Weiss waited, smartly dressed as before.

'What's the news, Albert?' His voice echoed between the walls.

Ryan looked to the gap between the double doors leading to the church itself, the glowing light from within. He saw no one inside.

'Six men died last night,' he said.

Weiss emptied his lungs, a despairing exhalation. 'Go on.'

Ryan told him about the body in the outbuilding, about the killing of Foss, about the dead guards in the trees. He did not mention Lainé's tattling or Skorzeny's shoving and baiting.

'Fuck,' Weiss said. 'Audacious, wouldn't you say?'

'Or stupid.'

'Maybe. What confuses me, and I imagine Colonel Skorzeny more so, is why they didn't come for him while they were at it. They've proved they can get to him if they want to. They've got the noose around his neck, so why not kick the chair from under him?'

The doors to the porch and the street beyond opened, and an elderly man entered the atrium. He went to one of the fonts that were mounted on each wall. He dipped his fingers in the holy water and made the sign of the cross before descending the steps. He nodded at Ryan and Weiss as he passed on his way to the church.

When the doors closed behind the old man, Weiss asked, 'How come you didn't do that? The water and the cross thing.'

'I'm not Catholic,' Ryan said.

'I see. Then I guess neither of us belongs here, do we?'

Ryan wondered for a moment if Weiss meant the church or something other. 'This isn't a good place to meet,' he said. 'It's too close to Merrion Street.'

'The government buildings? What, you think Mr Haughey's going to swing by to say a prayer for Skorzeny? Does he strike you as a man who likes to get his knees dirty?'

'No, he doesn't.'

For the first time, if only for an instant, Weiss's smile reached his eyes. 'So, why didn't Carter and his men kill Skorzeny last night?'

'Because they want him scared,' Ryan said.

'And is he?'

'Not on the surface, but underneath, yes, I think he is.'

'Scared enough to go running to Franco?'

'No, he won't run. He's got too much pride.'

'Good. But that doesn't answer the question. They've got him nervous, but that's not their goal. What is it they really want? Figure that out and we might be closer to tracking the sons of bitches down.'

'I have a lead,' Ryan said. 'A solid one.'

Weiss tilted his head, looked hard at him. 'What?'

'You'll know if it works out.'

'I'll know it now.' Weiss leaned in, his face darkening. 'Don't hold anything back from me, Albert. That would make me very unhappy.'

'I want to follow it up, but I can't have you breathing down my neck. Call off any tails you've got on me. When I need to talk, my car will be at the hotel along with the newspaper on the dashboard. I'll be in touch if I've got something.'

Weiss chewed his lip. 'Damn it, Albert, you're putting me in a difficult position.'

'If you want my cooperation, then you'll leave me alone. That's your only choice.'

Weiss curled his hands into fists, turned in a circle, his gaze far away. Eventually, he said, 'All right.' He extended a finger towards Ryan. 'But listen to me, Albert. If you cross me . . .'

He let the threat hang in the cool air between them.

Ryan walked away, saying, 'I'll be in touch.'

39

RYAN TOURED THE STREETS AROUND FITZROY AVENUE, TRAVELLED north and south along Jones's Road, skirted Croke Park stadium, passed under the railway line and back again. Few cars lined the pavements in front of the small red-bricked terraced houses.

Lainé's description had been far from precise, but close enough. The first time the Breton had talked to them, he had taken a train to Amiens Street Station where Carter and another man had met him. They had bundled him into the back of a van with no windows and driven for only a few minutes. When the van halted, they slipped a pillowcase over his head and led him out. They put him against a wall as they locked their vehicle, and a train passed overhead, shaking the ground beneath his feet. He heard the clack and rumble of the wheels, felt the force of it through the brickwork at his shoulder.

One man grabbed his elbow and led him through a gate and into a house. Once inside, they removed the pillowcase from his head and questioned him for two hours before putting it back on and leading him out to the van.

On the third visit, Lainé had seen the rickety stands of the stadium through a small gap between the van doors and heard the roar of the throng as a match played out. When the questioning was done, they made him wait for almost an hour. Let the crowds disperse, the other man had said.

Afterwards, Lainé had checked a street map, piecing together what he knew, and had established that the house they took him to stood on the most easterly block of Fitzroy Avenue, backing on to the railway line. He couldn't be sure which house, but he judged it to be closer to the stadium end.

Ryan parked north of the railway line beneath the trees on Holy Cross Avenue. Spring growth had scattered thick bright greens throughout the boughs even as the winter's dead leaves still gathered in the gutters.

He walked south, through the crossing with Clonliffe Road, and on towards the railway bridge. He lingered in the shadow beneath the line, watching Fitzroy Avenue. No pedestrians, the only sound the chirping of birds and barking of dogs.

An entry on the other side of the bridge opened onto the alleyway that ran along the back of the block Lainé believed he'd been taken to. Ryan passed it, glanced in as he did so, saw a Bedford van, and kept walking towards the corner shop at the junction of Fitzroy Avenue.

He turned left and kept a casual pace, glancing at the parlour windows, all of them shaded by net curtains, the glint of mirrors and glow of hearths from within.

Except for one.

Ryan barely slowed his step when he saw the blanket that had been hung on the other side of the net curtain. He walked to the end of the street, counted houses as he went, turned left again, and found the opposite end of the alleyway he had passed a few minutes before.

He paused there and found the back of the house, just visible from the street. Newspapers covered the insides of the windows. A small walled and gated yard separated by the alley from the bricked-up arches of the railway. A secret place, Ryan thought, a place of hiding.

He moved closer to the wall, out of sight of the windows, and thought. The rumble and hiss of a train approached along the elevated line above, the deep churning of its diesel engine swelling. The smell of oil lingered as it passed. Ryan edged along the yard walls and gates, deeper into the alley, closer to the van. As he reached it, he looked up at the railway track. At the other end of the block, beyond the arch of the bridge, was a green verge at the edge of the line, higher than the roofs of the houses, overgrown with bushes and weeds.

Ryan turned his attention back to the van. Burgundy in colour, rusted and battered, probably bought from someone's yard, not through an auto dealer. He worked his way along its length, keeping out of view of the house it stood behind. Trampled cigarette butts littered the ground around the passenger door. The cabin contained only a folded newspaper and a thermos flask. Through the glass, Ryan could see the newspaper was weeks out of date. A ruse, camouflage to make the van appear as if it belonged to workmen.

He made his way to the far end of the alley and slipped into the shadow under the bridge. The grey stone wall extended out perhaps six feet further than the line itself. Ivy clung to the stones, reared up in bushes at the top of the wall, formed a platform sheltered by thick foliage.

Ryan crossed under the bridge and came to a grassy embankment on the other side, bordered by the wall that followed its downward slope to the street beyond. He took a brief look in every direction then reached up, grabbed the wall's upper edge, and hauled himself onto the grass.

He scaled the embankment and reached the tracks. Another train approached, heading for Amiens Street Station. Ryan crossed the tracks to the patch of green on the other side. He crouched down in the ivy and scrambled to the edge of the wall. Lying down, he had a clear view along the alleyway below, and the Bedford van. He couldn't see the front of the house, but the junction of Fitzroy Avenue and Jones's Road, and the stadium, were visible beyond. No one could pass either end of the block without him seeing. Besides, if they kept their van in the alleyway rather than in a street with ample parking, that meant they came and went by the back of the house. Out of view of their neighbours as they went about their work.

A rush of displaced air swept over Ryan as the train roared and clattered past. When its rumble had receded, he crossed over the tracks, descended the embankment, and made his way back to the car.

Ryan asked Mrs Highland if he could speak to Celia. He pictured her grinding her teeth at the other end of the line before agreeing to his request.

'Hello?'

'Celia, it's me. Albert.'

'Hello,' she said. He hoped he heard a smile in her voice.

'I didn't get to say goodbye to you this morning.'

'I'm sorry,' she said. 'I didn't want to wake you. You looked so tired when you came in. Shall we meet tonight? We could talk.'

'I can't.'

'Oh,' she said, her voice falling.

'I mean, I have to go away for a day or two. For work.'

'I see. Will you call me when you come back? I hope so.'

'Of course I will.'

'Good. And, Albert?'

'Yes?'

'Whatever you're going away for, whatever work you're doing, be careful.'

'I will.'

Ryan returned at dusk and parked once more on Holy Cross Avenue. He slung his leather backpack across his shoulders and made his way down to the embankment. He wore a khaki canvas jacket and trousers and a black woollen cap. The backpack contained bread and cheese along with a bottle of water and a thermos of strong coffee, a small set of field glasses, a notepad and a pencil. He had also taken the Walther P38 from its hiding place in the bottom of the wardrobe in his hotel room. It sat snug in its holster against his ribs.

A two-minute walk took him to the wall and the embankment rising above it. One more glance around for curious pedestrians and twitching curtains, and he hauled himself up onto the grass. He ran at a low crouch up the slope, across the train tracks, and dropped into the ivy nest he'd found that afternoon.

Ryan lay down on his belly. A feeling crept up and surprised him: the familiarity of lying hidden in the green. He remembered his time dug into hedgerows in the Irish countryside, watching the comings and goings of men who couldn't accept that their war was over. Or the dense heat of the Korean jungles, scoping out positions, noting down numbers of men and weapons.

Ryan had stayed in Korea long after the armistice of July

1953, escorting shipments of the enemy's dead, bodies exchanged with the North Koreans as part of Operation Glory. He arrived back in Ireland in time to spend Christmas 1954 with his parents before reporting to St Patrick's Barracks in Ballymena on the first day of 1955. He spent four years there training recruits from all over the British Isles, many of them destined for posts in Germany where the army's role had turned from occupation to defence.

When Ryan received his discharge book in 1959, he spent a month in Belfast, sitting in a cramped bedsit near the city centre, scouring the jobs sections of the local newspapers. It took those thirty days to realise he held no qualifications of any use to the outside world, had no experience, had nothing to offer any employer.

He was ready to go back to the barracks in Ballymena, admit he couldn't hack civilian life, when he received a letter from an old friend in the Royal Ulster Rifles. Major Colm Hughes, like Ryan, had travelled north across the border from County Monaghan to join the British Army. They had promised to stay in touch when Ryan left the service, but he had doubted they ever would. The letter suggested they meet in the Rotterdam Bar in Sailortown, close to Belfast's docks.

Hughes sat at the bar, nursing a pint of Bass when Ryan entered. They shook hands, the warmth between them muted by the unfamiliarity of their civilian dress. Ryan realised he had never seen Hughes in anything but a uniform.

They took a table in a dark corner, exchanged a few stories about old comrades, some still alive, some not.

'So what have you been up to?' Hughes asked.

'Nothing,' Ryan said. 'That's the problem. Outside of the army, I'm no use to anyone.'

'Are you thinking of re-enlisting?'

'I don't know. What else is there for me?'

'How about settling down?' Hughes asked. 'Get married. Have some kids. Get fat and grow vegetables in your garden.'

Ryan couldn't help but smile at the image. 'Can you see me up to my ankles in fertiliser?'

Hughes laughed. 'I've seen you in worse.'

They sat quiet for a time, listening to the coarse jokes of the dock and shipyard workers who drifted in as their shifts ended. Hard, wiry men, tattoos of girls' names on their forearms, swollen knuckles and mighty thirsts.

'There is one way I could point you,' Hughes said.

Ryan leaned forward. 'What's that?'

'I was contacted a while back, when I was home visiting my mother in Monaghan. A fella in a suit came up to me in the pub near our old house, started talking all casual, acting like he knew me. He starts asking what I thought I might do when I left the army. I never talk about the job much back home. You know what it's like, some aren't too keen on Irish lads fighting for the Brits. So I didn't say much back to him.

'Anyway, after talking around it for half an hour, he says he works for the government. Says they're looking for Irish boys who've come out of the British Army, boys who've seen action. The lads in the Irish Army do plenty of square-bashing and exercises, but most of them's never slept in a trench or shot at anything but a paper target. He says they need boys like us for his department.'

'Which department?' Ryan asked.

'The Directorate of Intelligence,' Hughes said. 'G2, they call it.'

'So he was trying to recruit you?'

'No,' Hughes said. 'He knew I was in for life. But he wanted me to whisper in a few ears, talk to any lads that might be good material for them.'

'Like me,' Ryan said.

Hughes smiled, took a swig of ale, and took a pencil from his jacket pocket. He scribbled a name and a telephone number on a beer mat, slid it across the table.

'Think about it,' he said.

Ryan hardly thought about it at all. He called the number the very next morning.

40

SKORZENY WOKE EARLY, BATHED, AND ATE A STOUT BREAKFAST with good coffee. He walked in the fields for an hour or so, watched the sheep graze, observed Tiernan working on exercises with his dogs.

Lainé had kept himself out of sight since the night before last, holed up in his room, empty bottles gathering by the kitchen door the only visible sign of his passing. Skorzeny occasionally heard the pup's mewling, but little else.

In truth, he was glad of it. He did not find Célestin Lainé at all agreeable, but the Breton was useful, so he tolerated his presence in the house. Frau Tiernan found him less tolerable, had complained about Lainé several times since his arrival, but Skorzeny assured her he would move on before long and she wouldn't have to worry about the messes he and that damned pup left behind.

Skorzeny had spent much of the last thirty-six hours in thought, considering options, entertaining suspicions. Of course Ryan was correct, Skorzeny should simply board a flight to Madrid and stay there enjoying the sunshine until this foolishness was over. But if he had been the type to back down, to flee when danger thundered in the distance, he would not be Otto Skorzeny. He would never have tasted the glory, or the women, or enjoyed the power and the riches at his disposal. He would still be an engineer, toiling at a desk in Vienna, waiting for a pension or a heart attack, whichever came first.

Whoever these terrorists – yes, terrorists was the correct word – whoever they were, and whatever they wanted, he would stand here on his land, would not be dislodged by threat or action. If they wanted to come at him, they had better be prepared for a fight.

And Otto Skorzeny had never lost a fight.

Besides, Madrid might not be that welcoming for the time being, given recent events.

In Tarragona, Luca Impelliteri had sat across the table from Skorzeny eight hours after making his demands, smiling that damned smile of his as the rest of Franco's guests chattered around them. A young Spanish woman had sat by the Italian's side, her hand constantly brushing the tanned skin of his forearm.

Occasionally, Impelliteri spoke into her ear, causing her to smile and blush. Then he glanced up at Skorzeny, his looks a barbed reminder of the prize he believed he had won from the older man.

But he had won nothing other than the fate he deserved.

In the small hours of the following morning, Skorzeny was woken by a telephone call to his hotel room.

'SS-Obersturmbannführer Skorzeny?'

A woman's voice.

'Who is this?' he asked, though he knew the answer.

'I have come at the request of your old friend.'

'Good,' Skorzeny said. 'Where are you?'

'In a hotel at the far end of the Rambla Nova.'

'Do you know what I want from you?'

'I know what, but not who.'

As the Mediterranean lapped at the rocks beneath his window, Skorzeny gave her a name.

He made his way back to the house, cleaned his boots outside the door, and entered through the kitchen.

Frau Tiernan stood at the sink washing the breakfast things.

'I would like some coffee in my study,' he said in German. 'Have Esteban bring it to me when it's ready.'

She looked up from her scrubbing. 'Yes, sir. The post is on your desk.'

Skorzeny went to the study, sat behind his desk, and lit a cigarette. He leafed through the five envelopes. A letter from Pieter Menten in Holland, one from a bishop in Portugal, two from old *Kameraden* in Argentina.

And one with a Dublin postmark, the address typewritten to SS-Obersturmbannführer Otto Skorzeny.

His mouth dried. He drew hard on the cigarette, placed it in the ashtray, and opened the envelope.

One page, typewritten.

He read. Anger simmered in his gut. He clenched a fist, read the letter once more.

Then he laughed.

41

RYAN READ THROUGH HIS NOTES FROM THE NIGHT BEFORE, though there had been little to write about as the dark hours dragged on. Somewhere he had heard a baby cry every few hours, demanding its feed. A couple had argued loud and fierce on past midnight. A dog barked every so often. In the house closest to him, Ryan heard the rattle of a headboard through the open bedroom window, the grunts of a man's climax, the closing of a door, a woman's tears.

Ryan moved a few feet away from his nest when he needed to relieve his bladder, crawling slow and careful through the ivy.

As the night deepened, Ryan fought sleep with coffee. Still it slipped over him. He awoke from a nightmare, walls collapsing around him, burying him, as the dawn train screamed past. Once he'd gathered his senses, he checked his wristwatch. Not quite six-thirty.

Life stirred in the houses. The baby crying, dogs barking, mothers shouting at their children. Soon he spotted men leaving for work, trudging along the street, their jackets held tight around them against the early chill, cigarettes hanging from their lips, lunches wrapped in newspaper beneath their arms.

A milk float hummed onto the street. Ryan lost it behind

the houses, but he heard the clinking of bottles and the milk-man's whistling.

The corner shop below Ryan's vantage point opened not long after seven-thirty. The proprietor wiped down the windows and swept the floor.

A movement at the house caught Ryan's attention. He checked his watch: just past eight. A short, stocky man stepped out of the gated yard. He walked along the alleyway, coming directly towards Ryan. A soldier, there could be no question, with that hair, that gait. One who'd seen action. Ryan guessed he was around thirty years old, too young to have been in the Second World War, but very likely Korea.

The man rounded the corner and entered the shop. Through the glass, Ryan saw him nod at the shopkeeper, speaking as few words as he could get away with. He emerged with a packet of cigarettes and a box of kitchen matches, stuffing his change into his pocket, and jogged back up the alley to the gate.

Ryan had been correct about one thing: he came and went by the rear of the house, not the front.

Ten minutes later, two more men emerged. Ryan brought the field glasses to his eyes. He recognised one of them as Captain John Carter. Fuller in the face, his hair thinner on top, but it was him. The other stood a good five or six inches taller, and gave sharp deferential nods as Carter spoke. The face triggered Ryan's memory: one of the men standing along-side Carter in the photograph Weiss had given him. Carter went to the driver's side, unlocked the door, slid it back, and climbed into the cabin. He reached across and unlocked the passenger door. The other man finished his cigarette before getting in.

The clatter of the Bedford's engine echoed between the

houses and the railway arches. Carter watched his side mirrors, the alleyway barely wide enough to allow the van to pass.

As it approached, Ryan shrank back into the ivy. Through the vines and leaves he could make out the lines on Carter's face, and the other's. The tall man looked a similar age to his leader, around forty-five.

The van pulled out of the alley, and rounded the corner onto the avenue. The engine puttered and barked as it gathered speed on its way to Jones's Road and turned right towards the city centre.

Ryan noted the time.

All remained still until eleven-thirty when the shorter man left the house once more, again via the rear gate. He walked in the direction of Ryan's position, turned towards the corner shop, and came out a minute later with a bottle of lemonade.

Ryan held his breath as the man paused in the street below and unscrewed the cap. He brought the bottle to his lips, threw his head back, and gulped the fizzy liquid down. Wiping his chin, he let out a long belch. He went to the alleyway's entrance and leaned against the wall. There, he fished a packet of cigarettes from his pocket – the same one he'd bought earlier – and lit one.

The man remained at the end of the alley, sipping at his lemonade, long enough to smoke three cigarettes. All the while, he cast his gaze around, along the alley, up and down the street.

Ryan recognised the behaviour of a man not dealing well with being cooped up in his quarters. He had seen it everywhere he'd served, men finding any excuse they could to get outdoors, even if it meant simply walking circles around their barracks.

Finally, the man trudged back to the house, taking his lemonade with him, and let himself through the gate.

More than two hours passed before the van reappeared at the far end of the alleyway. It halted at the rear of the house, and the two men alighted without speaking to each other. They entered through the gate.

Three men in total. Ryan scribbled a brief description of each on his notepad. Height, build, hair colour.

The sun came out, warming Ryan's back.

On the street below, a group of five young boys rounded the corner, one of them carrying a soccer ball and a piece of chalk. He came to the gable wall of the house next to Ryan and disappeared from view. Ryan heard the scratching of the chalk on the wall, pictured the boy drawing a goal mouth.

One boy volunteered as goalkeeper, and the others split into pairs. Soon the sound of panting, kicking, leather scuffing on tarmac. Ryan watched them shove one another, their feet tangling over the ball. Every minute or two he heard the hard slap of its leather against the wall, the hollow ring as it bounced away, and one of the pairs would cheer.

Now and then the shopkeeper came to his window, glared out at them, shook his head, and retreated to his counter.

They played for more than an hour without a break, each pair's score reaching the dozens, before they stopped, breathless and sweating.

'I'm sitting down for a minute,' the boy who owned the ball said.

'Me too,' another said. 'I'm fucking knackered.'

The five sat on the footpath, in the shade, their backs against the red-brick gable wall opposite Ryan. They talked about school, and which of the Christian Brothers was the biggest bastard, and what they'd do when they were older and bigger and found one of the worst Brothers alone on the street. They talked about their mothers and fathers, and the girls they knew.

'Did you hear about Sheila McCabe and Paddy Gorman?'

'No, what?'

'She showed him her tits.'

'Fuck off. Sure, she's got no tits to show.'

'Yeah, she has, I saw her in town with her ma, they were buying her a bra.'

'Aw, shite, no you didn't.'

'I did. Anyway, she showed 'em to Paddy. He told me she let him have a suck on 'em and everything.'

The boys roared with laughter.

The shopkeeper came out onto the street. 'Here now, lads, I won't have that dirty talk outside my shop. Go on, the lot of you, before I go and tell your mothers what you were mouthing about.'

The boys stood, dropped their gaze to the ground, shuffled their feet. The shopkeeper went back inside. The boys laughed and recommenced their game.

They hadn't been playing long when the shorter man emerged from the house and into the alleyway. The boys glanced at him as he walked to the shop, and again when he left, a chocolate bar in his fingers. He went back to the mouth of the alley, unwrapped the bar, and ate. When the chocolate was done, he took his cigarettes from his pocket.

The boys paused in their play. They huddled around their leader, then parted.

The leader said, 'Here, mister.'

The man lit his cigarette, drew on it. The breeze carried away the smoke as he exhaled.

'Here, mister.'

He looked at the boy.

'Give us a couple of them, will you?'

The man hesitated then took two cigarettes from the packet and held them out. The boy approached and took them from his fingers.

'Thanks, mister.'

The boys ran off, taking their ball with them, their footsteps reverberating underneath the bridge as they went.

'What was that?'

The voice took Ryan by surprise as much as it did the man below.

Carter stood behind the man, his face hard with anger.

'Just some kids,' the man said, his accent Rhodesian or South African, Ryan couldn't tell which.

'We talked about this, Wallace.' Carter spoke through tight lips. 'Didn't we talk about this?'

'They're only kids. I didn't—'

Carter slapped Wallace's forehead with his open palm. 'I don't care if they're fucking leprechauns. You're drawing attention. How many times have you been at that shop today?'

Wallace scowled. 'A couple, that's all. I'm sick of sitting around that bloody house all day.'

'You'll sit wherever I fucking tell you to sit. Understand?'

Wallace sighed and nodded.

Carter leaned in close. 'Do you understand?'

'Yes.'

'Yes, what?'

'Yes, sir.'

'All right.' Carter stepped away. 'Now get back in the house. Go on, double.'

Wallace trotted away towards the gate.

Carter stood with his hands on his hips, watching him go. Then he looked in each direction along the street.

Ryan froze when Carter's gaze settled on the cluster of ivy at the top of the wall above. The Englishman stepped onto the road, squinting. Ryan held his breath.

Carter shook his head, spat on the ground, and followed Wallace to the house. Ryan let the air out of his lungs.

42

'I CAN'T REACH HIM,' HAUGHEY SAID, HIS VOICE CRACKLING IN the telephone's earpiece.

A soft ache settled behind Skorzeny's forehead. 'What do you mean?'

'What I mean is he hasn't been at the hotel since yesterday. Fitzpatrick, his boss, tried Gormanston Camp, and he hasn't been back there since all this started. I even had my secretary call that shop his father owns in Carrickmacree, she pretended to be his sweetheart, and they've seen no sign of him. In short, I don't have a baldy notion where the fucker is.'

Skorzeny drummed his fingers on the desktop. 'Minister, I don't believe I can stress the urgency of speaking with Lieutenant Ryan enough. This letter changes the nature of the work he is doing for us, and more importantly, the nature of the enemy we face.'

'*You* face, Colonel.'

'I beg your pardon?'

'*We* don't face any enemy,' Haughey said. 'That letter was addressed to you and nobody else. Your enemies are your own.'

'Trust me, Minister, you do not want to be one of them.'

'Likewise, Colonel. Think twice before threatening me. I can make Ireland a very cold house for you and your kind.

But let's not go down that road just yet. No need to fall out over Lieutenant Ryan. I'm sure he'll turn up before too long.'

Skorzeny returned the receiver to its cradle and rang the hand bell.

Esteban entered and lifted the telephone. He went to leave, but Skorzeny said, 'Wait.'

He sat silent for a few seconds, thinking, before he said, 'Fetch my coat, Esteban. I need to drive to the city.'

The woman asked, 'Is Celia expecting you?'

'No, madame,' Skorzeny said.

She smiled at the courtesy. 'Well, you'd better come in. You can wait in the parlour.'

He followed her through the hall and into the room.

'I won't be a minute,' she said, and left him there.

She returned two minutes later. 'Here she is.'

Celia entered. She stopped, one foot in front of the other, when she saw Skorzeny.

'Miss Hume,' he said.

Celia did not reply.

'Well, I'll leave you to it,' the landlady said.

'No,' Celia said. 'I'd rather you stayed.'

The landlady hesitated.

'It is a private matter,' Skorzeny said.

Celia gave a polite smile. 'Even so, I'd rather Mrs Highland stayed. Please sit down.'

The girl sat in the armchair opposite. Mrs Highland took the other chair. Skorzeny remained standing.

After seconds of silence, Mrs Highland asked, 'Would you like a cup of tea, Mr . . . Pardon me, I didn't quite get your name.'

'No thank you,' Celia said. 'Colonel Skorzeny doesn't need anything.'

'Oh.' Mrs Highland folded her hands in her lap. When no one else spoke, she said, 'Changeable weather we're having, isn't it?'

They both ignored her.

'What did you want to see me about, Colonel Skorzeny?'

'Our mutual friend,' he said, taking a seat on the couch. 'Lieutenant Ryan. I need to speak with him urgently, but I have been unable to reach him. I hoped you might know of his whereabouts.'

'I'm sorry, I don't.'

Skorzeny fixed his gaze on the girl. 'I must stress, Miss Hume, how important my business with Lieutenant Ryan is.'

'Again, I don't know where he is. I am sorry, but that's all I can tell you.'

He pinned her with his eyes. She looked down to her lap. 'Miss Hume, I will spare no effort – no effort at all – in finding Lieutenant Ryan. Do you understand my meaning?'

He watched her throat tighten, her hands tremble.

'I spoke with Albert yesterday. He told me he had to go away for a day or two. For work. He wouldn't tell me where or what for. That's all I know.'

Mrs Highland watched the girl's fingers knotting together.

Skorzeny leaned forward. 'Miss Hume, if you have neglected to tell me something, I will be most disappointed.'

Mrs Highland stood. She spoke with a tremor in her voice. 'Mr . . . I'm sorry, what was your name?'

'Skorzeny,' he said, also standing. 'Colonel Otto Skorzeny.'

'Mr Skorzeny, I don't think I like your tone. I don't know what your business here really is, but Miss Hume is under my care, and I can see you have made her nervous. I don't like it, and you are not welcome in my house. I would very much appreciate it if you would leave now.'

Skorzeny could not keep the smile from his lips.

'Of course, madame. Please forgive my intrusion. I will see myself out.'

He walked to the parlour door, turned, spoke to Celia. 'Miss Hume, please do call me if you should realise you know where Lieutenant Ryan is after all. I would be most grateful.'

She stared ahead, silent and still, save for the sharp rise and fall of her chest.

Skorzeny exited through the hall onto the street. He checked his watch and decided to head to one of the better hotels for dinner.

Perhaps the Shelbourne or the Royal Hibernian. Their food was at least tolerable.

His appetite roused.

43

THE VAN LEFT AGAIN JUST BEFORE SEVEN IN THE EVENING, this time with the three men on board, Carter at the wheel. When they returned, darkness had come, and the street lights glowed.

Ryan reached for his field glasses.

The men smiled and laughed, even Carter. Wallace grinned as he talked, his hands telling stories.

Saturday night. Ryan guessed they had gone out for dinner and a few pints. Even when stationed in a combat zone, men needed to unwind. Perhaps the excursion would ease Wallace's itch. But Ryan also knew Carter would keep them in check, not let a relaxing drink become anything more.

The men entered the house, and Ryan saw lights come on behind the newspaper that covered the insides of the windows. Within fifteen minutes, they had been extinguished, and the house stood in darkness.

Ryan checked his watch.

Eleven o'clock.

He burrowed into his nest, confident the men he watched had settled for the night. He tightened his jacket around him, placed the backpack beneath his head for a pillow. The sounds of the streets soothed him, the dogs barking, the distant shouting of drunken men, the begrudged lovemaking of the couple in the house nearest to him.

Ryan closed his eyes.

The early train woke him again, the roar pulling him from his dreams like a greasy tentacle, throwing him down in the ivy, a disorienting sense of weightlessness as his consciousness reassembled.

First Ryan looked for the van, saw it in the alley, then he crawled away from his hiding place to make his toilet. That done, he took the last of the bread and the nub of cheese from the backpack and ate his breakfast. The coffee had long since gone cold. He grimaced at the taste. Stubble abraded his fingers as he scratched his chin.

Sunday morning stretched on. Few residents ventured onto the street to break the monotony of Ryan's vigil. He yawned, flexed his fingers and toes, made up games to pass the time. Naming the birds he saw, laying bets on the colours of any cars he heard approaching.

No one came or went from the house.

His small supply of food had gone, and by the time noon crawled towards one o'clock, his stomach growled. For hours he had endured the smell of frying bacon, eggs and bread drifting from the houses all around. Had the corner shop opened, he might have risked leaving his position to buy something, but it remained stubbornly closed for the day.

Then something began to happen.

A trickle of men and boys, walking along Fitzroy Avenue and Jones's Road, drawing to the stadium. Some carried flags and banners, blue in colour.

Of course, Sunday, a football match at Croke Park. Ryan

did not follow sports, including those governed by the Gaelic Athletic Association, but he knew the season was under way and the National Football League was gathering pace. Dublin must be playing at home.

The streams of men and boys swelled, became rivers. Hundreds gathered around the stadium, filtering through the entrances, waiting shoulder to shoulder in the streets for their turn to go into the grounds.

By two o'clock, the crowds had mostly been absorbed by the stadium, and their noise boomed within, the voices raised and expectant. A sudden hush, then an explosion of cheers, and Ryan knew the game had begun.

He listened to the waves, a sea of voices, falling and rising with the currents of the match. Ryan imagined he lay on a beach, ivy for sand, the water lapping at the shore of his mind. His eyelids grew heavy, his head leaden with tiredness. He fought it, pushing the slumber back, but still it came, as inevitable as the tides.

Ryan drifted, found himself on the tiny cove he had discovered on the Sicilian island of Ortigia, the smooth stones and pebbles warm beneath his body, the glassy shallows reflecting brilliant sunlight.

The sound of the van's doors closing shocked him awake. His eyes struggled for focus. He lifted the field glasses.

All three of them in the van, Carter driving again.

Ryan shrank back into the ivy as the van reached the end of the alleyway below him. Carter pulled out onto the road, turned right, heading north. The engine strained as the van gathered speed. Soon, its clatter and thrum faded, drowned in the noise from the stadium.

Now, Ryan thought.

He stashed his belongings in the backpack, tucked it beneath the ivy, and climbed out of his hiding place. His joints and muscles protested, affronted at being asked to move after remaining still for so long. He crossed the tracks, descended the embankment on the other side, and dropped down from the wall onto the footpath. Checking for witnesses, he walked under the bridge and into the mouth of the alley.

Ryan kept tight to the yard walls, hidden from the rear windows of the houses as he approached the patch of oil-stained ground and its scattered cigarette butts.

He reached the gate, tried it, found it locked as he expected. It stood only a few inches taller than him. He reached up, grabbed the top edge, jammed his foot against the wood, and hauled himself up and over.

Dropping to the concrete on the other side, he saw an empty yard, too clean to belong to a house that civilians lived in. None of the detritus of family life cluttered the corners, no old prams left out to rot, no bicycles propped against the walls.

Ryan crossed to the outside toilet and pushed back the door. It smelled like it had been used not long before, but it was clean, squares of newspaper hanging from a peg by the bowl, a bottle of bleach on the floor.

He went to the back of the house. Like the upstairs windows, both the kitchen window and the glass pane in the door had been covered over by newspaper on the inside. He tried the door handle, knowing it was pointless, then attempted to squeeze his fingertips under the kitchen's sash window. Solid in its frame, it wouldn't shift. Nailed shut, he guessed.

Ryan stood back, studied the building, thinking through his options. There was no way to force entry into the house without leaving a trace of himself. So why bother being subtle?

He took the Walther from its holster and slammed the butt against the pane. The fragments cut through the newspaper, fell inside. He used the pistol's muzzle to clear the rest of the glass and newspaper away from the wood before returning it to its holster and gripping the sides of the opening.

Ryan hauled himself up and in, climbed over the sink, and lowered his feet to the tiled floor. The small kitchen smelled of stale food, the odours of meals long past. A selection of pots stood on the cooker, a stack of mismatched plates on a small table, a cardboard box packed with potatoes, onions, cabbages, and carrots.

No pictures hung from the painted-over nails on the walls. The floor had been swept, the surfaces wiped down, but dust clung to the cobwebs in the corners of the ceiling. The kind of clean that would not satisfy a woman.

Ryan opened the cupboards and drawers in turn and found them empty, save for a handful of utensils and a supply of tinned food.

He went to the door that led to the lounge, opened it, and stood there, taking it in.

In the light edging around the blanket suspended across the window, Ryan's eyes were drawn first to the corkboard mounted above the fireplace, and the photographs pinned to it. From the threshold he could make out several black and white images of Otto Skorzeny, two of them portraits, the rest taken from a distance, candid shots of the Austrian in the city or on his farm.

Ryan stepped into the room and approached the board.

He scanned the rest of the photographs, some he recognised, others he didn't, but each image carried the name of its subject. Hakon Foss, Célestin Lainé, Catherine Beauchamp, Johan Hambro, Alex Renders.

All of them dead except for Skorzeny and Lainé.

In the top corner, a hand-drawn map of the land surrounding Skorzeny's home, lines of attack drawn in red, each marked with a name: Carter, Wallace, Gracey, MacAuliffe.

Four names.

He had only seen three men enter or leave the house. Where was the fourth?

Ryan held his breath and listened.

Nothing stirred. If anyone was here, they would have been alerted by the breaking glass. They would have already come to investigate.

He let the air out of his lungs and continued exploring the items pinned to the board.

At the bottom, to the right, a sheet of notepaper.

Alain Borringer

Heidegger Bank

A/C 50664

Beneath the account digits, a telephone number written in thicker pencil. Ryan guessed it to be Swiss.

The same bank Skorzeny held his funds in.

Ryan thought of Weiss. Was he everything he said he was? Or more? Could Haughey be right? Could the Mossad have some hand in this?

He toured the rest of the room. Bare floorboards. A couch facing the corkboard, two armchairs that did not match, and an upturned crate for a table in the centre, an old typewriter resting on it. A transistor radio sat on the floor in the corner. No telephone.

Ryan moved into the small hallway, no more than a yard square between the front door and the bottom of the stairs. He mounted the steps and climbed. Three doors at the top. One stood open, showing a pair of cots, thin mattresses on low metal-framed beds, the kind Ryan had slept on for much of his career.

He stepped inside onto the bare floor. The room, like downstairs, was clean, but it had the stale and bitter odour of men. Each bed's blankets lay neatly folded at the foot, a wash bag placed on top. A photograph of a naked girl, cut from a magazine, was taped to the wall above one. Another crate served as a table between the cots. Two duffel bags sat propped in the corner.

The place felt and smelled like a barracks. Ryan wished it were untrue, but it made him homesick for his quarters in Gormanston Camp.

He left the room, crossed the small landing to the first closed door. It opened outward to reveal an airing cupboard containing towels and bedclothes.

And four automatic rifles, a Smith & Wesson revolver, and two Browning HP semi-automatic pistols, both of which had been adapted for the suppressors that lay beside them, nestled in an oily cloth.

'Jesus,' Ryan said.

He closed the cupboard and turned to the last door. It creaked as it opened. This bedroom was much like the other, except for the man lying on the farther cot, sweat forming a glossy sheen on his skin, his right arm tied in a splint, his fingers stained deep red with blood.

The man stared at Ryan, his eyes struggling to focus, his mouth open.

Ryan saw the first aid kit on the crate by the bed, the small brown bottle, the syringe.

Morphine.

'Hello,' the man said, the consonant L soft like cotton.

He lay naked from the waist up, skinny, two days' stubble on his chin, no more than thirty-five years old. A tiny spot of blood on the inside of his left forearm, a needle track.

Ryan took the Walther from its holster, held it at his side.

The man laughed, drool bubbling on his lip. 'What's that for?'

He had a Scottish accent, maybe Glasgow, it was too blunted by the morphine to be sure.

'Just in case,' Ryan said. 'Are you Gracey or MacAuliffe?'

His brow creased. 'What's going on? Who . . . Where's my . . .'

Ryan entered the room and sat down on the bed opposite the man. 'What's your name?'

'Tommy,' he said. 'My mam wanted to call me James, but my old man said, naw, he's Tommy. I'm thirsty.'

A half-full mug of water sat on the crate. Ryan lifted it, brought the rim to Tommy's lips, let him drink until he coughed. He splattered water over his bare chest.

Ryan returned the cup to the crate. 'What happened to your arm?'

Tommy looked down at the splint, the purple and yellow skin, the blood. His eyes widened as if he had not been aware of his injury.

'I fell,' he said.

'Where?'

'In the trees. I was running. I fell. It fucking hurts.'

'At Otto Skorzeny's farm?'

Tommy grinned. 'We'll scare the shite out of him.'

Ryan returned his smile. 'That's right.'

'We're going to be rich, boys.'

Ryan felt the smile crumble on his lips. 'Yes, we are.'

He thought of the account number scrawled on the notepaper downstairs.

Tommy tried to sit up. 'Did you send the letter?'

'Yes.'

'What'd he say?'

Ryan wondered if he should push the limits of Tommy's delusions any further. 'He hasn't answered yet. What was in the letter?'

Tommy smiled, waved the forefinger of his left hand at Ryan. 'Ah, you know.' He tapped the side of his nose. 'You know, boy.'

'No, I don't. Tell me.'

'The gold.' Tommy scowled as if talking to a wilfully stupid child. 'The fucking gold.'

'How much gold?'

'Fucking millions, boy. We'll all be rich.'

Ryan stood, his mind churning. Outside, the roar of the stadium rolled through the street.

When the other three men returned, they would see the broken window, know their lair had been discovered. They would surely clear out. What few belongings they had would fit into their van. They would simply load it up and leave. Ryan guessed they could clear the house within five minutes, probably less.

And go where?

They would not abandon their mission and flee the country, Ryan was positive about that. Too much blood had been shed to quit now.

Think, think, think.

If Ryan had been running this mission, he'd have had a backup place, another house in another part of the city. He would get there as fast as he could.

A wave of nauseous fear washed over him. He was out of his depth. He should have told Weiss what he knew, allowed the Mossad agent to take over.

Ryan knew full well what the Israeli would have done if he'd been here. He would have executed the injured man, lain in wait for the others, and killed them when they returned. That would have been the end of it. Ryan could have told Skorzeny and Haughey the threat had disappeared.

All over, just like that.

Could Ryan do such a thing? He had killed men before. More than he could count. But that had been war. Could he kill men for their greed?

No, he could not.

Yes, he could.

Ryan grabbed the Walther's slide assembly and chambered a round. He aimed at the centre of Tommy's forehead.

Tommy stared up at him, his eyes suddenly clear.

'No,' he said, his voice dry and thin like paper.

Ryan put pressure on the trigger, felt its resistance.

'No. Please.'

Dizziness swept over Ryan's forehead. He blinked it away. Breathed in through his nose, out through his mouth. Another rush of noise from the stadium.

'God, please, don't.'

Ryan thought of Celia and the warmth of her body against his. 'Christ,' he said.

He lowered the pistol, his hand shaking.

Tommy's chest rose and fell, his gaze locked on Ryan's. 'Thank you,' he said.

Ryan went to reply, though he did not know what words he had for this man, but the sound of a key in a lock trapped the breath in his lungs.

The opening of a door below, its banging against a wall.

A harsh whisper, a demand for silence.

Ryan looked back down at Tommy, put his finger to his lips, shush.

He moved towards the bedroom door, mindful of creaks from the bare floorboards. Stepping out onto the landing, he peered over the banister and listened. He could hear nothing but the noise of the crowds echoing down the street outside.

Then he saw a shadow move on the patch of floor visible inside the lounge.

Ryan stepped back into the bedroom.

Tommy called, 'Here! He's up here!'

Ryan closed the door, slid the small bolt across.

Quick footsteps on the stairs.

Ryan smashed the windowpane with the butt of the pistol, swept the muzzle around the frame to clear the fragments, and holstered the Walther as he slipped one leg through.

The door rattled in its frame, once, twice.

Ryan forced his other leg through, let his body follow. He saw the door burst inward, Carter barrelling in, as he let go of the ledge and dropped to the ground.

The pavement slammed into him hard, jarring his ankles,

then his shoulder as he landed on his side. Ryan cried out, rolled onto his belly, clambered to his feet as he heard a key working the lock of the front door.

He ran.

Behind him, the door opened, and footsteps thudded on the road. Ryan ducked left and right, keeping his head low.

'There!' he heard. 'Get him!'

The footsteps hammered the road surface. Ryan skidded right and dived towards the shadow under the railway bridge.

Up ahead, Holy Cross Avenue, and his car.

He pushed with his legs, harder than before, his arms churning. A glance over his shoulder – no sign of his pursuers.

The leafy greens of the avenue within reach, he ran.

Now he heard the feet – one pair, he thought – beating on the tarmac behind him. He ignored them, kept his pace, crossed Clonliffe Road and into the avenue, the car there, yards away.

Ryan skidded to the side of the Vauxhall, the key already in his hand, unlocked the door, in. He jammed the key into the ignition, turned, held it as the engine sputtered and finally kicked in. A dead end ahead. He jerked the gearstick into reverse, slammed his foot on the accelerator.

The pursuer, Wallace, sidestepped out of Ryan's path, made a grab for the door handle as he passed. Ryan fought the steering as he gathered speed towards the end of the avenue, straining his neck as he peered out the rear windscreen.

By instinct, he jammed his foot on the brake pedal as the Bedford van swung into the mouth of the avenue, blocking him. The car's chassis groaned as it halted.

Wallace at the driver's window, a Browning in his hand. He hammered at the glass until it shattered, spilling fragments over Ryan. The pistol's muzzle pressed against Ryan's temple.

'Don't fucking move,' Wallace said.

44

HAUGHEY'S TONGUE SLIPPED ACROSS HIS LIPS AS HE READ THE letter, a deep line between his thin eyebrows. He let out a short crackle of a laugh.

'Cheeky fuckers,' he said.

Skorzeny had driven to the city first thing. The traffic had been light despite it being a Monday morning, and he had made good time. Even so, he had waited close to forty minutes for Haughey to appear in his office. The minister's eyes looked heavy, and he had made a poor job of shaving, as if in a hurry.

'Are they serious?'

Skorzeny suppressed a sigh. 'Minister, they have killed very many men to arrive at this stage in their plan. So yes, I think we can assume they are serious.'

'Holy Jesus.' Haughey snorted, shook his head. 'The brass balls on them. One and a half million dollars in gold. How much is that in pounds? Christ, don't tell me, you'll make me cry.'

Skorzeny lifted the coffee from the desk, took a bitter sip, returned the cup to its place. 'It is a considerable sum.'

Haughey looked over the top of the paper, his eyes narrow. 'Can you really put your hands on that much?'

'That is hardly the question, Minister.'

'Fuck, then what is?' Haughey dropped the letter onto the desktop.

Skorzeny reached for the page. 'Please mind your language, Minister. It offends me.'

'Fuck yourself,' Haughey said, the consonants wet. 'This is my office. If you don't like how I talk, you can fuck off.'

The fibres of the paper rasped against Skorzeny's fingertips, the weight of it, the ink heavy on the page. He read it for the hundredth time.

SS-Obersturmbannführer Skorzeny,

You have seen our work. You have seen what we can do. You have seen that we can get to you.

The price for your life is $1,500,000 in gold kilobars, delivered in crates containing fifteen kilobars each.

Signal your intent to comply by placing a personal advertisement in the Irish Times, addressed to Constant Follower, no later than five working days from the date of this letter. If no advertisement is placed by this time, you will die as and when we choose.

Once your signal of compliance has been placed, you will be contacted by other means with instructions for delivery.

Your life hangs by a thread, SS-Obersturmbannführer Skorzeny. Do not test us. Do not run. We can get to you as easily in Spain or Argentina. No place on this Earth is safe for you now.

With Respect,

A large hand-drawn X criss-crossed the paper, a mockery of a signature.

'So?' Haughey leaned forward, his elbows on the desk. 'Are you going to pay them?'

'Perhaps.' Skorzeny folded the page along its creases and set it on the desk next to the coffee cup. 'Perhaps not.'

'You can't be thinking of saying no, can you? My office has done all it can to protect you, but there's a limit. These boys come after you, there's nothing I can do about it.'

Skorzeny took another sip of coffee. 'Minister, you must understand, this letter changes the nature of our situation.'

Haughey's eyebrows climbed the folds of his forehead. 'I'll say it does.'

'But perhaps not the way in which you think.'

The minister raised his palms. 'Then tell me.'

'Until I received this letter we believed we were dealing with fanatics, zealots, men driven by some misguided ideal. Now we know they are driven by greed. Now we know they are thieves.'

Haughey shrugged. 'So?'

Skorzeny had predicted the politician would not understand. Because Charles J. Haughey spoke of ideas, dreams, noble goals, but – as is the case with most men who seek power – those words were a shroud, camouflage for the man's true nature.

'A fanatic cannot be reasoned with,' Skorzeny said in slow, measured words, making sure their meaning penetrated Haughey's skull. 'A zealot has no concern for his own skin. He cannot be bargained with. He cannot be bought. He will have what he wants, or he will die, there is no other outcome. But a thief can be bargained with. A thief can be bought. A thief values his life above his honour.'

'So you're going to bargain with them? You're telling me you're going to haggle with these fuckers?'

'No, Minister. They have shown their weakness. I will use it to destroy them.'

Haughey's face stilled, became blank, as if he had slipped on a mask moulded from his own features.

'Colonel Skorzeny, there is a limit to my indulgence. I won't have you starting some fucking war in my country. If you intend to take these boys on, if you're going to fight them, then you'd best get on a plane to Madrid and see if Franco feels like putting up with you. Because I won't put up with it, I'll tell you that for sweet fuck all.'

Skorzeny smiled. 'Come, Minister, there's no need to talk in such terms. This problem can be resolved with your help. And that of your man, Lieutenant Ryan.'

Haughey shifted in his seat, his face mobile once more. 'Yes. Ryan. He hasn't turned up yet.'

'Of course not.'

'I'll have a few words to say to the bastard when I get my hands on him. I'll bury my toe up his hole.'

Skorzeny stood, lifted the letter from the desk, slipped it into his pocket. 'Lieutenant Ryan will return in good time. He knows more than he has told us. A clever man, and dangerous. I will question him myself.'

Haughey leaned back in his chair. 'Question him?'

'Good day, Minister.'

Skorzeny walked to the door. He gripped the handle, turned it, smiled at the secretary in the outer office.

Haughey called from behind. 'Colonel.'

Skorzeny turned. 'Yes, Minister?'

'A zealot or a thief.' The politician smiled, his lips thin and slick. 'Which are you?'

Skorzeny returned the smile.

'Both,' he said.

45

RYAN BLINKED IN THE DARKNESS, JARRED AWAKE BY SOMETHING, his eyelids clicking wetly. The floor's chill crept through his skin and into his cheekbone. His bare shoulder and hip ached with the coldness of the packed earth. The fingers of his right hand traced the lines of his face, as if the assurance of touch might confirm that he yet lived.

How long?

The stubble on his chin scratched at his fingertips, heavier than before.

At least a day, maybe thirty-six hours.

Ryan searched his mind for the pieces, gathered them, set them in order.

Wallace had dragged him from the car, the Browning's muzzle jammed hard against his neck. The van's rear doors had opened, swallowed him, then darkness as something slipped over his head.

They beat him.

First in the back of the van, clumsy blows, angry fists and feet landing on his body, his head, his thighs, his gut. He had tasted blood. He had gagged as it welled in his throat, coughed, felt the hot wetness on the material that covered his face.

Something, someone, had locked his hands behind his back. A bomb had landed on his temple. Buzzing, floating, suspended on the sickly wave of pain. Another explosion, then black nothing for a time that stretched out like spit clinging to a wall.

Vague smears of memories connected then to now. Being dragged from the van, his head still covered, across grass, into a building with wooden floors.

His clothes pulled from his body. A leather strap, maybe a belt, whipping across his naked shoulders and buttocks.

Then falling, weightless for a moment before the floor knocked all the air and sense from him.

He had woken where he fell. He had pulled the canvas sack from his head, looked around, saw nothing he could distinguish from the sea of black. On his hands and knees, he had explored the limits of the room, the dirt floor, the slimy damp of the brickwork.

But no door.

Eventually, it could have been minutes or hours later, he slept. Until now, woken by a sound he could not remember.

There, a key turning in a lock.

Ryan's gaze darted left and right, searching for the door he had been unable to find with his hands.

A creak, and light trickled in.

He struggled through the confusion, the disorientation, until he looked up and saw the open doorway strangely suspended eight feet above the floor. In the feeble light, he made out the zigzag that cut down through the wall's faded whitewash, the remnants of a staircase that had been removed to make this cellar a pit.

'He's awake.'

Ryan recognised Wallace's southern African accent.

A ladder descended until its feet rested on the floor in front of him. He looked back up to the doorway. Wallace held the Browning pistol, levelled the suppressor at Ryan.

'On your feet.'

Ryan pushed himself onto his knees. Nausea rolled up from his belly and through his head. He retched and spat on the floor.

'Up,' Wallace said.

Ryan hauled himself upright, listed to the side, found his balance. He placed his left hand over his genitals, feeling like a child caught in some shameful act.

'Back against the far wall.'

Ryan did as he was told, keeping his eyes on Wallace, until the cold damp brickwork pressed against his shoulders. He coughed and shivered.

Wallace kept the pistol's aim on Ryan as he stepped back to allow Carter to pass, turn, and climb down the ladder. The tall man followed, then finally Wallace slipped the Browning into his waistband and joined them in the cellar.

The three men faced Ryan, each staring hard.

Wallace took the pistol in his grip once more, brought it up two-handed, finger on the trigger.

Carter said, 'Take one step forward.'

Ryan obeyed.

'Put your hands on your head.'

Ryan breathed what little air the room had left in it. He placed his fingers on his scalp, felt his testicles retreat from the chill.

Wallace smirked. The tall man kept his gaze on Ryan's face.

'Legs apart,' Carter said.

Ryan shuffled his feet on the packed earth, his stomach already tightening against what he knew was coming.

Carter made him wait for it, the only sound in the room the air ripping in and out of Ryan's chest. Then Carter took one long stride and swung his boot upwards.

A fleshy slap followed by numbness in Ryan's groin. The heavy heat came after, the pressure in his bowel, the molten lead in his stomach. His knees folded and he sprawled on the floor. His gut clenched, sending bile into his mouth and nostrils. He coughed it out. A long groan rose from the hot pit of his abdomen and gurgled in his throat.

Carter and the tall man went to work. Not the florid rage of the beatings they had given him before, but precise blows, sharp knuckles and booted toes delivering pain to the most tender parts of Ryan's body.

They asked no questions and he screamed until his voice cracked. After a time, Ryan's consciousness withdrew so that the pain belonged to someone else, some other man crawling and bleeding in the dirt of some other cellar.

Ryan drifted into waking, back to darkness again, the tide ebbing to reveal the pain that had sunk beneath the surface. He lay still, listening to his own heart, the thudding in his ears. When he could resist no longer, he inhaled.

His sides and his back shrieked. The clamour of it reached his mouth as a whimper, and his mind retreated to the darkness.

Time dissolved and reformed, the sediment of minutes and hours settling on the cellar floor. Ryan became dimly aware of lying in a cold wetness, and a sour odour. He knew it was his own urine tainted by the smell of blood. The thought of lying in his own waste got him moving. He fought to bring his elbows and knees under him, every movement punished by a new stab of pain in his midsection.

Three feet of crawling and he lay flat on the floor, his shaking limbs unable to carry him further. When the tremors and the nausea eased, he moved again, kept crawling until he felt the wall with his fingertips. He rested there, he had no idea how long, before tracing the brickwork to the corner.

Once there, Ryan squatted, his back pressed into the angle formed by the meeting of the walls. He hissed through his teeth as the stinging heat sputtered between his legs, gagged when the smell rose to him. As dizziness rushed over him, he placed his hands on the walls to steady himself, desperate not to pass out and collapse in his own foulness.

Empty, drained, Ryan crawled as far away from it as he could before his arms and legs gave out. The coarse floor grazed his cheek. He sank into it, let it swallow him whole.

As his mind fell into blackness, Ryan swore he would kill them all.

The light stirred him.

'Jesus, he stinks.'

Ryan looked up, saw Wallace blurred in the doorway. The squat man held something in his hand, not a pistol, something else.

'Stand up,' Wallace said.

Ryan got to his feet, trapping his cries behind his teeth as pain shot through his groin and stomach. He blinked, tried to focus on what lay in Wallace's hand. His mind grasped what he saw just as the stream of cold water hit him.

A howl escaped him as the shock coursed through his body. He fell and scrambled back.

'Get back here,' Wallace said, flicking the hose so the water lashed at Ryan.

Ryan crawled forward and got to his feet. He hunched his shoulders against the cold as Wallace ran the water over his body.

'Turn around.'

Ryan did so and felt the freezing punch of the water against his back. Wallace focused the stream on Ryan's buttocks and thighs, washing away the stench.

'Dirty bastard,' he said. 'Take a drink if you want it.'

Ryan turned back to the doorway. He opened his mouth and lapped at the stream, swallowing more air than water. He coughed, and doubled over as the spasm seemed to tear him in two.

The flow of water died and a tin bucket clattered to the floor, rolled across the sodden earth.

'Use that next time.'

Something small and solid struck Ryan's chest and bounced away. He looked for it in the puddles at his bare feet. There, a chocolate bar.

'Eat that. It's all you're getting.'

The door closed, sealing out the light, locking in the darkness. Shivers rippled through Ryan's torso. He dropped to his knees on the wet earth, ran his fingers over the slick floor, found the chocolate bar.

He ate in the blackness, blinded, swallowing despite the pain it caused.

They beat him again, Carter and the tall man, as Wallace kept the pistol trained on him.

Every time the light faded, a hard slap dragged Ryan back to its harsh glow. Carter's open hand left stinging shadows on Ryan's cheek. An anchor in the waking world, mooring him to the pain.

When they were done, Carter crouched over Ryan's shaking body. He reached out and grabbed a handful of Ryan's hair.

'Get some rest, son. Tomorrow, you and me are going to have a talk. And we'll settle this. Now, you have a good long think about what you're going to tell me. Because if you don't tell me what I want to know, you're going to think everything up to now was just a tickle fight. Understand?'

With his free hand, Carter gave Ryan one last slap to the cheek.

'Good boy,' he said, and released his grip on Ryan's hair.

He stood and went to the ladder. Wallace and the tall man followed him up to the doorway. The tall man pulled the ladder up behind them and closed the door.

In the darkness, Ryan wept.

46

SKORZENY FINISHED THE CIGARETTE AND STUBBED IT OUT IN the crystal ashtray. He heard the rustling of a newspaper at the other end of the line.

'Here it is,' Haughey said. 'Exactly like you wrote it.'

'It's done, then,' Skorzeny said.

'I don't like it. These boys are dangerous, and you're goading them.'

'I am simply playing them at their own game. Their weakness is greed. It will destroy them.'

'I pray you're right,' Haughey said.

Skorzeny smiled. 'Minister, I have never been wrong.'

He returned the receiver to its cradle.

It was as if Haughey believed no one had ever attempted to blackmail Skorzeny before. Several had tried over the eighteen years since the war had ended, and none had succeeded. Indeed, none had survived.

Though Luca Impelliteri had almost escaped death. Almost, but not quite.

A tour of Tarragona's Roman amphitheatre, undergoing restorations since the previous decade, had been arranged for Skorzeny and the rest of Franco's guests, with the mayor himself acting as guide. The guests clambered across the arced stone seating, built eighteen hundred years ago, where the region's wealthy would have watched gladiators spar or Christians burn.

The ruins of the amphitheatre clung to the edge of a cliff not far from the hotel where Franco's guests stayed, a sheer drop to the sea beyond its eastern walls.

The mayor stopped his lecture on the sins and virtues of the Romans, pointed, and cried, 'You! Yes, you!'

A young woman, petite and full-bosomed, bare-legged in shorts, turned to his voice. 'Me?'

'Yes, you,' the mayor called to her. 'Who let you in? This area is not open to the public.'

A frown broke on her face. 'I'm sorry, I didn't know.'

She spoke her Spanish with an accent that might have been French.

'Well, now you do,' the mayor said. 'Out you go.'

Skorzeny watched as she descended the rows of stone seats, dropping from one to the next, her arms held out for balance. As she passed Luca Impelliteri, she slipped. He caught her before she could fall into the gladiatorial pit below, his hands at her slender waist, pushing up beneath her breasts.

She smiled up at him, said thank you, brought her hands to his.

'My pleasure,' he said.

Skorzeny turned his attention back to the mayor, whose lecture droned on.

At that night's dinner, the girl with the French accent replaced the young Spanish woman at Impelliteri's side. She laughed at his jokes, let her hands wander beneath the table, and made no eye contact with Skorzeny.

As midnight passed, Skorzeny stood on the small balcony of his hotel room, his shirt open, enjoying the breeze on his bare chest and belly. He drew on his cigarette, wondering if Luca Impelliteri still lived. A crash and a scream from the floor above stopped his thoughts dead.

He remained still and listened.

Shouting, glass breaking. A door slamming.

More voices. Alarm, cries for help, calls for someone to stop her, she's escaping.

Skorzeny's throat tightened. He flicked the cigarette over the balcony and buttoned his shirt before going to the door. Opening it, he found other guests peering into the corridor, drink and sleep clouding their eyes.

'What's going on?' a man asked in English.

'I don't know,' Skorzeny said. 'Perhaps someone had too much champagne.'

The Englishman smiled and nodded.

Then the voices from the stairwell at the end of the corridor, and the gunfire, and the girl's dying cry.

47

'BACK AGAINST THE WALL,' WALLACE SAID.

Ryan obeyed, taking careful steps, his innards seeming to writhe with each one. He kept his genitals, still tender, cupped in his hand.

The ladder touched the floor.

Ryan waited, ready to strike at any man who came near him. None did.

Carter appeared in the doorway.

'Up you come,' he said.

Ryan blinked at him.

'Come on, let's have you.'

Ryan shook his head. 'No.'

Carter nodded to Wallace. Wallace raised the Browning and took aim. The pistol spat, the report deadened by the suppressor. The earth by Ryan's toes exploded. By reflex, he hopped aside. Wallace giggled.

'No messing about,' Carter said. 'Up here. Now.'

Ryan shuffled towards the ladder. He gripped the stiles with his hands, placed a foot on the second rung, and hauled upwards. Another rung, and another, and more until he had to stop, the effort tearing through him. His head lightened, and he hugged the ladder close to keep from falling back to the floor.

Carter leaned out from the doorway. 'Move it.'

Ryan climbed until he could crawl out onto the hall. He stayed there, hands and knees on the wooden floorboards, as he recovered his breath.

Wallace stayed back, the Browning up and ready.

Carter grabbed Ryan's hair and pulled. Ryan hissed at the stinging of his scalp. He followed it up until his feet were under him, reached out to the walls to steady himself.

Something cold and hard pressed against the skin beneath his ear. Slowly, he turned his head and saw the tall man, a pistol in his hand.

'Come on.' Carter walked through a doorway into a small room. The tall man jabbed the suppressor against Ryan's ear, telling him to follow.

The room dripped with damp, the wallpaper long rotted and blackened. Through the tiny square of a window, Ryan saw overgrown hedges and shrubs, heard the singing of birds. A cottage somewhere out of the city.

A wooden chair had been fixed to the floor with nails.

'Sit down,' Carter said.

Ryan did so. Carter set about binding his wrists and ankles to the chair's arms and legs with rope. Ryan smelled his sweat. The hard base of the seat chilled Ryan's thighs and testicles.

Wallace and the tall man took up their positions, one at each side of the room, weapons held loose at their sides. Carter walked to another door, exited through it, and re-emerged a moment later carrying a metallic block and something that looked like a wand made of aluminium and bright orange rubber. Two cables joined the wand to the block.

Ryan's heart raced. He steadied his breathing.

Carter set the block on the floor. Ryan felt the impact of its weight on the floorboards through the soles of his feet. He saw the terminals, and the wires wrapped around them, and knew it was a car battery. A small black box with a knurled dial was fixed to the battery with sturdy tape. The wires joined the box to the terminals, and two more wires led from the box to the wand in Carter's hand.

'Tell me what you want,' Ryan said.

The wand had a rubber handle, a metallic shaft, and a rubber tip that bore two copper-coloured prongs. Carter set it on the floor. He went back to the other room then returned carrying a bucket of water in one hand and a packet of table salt in the other. He placed them both next to the battery.

Ryan asked, 'What do you want?'

Carter crouched and poured salt from the packet into the water. He lifted an enamel mug from the bucket and used it to stir the solution. When he was satisfied, he stood and splashed salted water across Ryan's torso. He dipped the mug into the bucket once more, and again threw the liquid over Ryan's body.

That done, he returned the mug to the bucket. He reached for the dial on the small black box and turned it.

Ryan's bladder ached. His chest rose and fell in a rhythm he could not master. 'Please tell me what—'

Carter lifted the wand and touched its tip to Ryan's chest. It sparked like a cap gun and felt like a fist rammed into Ryan's ribcage. His jaw muscles bunched and ached as he held back the cry that tried to escape him.

Carter smiled. 'Hurts, doesn't it?'

Ryan closed his eyes tight. He growled deep in his throat then fought his lungs, slow breaths, even breaths.

Carter touched the prong to Ryan's belly.

His abdominal muscles flexed of their own accord, a spasm that might have been a knife piercing the flesh. Ryan cried out.

Carter nodded. 'That's more like it. You'll answer me when I ask you a question. Is that clear?'

Ryan would have answered had there been enough air in the world. Instead he coughed out what little he had left, a string of bile and saliva spilling from his lip.

Carter brought the tip to the billow of hair above Ryan's groin. Ryan doubled over, his chin almost to his knees, as the pain swelled in his abdomen. He smelled the singed hair as his bladder let go.

Carter stepped back to avoid the weak trickle as it pattered on the floor. Wallace sniggered.

'Now, the question I asked was: It hurts, doesn't it?'

Ryan forced himself upright in the chair, pushing against the sickening torrents that thundered through his head. Carter tapped his shin with the toe of his boot.

'Answer me.'

'Yes,' Ryan said, the word seeping out through his lips.

'That's better.' Carter held the wand up before Ryan's eyes. 'You seen one of these before?'

Ryan could not answer.

Carter brought the pronged tip close to Ryan's face.

Ryan jerked his head back. 'No.'

'Didn't think you would have.' Carter withdrew the wand, took a step away. 'First time I saw one was in Korea. The bastards strung me upside down from the pipes in the ceiling.

It was a bigger one than this, more power. They didn't mess about, went straight for my goolies. I lasted twenty minutes before I told them everything. Not that I knew much. I didn't find out till after it was called a *picana eléctrica*. They're popular in South America, places like Argentina and Paraguay, the kinds of places your friend Otto Skorzeny and his sort like to hang out.'

Ryan spat a glob of reddened sputum on the floor. 'Skorzeny is not my friend.'

'Really? So you were just sneaking around my house for the good of your health?'

'I was given a job to do.'

'By who?'

Ryan scrambled through his thoughts. They had guessed he worked for Skorzeny, but what else did they know?

'By Skorzeny.'

Carter smiled. 'So he just put an ad in a shop window, help wanted, something like that?'

Ryan nodded. 'Something like that.'

The smile on Carter's lips flicked off like a light. He took a wallet from his pocket, let it flap open. Ryan recognised it as his own.

Carter read the identity card aloud. 'Lieutenant Albert Ryan, G2, Directorate of Intelligence.' He returned the wallet to his pocket. 'So I can assume you were ordered by your superiors to intervene.'

'Yes.'

'How much have you learned?'

'Your name. Captain John Carter. You were SAS. I know his name is Wallace.' Ryan nodded towards the tall man. 'He's either MacAuliffe or Gracey.'

'Tommy MacAuliffe is no longer part of this team,' Carter said.

'He was hurt. He needed a doctor.'

'MacAuliffe was a good lad, but he was no more use to us.'

Ryan looked up at Carter, saw the blank expression in his face. 'What did you do with him?'

Carter didn't reply. He scooped another cupful of salt water from the bucket and splashed it onto Ryan's groin. He brought the prongs to Ryan's scrotum.

Ryan screamed and writhed, twisting his body, pulling at the ropes that bound him to the chair. When the pain receded, he slumped, gasping for breath.

Carter leaned over him. 'Let's be clear about one thing. I'm asking the questions, not you. Do you understand me?'

When Ryan did not respond, Carter slapped him hard across the ear, rocking his head to the side.

'Do you understand me?'

'Yes,' Ryan said.

Carter moved away. 'Good. So you know who we are. What else?'

'I know you're after money. Gold. MacAuliffe told me.'

Carter paced. 'How much of this have you passed back to Skorzeny?'

'None,' Ryan said. 'I haven't reported to him since I found your house. The rest I held back.'

'Why?' Carter stopped.

'I told you, Skorzeny is not my friend.'

'But you're working for him. What's your angle?'

'No angle. I don't trust him. I wanted to know everything before I decided whether I'd tell him or not.'

'I don't believe you.' Carter watched him from across the room. 'There's something else. How did you find us?'

Ryan did not hesitate. 'Célestin Lainé. He told me where to find you.'

The three men exchanged glances.

'How did he know?' Carter asked.

'He worked it out,' Ryan said. 'The railway line and the stadium.'

Carter nodded. 'He's smarter than he looks. So why did he talk to you?'

'I said I'd tell Skorzeny he was the informant. He's terrified of Skorzeny.'

'With good reason. And how did you figure out it was Lainé?'

Ryan searched for a lie. 'Because you let him live. When you killed Elouan Groix and the other man. There was no other reason to let him go. It had to be him.'

'All right,' Carter said. 'I'll accept that. But there's more. You're holding something back.'

Ryan closed his eyes, thought of Goren Weiss. 'There's nothing.'

Quick footsteps on the floorboards as Carter approached, then pain exploded in Ryan's groin, and again before he could scream, and a third blast. The smell of burning skin reached his nostrils. He coughed and gagged, his stomach clenching tight. Pressure ballooned inside his head, pushing against the walls of his skull, the backs of his eyes.

The world tilted, pitching Ryan to the side. The ropes held him to the chair, and the nails held the chair to the floor. A sharp slap to the cheek brought his mind back within reach.

'Who put you in contact with Skorzeny?'

Ryan let his chin sag down onto his chest.

Carter grabbed his hair, pulled his head back up.

'Who put you in contact with Skorzeny?'

'Charles Haughey,' Ryan said.

'The politician? How much does he know?'

'Less than Skorzeny.'

Carter hunkered down, looked into Ryan's eyes. 'Who are you protecting? There's someone else, isn't there?'

All Ryan had to do was speak the Mossad agent's name. Tell Carter about the talk they had, and the newspaper on the Vauxhall's dashboard. And it would be over.

Over.

They would kill him once they had what they wanted. Ryan knew the only thing keeping him alive was the truth he hid from them. If he talked, he would die.

'No one,' Ryan said.

Carter sighed and took another scoop of water from the bucket and threw it in Ryan's face.

Ryan spat salty water, said, 'No,' but the lightning struck beneath his eye, throwing his head back to crack against the wood of the chair. Another bolt of pain in his groin, another in his belly.

Consciousness shook and crumbled, dissolved, then reformed. Ryan saw the men as stretched figures, like a fairground hall of mirrors, colours bleeding together.

'Who are you protecting?'

'No one.'

Another blast beneath Ryan's navel, another to his chest, another beneath his eye. A slap across his cheek, more water thrown over his torso.

'Who are you protecting?'

Ryan's tongue seemed to swell inside his mouth, blunting the words. 'No . . . one.'

Carter held the wand's pronged tip against Ryan's belly, kept it there, sparking, as Ryan's abdominal muscles flexed and clenched through no will of his own, each spasm like a wild animal's teeth sinking deep into his flesh, tearing at the meat.

It came clear in his mind, a lion, a wolf, whatever it was, snarling and snapping at his midsection. Feasting on him, eating him alive, watched by men who towered up to the heavens, and then all was darkness, the sound of a hurricane in the distance, and someone screaming who could not possibly have been Albert Ryan.

He stayed there, in the swirling black and greys, until he felt them dragging him down, deeper into the dark. Ryan fought his way up and out, dragging himself towards consciousness. And there, the pain, muscles still convulsing, his skin burning. He opened his eyes, strained to focus.

Carter spoke to Wallace, said, 'That's all he's got. Finish him off.'

Wallace nodded, smirked, and stepped forward. He raised the Browning.

Ryan saw the suppressor's mouth opening before his eye, seeming to suck all the air from his lungs and the light from the room. He saw Wallace's finger on the trigger, the knuckle whitening.

'Wait,' a voice said.

Wallace looked somewhere behind Ryan. 'Why? We've wasted enough time on him already.'

'Step away,' the voice said. 'Now.'

Wallace hesitated for a moment, then exhaled and shook

his head. He lowered the pistol and moved back to his position across the room.

The owner of the voice stepped into Ryan's vision. One hand in his pocket, the other holding a newspaper.

Goren Weiss said, 'Hello, Albert.'

III

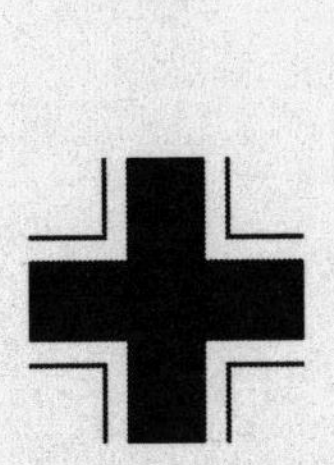

COLLABORATOR

48

GOREN WEISS WATCHED RYAN BLINK, HIS FACE CONTORTED WITH confusion, his eyes unfocused. The Irishman shook his head as if trying to dislodge some veil.

Weiss asked, 'How are you holding up?'

'I . . . I don't . . .'

Weiss raised a hand, silenced him. 'Okay, save your energy.'

Carter came to Weiss's side, spoke in a low voice. 'What are you doing? Let's just finish him and get out of here.'

'No,' Weiss said. 'Bear with me just a little while. Let me have a word with him.'

Carter looked from Weiss to Ryan and back again. 'All right. Five minutes, then I'm putting him out of his misery.'

Weiss nodded. Carter went to the window and sat on the sill, glowering like a wilful child who thought he'd got his way.

Ryan's eyelids rose and fell like heavy curtains. 'What's happening?' he asked.

Weiss placed his free hand on Ryan's shoulder. 'It's okay, Albert. I just want to have a talk with you. Take your time. Gather yourself. These gentlemen will wait.'

Ryan closed his eyes. Weiss fetched the chair from the far side of the room, dragged it back and sat down in front of Ryan, the newspaper in his lap.

'Seems like we've been here before,' Weiss said. 'The last time wasn't quite so trying, though, was it?'

'What's happening?' Ryan asked again.

'Captain Carter insisted on questioning you in his own particular way. I regret allowing him to do so, Albert, but I had to know if you'd give me up or not. Please accept my apology.'

'What are you doing here?'

'Making sure things don't get out of hand. I probably should have stepped in sooner. But you conducted yourself well, Albert. I'm impressed.'

'Tell me what's going on. Please.'

Weiss nodded. 'Okay. So you know what all this is about by now. It's a business enterprise. Otto Skorzeny is sitting on a great big pile of money, and we want some of it. Not all, not even most of it. Just a taste.'

Ryan shook his head once more. 'But you said . . . your mission.'

'My mission still stands,' Weiss said. 'This is just a little side project. I'm not on company time, as it were. This project was undertaken initially by Captain Carter, he recruited his team, and I came onboard last. I still get control of Skorzeny's ratlines, and I add a little something to my pension pot. Where's the harm in that?'

'But those people. They died for this?'

Weiss smiled. 'They were fucking Nazis, Albert. They did not deserve to walk and breathe among human beings.'

'Catherine Beauchamp. She didn't deserve to die.'

Weiss shrugged in acceptance. 'Maybe so, but she died by her own hand. If you hadn't called at her door, she'd still be alive. You can't hold that over me.'

'All this. For money.'

'Of course. What other reason do you need?'

Ryan did not answer. Instead, he asked, 'Why did you bring me into this?'

'I didn't. Charles Haughey brought you into this.'

'But you contacted me. You came at me in that bar.'

'True. When I found out you were sniffing around, I wanted to get the measure of you. Then I thought, why not draw you in? You were my inside man, Albert, the best kind. The kind who doesn't even know it. So I dropped a few crumbs for you along the way. We'd gotten everything we could from Célestin Lainé. You would have figured out he was the informant eventually, and I wanted to see if that would lead you to Carter's doorstep. I wanted to see if you could possibly endanger this project. Turns out you could, and I'm glad I reined you in before you did any more damage. And you might be of use to me yet.'

Weiss leaned across the gap between them, held the newspaper in front of Ryan's eyes. Ryan squinted at the page, his mouth hanging open.

Weiss leaned back. 'All right, I'll read it for you.' He drew a breath and began. 'To Constant Follower – that's us, by the way – I do not agree to your terms. I will, however, agree to one third of the amount for whichever one of you can prove he is the last of his kind.'

Weiss looked over the top of the newspaper. 'Do you understand what this means?'

'No,' Ryan said.

'It means that Colonel Skorzeny is clever, but perhaps not as clever as he thinks. In thinly veiled terms, he has said that he will pay half a million dollars to whichever one of us is willing to betray the others, kill them, and bring proof of it to him.'

Ryan's gaze travelled between the four men in the room.

Weiss tapped his knee to regain his attention. 'But of course I anticipated this. We have discussed it in detail, and agreed against any such betrayal.'

Ryan laughed, winced at whatever pains it stoked. 'Do you really think you can trust these men?'

'Trust has nothing to do with it. It's a matter of logic. Say I kill everyone in this room and bring their heads to Skorzeny. You think he'll honour his offer? Or do you think he'll cut my balls off and choke me with them? I suspect the latter. No, the smart strategy is for us to stick together. As a unit, we can break him. If one man goes it alone, then Skorzeny will destroy him. Don't you agree?'

'It's insane. You're all crazy.'

'Maybe so. But if I was given to entirely rational thinking, I'd still be managing my father's drugstore in Brooklyn instead of fighting for Israel.'

'This isn't fighting for Israel. This is greed.'

'We'll have to agree to disagree on that point. We have a more urgent question at hand.'

Ryan waited.

'Aren't you going to ask me what the question is?'

'I don't care,' Ryan said.

Weiss leaned forward. 'Well, you really should. You see, the question is this: What shall we do with Lieutenant Albert Ryan?'

49

RYAN KNEW WEISS WANTED HIM TO REACT, TO MAKE SOME angry or fearful reply. He kept his mouth shut.

'Of course,' Weiss said, 'the smart thing to do would be to kill you and dump your corpse on Skorzeny's doorstep. Let him know he can't bargain with us.'

Wallace grinned. Carter and Gracey stared.

'Then what are you waiting for?' Ryan asked.

'Well, that was the plan,' Weiss said.

Carter stood up from the windowsill. 'It still is.'

Weiss raised a hand to silence him. 'Now I'm not so sure.'

'Bollocks to that.' Carter came to Weiss's side. 'We agreed on this. We put a bullet in his head and a note in his pocket. We've been over and over it for two days, for Christ's sake.'

Ryan watched the anger burn on Carter's face, the cool calm on Weiss's. Which of these men held command?

'Let's go over it one more time,' Weiss said, his voice even and smooth like still water.

Carter put his hands on his hips. 'No. There's been enough talk already. Do it, Wallace.'

Wallace snapped into action, raised his pistol, marched towards Ryan, aim centring on his chest.

Weiss moved with such speed, Ryan couldn't be sure what he'd seen. The agent had been seated, hands and newspaper in his lap, as Wallace came alongside him. Then he was upright. Ryan's eyes followed the newspaper's drift to the floor, caught an impression of Weiss seizing Wallace's outstretched arm with one hand, the pistol with the other. When Ryan looked back up, Weiss held the suppressor's muzzle to the Rhodesian's forehead.

Carter stepped back. Gracey went to raise his own weapon. Carter waved a hand to stop him.

Weiss spoke, his voice soft and gentle, carrying only the slightest tremor from the exertion. 'Like I said: Let's go over it one more time.'

Wallace backed away, his hands flexing, his face flushed with anger.

'Leave it, Wallace,' Carter said.

Wallace bared his teeth. 'I'm going to kill the Jew bastard.'

'I said leave it. That's an order.'

Wallace clenched his fists.

Carter crossed the room and put a hand on Wallace's shoulder. 'Step outside and cool off. Now. Gracey, you go with him.'

Gracey holstered his weapon and took Wallace by the arm. As they left the room, Ryan heard Wallace whisper, 'I'll fucking kill that Jew bastard.'

Carter and Weiss stood in silence for a time before Weiss smiled and said, 'Got a little heated, there, didn't it?'

He handed Wallace's pistol over.

Carter took the weapon, stowed it in his waistband, and pointed a finger at Weiss. He stabbed the air as he spoke. 'Don't you dare undermine me in front of my men again. Ever. I'll fucking kill you myself.'

'Your men?' A wide grin cracked across Weiss's face. 'You

don't own them. You bought them, but they have no loyalty to you. They'd cut your throat for a dollar. Don't forget that.'

'I've had just about enough of your mouth. Now say whatever you've got to say so I can shoot this bastard.'

'All right. Just hear me out. If you still don't see things my way, then by all means, do what you have to do.'

Carter returned to his seat on the windowsill. 'Let's have it, then.'

Weiss paced the room as he spoke. 'So, poor Tommy MacAuliffe's demise has left us a man down. Not only that, our only other man on the inside has been compromised. Célestin Lainé gave you up the second Ryan here got hold of him. He's no good to us any more. He'll tell Skorzeny everything sooner or later.'

'Then we kill him,' Carter said.

'Is that your answer for everything? Actually, in this instance, it's probably the best option. But here's the thing: we've got a great big hole in our operation now. And I know how to fill it.'

Ryan watched the workings of Carter's mind play out on his face. At last, his features hardened. 'No,' Carter said.

'Yes,' Weiss said. He aimed a finger at Ryan. 'This man right here.'

'No,' Carter said again, shaking his head.

'Don't you see? It's the perfect solution. He can get right next to Skorzeny, tell us what he's thinking. More than that, he can influence Skorzeny, push him in whatever direction we want him to go.'

'It's madness,' Carter said. 'He'll turn us over.'

'I don't think so. You won't, will you, Albert?'

Ryan had no reply. He stared up at the men, blinking.

'Of course he will. He's taking his orders from a Nazi bastard, him and that politician. He's one of them.'

Weiss turned back to Ryan, leaned over, hands on his knees. 'Is that so, Albert? Are you in bed with the infamous Nazi Otto Skorzeny? Are you a collaborator?'

The word stung Ryan. 'No,' he said.

'Yes you are,' Weiss said. 'A collaborator. Just like Elouan Groix was, or Hakon Foss. Or Catherine Beauchamp.'

'Shut your mouth,' Ryan said, the words hissing between his teeth. 'I am not one of them. I am not a collaborator.'

'But you take orders from Otto Skorzeny.'

'I take my orders from the Directorate of Intelligence. I was given a job to do.'

Weiss straightened. 'Funny, a lot of people said that after the war. It was only a job.'

'I was given an assignment. I wish I hadn't taken it, but I had no choice. I fought men like Skorzeny in Europe and North Africa. It cost me everything, but I did it anyway. I am not one of them.'

'You hear that, Captain Carter? Lieutenant Albert Ryan is not a collaborator. He's a soldier. Like you. Like I used to be. He might have fought alongside you, for all we know.'

Carter folded his arms across his chest. 'What, should we give him a medal?'

'No. We should give him a place on our team.'

'My arse, we should.'

Weiss hunkered down in front of Ryan. 'What do you say, Albert? You want to regain your honour by shafting Skorzeny? And get filthy fucking rich in the process, I should add.'

Carter leapt from the windowsill. 'Now hold on a bloody minute. There's no way he's getting a piece of this.'

Weiss ignored him. 'What do you think, Albert? It's time to take a side. Do you want to help me bring Skorzeny down? Do you want to make more money than you've ever seen before?'

Ryan looked from one man to the other, Carter furious, Weiss smiling.

'What are you doing, Weiss?' Carter asked. 'My boys won't have it.'

Weiss placed his hand on Ryan's knee, words soft as air. 'What's it to be, Albert? Are you with me?'

'Yes,' Ryan said.

50

LAINÉ SAID, 'NO, I WON'T.'

'Why not?' Skorzeny asked as he took his seat across the desk.

Lainé couldn't meet the Austrian's gaze. He drew deep on one of Skorzeny's cigarettes. 'She is innocent. She has nothing to do with any of this.'

'Celia Hume took the assignment. She willingly involved herself.'

'I don't care. I won't help you question her.'

'Come, Célestin, questioning women has never troubled you before.'

Lainé looked up through the smoke. 'It troubles me now. Interrogate her yourself. I want nothing more to do with it.'

Skorzeny leaned back in his chair, lips upturned in a mockery of a smile. 'I'm beginning to question your loyalty, Célestin. Have I not been generous to you?'

'You have. And I'm grateful. But I will not torture this woman for you.'

Skorzeny's face darkened. He was about to speak, but the telephone's clamour stopped his tongue. He lifted the handset, said, 'Yes?'

Lainé watched as Skorzeny's eyes made tiny quick movements, his lips parted as he listened.

'Very well,' Skorzeny said. 'I will expect the minister's call tomorrow.'

He replaced the receiver and gave Lainé a slithering smile.

'It seems we no longer require Miss Hume's assistance. That was Charles Haughey's secretary. Lieutenant Ryan has surfaced. He wishes to debrief the Minister for Justice tomorrow afternoon. After that, I will see to it that I question Lieutenant Ryan myself, in private. Do you object to assisting me in his interrogation?'

Lainé said, 'No, I do not.'

51

A KNOCKING AT THE HOTEL ROOM'S DOOR PULLED RYAN FROM the swirling terrors of his dreams. He started awake, cried out at the pain that tore through him. Darkness filled the room. How long had he slept?

'Albert?' she called.

'Celia,' he said.

The door opened, a slash of light, Celia held within it. She found him with her eyes.

'My God, Albert.'

She entered, closed the door behind her.

'Lock it,' he said.

Ryan listened to her fumble with the bolt and chain until they clicked and rattled into place. The light came on, burning from the ceiling. Through the glare, he saw her frozen by the door, one hand on the switch.

'Christ, Albert, what happened to you?'

He lay on top of the bedclothes, naked but for a towel he had draped around his waist. Bruises like maps of foreign lands, purples and browns and yellows, flared across his torso. Dried blood crusted in the folds of his skin, under his arms, around his neck. And the burns, blistered and red, dotted across his chest, his belly, his thighs, his face. The worst of them on his stomach, a scorched cluster by his navel. He could smell his own seared flesh.

Celia came to the bedside and knelt. Fat tears fell from her eyes onto his forearm, warm and heavy.

'Oh God, Albert, what did they do to you?'

'I'll be fine,' he said.

Her fingertips skimmed his stomach and chest, circled the charred places. 'You need a doctor. We'll get a taxi to the hospital.'

'No.' Ryan tried to sit up, managed only to lift his head. 'No doctor. No hospital.'

'But you must—'

'No.' He took her wrist in his hand. 'Help me up.'

Celia slipped an arm under his back and supported him as he hoisted himself up on the bed. He lowered his feet to the floor, fought the nausea and dizziness that swelled in him.

'Are these burns?' she asked. 'We need to clean them.'

Celia noticed the pistol resting on the bedside locker. Weiss had returned the Walther to Ryan before they pushed him out of the van. She opened the drawer, set the pistol inside, and pushed it closed.

She sniffed back tears and went to the washbasin in the corner, put the plug in its hole, turned the taps. She came back to him, bent down, put her arms beneath his.

'Come on,' she said. 'Up you get.'

Ryan pushed up with his legs, allowing her to take the weight of his torso. They staggered together to the corner. Celia dipped a hand in the water to test the temperature, then shut off the taps.

She soaked a facecloth and reached for the towel at his waist. 'Take that off.'

Ryan held it in place. She pulled harder. He resisted.

'I have three brothers and a subscription to *National*

Geographic,' she said, forcing a scolding smile. 'There's nothing under there I haven't seen before.'

Ryan let her pull the towel away. She dropped it to the floor, brought a hand to her mouth to smother the gasp. He covered the burnt skin of his scrotum with his hands as she sobbed.

'I want to kill them,' Ryan said.

Celia wiped the tears from her cheeks and wrung out the facecloth.

'I know,' she said.

52

GOREN WEISS SAT ACROSS THE TABLE FROM CARTER, STUDYING the Englishman. The stuttering light of the kerosene lamp made him look older, the lines on his face deeper. A bottle of vodka, half empty, sat between them. Weiss lifted it, poured a measure into each of the two shot glasses.

Carter reached for his, brought it to his lips, downed the alcohol, and coughed.

Something rustled and scratched in the darkness around them, some vermin seeking shelter in the old derelict cottage. Gracey and Wallace slept in the room at the other end of the building.

'You think you're smart,' Carter said, his words dulled by the vodka.

'Yes, I do,' Weiss said.

It was not a lie. Goren Weiss knew he was smarter than just about anybody he'd ever met. Not smart in the way a studious schoolboy is – he'd never passed a real exam in his life – but he possessed an intelligence born of instinct and experience.

His instinct told him Carter was a good soldier, but incapable of pulling off this job on his own. Wallace and Gracey were nothing more than infantrymen, albeit highly trained infantrymen. MacAuliffe had been the best of Carter's men. It had made Weiss sad to put a bullet in his head.

Carter sneered at him from across the table. 'Not smart enough to set this job up.'

'But smart enough to see it works.'

Weiss had stopped over for a couple of days in West Berlin on his way to Dublin to meet with Thomas de Groot, the South African. Weiss enjoyed Berlin every time he visited. He liked the idea of its suspension, a bubble of Western decadence trapped inside a hostile communist power. The barrier that split the city in two fascinated him. The brutal obscenity of it. He walked long stretches of the construction, wire fence and crude concrete blocks. Dour-faced GDR soldiers watched him as he passed, automatic rifles slung across their stomachs.

Even though he knew the true geography of the land did not allow for it, he imagined the city of his birth lay on the other side of the barrier. Zwickau, where they now made rickety Trabant cars for those East Germans privileged enough to be able to purchase one. Weiss's father had left for America the moment he sensed the coming storm that would sweep away so many of his kind. Benjamin Weiss had settled in Brooklyn, leaving behind two brothers and his wife's grave to find a new beginning across the Atlantic.

At one time, before the war, when Goren Weiss was still a feckless kid bottling pills and potions for his father, he had entertained ideas of socialism. He had even attended a few Communist Party meetings at Brooklyn College. Mostly, he went so he could ogle college girls. Something in their serious and sincere demeanour caused heat in him, the creases in their brows as they listened to the speeches and made astute observations on the cost of capitalism to the American working classes.

When he had gathered sufficient nerve, he asked one of the

girls out. Ice cream, he had said. She had blonde hair tied back tight to her head and a scattering of pimples on her chin. He thought her name was Melissa. She had politely said that's sweet, but no, thank you, and returned to her cluster of friends. He had stood with a bundle of pamphlets in his sweating fingers as they walked away giggling.

He heard the word 'kike' and they erupted in laughter, glancing back over their shoulders at him. Young Weiss tore the pamphlets up and dumped them in the nearest garbage can. He was no longer a communist.

By the time Weiss first visited Berlin, he had lost any notions that either the left or the right had moral superiority. He earned that knowledge as he fought his way across Europe, the hardest lesson learned a few miles from the city of Weimar, in what first appeared to be some kind of fenced-in village. The men fell silent as they neared the place, Buchenwald as Weiss discovered, and above the thrumming of their engines they heard the thin and pitiful cries.

Weiss had felt for a moment that he had lost his sanity, that the stick figures beyond the fence were night terrors escaped from his mind into the waking world. Men and women and children, so shrivelled he couldn't fathom how they still lived.

The soldiers, his comrades, gasped and wept, covered their mouths and noses against the stench. They stepped down from their vehicles and walked amongst the shambling hordes, the mounds of bodies discarded by the Germans who had fled minutes before.

Weiss took photographs with the small Brownie Six-16 folding camera he carried, images of children staring at the sky, flies on their dead lips.

When the Germans had surrendered, Weiss learned the Soviets were every bit as cruel as the common Nazi enemy. Barbarians, a member of Weiss's regiment had said. Goddamn animals. He saw the evidence of it himself in the weeks after Berlin fell, heard the stories from the mouths of those Russian soldiers who had fled to the Americans, and the civilians surviving among the ruins of the city. Women cowered in basements and attics, dreading the roving parties of drunken Soviet men who would rape anything that breathed.

Not long after the Allies had carved up Germany's corpse, the Soviets took over Buchenwald labour camp and put it to much the same use as it had been built for.

In the end, for all of Hitler's deranged evil, Stalin proved little better. So Weiss had learned that fascism and communism were brother and sister, each born of the same poison seed. And when those creeds met with nationalism, only bloodshed could follow.

As it did in 1948 when Weiss fought for the creation of the state that was now his home. He had spent a year back in Brooklyn, helping his father around the drugstore, but he passed every moment of his spare time at meetings around the city, where young men like him talked about Palestine and their brothers who fought there. Soon he travelled back to Europe, through Italy, ferried across the Mediterranean to be smuggled under the noses of the British. He joined the swelling ranks of the Haganah and was soon a member of the elite Palmach fighting force. He had shed joyful tears with his comrades as they listened to the radio broadcast of David Ben-Gurion reading Israel's Declaration of Independence, the words that made his country real. He had fought for Israel's existence ever since.

Six months ago, Weiss had met Thomas de Groot in a cafe on Kochstrasse, not far from Checkpoint Charlie. De Groot was a large man, tall, and generous at the waist, who sweated a great deal. One would have thought a South African used to the arid heat of his homeland might have found early winter in West Berlin cool. Weiss certainly did, but de Groot's shirt was darkened by perspiration nonetheless.

Thomas de Groot did not work for any government. At least, not any *single* government. He had neither allegiances nor enemies. He simply provided a service to anyone willing to pay. That service was the sourcing of information.

De Groot handed a manila file across the cafe table. Weiss opened it, leafed through the contents, and closed it again. He passed a fat envelope back to de Groot.

'You've been a good client,' de Groot said.

'I know. I'm surprised that hasn't qualified me for a discount.'

De Groot smiled, showed his small, blunt teeth. 'Not a discount. A free gift, more like.'

Weiss studied the South African for a moment. 'Oh?'

'You know I like to avoid disagreements, conflicts of interest, that sort of thing. Doesn't do anyone any good to be tripping over each other out in the field.'

Weiss nodded. 'Indeed it doesn't.'

'Well, something came up, and I thought it best to make you aware of it. Just in case.'

'What is it?'

A waitress set about cleaning the table next to them. They held their silence until she had finished.

'Someone else has been asking after Otto Skorzeny,' de Groot said.

'Who? Which agency?'

De Groot shook his head. 'No agency. No government. No one official.'

'A freelancer?'

'An Englishman. Captain John Carter, formerly of the SAS. He's been seeking information on Skorzeny and his associates in Ireland. Not directly from me, you understand, but a friend of mine in Amsterdam was approached some time ago. I wouldn't have been too concerned – after all, information is information, I just find it lying around and store it up to save men like you the trouble of finding it for yourself.'

'But?'

'But it seems Captain Carter has also been spending time in procurement and recruitment.'

'Weapons?'

'Small arms. Clean, never used in anger. My friend was able to help him with that. And manpower. He was looking for someone to complete a team. Someone experienced in commando operations. He let it be known it was interesting work and potentially lucrative.'

'I see. Thank you. I'll arrange for a small bonus to be wired to you.'

De Groot smiled and stood. 'Not too small, I hope.'

Weiss shook his hand. 'I'll see what I can do.'

It took a month of investigation to track Carter down, and another six weeks of observation before Weiss was confident of his next move: introducing himself.

Carter had been flying back and forth between Dublin and London, a week in one city, a fortnight in the other. He had been eating alone in a pub on the Vauxhall Bridge Road when Weiss first approached him.

The first conversation had not gone well. In fact, it had

developed into a fist fight on a path by the Thames riverbank, but eventually, with a knee planted between the Englishman's shoulder blades, Weiss had been able to convince Carter to see things his way.

Carter's original plan had been a mess. It had involved little more than storming Skorzeny's farm, taking him prisoner, and forcing him to hand over the money. The subtlety, if such a word could be applied, of using Skorzeny's *Kameraden* as statements of intent had been Weiss's contribution to the plan. Carter and his men were excellent soldiers, Weiss had no doubt of that, but they were not tacticians. Not like him.

Now, in this damp and stinking cottage, Carter glared across the table at Weiss with all the hatred of a man who knows the object of his attention is better than him.

'You're not so clever,' he said, reaching for the vodka bottle.

Weiss snatched it away from his grasp. 'Go easy, my friend.'

Carter bared his teeth, his breathing deepened, then a grin spread across his face. 'You know, Wallace wanted to kill you today. He took me aside. He said, why don't we just blow that Jew bastard's head off? And I thought about it. I really did. You and that Mick you're so fond of. We could have got rid of both of you, left you out here in the arsehole of nowhere. We could see this thing through ourselves.'

'So why didn't you?'

Weiss took a sip of vodka while he waited for Carter to think his answer through.

Carter sat back and spread his arms wide, a gesture of magnanimity. 'Because I am a man of my word. I agreed to your bloody scheme, fool that I was, so now I'm going to stick to it.' He leaned forward, waved his forefinger at Weiss. 'But don't push me. You pull another stunt like you did today, and I'm going to start seeing things Wallace's way.'

'That would be a mistake, my friend.' Weiss poured Carter another shot of vodka. 'I have concerns about young Mr Wallace.'

Carter took the glass, downed the vodka. 'Stop calling me your friend. Wallace is a good lad. He's hot-headed, but he's tough and he follows orders. He's loyal.'

'So loyal he wouldn't give you up to Skorzeny?'

'Bollocks.' Carter slammed the glass down on the table. 'He's a good soldier. Him and Gracey. And so was MacAuliffe.'

'Not any more.'

Weiss almost regretted saying it, but then the look of hurt on Carter's face turned to anger, and the Englishman stood, throwing the chair back to clatter against the wall. He hovered there for a moment, his chest rising and falling, his cheeks reddening, before leaving the room, cursing under his breath.

In the warm yellow glow of the lamplight, Goren Weiss smiled.

53

FITZPATRICK FOLLOWED HAUGHEY INTO RYAN'S HOTEL ROOM.

The director stopped in the doorway, his mouth agape. 'Dear God, Ryan, what happened to you?'

Ryan lay on the bed wearing a vest and trousers. Celia sat alongside him, a bowl of warm water on the bedside locker, muslin cloths ready to dab at his wounds. They had discussed this for some time, the effect, how disabled he should appear.

'Close the door,' Ryan said.

Fitzpatrick obliged.

Haughey scowled. 'I don't like this, Ryan.' He gave the director a sideways glance. 'When someone calls me to a hotel, I expect to have my lunch bought for me, not to wind up at somebody's sickbed.'

'He needs to rest,' Celia said.

Haughey shot her a hard look. 'And what are you doing here? Aside from playing doctors and nurses.'

'This concerns Celia as much as anyone,' Ryan said.

'My arse, it does.'

Celia stood. 'Minister, if you remember, it was you who involved me in the first place by asking Mr Waugh to approach me.'

Fitzpatrick's face paled. 'Waugh's department is mixed up in this?'

Haughey dismissed the director's concern with a wave of his hand. 'I asked him for a favour, that's all.' He turned back to Ryan. 'Either way, I don't think Miss Hume needs to be here.'

Ryan paused, then reached out to touch Celia's hand. She nodded, went to the door and exited the room.

'Now can we get on with this?' Haughey asked. 'Where in the name of Christ have you been?'

Ryan kept his gaze fixed on the minister, his voice flat. 'I located the men who've been carrying out attacks on Colonel Skorzeny's associates. I had them under surveillance when they captured me. They tortured me for two days before releasing me with a message for Colonel Skorzeny.'

Haughey looked from Ryan to Fitzpatrick and back again. 'Tortured you?'

'Yes, Minister. First they beat me, then they used an electrical device, something like a small cattle prod.'

Fitzpatrick winced.

'Christ Almighty.' Haughey shook his head.

'Minister,' Fitzpatrick said, 'I would not have put one of my men under your command if I'd thought there was the slightest chance of—'

'Who were they?' Haughey asked.

Fitzpatrick stepped between Haughey and Ryan. 'Minister, at this point I'm more concerned about the well-being of Lieutenant Ryan.'

'Who were they?' Haughey asked again.

Ryan answered. 'Three men. Two English, one Rhodesian. All military. All skilled and experienced. The senior man, English, was around forty-five years old, an officer. The other two aged around thirty and forty, the Rhodesian the youngest. They did not address each other by name in my presence.'

'How did you find them?'

'Catherine Beauchamp told me they were based somewhere close to Croke Park stadium. I scouted the area over two days until I found them.'

Haughey's eyes narrowed. 'I think that's a lie.'

'That's right.' Ryan met Haughey's hawk gaze. 'But it's all I'm going to tell you. Director, Minister, I'd like to be clear about something.'

Fitzpatrick said, 'Go on.'

Ryan did not avert his eyes from Haughey's. 'I have witnessed Colonel Skorzeny and his associate Célestin Lainé torture and kill a Norwegian national whom they suspected of being an informant.'

Haughey could not hold Ryan's stare.

Ryan continued. 'I have reason to believe that at some point in the next twenty-four hours, Colonel Skorzeny will try to imprison me, and he will torture me to learn anything that I have not told you this afternoon.'

Haughey wetted his lips. 'That's a hell of an accusation, Lieutenant Ryan.'

'There is also a risk that Colonel Skorzeny may try to do the same to Miss Hume in order to coerce me into providing him with more information.'

'So what do you want from me?' Haughey asked.

'I expect the protection of the Department of Justice and the Directorate of Intelligence. If any harm should come to me or Celia Hume in the coming days, if any accident should occur, or if either of us should go missing, your first line of enquiry should be with Colonel Skorzeny.'

Ryan stopped talking and let the silence thicken between them.

Eventually, Haughey nodded and cleared his throat. 'All right. I'll tell Colonel Skorzeny he's to have no direct contact with you. If he wants to talk to you, it'll be through me. Good enough?'

'No, Minister. I want your guarantee that I have the protection of your department, and of the Directorate of Intelligence.'

Haughey and Fitzpatrick exchanged a glance.

'Fine,' Haughey said. 'You have my word. If anything happens to you or Miss Hume, then Colonel Skorzeny will answer to me. So, what message did these boys send back?'

'They rejected the Colonel's counter-offer.'

Fitzpatrick's eyebrows rose. 'Counter offer?'

'Colonel Skorzeny made a thinly veiled suggestion that one of them would receive a payment only if he betrayed the others. If he killed them, and presented proof to Skorzeny.'

'Is this true, Minister?' Fitzpatrick asked.

Haughey's face reddened. 'An advertisement was placed in the *Irish Times*. I did not approve, I made that clear to the colonel.'

'My God, you knowingly allowed Skorzeny to place an ad soliciting murder?'

Haughey fidgeted. 'Like I said, I did not approve. Perhaps in hindsight I should have made my objection more strongly.'

'I'll say. I've a good mind to go to the Taoiseach about this. I imagine your father-in-law might have something to say about it.'

Haughey moved close to Fitzpatrick, their bodies almost touching. 'Now hold on, Director. Don't go thinking you can threaten Charlie Haughey. Push me, and I'll have you run out of your fucking job by the end of the day.'

Fitzpatrick stepped away, straightened his tie, smoothed his suit jacket. 'Gentlemen, I think I've contributed all I can to this discussion. If you'll excuse me, I have quite an amount of paperwork to see to.'

He walked to the bed and placed a hand on Ryan's shoulder.

'Come to me if you need anything, Ryan. Anything at all.'

'Thank you, sir.'

Fitzpatrick left the room. Haughey watched the door close.

'So, what now?' he asked.

'Make sure Skorzeny pays them,' Ryan said.

Haughey sighed, his shoulders falling, his body seeming to deflate. 'I don't know if he'll agree. He's a stubborn bastard.'

'It's either that, or you let them fight it out. These men are serious. They won't give up. I've done everything I can for you, Minister, and more. You have twenty-four hours to convince Skorzeny. If you can't, you'll have my final report and then you're on your own.'

Haughey walked to the door. 'I'll see what I can do. Stay out of trouble, Ryan.'

He nodded at Celia as he left. She entered and closed the door.

Ryan eased his legs off the bed, every part of him protesting at the effort, and sat upright. He placed one hand on the bedside locker to support himself.

Celia came to the bed, got down on her knees. She reached beneath and slid out the portable Grundig tape recorder she had purchased that morning with the last of the money Ryan had been given by the director. She pressed the stop button and the reels ceased spinning. A small microphone peeked out from its hiding place between the pillows on the bed, the cable snaking down behind the headboard.

She got back to her feet, went to the wardrobe, and opened the mirrored door. She crouched down, reached inside.

'Careful, it's heavy,' Ryan said.

'I know it is,' she said. 'I bloody carried it here all the way from the office. I'll be in terrible trouble if anyone notices it's missing.'

She kept her back straight as she brought the Olivetti typewriter to the bed.

'Can you type?' Ryan asked.

'Of course I can.' She took a stack of paper from the wardrobe, sat on the bed, fed a sheet into the typewriter. 'Now, what date is it today?'

54

SKORZENY HAD BEEN WAITING ALMOST HALF AN HOUR IN Haughey's office when the minister returned. He did not greet the politician as he entered, nor when he sat down.

Haughey remained silent for a time. Skorzeny lit another cigarette and waited, enjoying the quiet and the gritty heat of the tobacco in his chest.

Eventually, Haughey said, 'What a fucking mess.'

Skorzeny did not respond. He took another draw on the cigarette, exhaled a pungent cloud, watched it hang in the air, drifting with the currents of the room.

'A disaster. That's what you've landed me in. A bloody disaster.'

'Lieutenant Ryan did not bear good news?'

Haughey glared from across the desk. 'No he did not.'

He told Skorzeny about Ryan's condition, about his capture, his torture, the rejection of the offer. And that the head of the Directorate of Intelligence now knew too much.

When he finished, Skorzeny said, 'The Directorate of Intelligence is your concern, Minister, not mine. I will speak with Lieutenant Ryan myself. I'm sure I can persuade him to be more open with me than he was with you.'

'No,' Haughey said, pointing a finger. 'Not a bloody chance. You stay away from Ryan, and that fancy piece of his. I gave him my word. Now, I want this business over with.'

'Be patient, Minister. Their greed will overcome them. Perhaps not today, or tomorrow. But soon. And the problem will have disappeared.'

Haughey got to his feet. 'No, my problem won't have disappeared. It'll still be sitting there smoking its bloody cigarettes.' He paced the room, his hands in his pockets. 'Old Dev should never have let any of you boys set foot in Ireland. And I'll tell you what, it's not too late to turf the lot of you out. Go back to Spain or Argentina or whatever stone you came out from under.'

'What do you suggest, Minister? Should I give in to extortion?'

Haughey stabbed a finger at him. 'Yes you bloody should. And that's exactly what you're going to do.'

Skorzeny stubbed the cigarette out. 'I beg your pardon?'

'Pay the bastards. Ryan's right. Give them what they want and be done with it.'

'Minister, do you think I'm the kind of man who surrenders to his enemies?'

'Oh, give over with this battlefield shit. This is not a war zone, and I won't let you turn it into one. We have the President of the United States coming in a few weeks, and I won't have any more bodies showing up on account of you and your bloody Nazi friends.'

Skorzeny stood, used his full height to tower over the politician. 'Minister, please do not push me. You have been a good friend to me, and I to you. We should not become enemies.'

'Enemies?' Haughey gave a hard laugh. 'I've no shortage of enemies, Colonel, and one more won't cost me any sleep.' His forefinger jabbed Skorzeny's chest. 'Now you listen to me, and you listen well. Stay away from Ryan. You go near him and I'll put you on the next flight to Spain myself.'

Skorzeny smiled, buttoned his jacket, and walked towards the door.

'You have my word, Minister. Good day.'

He passed Haughey's secretary without acknowledging her, an angry laugh trapped in his throat. The very idea that he would give in to blackmail.

The last man to try such a foolish thing had died badly.

Along with the head of Franco's personal security team, Skorzeny had inspected the hotel room where Impelliteri had met his end. Sebastian Arroyo stood over the bloodstains on the carpet, shaking his head.

'She stabbed him in the gut,' Arroyo said. 'Tore him right open. The Generalissimo's own doctor tended to him, but it was no good. Señor Impelliteri died in great pain.'

Skorzeny was careful to show no pleasure at that observation.

'An assassination, pure and simple,' Arroyo continued. 'They were both naked. My guess is she meant to kill him in his sleep, but he woke up, and there was a struggle. We trapped her in the stairwell. A beautiful girl. Who would think she could do a thing like this?'

'Did she say anything?' Skorzeny asked.

'I shot her before she could speak,' Arroyo said. 'The kindest thing, really. She would have suffered terribly if she'd been captured.'

Skorzeny nodded in agreement. 'True.'

'An odd thing, though.'

The sweat on Skorzeny's back chilled. 'What's that?'

'I had the room at her hotel searched. She had packed for a holiday, it seems, some clothes, swimwear and so on. She travelled on a Swiss passport, by the way. The odd thing was a note she had tucked inside some underwear in her suitcase.'

Skorzeny shifted his weight on his feet. 'A note?'

'A small piece of paper. It had your name and the telephone number of this hotel written on it. Oh, and your room number.'

Skorzeny said nothing.

'I did not like Señor Impelliteri,' Arroyo said. 'The Generalissimo made me hire him. As if I didn't know my own job.'

Arroyo turned and walked to the door. He paused.

'Colonel Skorzeny, you would be wise to return to Ireland and stay there for a while.'

Skorzeny nodded. 'Perhaps so.'

A month later, he made a generous gift to Arroyo. After all, there was a clear distinction between bribery and blackmail.

55

RYAN FOUND WEISS SITTING ON A PEW IN THE UNITARIAN Church, on the western side of St Stephen's Green. He noted the concern on Weiss's face as he approached.

'Is it bad?' Weiss asked.

'I'll live,' Ryan said. He eased himself down onto the wooden bench, straining to keep the pain from showing on his face.

'Is this a more suitable place than the University Church?' Weiss asked. 'It's non-denominational, you know. Both of us are welcome here. What are you? Anglican, Baptist, Methodist?'

'Presbyterian,' Ryan said. 'I don't go to church much.'

'Me neither. I guess we don't belong here, after all. So how did your little meeting go?'

'I gave them twenty-four hours to get Skorzeny to agree.'

'You think he will?'

Ryan shook his head. 'I don't know if his pride will allow it.'

'Yes, he's stubborn and proud, but he's also smart. He knows this isn't a war worth fighting. Mark my words, he'll have agreed by this time tomorrow.'

Ryan turned to look at Weiss. 'Can you keep control of Carter and his men that long?'

'Of course I can. They're a good team.'

Weiss looked up at the stained-glass windows above the pulpit, his eyes betraying the doubt in his own words.

56

WEISS FOLLOWED THE SINGLE TRACK ROAD AS THE WHITE SHEET of sky overhead darkened to grey. The raindrops on his windscreen fattened. He flicked the wipers on. They smeared the water across the glass.

He had left Remak at the airport. A few days' furlough, Weiss had said. Get some rest while Weiss revised his notes for presenting to their superiors back in Tel Aviv. Next week, he told him, when they had final approval from the top, they'd move on Skorzeny. He'd booked the flight out of his own pocket. First class.

The cottage appeared through the trees ahead, a low tumble-down building, whitewash turned to grey and brown, the paint on the door reduced to a few flakes of green on bare wood. He pulled the car onto the small patch of clear ground in front of the house, alongside the Bedford van. When the engine shuddered and died, he heard the voices.

Hard, angry voices.

He recognised Carter's first, the harsh barks, like a guard dog that had caught scent of an intruder. Then Wallace, his mocking tone, his arrogance.

Weiss put a hand to his pistol and climbed out of the car. He closed the door over, pressed it gently until it sealed shut. The voices rose in pitch and volume.

'He'll shaft us.'

'Maybe, maybe not, but I say what goes, and I say we wait it out.'

'You say what goes? Under what authority?'

'I'm your superior officer, I don't need any other authority.'

'Superior officer? I'm not in your bloody army. You've got no bloody say over me or him.'

'If you want paid, you'll do what I tell you.'

'Yeah, I want paid, but what with? Where's the fucking money? Eh? You told me you'd make me rich, and I haven't seen a bloody penny yet.'

Weiss opened the cottage door, stepped inside. The damp in the air fell on him like a chilled cloak.

Carter and Wallace stood toe-to-toe at the centre of the room. They both turned to look at Weiss, shame on their faces, like children caught in mischief. Gracey watched from the corner, weariness in his eyes.

Weiss took a wad of bills from his pocket, held tight by a money clip. He counted out five, ten, twenty of them and held the money out to Wallace.

'A thousand dollars,' Weiss said. 'You want to be paid? Okay, then take it as a severance package and get the hell out of here.'

Wallace looked at the cash, then back at Weiss.

'Take it.' Weiss shook the bills at him. 'Or shut the hell up.'

'So now you think you're in charge, eh?'

'Captain Carter and I are running this operation. You don't like it, here's the money, there's the door.'

Wallace sneered. 'If I wanted the money out of your pocket, I'd kill you and take it. That's not what this is about. I'm sick of sitting on my arse waiting for something to happen. If we'd stuck with the original plan, we'd have been out of this shit pile of a country weeks ago.'

'If you'd stuck with your original plan, you'd have got nothing, except maybe a bullet up your ass.' Weiss stuffed the cash back into his jacket pocket. 'This is the only show in town. Either you're with us or you're out of here.'

Wallace took a step closer. 'See, that's where you're wrong. Might be I'm still considering Skorzeny's offer. If I have to sit around here much longer, I might have to serve you bastards up to—'

Weiss snatched his pistol from its holster as he crossed the few feet between him and Wallace. Before Wallace could raise his hands, Weiss whipped it across his cheek. He felt the force of the blow in his wrist, charging up through his elbow to his shoulder.

Wallace spun around, staggered two steps, then landed hard on all fours. Weiss swung his shoe into the Rhodesian's gut. He curled into a ball on the floor, face red, coughing.

'That's enough,' Carter said.

Gracey straightened, his hand going to his trouser pocket. He produced a lock knife, flicked open the blade.

Weiss looked at Carter. 'Tell your boy to put that knife away.'

Carter kept his voice steady. 'Do as he says.'

Gracey hesitated for a moment, then closed the blade and returned it to his pocket. He kept his arms by his sides, hands open and ready, his weight on both feet.

Weiss knelt down beside Wallace. 'Now let's get something straight, my friend. You talk like that one more time, even as a joke, and I will kill you right where you stand. Are we clear?'

Wallace spat on the floor. 'Jew bast—'

Weiss placed the pistol's muzzle against Wallace's eye. He froze.

'Are we clear?'

'Yes.'

Weiss stood upright. Wallace crawled away, reached the wall, rested his back against it as he rubbed his eye with the heel of his hand.

'All right,' Weiss said. 'Now, if you ladies can keep from scratching each other's eyes out for a couple days, then we might just see this thing through.'

Carter held Wallace in his hard gaze for a moment before turning to Weiss. 'Well? What did your friend Ryan say?'

'He gave Skorzeny twenty-four hours to agree to our terms or he'll quit the assignment.'

'And if he doesn't agree?'

'Then we're no worse off than we were before, are we?'

Wallace wiped spit and snot from his chin. 'We should've got rid of Ryan. He's going to shaft us.'

'Ryan's tougher than you think,' Weiss said. 'Carter put him through hell and he didn't give me up. Frankly, I don't give a shit if you trust him or not. That's a risk I'm willing to take.'

'That's the trouble, isn't it? We're the ones risking our arses. Not you.'

Weiss put his hands in his pockets. 'Right now, Lieutenant Ryan is risking more than any of us.'

57

FROM HIS WINDOW, CÉLESTIN LAINÉ WATCHED THE SUN MOVE across the sky, dipping closer to the treetops. For the last few days, he had remained in his room, emerging only to fetch food for himself and the dog, and several bottles of wine.

The puppy whimpered with boredom almost constantly. A mound of excrement had gathered in the corner, and the smell had become unbearable. After a day of it, Lainé had resorted to scooping the foulness up and throwing it out of the window. He had stolen towels to soak up the urine.

Still the room stank, but until now Lainé had had no wish to venture out. To do so would have meant facing Skorzeny, and he felt sure the colonel would see the betrayal written clear on his face.

He had slept for no more than one or two hours every night, the fear and anger keeping him awake and shivering. The fear of Skorzeny, and the anger of knowing that Carter, and now Ryan, had abandoned him.

The Englishman had promised money, more than Lainé had ever imagined he could possess. He had spent days and weeks dreaming of it, how he would spend it, the life he would have. A cottage by the sea, where perhaps Catherine could have visited him, and they would have passed hour after hour smoking cigarettes, drinking wine and speaking in Breton while the sea spray hissed on the windows.

All gone.

So he had confessed his sins to Ryan, expecting the Irishman to hand Carter and his men over to Skorzeny. Days had passed, and still nothing. One betrayal after another had been rewarded with betrayal in return.

So Lainé had stayed in this shit-smelling box, feasting on his own rage, until he resolved to act the traitor one last time.

He closed his eyes, uttered a prayer for courage, then let himself out of the room. He descended the stairs and went to Skorzeny's study, stopped outside the door, listened to the colonel's hard voice on the other side of the wood. He opened the door without knocking.

Skorzeny sat at his desk, the telephone receiver pressed to his ear. He watched Lainé enter, close the door behind him, and take a seat. He finished his conversation and hung up.

'Célestin. You look unwell.'

Lainé said, 'We need to talk.'

Skorzeny nodded. He offered a cigarette. Lainé accepted, unable to quell the shaking in his hands as he brought a flame to the tobacco.

'So, what is it?' Skorzeny asked as he lit his own cigarette.

Lainé coughed, his eyes watering. 'I want to tell you something.'

'Oh?'

'But first, I need you to make an oath.'

Skorzeny's eyes glittered. 'Tell me the oath, and we'll see.'

Lainé went to flick ash into the ashtray, but the tremor of his hand sent the powdery flakes drifting to the floor.

'You must promise to let me live.'

A sharp bark of a laugh escaped Skorzeny. 'How can I make such a promise?'

'You must, or I won't tell you.'

'Célestin, there's nothing you can keep from me. You know I'll torture you if I must.'

With his free hand, Lainé reached into his pocket and retrieved the filleting knife he had taken from the kitchen the day before. He brought the blade to his throat. He felt the cold of it, then the hot sting as it pierced his skin.

'Promise me,' he said, holding Skorzeny's gaze firm. 'Make an oath that you will let me live, that you won't allow anyone else to kill me, or you will never know what I had to tell you.'

The laughter faded from Skorzeny's eyes. 'Célestin, you're bleeding. Put the knife away.'

'Promise or you'll never know.'

Anger flashed on Skorzeny's face, then faded as his cold calm returned. He nodded once. 'As you wish. I give you my word you will not be killed by me or anyone else.'

Lainé took the blade away from his throat, felt something warm trickle down inside his shirt to his chest.

He talked.

He told Skorzeny everything. He talked about the sick anger that haunted his days in Ireland, the hatred of his own impoverished life, the jealousy that bit at him when he saw the riches men like Skorzeny enjoyed. Then he spoke of the Englishman who came to him with promises of wealth beyond imagining, the things the man wanted to know, the van they drove him away in, the secrets Lainé whispered to him.

And he talked about the deaths of Elouan Groix and Catherine Beauchamp, and how they tormented him.

Finally Lainé told how Lieutenant Albert Ryan had cornered him on the landing upstairs, how he knew Lainé was the traitor they sought, that Ryan knew the identities of the killers who had picked off Skorzeny's *Kameraden*, and how the Irishman had conspired to keep it secret.

When Lainé had finished talking, Skorzeny sat still and quiet for a time. He had finished one cigarette and started another, but it now burned forgotten between his fingers.

Eventually, Skorzeny stubbed out the cigarette, stood and said, 'Thank you, Célestin.'

He walked around the table and came to Lainé's side. There, he lifted the heavy crystal ashtray from the desktop. Lainé opened his mouth to speak, but the ashtray slammed into his jaw.

Consciousness flickered like a faulty light bulb as the floor rushed up to meet him. In the dim swirl of his mind, he became aware of hard jagged things on his tongue, fragments of teeth. He spat them out, saw the yellowed enamel's dull sheen amongst the blood.

Skorzeny, his voice thick with rage, hunkered down beside him and said, 'I'll keep my promise. You'll live. But when this is settled, you will leave this house and never return. You will have no contact with me or anyone who calls me their friend. Do you understand?'

Lainé spat blood and nodded.

Skorzeny straightened. 'Now leave me. I have some calls to make.'

Lainé made his way back to his room, and lay down

on the bed. He ran his tongue around his mouth, seeking out the jagged remains of the broken teeth. The puppy nestled beside him, licked at his fingers, whimpering in sympathy.

58

THEY HAD WORKED UNTIL LONG AFTER DARK, LISTENING, transcribing, Ryan dictating, Celia typing. Now they lay on the bed, fully clothed except for the shoes they'd kicked off.

'Charlie Haughey will never forgive you,' Celia said, her breath warm on Ryan's neck.

'I don't care,' Ryan said.

'He'll never forgive me. He'll run me out of my job.'

'Not if we play it right.'

Her lips pressed against his ear. He turned his head, kissed her. Her fingertips skated across the stubble on his cheek.

'If we get it wrong,' she said, 'Skorzeny will kill us both.'

The following morning, Ryan headed north out of the city, the package on the passenger seat beside him. He had kissed Celia goodbye at Amiens Street Station, a similar package held under her arm. They had agreed she would stay with her parents until it was over. When they had stopped off at the boarding house for Celia to collect a few things, Mrs Highland had scowled and told her she would no longer be welcome there.

Celia had smiled and said, 'Fine. Albert and I have decided to live in sin, anyway.'

On the way out, Celia had taken Mrs Highland's

hand, leaned in close, and whispered, 'He's an extraordinary lover.'

Mrs Highland had gasped as Celia giggled. She laughed all the way to the station.

The world turned from grey to green as Ryan left Dublin behind, and with it, the grind of recent days. Wind from the broken driver's window swept across his face. As the car crested each rise, weightless for those moments, Ryan's spirit remained suspended.

He knew it was an illusion, a temporary respite from fear as he chose a course and acted on it. The crushing pressure of it all would come back soon enough. For now, he savoured the lightness of being that came with the rise and fall of the road.

Ryan parked behind his father's delivery van in the alleyway to the rear of the shop. The back gate was locked, so he walked around to the street. It seemed strange to approach the place in the morning light after so many years of slipping in and out at dusk or dawn.

The bell above the door jangled as Ryan entered. The shop seemed smaller now than it had when he was a boy, as if the walls had closed in. His confrontation with Mahon appeared to have worked. The shelves were well stocked, no shortage of bread, bottles of milk filling the large cooler.

But no one behind the counter.

Ryan stood for a moment, held still by the quiet, before he called, 'Hello?'

He listened.

Nothing. He moved deeper into the shop, its warm light turning to gloom. The cooler thumped and hummed as its thermostat kicked in. Ryan started at the noise. The milk bottles rattled against one another. He lifted one, burst the foil cap with his thumb, took a long swallow, felt the chill run down his throat to his stomach.

'Hello? Da? Ma?'

A feeling of childishness came over him as he called, as if he had just got off the bus from the school he'd attended in Monaghan town. Once when he was twelve or thirteen he had come home from Monaghan Collegiate and found the shop empty like this. He had walked around the counter and pulled aside the curtain that cloaked the doorway to the back room. He had found his parents in there, knotted together. His mother had squealed and pushed his father away with one hand while she fumbled at the buttons of her blouse with the other. His father had clipped him round the ear, hard enough for it sting for half an hour. Since then, he had always made a point of calling out for them if he found the shop empty.

Ryan called once more. When still no answer came, a crackle of worry mixed with the childishness. He set the milk bottle on the counter and went around. He reached for the curtain, pushed it aside, and stepped through.

The back room was empty save for the sparse furnishings and the stacked boxes of tinned and packet goods. A small table and two chairs took up the centre of the floor. A long white enamel sink and drainer clung to the far wall, the cold tap hissing and dripping as it had done for as long as Ryan could remember.

'Anyone here?'

Ryan's worry might have turned to fear, might have set him running up the stairs shouting for his parents, had he not heard the clattering flush of the privy out in the yard. He exhaled and cursed.

The back door opened and the young boy who worked for Ryan's father after school and on Saturdays entered. Barry something, Ryan thought. A good wee grafter, his father had said. He was fond of the lad and paid him more than he should.

The boy stopped in the doorway, stared at Ryan.

'Where's my father?' Ryan asked.

The boy kept staring, his lip trembling.

'Where is he?'

The boy shook his head, his eyes watering. He asked, 'Haven't you heard?'

Ryan followed the sound of his mother's weeping through the hospital's corridors and wards until he found her at his father's bedside beneath a tall window. He stopped when he saw the purple skin, the puffy swollen fingers protruding from the casts on each arm, the bloodied gauze taped above the eyebrow.

His mother looked up, her eyes red and wet.

'Albert. I've been trying to get you since last night. I rang the camp. They didn't know where you were. I've been ringing everywhere I can—'

'What happened?' Ryan asked. He dared not step closer.

'Men came. IRA, I think. They had hurling sticks and a metal bar. They said it was a message for you. From a friend of yours.'

A deep chill spread from Ryan's belly up through his chest and into his throat, the milk he'd drunk threatening to expel itself from his stomach. His hands hung useless by his sides.

'Dear God, Albert, what have you been involved in? Who did this to my husband?'

She stood, her shoulders quivering. Ryan wanted to flee, but he kept still and silent. She crossed to him, her gaze flitting over his face, registering the injuries there. Then she opened her right hand and slapped him across the cheek.

Ryan's head rocked, the heat and the sting flaring on his skin.

'What have you got us mixed up in?'

He had no answer. She slapped him again, harder this time.

'Who did this to your father?'

Ryan took her in his arms, wrapped them tight around her. She fought him, tried to pull free, but he would not release her. Her body softened against his and he felt the damp heat of her cheek against his neck, her eyelashes fluttering on his skin.

Her hand moved across his chest, found the hard butt of the Walther beneath the fabric of his jacket.

'My God,' she said, her voice muffled by his embrace.

'I know who did this,' he said. 'They won't touch you again. I promise.'

59

WHEN RYAN PULLED UP AT THE GATE OF SKORZENY'S PROPERTY almost three hours later, the package no longer lay on the passenger seat. He had stopped at a telephone box on the journey south and called Celia's home near Drogheda. Her father had answered, his response curt when Ryan asked to speak with his daughter. She told him she had done as they discussed, and the package and its instructions had been delivered.

He did not tell her about his own father, or that he was heading for Skorzeny's farm.

A heavyset young man stopped Ryan at the gateway. Another lurked in the trees, watching.

'No one's coming in,' the young man said. 'If you've got a delivery, you can leave it here.'

A local accent. Ryan guessed him to be IRA, a replacement for the guards who had perished a few nights before.

'My name is Lieutenant Albert Ryan. Tell Colonel Skorzeny I'm here.'

The young man leaned on the roof of the car, his round boulder of a head close enough for Ryan to smell his breath.

'I told you, no one's coming in. Doesn't matter a shite who you are.'

Ryan reached up, slipped his right arm around the young

man's neck, and pulled him down to the Walther which he held in his left hand. The muzzle made a dimple in the young man's fleshy cheek.

The man in the trees came forward, concern on his face as he tried to see what was happening at the car. Ryan saw the shotgun in his arms.

'Tell your friend to stay back.'

The young man waved a hand at his colleague. The other man stopped.

'Now, please let Colonel Skorzeny know that Lieutenant Ryan is here. Trust me, he'll want to see me.'

Skorzeny stood waiting in his study.

'Good afternoon, Lieutenant Ryan. My gatekeeper informed me that you are armed. He lacked the intelligence to relieve you of your—'

Ryan's open palm caught him hard across the mouth. He took one step backward.

'Don't touch my family again,' Ryan said, 'or I will kill you myself.'

Skorzeny raised a hand to his lip, checked his fingertips for blood. 'It was a warning, nothing more.'

Ryan drew the Walther from its holster, raised it to aim at Skorzeny's forehead.

The Austrian smiled. 'As I was saying, my gatekeeper had not the intelligence to take your weapon from you. Good men are hard to find.'

'Give me one good reason why I shouldn't blow your brains out right now.'

'If you had the will to kill me, you would have done it by now.' Skorzeny walked around his desk, fishing a handkerchief from his pocket. He dabbed at his lip and sat down. 'But I do have a reason.'

Ryan kept his aim steady. 'Let's have it, then.'

'In a moment. Please lower your pistol and sit down, Lieutenant Ryan. I really see no need for such dramatics.'

Ryan held firm for a moment, anger battling reason. He lowered the Walther, but kept his finger on the trigger guard.

'Sit, please,' Skorzeny said.

Ryan stayed on his feet.

'Would you care for a drink?' Skorzeny asked. 'You seem stressed. A brandy, perhaps? Or whiskey?'

'Nothing,' Ryan said.

'Very well. Now, regarding the injuries to your father. I must apologise. I had asked my contact in the IRA to have some men visit your parents. I wanted only that they should be frightened. It seems matters got out of hand. But the message was necessary.'

'You had no cause to harm my father.'

'Oh, but I had.' Skorzeny returned the handkerchief to his pocket. 'You see, the situation has changed.'

'I don't care.' Ryan raised the pistol for emphasis. 'If you, or anyone else, come near my parents again, I promise you will suffer.'

'I understand your anger,' Skorzeny said. 'But if you'll listen for a moment, you'll see there's no reason for anyone else to come to harm.'

'Go on.'

'Against my better judgement, I have decided to pay the men who have been causing us such problems. An advertisement will appear in tomorrow's *Irish Times*.'

The Walther grew heavy in Ryan's hand. He lowered it to

his side once more and sat down, jaw clenched against the pain that shifted from his groin to his stomach.

'There will be one condition,' Skorzeny said.

'What?'

'That you, and only you, shall act as courier for the gold. I am confident you won't try to steal it for yourself.'

'How can you be so sure?'

Skorzeny smiled and said, 'How? I can be sure because the men who attacked your father are watching the hospital he's in. They know which ward and which bed. They know your mother wears a red coat and carries a black leather bag. Do I need to continue?'

Ryan fought to keep his hands at his sides, to keep his finger off the trigger.

Skorzeny smirked. 'Would you like to point your gun at me again? Or will you agree to my request so we can have this over and done with?'

Ryan returned the Walther to its holster.

60

GOREN WEISS CIRCLED BACK AROUND TO DRIVE PAST BUSWELLS once more. Yes, the newspaper sat on the dashboard of Ryan's car. He parked further along the street and walked back to the hotel.

He gave the receptionist Ryan's name and room number. She smiled and lifted the telephone.

'Mr Ryan will be down presently,' she said, that smile fixed to her face like a man clinging to a cliff edge. 'Please take a seat in the lounge.'

Weiss thanked her and walked through to the high-ceilinged room where a few suited men read newspapers while they drank their tea and coffee. He found a comfortable seat close to the window.

A pudgy waiter approached. 'Can I get you some refreshment, sir?'

'You got any Jack Daniel's?'

'Sir?' The waiter's bottom lip drooped, his breath sounding like cough syrup sucked through a straw.

Weiss sighed. 'I guess not. Glenfiddich, then. A double, neat, on ice.'

The waiter leaned in close, spoke in a confidential tone. 'Sir, this is a temperance hotel.'

'A what?'

'We don't serve alcohol. I can get you a nice cup of tea, if you like.'

Weiss wiped his hand across his eyes. 'No, thank you, just a glass of water, please.'

The water arrived at the same time as Ryan. The Irishman lowered himself into the chair next to Weiss's, his features contorting with the pain it caused him.

'Still hurting, huh?' Weiss asked. 'You want some tea? They might even run to something as strong as coffee.'

'Nothing,' Ryan said.

'So, what is it?'

'I saw Skorzeny today.'

Weiss studied Ryan as he waited for him to continue, saw something hiding behind his eyes. When he remained silent, Weiss said, 'Spit it out, Albert. I don't like it when people keep things from me.'

Ryan let the air out of his lungs, a long and weary sigh.

'Skorzeny had my father beaten. As a warning.'

'And I guess you're kind of sore about that.'

Ryan did not answer.

'That's understandable. But don't let your anger get the better of you. So what did the colonel have to say for himself?'

'That he's going to pay. There'll be an ad in the *Irish Times* tomorrow.'

Weiss raised his glass in a toast. 'Good news. I told you he'd come around.'

Ryan shook his head. 'It was too easy. Something's not right.'

'Oh, come on, Albert. Don't be so negative. I told you, Otto Skorzeny is a smart man. One and a half million is pocket change to him. Paying up is the only option that makes sense.'

‘I’m not so sure,’ Ryan said. ‘We need to watch our step. He could be setting a trap. He’s too proud to give in like this.’

‘Perhaps the colonel isn’t as all-powerful as you think he is.’ He locked eyes with Ryan.

‘What do you mean?’

Weiss couldn’t keep the smile from his lips. ‘Did it ever strike you that Skorzeny’s war record is a little too good to be true?’

‘You know something,’ Ryan said. ‘Tell me.’

‘I have a contact, a former member of Himmler’s staff. He’s given us some good information, so we let him live. Anyway, he was there when they made that film reconstruction of the Gran Sasso raid, where they show Skorzeny and his crew swooping in on their gliders and snatching Mussolini. Thing is, the bold colonel was only supposed to be there as an observer.’

‘He planned the raid,’ Ryan said. ‘I read about it. There’s books written about—’

‘Propaganda,’ Weiss said. ‘All he did was reconnaissance, and poorly at that. The Reich was in trouble by ’43, and the SS needed a hero. Skorzeny fell ass-backwards into the role. He was supposed to be on one of the last gliders to land, but something fucked up, and he wound up landing first, right at the front door of the hotel where they were holding Mussolini. Scared the shit out of the *carabinieri*, and they dropped their weapons right there and then.

‘So, my German friend tells me, the front door of the hotel is barred, and Skorzeny goes running around the building trying to find another way in, dodging guard dogs, trying to climb over walls. In the end, against orders, he got inside, ran up and down corridors until he found Mussolini. Made damn sure he got the credit for it. The Italians put up no resistance, hardly a shot was fired. The only injuries were caused by a couple of the gliders crash landing. Hardly the daring feat the SS propaganda team made it out to be. Almost everything you read in those books is fiction, not history. Skorzeny is not Superman. He's a middle-aged fraud living off a reputation he didn't earn.'

'He's still dangerous,' Ryan said.

'Yes, he's dangerous. Very dangerous. But he is not invincible. Just remember that. We can beat him.'

Ryan took a breath. 'He wants me to be the courier.'

'I have no problem with that. Come on, Albert, lighten up. A few days from now, you'll be one of the richest men in this godforsaken country. All you got to do is hold your nerve.'

He stood, reached for the glass, and downed the rest of the water.

'I need a real drink.' He patted Ryan's shoulder. 'We're almost home, Albert. Let's talk tomorrow.'

Weiss left Ryan sitting in the lounge, a warm glow in his chest, despite the lack of whisky and the look of hollow dread on the Irishman's face.

Weiss approached the cottage at the end of the overgrown lane. He stopped the car short of the clearing when he saw Carter sitting on the doorstep, his head in his hands.

Weiss climbed out, shut the door.

Carter looked up at the sound, startled, as if he had been unaware of the car's approach.

A queasy knot tightened in Weiss's stomach. 'What's wrong?'

Carter shook his head and stared off into the trees. His Browning pistol lay on the worn stone step beside him.

'Come on, Carter. What is it?'

The Englishman jerked a thumb back towards the open door behind him. 'In there.'

Weiss crossed the clearing. Carter leaned aside to allow him to step over.

The smell first, the metal odour, then as his eyes adjusted to the gloom inside the cottage, he saw the upended table, the tin plates and cups scattered, the chairs on their backs and sides.

And he saw the bodies.

'Goddamn it,' Weiss said. 'Goddamn it.'

Wallace sat propped against the far wall, a chunk of his face and skull ripped away, two holes torn in his chest. The one remaining eye, dull as a raincloud, gazed across the room at the other man.

Gracey lay face down, a neat hole between his shoulder blades, another in the back of his head. His fingers still clutched an automatic rifle.

'Goddamn it,' Weiss said.

He went back outside and sat down on the step beside Carter.

'What happened?'

Carter ran a hand across his face, wiped his mouth and his eyes.

'It was Gracey. Fucking idiot. He'd been quiet since we let Ryan go. But he's always been quiet, even back when we were in North Africa together, so I didn't think much of it. We'd just eaten a bit of lunch. Wallace cooked it. We'd been talking about the money, divvying it up in our heads, what we were going to do with our shares.

'Then Wallace makes some stupid joke, how Skorzeny had

offered a third of the price, and that was more than any of us would get if the whole thing was split five ways. I told him to shut his stupid mouth, it wasn't funny, but he wouldn't let up. Gracey just sat there saying nothing, pushing his food around his plate.

'Then he grabs for his rifle and lets Wallace have it. Only I had my Browning out for cleaning, I would've got it too. Fucking idiot.'

'Yeah,' Weiss said. 'A fucking idiot. Skorzeny agreed to pay.'

Carter turned his head to Weiss, his eyes wide.

'Yep. Ryan just told me. There'll be an ad in the paper tomorrow morning. You got any of that good vodka left?'

Carter climbed to his feet and went inside. He returned a minute later with two bottles, one almost empty, the other almost full. He gave the first to Weiss.

They sat in silence for a time, Weiss sipping at his drink, Carter swigging mouthfuls of his.

'I used to be a soldier,' Carter said.

Weiss shrugged. 'So did I.'

'It used to mean something. For king and country, all that. You give your life to it. Then one day there's no more wars to fight and you're left sitting on your hands, counting the days, no bloody use to anyone.'

Weiss felt the vodka warm his chest and his tongue. 'My war never ends. I fight for a tiny patch of land surrounded by a dozen nations that want to scorch every trace of us from the face of the earth. If it wasn't for the fact they hate each other almost as much as they hate us, they'd have driven us into the sea ten years ago. Be grateful for the peace you've found, my friend. Not everyone gets to go home alive.'

He clinked his bottle against Carter's.

'And what happens if your war does end?' Carter asked. 'Or you're too old to fight any more? What do you do with the rest of your life?'

Weiss thought about it. He had done so many times, but never during daylight, only in the dark hours as he chased sleep. He returned to the only answer he'd ever found.

'I don't know,' Weiss said, hoping the terror of it didn't tell in his voice.

61

A COPY OF THE *IRISH TIMES* WAITED OUTSIDE RYAN'S HOTEL ROOM door when he awoke. He brought it inside and leafed through the pages until he found the classified ads. There, in the personals section, among the listings of lonely country gentlemen seeking ladies of good character, he found it.

Constant Follower: I agree to your terms, but with conditions. I await your instructions.

'Too easy,' he said, his voice sounding brittle in the small room.

He set the paper aside and went to the full-length mirror and studied the burn on his cheek. It had scabbed over, the healing begun. Aches still lumbered through his body, pains whose location he could not pinpoint, that shifted from one part of him to another.

Ryan went to the bathroom on the next floor up to empty his bladder. He felt a quiet relief when his urine ran clear, not the muddy reddish brown of the last two days. Perhaps, if he was fortunate, his bowel movement might also be clear of blood. He did not relish finding out, given the pain it caused to pass anything more than water.

He plugged the bathtub and turned the taps, stopping the

flow of water when it was deep enough for him to kneel in and cleanse his wounds. That done, he dried himself off and shaved, careful of the raw and tender parts of his skin.

Once dressed, he returned to his room, sat on the edge of the bed, and dialled an outside line.

Celia's father answered, gruff and obstreperous.

'Is this Ryan?'

'Yes.'

'I'm not sure if she's available at the—'

A rustling, muffled voices, the sound of the receiver passing from hand to hand.

'Bertie?' she asked.

'What? No, Albert.'

'I think you should be a Bertie.'

'And what if I don't want to be a Bertie?'

'I shall call you what I like.' The teasing in her voice pleased him. She said, 'That's settled, then. Bertie it is.'

'Have you seen the paper?' he asked.

'Yes,' she said, the teasing gone. 'Daddy, can I speak in private?'

Ryan heard an offended grumbling, then the closing of a door.

'What happens now?' she asked.

'They'll have me deliver the instructions to Skorzeny. He wants me to be the courier.'

'No. It's too dangerous.'

'I can't refuse.'

'Yes you can. You can tell him—'

'No, I can't.'

'But what if something happens to you?'

'It won't,' Ryan said, though he didn't believe it.

'But what if it does?'

'Then you go to the travel agent like we talked about, but you buy a ticket just for you.'

She fell silent, but he knew her thoughts as he knew his own. If something went wrong, if he did not return, then Skorzeny would not spare her. Neither he nor Celia had said it aloud, but they both knew it to be true.

'Promise me you'll go,' he said.

'I promise.'

'Good. It's nearly over.'

'I hope so. Call me soon.'

'I will,' he said. He hung up.

Before he'd taken a breath, the telephone jangled. He lifted the receiver.

'A caller for you, Mr Ryan,' the receptionist said. 'He refuses to give his name, but he sounds American.'

'Put him through.'

'Good morning, Albert,' Weiss said. He sounded hoarse, but it might have been the line. 'Looks like we're in business.'

'I saw the ad.'

'Just like you said. Now, here's how we'll play this out. You and I will have no more face-to-face contact. Every communication will be by telephone or letter drop. We play it for real from here on. At eleven a.m., there'll be a note waiting under the windscreen wiper of your car. You will be surprised to find it there. You will read it, then take it to your superiors. Are we clear?'

'We're clear.'

'Good. Hold your nerve, Albert. We're almost there.'

* * *

At five minutes past eleven, Ryan left his hotel room and went downstairs. He exited onto the street and walked the few yards from the hotel entrance to his car.

A brown business-sized envelope curled in the breeze, held in place by the windscreen wiper.

Ryan lifted the wiper blade and retrieved the envelope. The words LIEUTENANT ALBERT RYAN were typewritten across its face. He slipped his fingertip beneath the flap and tore the envelope open.

62

ONCE AGAIN, SKORZENY TRAVELLED INTO THE CITY AND CHARLES Haughey's office. The minister greeted him at the door with a firm and serious handshake.

'I'm glad you took the sensible course,' Haughey said.

'I simply want an end to the bloodshed, Minister.'

Haughey ushered him inside. Ryan waited facing Haughey's desk, his back to the door. He did not turn to acknowledge Skorzeny's entrance.

Haughey took his seat behind the desk. Skorzeny sat next to Ryan.

The minister placed an envelope on the desk in front of Skorzeny. He lifted it and removed the single page from within.

At dawn two days from today, you will deliver the agreed payment to us. It will be carried aboard a small-engined boat that will anchor at the following coordinates:

'Where is this?' Skorzeny asked.

'About five miles off the east coast,' Haughey said, 'south of Dublin.'

The boat will carry no more than two people: your courier, Asif Hussein, and the boat's pilot. They will place a light at the boat's fore and stern, and they will wait on the deck in plain sight with their hands on their heads.

If they follow these instructions, they will not come to harm. Otherwise, they will be killed. Both men will be aware of the danger of the situation. If they follow instructions, they will each be paid from the cargo.

If any other person is found to be aboard the boat, everyone aboard will be killed.

We will approach the boat from the west. The cargo will be transferred to our vessel. We will have other boats in the area. If any attempt is made to attack our vessel, the consequences will be serious.

Lieutenant Ryan will wait at the telephone kiosk in the foyer of the Royal Hibernian Hotel at 3:00 PM today to confirm details of delivery.

Skorzeny folded the paper and returned it to the envelope. 'Lieutenant Ryan, you will tell them I agree to all their instructions with the one exception we discussed: you will act as courier, not Mr Hussein.'

'And if they don't want me?'

'Then they will not be paid. You will observe everything that happens, how many men, their appearance, their accents. What kind of boat, its name, its markings.'

'What for?' Haughey asked. 'Once the gold's handed over, that's that. You won't be chasing after them, I can tell you that for nothing.'

'Of course not, Minister. But still I would like to know who has robbed me. For my own curiosity, you understand.'

Haughey gave him a long stare. He raised a finger. 'It goes

any further than curiosity, I'll have you out of this country and packed off back to Spain.'

Skorzeny smiled and bowed his head in deference. 'You need not worry, Minister.'

Haughey held Skorzeny's gaze, the mockery of the gesture not lost on him. He turned his attention to Ryan.

'Are you happy to go along with this, Lieutenant Ryan?'

Ryan kept his silence, his gaze still fixed on the window.

'Well?'

'Yes, Minister,' Ryan said.

63

RYAN ENTERED THE TELEPHONE KIOSK AT ONE MINUTE TO THREE and sat on the leather-upholstered stool. A folded scrap of paper peeked out from beneath the receiver's earpiece. He pulled it free, unfolded it.

Telephone box at the northern end of Kildare Street. You have two minutes.

He exited the kiosk and ran.

The telephone rang as he approached, running with a lopsided gait, ten yards between him and the box. A young man smoking on the corner turned and reached for the door.

'It's for me,' Ryan called.

The young man let go of the door and backed away.

Ryan slipped inside, lifted the receiver, and spoke his name.

'Does Colonel Skorzeny agree to our instructions?'

Weiss's voice. Play it for real, he'd said. Assume they're watching and listening to everything. Act like we've never met.

'Yes,' Ryan said. 'But one change.'

'What?'

'I will act as courier.'

'Our instructions are to be followed to the letter. No variation.'

'I'm the courier. That's what Skorzeny wants. If not, then no deal.'

Silence for a moment, then, 'Very well. You have the coordinates. You know what will happen if you try anything. Dawn, day after tomorrow.'

A click, and the line died.

64

OUTSIDE THE AIRPORT TERMINAL, ASIF HUSSEIN WAITED IN A grey Citroën van, its headlights glaring.

'Mr Ryan?' he asked.

Hussein wore a well cut suit that clung to his wiry body, and a silk tie loosened at the open collar of his shirt. His jaw was clean shaven, but a thick moustache covered his lip.

Hussein reached over and opened the passenger door. Ryan climbed in. He had carried no luggage from Dublin, flying first to London, then on to Zurich.

As Ryan settled into the passenger seat, Hussein slipped his hand across, felt around his torso, down to his thighs.

'I'm not armed,' Ryan said.

Hussein did not reply. He continued his search until he gave a satisfied grunt.

A metal wall separated the van's cabin from its rear, a hinged door open at the centre. In the dimness beyond, Ryan saw two hulking dark-skinned men, their eyes reflecting the bright lights of the terminal building as they stared back at him.

'Habib and Munir,' Hussein said. 'They will look after us until we reach Camaret-sur-Mer.'

Sheets of steel had been welded to the van's interior walls, armouring it from within, slots cut in those that covered the rear windows allowing spindles of light through.

Hussein lit a cigarette, its smoke thick and pungent. He put the van in gear and pulled away.

The Heidegger Bank stood enclosed by a high wall on the outskirts of a village hidden in the forested hills that overlooked Lake Zurich, less than forty minutes from the airport. A solid metal gate sealed the only entrance, an archway in the stonework. A guard with a pistol holstered at his hip examined the letter that Hussein handed to him, reading it by torchlight. He shone the torch's beam at each of the van's occupants in turn. Satisfied, he nodded, and spoke into a radio.

The gate opened outward. Hussein eased the van through the archway and parked by the plain single-storey building at the centre of the compound. He checked his reflection in the rear-view mirror, buttoned his collar, straightened his tie. He took a comb from his pocket and smoothed the wild curls of his hair.

'Come,' he said, returning the comb to his pocket, and climbed out of the van.

Ryan followed.

A thin, smartly dressed man waited at the building's entrance. He extended his hand as the Arab approached.

Hussein shook it. 'Monsieur Borringer, please forgive the lateness of the hour.'

'Monsieur Hussein, it is a pleasure to see you at any time.' He glanced at Ryan, but did not greet him. 'I feared I might not be able to source sufficient gold in time, but I called on some colleagues in other institutions for assistance. The Heidegger family is held in high regard in our industry, so my colleagues were glad to help.'

Borringer turned and led Hussein and Ryan inside the

building, Habib and Munir following behind. The foyer was modern but tasteful, with a large reception desk facing the entrance. Doors led to offices beyond, two guards barring entry. Portraits of grey-haired men lined the walls, all of them with the same stern expression, long nose and pale blue eyes. Eight in total, the mode of dress going back from twentieth to eighteenth century.

Ryan could make out small brass plates beneath each of them, all bearing the name Heidegger.

'Please follow me,' Borringer said.

'Wait here,' Hussein told his bodyguards. He turned back to Borringer. 'Mr Ryan will join us.'

Borringer looked first at Ryan's shoes, then his watch, before settling on his face. Ryan saw the measures and valuations working behind his eyes.

'As you wish,' Borringer said, making no effort to hide his distaste, and walked towards a gated elevator. He pushed the gate aside and waved Hussein and Ryan in before following after and pulling the gate closed.

Borringer took a silver chain from around his neck and selected one of the keys attached to it. He inserted the key into the elevator's control panel, turned it, and pressed the single button.

The elevator lurched downward, brickwork sliding past its cage, and came to a halt below ground. Borringer removed the key and placed the chain around his neck once more before opening the gate.

A guard sat at a small desk in the centre of the room. He stood, his hands rigid at his sides, and stared straight ahead. Nine steel doors, three to a wall, each bearing a combination lock and a heavy handle.

Borringer walked to the centre door on the wall facing the elevator. He stood with his body between the lock and the visitors as he worked. Ryan listened to the clicks and ticks as the dial turned, the solid clank as tumblers aligned. Borringer stood back to allow the guard to haul the door open.

'Gentlemen, your cargo.'

Countless numbered drawers lined the vault, all with pairs of locks, many with wax seals across them. On the floor stood a flatbed trolley laden with wooden crates. Dozens of them, each no more than a six or seven inch cube.

Borringer cleared his throat before he spoke. 'Eighty-nine crates, each containing fifteen gold kilobars, a value of sixteen thousand, nine hundred and twenty-two dollars per crate, making a total of one million, five hundred and six thousand, and fifty-eight dollars.'

His voice thinned as he ran out of breath. He took a deep inhalation before speaking again.

'Monsieur Hussein, please inspect the crates before the remaining few are sealed.'

Hussein and Ryan stepped forward. Ryan caught sight of a glistening within the five open boxes on top of the stack, saw the words *Credit Suisse* stamped in the metal. His heart quickened.

Borringer held a hand up. 'Monsieur Hussein only, if you please.'

'Wait there,' Hussein said at the vault's threshold.

Ryan obeyed.

The skin beneath Hussein's chin glowed yellow with reflected light. He must like butter, Ryan thought, the foolish memory of a fairy tale flitting through his mind before he chased it out. Hussein examined the open crates in turn while Ryan listened to the low, insistent thrum of air vents. A draught cooled his neck.

'They're good,' Hussein said. 'You may seal them.'

Borringer nodded, and the guard lifted the hammer that sat next to the stacked wooden lids. He set about nailing them in place, three firm taps for each nail, six nails for every crate.

Ryan couldn't help but feel he was witnessing a ceremony, some obscene communion in a church of concrete and steel, the blood of Christ turned gold.

Habib and Munir loaded the crates onto the van while Borringer waited with his hands folded at the small of his back. Ryan stood alongside him, stifling yawns.

Hussein conferred with the driver of the first escort car, tracing a route on the map with a pencil. Two cars, one ahead, one following, would accompany them to the French border. Once there, the armoured van and its load would travel on guarded mostly by Hussein's men. Two more cars would occasionally pass them on the French roads, Hussein explained, just to ensure no one followed.

When the crates were aboard, Habib and Munir climbed in and closed the rear doors behind them.

Borringer shook Hussein's hand before the Arab climbed into the driver's seat. Ryan took the passenger seat with no farewell.

Stars glittered above the walls of the compound, and before Hussein fired the van's engine, Ryan shivered at the silence that lay across the world. He checked his watch. Approaching two in the morning.

The convoy left the walls of the Heidegger bank behind in the darkness. Ryan watched the lead car's lights wavering ahead as the Citroën's engine droned. His eyelids dropped and his head nodded forward before jerking up.

Hussein blew cigarette smoke from his nostrils. 'Get some sleep, Mr Ryan. We have a long journey ahead.'

Ryan leaned back into the corner formed by the passenger seat and the door, allowed the engine's drone to soothe his mind. He dreamed of gold stolen from skeletal corpses and pulled from dead men's teeth, and how heavy it weighed in his hand.

The sound of the driver's door slamming shut pulled him from his unsettled sleep. The sky had lightened from black to deep blue, but the sun remained hidden beyond the horizon.

The van stood at the side of a narrow road, one of the escort cars parked some yards ahead. Ryan could barely make out the driver leaning against its roof. He guessed the second car had parked behind the van. Trees surrounded them, stretching into the distance as far as Ryan could see.

Hussein's guards joined him at the roadside, each of the three men carrying a rolled rug. Habib or Munir, Ryan couldn't be sure which was which, set a plastic gallon drum on the verge. They kicked off their shoes and socks, rolled up their sleeves, put woollen caps on their heads. They doused their hands with water from the drum, rinsed their faces, their heads, their arms up to the elbows, and finally their feet.

Ryan watched as they unrolled their rugs on the ground, stood with their hands lifted to heaven, and chanted. He had seen the ritual in Egypt as a young soldier. There, he had observed some performing the ritual ablutions with sand when no water was available.

He listened to the drone of their prayers and watched the orange glow on the horizon burn away the darkness.

The air had developed an icy chill by the time the lead car had pulled over to the side of the narrow road and stopped. Its driver waved as the Citroën van passed. Hussein raised his hand in return before turning onto a path so slender and overgrown it could barely have been described as a track, let alone a road. Ryan braced his hands against the dashboard as the van juddered and lurched over coarse ground. By the time the wheels found good footing on a decent surface, they had crossed into France.

The mountains rose up beyond Ryan's vision, mist veiling the slopes. He had not seen another car since the last village they had passed through, a loose gathering of chalets and farm buildings. Goats and horned cattle had watched them drive by. Now a vehicle appeared up ahead, travelling slow enough for Hussein to catch it up.

When the car was close enough, Hussein raised a forefinger from the steering wheel, a small gesture, but enough to tell the driver of the car to accelerate away.

Ryan felt pressure in his ears as they climbed. Hussein had not spoken since they left the bank's compound, but now he took a breath.

'Soon, you will drive. We will stop and eat, then you will take us to Crozon.'

'All right,' Ryan said.

Eighteen years since he'd been in France, and like today, he'd mostly seen it from the inside of a vehicle. He thought of Celia, and the time she had spent in Paris, and the smoky look of her eyes when she talked about it.

Perhaps they would return here, when it was all over. Part of Ryan rejoiced at the idea, while another told him it was a foolish notion. He could not think beyond the rendezvous, handing over the crates to Weiss and the others.

In his mind, Ryan's life ended at that point, though he did not imagine his own death. He simply could not conceive of an existence that stretched further, a time after the act.

Fear would be the proper emotion. But he did not feel fear, or excitement, only the cold that leaked through the seals of the Citroën's doors.

He pulled his coat tight around him, folded his arms across his chest, and closed his eyes.

65

THEY REACHED CAMARET-SUR-MER AT DUSK. THAT AFTERNOON, they had pulled in at a village cafe and taken it in turns to leave the van and eat. Ryan had chosen a rabbit stew with chunks of coarse bread. The meat had been dry and bland, the stew watery, but hunger had made him devour it all the same. Now his stomach grumbled, eager for food once again.

Habib and Munir passed some form of flatbread back and forth, cutting chunks with a vicious looking knife. They offered none to Ryan. Hussein seemed able to exist purely on tobacco and prayer.

Despite the evening chill, Ryan had rolled down the window to release the pent odours of men and cigarettes. As he pulled up to the small harbour, he smelled salt and heard the tide pushing against its walls, gulls calling as they scavenged the last of the day. Fishing vessels and pleasure boats swayed on the dark water.

'There,' Hussein said, pointing to the aged fishing boat moored closest to a set of steps that descended into the water. Weathered blue paint flaked off its wooden hull. A heavyset man with wiry grey hair and florid cheeks watched from its bow, one hand leaning on a rusted winch. He touched a finger to his brow in a casual salute.

'His name is Vandenberg,' Hussein said. 'He is not a friendly man.'

Given how little the Arab had spoken on the journey, Ryan wondered what his idea of friendly was.

They climbed out of the van. Ryan stretched his back and arms.

'Who is the passenger?' Vandenberg asked, his sing-song accent sounding to Ryan like Dutch or Flemish, possibly Danish.

'This man,' Hussein said, indicating Ryan. 'Come help us. The cargo is heavy.'

Vandenberg shook his head. 'No. I am paid to sail the boat, not to lift things. You lift things.'

Hussein grumbled and spat. He tugged Ryan's sleeve, guided him to the back of the vehicle. Soon, they had established a chain, Habib bringing each crate from the van to Ryan's hands, Ryan passing it to Munir, who then descended the steps and handed it to Hussein, who stood on the boat, stacking each box as it arrived.

Ryan's hands were raw and bloody by the time it was done, his back aching, sweat slicking the skin beneath his clothes. He considered crying off, telling them of the injuries he'd received only a few days ago, but his pride would not allow it.

As the sun kissed the horizon, Hussein pulled a fat envelope from his pocket and tossed it to Vandenberg. He opened the envelope and thumbed through its contents. Satisfied, he stashed it inside his coat and nodded to Hussein.

Without a word to Ryan as he passed, Hussein returned to the driver's seat of the van while Habib and Munir climbed into the back. The Citroën's engine barked as it caught, then pulled away from the harbour.

Ryan watched its tail lights fade.

'Come,' Vandenberg called from the boat. 'Is time for going.'

Ryan huddled on the cabin's single bunk, wishing he had brought warmer clothes as Vandenberg navigated the channels and sandbanks from Camaret-sur-Mer, away from the Crozon peninsula and towards the open sea.

The crates had been covered in a canvas tarpaulin and lashed in place with ropes and hooks. The tarpaulin's corners fluttered in the breeze.

Soon, the boat gathered speed as it moved into open water, rising and falling with the waves.

Ryan had never minded travelling by boat. Back in the war, he had found the movement soothing, even while many among his comrades hung retching over the sides. The boat creaked and groaned as its wooden hull cut through the waves.

Above, visible through the cabin's grimy windows, the sky cleared, a sheet of deepest black, a hint of orange and blue on the far horizon. Stars emerged, hard bright points beyond number, made clear away from the haze and the lights of mankind. Ryan picked out constellations, searching his memory for their names.

A brilliant streak shot across the black, and he wished for the warmth of Celia's body next to his.

He awoke with the sensation of drifting. The boat rose and fell, but there was no sense of speed, no forward movement. Ryan opened his eyes, saw the deck outside the cabin doused in blue moonlight.

There, Vandenberg pulling back the tarpaulin to expose a crate. He tried its lid with his thick fingers, found it solid.

He harrumphed and opened a long box on the deck. He rummaged through its contents until he found a short crowbar. Ryan watched as Vandenberg began prising the crate open.

'Leave it alone.'

Vandenberg spun to Ryan's voice.

Ryan got to his feet, went to the cabin's doorway, steadied himself against the boat's sway.

'Is my boat,' Vandenberg said. 'I will know what I carry.'

'The Arab paid you. That's all you need to know.'

Vandenberg straightened, puffed out his chest, the crowbar held at his side. 'He is no Arab. He is Algerian. I will know what I carry.'

'I don't care what he is. Those crates are none of your concern. Your job is to sail this boat. I suggest you do it.'

'No,' Vandenberg said, turning back to the crates. 'I am the captain. I will look inside.'

Ryan stepped towards him. 'Leave them alone.'

Vandenberg raised the crowbar. 'You go away from me.'

'Put it down,' Ryan said, taking another step.

Vandenberg swiped the air between them.

Ryan moved closer. He smelled whisky.

'Go away from me.' Vandenberg held the crowbar high, ready to bring it down on Ryan's head.

'I'll tell you once more,' Ryan said. 'Put it down.'

Vandenberg swung the crowbar, and Ryan raised his left forearm to block it. Metal displaced air by Ryan's ear as he seized Vandenberg's wrist, took his balance. Ryan's right fist connected with Vandenberg's jaw, and the sailor sprawled on the deck.

Reaching down, Ryan grabbed the crowbar with his right hand. Vandenberg crawled past him, towards the cabin, panting and gasping. Ryan followed. Vandenberg clambered to his feet and stumbled through the doorway, grasping for something beneath the radio set.

Ryan brought the crowbar down hard on Vandenberg's outstretched hand, felt bones give under the force of it, saw the small pistol fall to the floor.

Vandenberg screamed and dropped to his knees as Ryan kicked the gun away. The sailor cowered on the cabin floor and clutched his ruined hand to his chest.

Ryan held the blade of the crowbar to the other man's jaw. Vandenberg blinked up at him, sucking air through his rotted teeth.

'Enough,' Ryan said. 'Now do what you were paid to do.'

The sky lightened on the far horizon and the stars faded, lost behind thickening cloud. In the distance, Ryan imagined he saw a vague dark band of land, but he could not be sure.

Vandenberg slowed the engine to a halt, struggling with one hand held in an improvised sling at his chest. Ryan watched from the deck as he checked his maps and instruments for a time before emerging.

'Is here,' Vandenberg said. 'What now?'

Ryan rested against the crates. 'We wait.'

Weariness invaded Ryan's limbs, and the world seemed quieter, even the sound of the water muted by the stillness and the grey. Vandenberg placed a kerosene lamp at one end of the boat, a battery powered light at the other. Ryan fought to keep his eyes open, his head nodding with the gentle rise and fall of the sea.

His mind had begun to drift, flitting through images of slender freckled wrists and glistening lips, when Vandenberg said, 'They come.'

66

RYAN'S HAND WENT TO THE PISTOL THAT NESTLED IN HIS COAT pocket. He scanned the expanse of grey until he spotted the boat to the north-west, circling around towards them.

A white plume of foam arced in the cabin cruiser's wake, matching the boat's paintwork, the powerful engine's thrum audible across the waves. As the cruiser drew closer, Ryan made out the shape of a man at the wheel. He studied the form until he was sure it was Carter.

Ryan checked his watch. Seven thirty-five. He remembered his thoughts of the day before, that he could not imagine a time beyond this exchange. Unease gnawed at his gut. He put his hand back in his coat pocket, felt the hard lines of the pistol, the curve of the trigger.

The boat's engine dropped in pitch as it slowed. In the cabin window, the silhouette of a man who could only be Goren Weiss.

Ryan turned his gaze to Vandenberg, who watched the cruiser with worry in his eyes. He rubbed his lips with his uninjured hand. He noticed Ryan's attention on him.

'What is in these boxes,' Vandenberg said, 'will men kill to have it?'

'Yes,' Ryan said.

'You have my gun?'

'Yes.'

'Is must be careful.'

Ryan nodded.

Carter steered the boat away in a wide circle, then brought it around so that its port side aligned with Vandenberg's starboard. He slowed it further and manoeuvred alongside. Weiss climbed up and out of the cabin, fixed a rope to a cleat on the side of the boat, then threw the other end up and over to Ryan. Ryan pulled, brought the two vessels together, and tied the rope to his own side. The fishing boat sat higher in the water than the cabin cruiser.

Carter lifted an automatic rifle and trained it on Vandenberg. 'Stay where I can see you.'

Vandenberg raised his one good hand. 'Where do I go?'

Weiss asked, 'Is everything in order?'

'Yes,' Ryan said.

'What happened to his hand?'

Ryan sensed the truth would not do well for Vandenberg. 'He fell.'

'Shit,' Weiss said. 'Step away.'

'Why?'

'Just do it, Albert.'

Ryan took two steps away from Vandenberg. Weiss looked to Carter and nodded.

A burst of rifle fire, and Vandenberg fell.

Ryan closed his eyes, swallowed, opened them again. 'You didn't need to do that.'

Weiss hoisted himself up onto the fishing boat. 'I wouldn't have if he'd had two good hands to help us move these crates.'

'So when I'm no more use to you,' Ryan said, 'you'll shoot me too?'

Weiss laughed. 'Really, Albert, is that what you think of me?'

'Yes.'

'I'm hurt, I truly am. Now let's get to work.'

Carter left the wheel and Weiss started handing crates over to him. Carter carried each one down into the cabin while Ryan scanned the horizon, from the strip of land in the north-east, to the west, to the south.

'It's clear,' Weiss said. 'We've been circling for an hour. There's no one else out here. Help me with these, goddamn it.'

'It's too easy,' Ryan said.

'Stop worrying, Albert. We're almost home and dry. Now shut up and start moving these crates.'

The grey sheet of sky faded to dingy white above them as they stowed the cargo.

Carter passed a canister across to Weiss.

'I'd stand clear if I were you,' Weiss said. He splashed liquid onto the deck, over the walls of the cabin, across Vandenberg's body.

Ryan smelled petrol. He climbed over to the other boat, hurrying to avoid Weiss's aim. Weiss followed, taking the canister with him. He untied the rope from the cruiser's port side and tossed it to Carter to hold Vandenberg's fishing boat close by.

Weiss pulled a handkerchief from his pocket, tipped up the canister to wet the fabric, then stuffed the handkerchief into its neck. Next, he produced a Zippo lighter, touched its flame to the handkerchief, recoiled as it caught, and tossed the canister across to the other boat.

The petrol on the deck ignited with a soft *whump!* and Weiss said to Carter, 'You might want to let go now.'

Carter dropped the rope and gave Vandenberg's boat a shove. The two vessels drifted apart, five feet, ten feet, before the petrol canister blew. Carter went to the wheel and restarted the engine. Ryan felt its grumble through the soles of his shoes, and the boat pulled away.

As they gathered speed, he watched the growing tower of black smoke climbing to the sky, chased by dirty orange flames. Finally, the dull thump as the boat's fuel tank exploded. Ryan felt the rush of hot air, saw timbers and sparks scatter.

Weiss came to his side. 'How does it feel to be a rich man, Albert?'

His hand felt cold on Ryan's shoulder.

'Where are Wallace and Gracey?' Ryan asked.

When they moored at the rear wall of Balbriggan harbour a little more than an hour later, a mist lay heavy on land and water. The Bedford van stood waiting above, parked sidelong to the sea, the raised bridge of the railway line climbing beyond it, dark grey concrete and stone surrounding them on three sides.

Quiet hung over the harbour, the local fishing boats gone to sea, the pleasure boats tied up and idle. Ryan guessed Weiss and Carter had stolen the cabin cruiser from here. Waves hissed and rumbled against the beach beyond the northern wall.

Carter climbed the rusted ladder and Ryan hoisted crates up to him. His shoulders and back screamed with pain by the time they had all been loaded. The three men leaned against the van for a time, chasing their breath.

Carter said, 'If I'd known it was going to be such hard work, I never would have started this.'

Weiss spat on the ground. 'You'll never have to work again. Come on, let's see what we've got.'

Carter packed his rifle into a canvas sack and stowed it beside the crates. They stood at the rear doors of the van, each regarding the load.

Weiss took a last look around, then climbed up into the van. He pulled a long-bladed screwdriver from the small toolbox that rested on the plywood flooring. He wedged it beneath the lid of the nearest crate and pulled up.

Ryan heard wood creak and crack.

The lid fell away and he saw the colour drain from Weiss's face. His smile widened for a moment, flickered, then faded. He shook his head.

Carter asked, 'What's wrong?'

Weiss lifted a dim grey obelisk from the crate, then another.

Carter leaned in. 'What in the name of . . .'

Weiss dropped them to the van's floor. They clanked together. Carter lifted them, tested their weight.

'What's this?' he said. He turned to Ryan. 'What the fuck is this?'

Weiss laughed once, a deep guffaw that rose from his belly. But it rang hollow in the van. He laughed again, a high peal edged with madness.

Carter's voice wavered as if he verged on tears. 'What's going on? Where's the fucking gold?'

Weiss brought his hands to his face, the laughter coming thick and strong now, rolling from him, his shoulders shuddering.

'Where is it?' Carter asked.

But Ryan knew. Before Weiss had reached down into the crate Ryan knew, but he had no desire to laugh.

Carter leaned into the van, grabbed the edge of the crate, pulled it away from Weiss. 'For Christ's sake, where's the gold?'

He peered into the crate, shook his head. 'No.'

Weiss hooted and cackled. 'Oh, yes, my friend. Oh, yes.'

He lifted another two bars of lead from the crate, clanked them together, and laughed until his eyes watered.

67

WEISS'S SIDES ACHED AND HIS VISION BLURRED WITH TEARS. Giddiness washed through him and his stomach threatened to empty itself.

He dropped the bars to the van's plywood floor and pushed the crate away. It toppled and spilled onto the ground outside, Carter and Ryan skipping aside to save their toes. Fifteen blocks of worthless metal scattered on the ground.

Weiss grabbed the next crate, rammed the screwdriver beneath its lid, and heaved. The wood splintered and cracked. Inside, the same, nothing glittering, only the dull sheen of lead.

He collapsed back against the van's wall, the air gone from his lungs, the strength deserting his legs. Still he laughed, wave after ridiculous wave, he couldn't stop it, even as it all went to shit before his eyes, all he could do was laugh.

A sharp hot sting across his cheek.

He wondered for a moment who had struck him before realising it had been his own open hand. He slapped himself again, bit down on the clarity it brought.

'Goddamn it,' he said.

He reached beneath his coat, seized his pistol, and brought it up to aim at Ryan's forehead. He blinked the tears away.

'Goddamn it, Albert, didn't you check?'

Ryan's face showed no emotion, not even surprise.

'I only saw a few crates. I saw the gold. It said *Credit Suisse* on them. Skorzeny's courier checked. I wasn't allowed into the vault to see them up close.'

Carter fought his own breathing. 'I knew he'd shaft us. I told you, didn't I? I told you, but you—'

Weiss shifted his aim to Carter. 'Shut up.'

'I knew it was too easy,' Ryan said.

'Don't point that at me,' Carter said.

Weiss held his aim steady. 'Both of you, shut up and let me think.'

'I said, don't point that at me.'

'Shut your mouth, Carter, or I swear I will shoot you in the face.'

Carter grabbed for Weiss's wrist, but Weiss snatched his arm away. He brought the pistol back around, squared it on Carter's forehead, pressure on the trigger.

'Don't push me, Carter. You know I'll—'

'Everyone away from the van.'

The voice came from above, a harsh distorted bark followed by a squall of feedback.

'This is Chief Inspector Michael Rafferty, Garda Síochána. You're surrounded. I've got a dozen Guards here, all armed, and an army sniper team. Any messing about and I'll give the order to fire. Now, everyone out of the van.'

Weiss leaned out, looked up, saw the hulk of a man standing on the railway bridge above, a loudhailer in his hand. Two policemen stood alongside him, pistols drawn and aimed, the mist hazing them.

Further along the bridge, a prone man, a rifle's telescopic sight trained on them. In the shadows beneath the bridge, in the dark pools between the arches, more cops, more weapons.

'Lieutenant Albert Ryan, make yourself known.'

'Bastard,' Carter said. 'You bastard.'

Weiss looked at Ryan, saw the shock on his face, and said, 'He didn't know.'

Carter glared. 'My arse, he didn't.'

Ryan said nothing. He stepped away from the van, his hands up.

Carter's eyes went to the canvas bag he'd wrapped his automatic rifle in.

'Don't,' Weiss said. He dropped his pistol, put his hands above his head, and edged towards the van's rear.

'Bastard,' Carter said.

The loudhailer crackled again.

'Down on your knees, Ryan, your hands on your head. The rest of you, step away from the van.'

Carter kept his back to the cops, his hands busy undoing the canvas.

'Don't,' Weiss said. 'They'll kill us both.'

Carter freed the rifle from the bag, hoisted it up, spun towards Ryan, his finger going for the trigger.

His skull cracked open a fraction of a second before Weiss heard the shot and felt the warm spatter on his face. Carter fell, his limbs loose, his eyes and mouth wide open.

'All right,' Weiss called. 'I'm coming out.'

The loudhailer squealed. 'How many are there?'

'Just Ryan and me. That's all.'

'Get out of the van, your hands on top of your head.'

Weiss eased out, got his feet under him, and took half a dozen steps, avoiding Carter's blood on the wet concrete.

'On your knees, beside Ryan.'

He did as he was told. Ryan stared ahead, his expression blank.

'I have a suite at the Shelbourne,' Weiss said, his voice low. Ryan turned his head towards him. 'Under the name of David Hess. Everything I have on Skorzeny is there, locked in a metal file box. If I don't get out of custody, if they deport me, you go there, you get it. Take it to Hedder and Rosenthal, a law firm in Ballsbridge. Give it to Simon Rosenthal. No one but him. You hear me?'

Ryan did not reply.

Policemen advanced from the shadows, fear on their faces, their weapons quivering in their hands.

'You hear me, Ryan? Take the information to Simon Rosenthal. Get Skorzeny for me.'

'No,' Ryan said. 'I'll get him for myself.'

68

RAFFERTY LOWERED HIS BULK INTO THE CHAIR OPPOSITE RYAN, huffing as he did so, his face red. He set one mug of steaming tea on the table, took a sip from the other.

'Jesus, this is a bit too much like hard work,' he said. He nodded at the mug in front of Ryan. 'Go on, drink up.'

Ryan reached for it, brought it to his lips.

'There, now, isn't that better?'

The policeman fell silent, watching from across the table. Moisture beaded on the bare concrete walls of the interview room. A tape recorder sat idle between them, no reels loaded on its spindles.

'Your friend, the American fella. Or Israeli or whatever the hell he is.' Rafferty placed his mug back on the table and pulled a packet of cigarettes from his jacket pocket. 'All he'll tell me is his name. He keeps asking for some lawyer called Rosenthal. What's he up to? What's he doing here?'

'He's Mossad,' Ryan said.

'He's what?'

'Mossad. Israeli intelligence.'

'Like a spy?'

'Something like that.'

Rafferty snorted. 'Holy Mother of God. Here?' He pulled a cigarette from the packet and lit it. 'I tell you, this is too much excitement for me. The worst I'm used to dealing with is a spot of livestock theft or a fight in a pub. Not this sort of carry-on. I don't get paid enough to be doing with spies and smuggled gold. Well, more lead than gold, as it happens. Five of the crates had three gold bars on the top. Anyway, my point is, do I look like James bleeding Bond?' He leaned forward, his cigarette held between fat fingers. 'Did you see that film?'

'Yes,' Ryan said.

'I took the missus. She put her hand over my eyes when that lass came out of the sea, all wet like. I gave her something to smile about that night, I can tell you.'

Rafferty's belly jiggled as he laughed, smoke leaking out between his teeth.

Ryan cleared his throat. 'I need to speak with Ciaran Fitzpatrick at the Directorate of Intelligence.'

'I was told you'd say that.' Rafferty took a folded piece of paper from the cigarette packet. 'Unfortunately, Mr Fitzpatrick isn't available at the moment. But you do have friends in high places.'

He unfolded the paper, revealing a few typewritten sentences and a looping signature.

'This here is a note from none other than the Minister for Justice, Mr Charles J. Haughey, the very same man who ordered that van to be followed and its occupants to be arrested after they came back ashore. This arrived by courier about twenty minutes ago. It says you aren't to be questioned about all this, that no statement of any kind should be recorded, and I should release you at my own discretion. He wants things to be handled on the quiet. Just in case we upset the Americans and they decide President Kennedy isn't going to pay us a visit after all. What do you think of that?'

'I think you should let me go.'

Rafferty nodded. 'I could do, I suppose. But it does say at my discretion, and my discretion says not just yet. I think I'll let you stew a while, Mr Ryan.'

The policeman hauled his bulk out of the chair, wheezing at the strain.

'Why?' Ryan asked. 'You can't question me, so why keep me here?'

Rafferty leaned across the table until Ryan felt the heat of his breath.

'Because I don't like trouble on my doorstep, and I especially don't like government bastards telling me my job in my own bloody station. But mostly, I'm going to keep you here just because I can. Is that good enough for you?'

69

THE OPENING OF THE CELL DOOR SHOOK GOREN WEISS FROM his shallow slumber. He turned his head, expecting to see the fat cop back for more clumsy attempts at interrogation. Instead, three suited men entered, none of whom he recognised.

'Who are you?' he asked.

'Stand up,' the eldest said. He closed the door behind him. A man of around fifty, cropped hair greying, his charcoal-coloured suit neat across his broad shoulders. The other two were younger, mid thirties, but had that same physique.

Weiss's gut tightened as he stood. 'I want to speak with my lawyer, Simon Rosenthal at Hedder and Rosenthal.'

The two younger men came to Weiss's sides. Each took a wrist.

'I suggest you contact him right now, or I can promise you, there will be trouble.'

The younger men tightened their grip on Weiss's arms. The older man went to the bed Weiss had just got up from. He tugged at the sheet until it came free.

Weiss tried to jerk his right arm away, but the young man's grip was solid like a manacle.

'Goddamn you, the Israeli government will not sit still for this. You are bringing a war upon yourself.'

The older man stretched the sheet out and rolled it into a thick rope.

Weiss kicked at one of the younger men's legs. They shifted their feet, avoided his, then pushed him down on the floor. Concrete slammed into his cheek.

The older man made a loop at one end of the sheet, tied a crude slip knot.

'Hold him steady,' he said as he crouched down.

Weiss screamed. He threw his weight to one side, then the other. A knee pressed into his back, pinning his chest to the floor. He screamed again, a word that might have been 'No.'

The loop slipped over his head, snagging on his nose and mouth. Cool fabric tightened beneath his chin, choking the curses from his mouth.

The noose gripped his neck, closing his throat. Pressure built inside his head. He felt it swell behind his eyes. His vision reddened. A roaring in his ears.

The cell door opened. Weiss saw the fat cop's boots, along with two other pairs.

The pressure in Weiss's head eased.

The fat cop asked, 'What in the name of Christ is going on?'

70

'WE HAVE A MUTUAL FRIEND,' THE MAN SAID.

He stood with his hands in his pockets. Ryan noticed the grime on his knees.

He had entered the interview room alone, carrying a leather satchel, closed the door behind him, and grunted as he hoisted the satchel onto the table. It had settled on the wood with a muted clunk.

'Who are you?' Ryan asked.

'My name is James Waugh. Your young lady friend Celia Hume has run a few errands for me in the past.'

The words glided across the soft contours of his accent, south-west of Dublin, north-east of Cork.

'She mentioned you,' Ryan said. 'You told her to report on me.'

Waugh sat down across the table, the satchel between them. 'Truth be told, I wish I hadn't. If I'd known the kind of mess the minister was getting mixed up in, I wouldn't have allowed it.'

'Who do you work for?' Ryan asked.

'I run my own department, very small, less than two dozen on the staff. We don't answer to the Directorate of Intelligence or the Department of Justice, but we do odd jobs for them now and again. Imagine us as handymen, doing the dirty work for other departments so they don't have to.'

'What do you want?'

'To tell you you're free to go, for one thing.'

'What about Weiss?'

Waugh pursed his lips. 'Mr Weiss attempted suicide in his cell about an hour ago. He tried to hang himself with a bed sheet. Thankfully we intervened in time to save him.'

Anger flared in Ryan's chest. 'I think that's a lie.'

Waugh's eyelid flickered. He took a breath. 'Mr Weiss has been taken to hospital for treatment. Now, the Minister for Justice has asked that you bring all materials relating to your investigation to his office tomorrow afternoon at two. You will give your final debriefing, and that will be an end of it.'

'Does Haughey know you tried to kill Weiss?'

Waugh smiled. 'As I explained, Mr Weiss attempted suicide. But I'll repeat, neither I nor my staff report to the Department of Justice. I act independently with my own objectives. Does that answer your question?'

Ryan watched Waugh's face, the eyes grey and cold like slate. 'You said "for one thing". What else did you want?'

Waugh stood and fetched a business card from his pocket. He placed it face up on the table, next to the satchel, pushed it towards Ryan with his fingertips. It bore only Waugh's name and a telephone number.

'I have an opening in my department,' he said, a warm smile on his lips that did not soften his stare. 'More interesting work than the Directorate of Intelligence has to offer. I could use a man like you.'

Ryan looked down at the card. He pushed it away. 'No, thank you.'

Waugh pushed it back. 'Think about it.'

He went to the door, paused, turned, as if he had remembered some minor detail. He pointed to the satchel.

'I wasn't sure what to do with that. I suppose you ought to take care of it.'

Waugh exited, closed the door behind him.

The satchel's leather glowered in the interview room's fluorescent lighting. Ryan undid the single buckle, pulled back the flap.

He saw the yellow glistening within, felt his mouth dry.

71

'I THOUGHT YOU IRISH COPS DIDN'T CARRY GUNS,' WEISS SAID. The words rasped in his throat like sandpaper.

Rafferty sat down at the foot of the hospital bed, the only other person on the ward. He had dismissed the lone Garda officer as he entered. His hand went to the pistol at his hip.

'We do the odd time,' he said. 'If the situation calls for it.'

'And this one does?'

Rafferty smiled. 'I'd say so, wouldn't you?'

'I would.'

Weiss put his right hand behind his head, lay back on the bed. A pair of handcuffs bound his left hand to the bed frame. He wore his vest and trousers, socks on his feet. His neck had already begun to bruise.

'So when are you going to let me go?' he asked.

'You can stay here until the quack says you're fit,' Rafferty said. 'After that, you'll come back to the shop with me. Then we'll have to see. That government fella didn't seem too impressed at there being a . . . what you call it? Mossad? That's it. He didn't like there being a Mossad man arsing about this part of the world. I wouldn't be surprised if someone wanted you put on a plane out of here, would you?'

'I guess not. What about Lieutenant Ryan?'

'He's gone. That government fella gave him a leather bag and told me to turn him out.'

Weiss wet his lips. 'A leather bag?'

'That's right.' Rafferty nodded, the folds under his chin squashing and bulging.

'What do you suppose was in it?'

'I couldn't say. It looked right and heavy, though.'

Weiss's gaze flitted once more to the revolver at Rafferty's hip.

'Here's a funny thing,' Rafferty said. 'After the government fella left, I put in a call to that Rosenthal chap you were busting to talk to. The lawyer. He knew who you were, all right, said you were a client and all, but when I told him where I'd picked you up, what you'd been up to. Well, he seemed a bit surprised, like. And maybe annoyed, too. Why would that be, do you think?'

'No idea,' Weiss said.

'Want to know what I reckon?'

'Not really.'

'I reckon this Rosenthal is your contact here in Ireland. Seeing as Israel has no embassy in Dublin, you'd need someone to run to when things go tits up. Am I near the mark?'

Weiss did not reply.

'Anyway, I think you've been up to badness behind your man's back. I think you've shit in the nest, as we say around here. Otherwise, I reckon your man Rosenthal would've been down here screaming for your release the second I put the phone down. Is that about the size of it?'

Before Weiss could respond, the doctor entered the ward.

'Are you the officer in charge of the patient?' he asked Rafferty.

'That's right,' Rafferty said, standing.

'He's got some bruising to the neck, but I don't think there's any damage to the larynx or the windpipe. You got to him before he did any real harm. I'm happy to hand Mr Weiss back to you now.'

'All right, so,' Rafferty said. 'Thanks.'

The doctor left, and the fat cop approached the bedside. He fished a set of keys from his pocket and set about loosening the handcuffs.

Only when he reached for them, he discovered they were already undone. They had been for some time. Weiss had taken the paper clip from the doctor's desk in the examination room, simple as that.

Rafferty's eyes widened as Weiss seized his wrist. His free hand grabbed for the revolver at his hip, but it was already too late for him.

72

THE RECEPTIONIST, A SKELETAL MAN OF MIDDLE YEARS, WATCHED Ryan approach the desk with something close to horror on his face.

'Can I help you, sir?'

'You have a guest by the name of David Hess,' Ryan said.

The receptionist flicked through page after page of the registration book until he found what he was looking for. 'Yes, Mr Hess. But I'm afraid he hasn't been here for a few days. Can I take a message?'

Ryan noted the room number written next to Mr Hess's registration. 'No, thank you,' he said.

He walked away from the desk, waited until another customer claimed the receptionist's attention, and went to the stairs.

Ryan looked both ways along the corridor, then wedged the screwdriver's sharpened blade between the door and its frame where the lock joined the two. He put his weight behind the handle, pushed, pulled it back, pushed again. Wood splintered and cracked.

The door opened, and Ryan stepped inside. He returned the screwdriver to his pocket and pressed the door back into its frame.

A couch and two armchairs surrounded a coffee table, a sideboard against one wall, a writing desk at another. Every surface sparkled, not a trace of dust or use. He toured the room, checking drawers, lifting cushions, and found nothing.

The bedroom was just as immaculate, the blankets and sheets crisp and undisturbed.

Ryan went to the large wardrobe and opened it. A suit wrapped in cleaner's plastic and half a dozen ironed shirts hung inside. At the bottom, a metal file box. He lifted it out and placed it on the bed.

A lock held the box closed. Ryan took the screwdriver from his breast pocket and forced the blade beneath the clasp. He prised outward until the lock gave, then returned the screwdriver to his pocket. Inside, a cluster of suspended files, folders and loose sheets of paper. He sorted through them, lifting pages out, scanning them, returning them to their places. Two passports, one German, the other American, both in the name of David Hess.

Towards the back, he found what he wanted: a file containing the facsimiles of Skorzeny's accounts. Ryan ran a finger down the columns, tracing the movements of money from one account to another, interest accruing, a few tens of thousands slipping away here, another hundred thousand or so turning up there.

He folded the pages, slipped them into his jacket pocket, and closed the file box before returning it to the wardrobe. Fatigue dragged on his arms and legs as he straightened and went to the bedroom door. He stepped through to the sitting room.

Goren Weiss stood at its centre, a revolver in his hand, its muzzle pointed at the floor.

'What are you doing here, Albert?' he asked.

73

WEISS LET THE PISTOL HANG LOOSE AT HIS SIDE. NO NEED FOR things to turn ugly. Not yet.

Ryan's face remained impassive. 'I wanted those papers you told me about.'

'Did you get them?'

Ryan's right hand went slowly to his breast pocket, beneath his jacket. 'Yes.'

'That's all right,' Weiss said. 'They're no good to me now. You going after Skorzeny?'

'Maybe,' Ryan said, easing his hand away from his pocket.

'Good luck,' Weiss said.

Ryan stood still in the bedroom doorway, did not reply.

'There's something I do need from you, though.' Weiss took a step closer, kept the pistol lowered.

Ryan visibly tensed. 'What's that?'

'You were given a satchel. What was in it?'

'I think you know.'

'I guess I do. Where is it?'

Ryan shook his head. 'It's not here.'

Weiss laughed and raised the pistol to aim at Ryan's heart. 'I guessed as much, Albert. I didn't ask you where it's not. I asked you where it is. This is not the right time to play stupid, my friend.'

'It's not here.' Ryan held his hands out from his sides. 'I don't have it.'

Weiss took two steps forward, the muzzle of the revolver a foot from Ryan's chest. He thumbed the hammer, cocked it.

'I need that bag, Albert. How much do you think was in it? Whatever they used to cover the lead in those crates. I'd guess fifteen, sixteen thousands' worth, maybe more. What do you think?'

'I don't know.'

'I'm a dead man without that bag, Albert. My superiors know what I was up to. They'll take me for treason. I have to run, and I need that gold to do it. I want you to know how important this is to me, Albert, so you know I won't give up on it. Now tell me where it is.'

'No,' Ryan said. 'I won't.'

Another step, the pistol's sight aligned on Ryan's forehead. Inches away.

'I bet it's in your room at Buswells. Am I right? It's there with your girl, that redhead. If I have to, I'll put a bullet in your brain. Then I'll walk to your hotel, go to your room, and take it from her. And you know I won't be able to let her live. Don't make me do that, Albert. Please.'

Ryan took a step to the side, away from the door, his left hand raised in front of his face, his right still held out from his side.

'I can't make you do anything,' he said. 'If you pull that trigger, it'll be your own choice.'

'Goddamn you, Albert.' Weiss increased the pressure on the trigger. Cocked, the pistol would fire with the slightest twitch of his finger. 'Goddamn y—'

The movement of Ryan's hand was so small, hardly anything

at all, just a tap to the inside of Weiss's wrist, and the shot missed Ryan's head, buried the bullet in the wall.

And that deep hot pain in Weiss's belly.

As the strength ran from his legs into the floor, he looked down, saw the screwdriver in Ryan's grip. Had his mind worked faster, he might have brought the pistol back around, taken Ryan's head off, but instead the blade of the screwdriver pierced his flesh once more, higher this time, beneath his sternum.

Weiss dropped to his knees, clutching at himself, feeling the warmth spread across his stomach, spilling into his lap. The pistol fell useless beside him, out of his reach. He rolled onto his side, his legs no longer able to support him.

Ryan backed away. He went to the window, wiped the screwdriver's blade clean on the curtains before returning it to his pocket.

'Albert,' Weiss said.

Ryan paused on his way to the door.

'Get me a doctor, Albert. I don't want to die. Please, Albert.'

Ryan came back, stopped short of the red creeping across the carpet. He hunkered down.

'You let them torture me,' Ryan said. 'You watched them do it.'

'Albert.' Weiss reached for more words, but they were lost in the storm that raged behind his eyes. His head grew heavy, and he lowered it to the carpet.

He watched as Ryan examined his clothing then left the room, pulling the door closed behind him.

74

NO ONE OBSERVED RYAN AS HE LEFT WEISS'S ROOM, NO ONE ventured into the corridor to investigate the sound of the gunshot. He exited on to St Stephen's Green, his ears ringing from the pistol's roar, dropped the screwdriver into the first litter bin he found.

A few minutes' walk brought him to the car outside Buswells. He climbed in, started the engine.

Ryan paused, closed his eyes, slowed his breathing. He steadied his mind by reciting the things he needed to do.

He took control.

Two hours had passed by the time Ryan returned to Buswells. Celia waited for him in the room. It seemed dowdy and cramped compared to the suite Weiss had kept at the Shelbourne just a few streets away, but Celia brightened it, the late morning light catching fire in her hair.

She reclined on the bed, her long body stretched out.

'Did you get it?' she asked.

'All of it.' He took off his jacket, hung it up in the wardrobe.

'Any trouble?'

'None at all,' he said.

Celia reached up her hand, beckoned him down to the bed.

He lay down beside her, his chest against her back, slipped an arm around her waist. She took his hand in hers, guided it to the hollow between her breasts.

'How long do you have the room for?' she asked.

'Until the meeting this afternoon,' he said. 'After that, they'll kick me out.'

She turned onto her back, pushed his hand down between her thighs.

'We'd best make the most of it, then,' she said.

Ryan walked through Haughey's outer office, did not wait for the secretary to announce his arrival, opened the door without knocking.

Haughey and Fitzpatrick looked up at him, surprise on the director's face, anger on the minister's.

'You're forgetting yourself, big fella,' Haughey said. 'Or didn't your mother teach you to knock?'

Ryan closed the door behind him then dropped the file on Haughey's desk.

'Is this everything?'

'All of it,' Ryan said, feeling no shame in the lie.

'All right, sit down.'

Ryan took the chair next to Fitzpatrick.

Haughey gave him a hard stare, the hawk eyes blazing. 'So, what have you got to say for yourself?'

'Nothing, Minister. Everything you need to know is in the file.'

Haughey nodded. 'I wish I could say it was a job well done. But it's over with, that's the important thing.'

Fitzpatrick held out a hand. 'I'll have the keys to the car, thank you.'

Ryan said, 'I think I'll hold on to the car, thank you, sir. It's got a broken window anyway.'

Fitzpatrick's mouth dropped open. He looked to Haughey.

'Look here, big fella, I don't like your cheek.'

'Minister, I don't care what you like. I no longer answer to you.'

Haughey stood, his face reddening. 'Now listen to me, Ryan, you're heading for a fall, I'll tell you that for nothing. I'll fucking destroy you.'

'Minister, two solicitors are currently in possession of identical packages. Those packages each contain a recording of the conversation we had in Buswells a few days ago. The conversation in which you admit to allowing Colonel Skorzeny to place an ad in the *Irish Times* inviting persons unknown to commit murder. The packages also contain a signed letter in which I describe the nature of the work I carried out on behalf of this office. These solicitors are under instruction to pass the contents of these packages along to the press, the Garda Síochána, and Matt McCloskey, the American ambassador, in the event of any injury befalling me, or at any time of my choosing.'

'You dirty little bastard,' Haughey said. 'You will rue the day, big fella. Mark my words.'

Ryan stood. 'Any time I choose, Minister. Remember that. Excuse me, gentlemen.'

He left them there, staring after him.

Ryan took his time walking back through St Stephen's Green towards Buswells. He felt the warmth of the sun on his skin, relished it, and the clarity of the air. Passers-by glanced at the still healing burn on his cheek, the slight awkwardness of his step, but he did not mind.

It seemed like weeks since he had last been able to breathe freely, no tightening ring of guilt and fear around his chest. He was no longer beholden to Haughey and his money, no longer frightened and awed by Skorzeny's strength.

Despite their power, their contacts, their spheres of influence, they were only men.

He did not think of Goren Weiss at all.

Ryan walked north along Kildare Street, seeing the gardens of Trinity College up ahead, the university standing beyond like some royal palace, indifferent to the traffic that streamed around it, the people who milled in its shadow but who would never step inside. He turned left into Molesworth Street, and entered the hotel.

'Mr Ryan,' the receptionist called.

Ryan approached the desk. The receptionist gave a regretful smile.

'Mr Ryan, I've received a call from Mr Haughey's office, and they wish your stay with us to end today.'

Ryan nodded. 'That's fine. My bag's already packed.'

The receptionist's smile grew more pained. 'Unfortunately, checkout time is twelve noon, and it's now past three. Can I ask you to vacate the room as soon as possible so it can be cleaned?'

'Of course,' Ryan said. 'I wouldn't want to cost Mr Haughey any more money than absolutely necessary.'

He turned to go, but the receptionist called, 'Sir, one more thing.'

Ryan stopped.

'You have a caller,' the receptionist said. 'A Mr Skorzeny. He's waiting in the lounge.'

75

SKORZENY WAITED IN THE SAME CHAIR GOREN WEISS HAD SAT in just a few days before, close to the window overlooking Molesworth Street. The leather satchel rested on the table in front of him. Only two other patrons sat in the lounge, an elderly couple on the far side of the room.

From the chair next to Skorzeny, Celia watched Ryan approach, her lower lip reddened and swollen. She wrapped her arms around her body. 'Bertie, I'm sorry. I thought it was the maid when he came to the room.'

'It's not your fault,' Ryan said. He quelled the anger that burned in his heart. 'What did he do to you?'

She brought her fingertips to her lip. 'I'm all right.'

'Miss Hume did not wish to cooperate,' Skorzeny said. 'I was forced to use more physical persuasion.'

Ryan asked, 'What do you want?'

Skorzeny laughed. 'What do you think? You betrayed me, Lieutenant Ryan. Célestin told me everything. That you knew who was trying to blackmail me, and you kept the information to yourself. Then I learned that you aligned yourself with a Zionist against me, and that same Zionist came ashore with the cargo you were to deliver.'

'Goren Weiss is dead.'

'As he should be,' Skorzeny said. 'You would have stolen

from me too if Célestin had not repented, if Monsieur Borringer had not followed my instructions, if Mr Haughey had not mobilised the police against you and your friends.'

'So you want me dead,' Ryan said.

'Of course. But not now, not here. Besides, there is more I need to know. Please sit.'

Ryan took the chair across the table from Skorzeny and Celia. She reached for his hand, let her fingertips graze his.

A waiter walked towards them, but Skorzeny waved him away.

'Go on,' Ryan said. 'Ask your questions.'

'The Zionist, Weiss. He worked for the Mossad. The Mossad are many things, but they are not thieves. Why was he on that boat? What was their involvement?'

'Weiss had his own agenda. He found out what Carter was up to, and he wanted a taste for himself.'

'Greed,' Skorzeny said, his eyes glittering as he smiled. 'I told Mr Haughey greed would destroy them. But tell me, Lieutenant Ryan, how did this Weiss come to know of Carter's plan to blackmail me?'

'He was leading a Mossad team in an operation against you. His investigation took him to Carter.'

Skorzeny's smile faded. He leaned forward. 'A Mossad operation against me? What was this operation? Did they plan to assassinate me?'

'No,' Ryan said. 'Weiss didn't want to kill you. He said you were no good to him dead.'

'Then what?'

Now Ryan smiled. He held Skorzeny's brilliant gaze, spared him none of the savage pleasure in his heart.

Skorzeny leaned closer, casually pulled his jacket aside to reveal the butt of a pistol. 'Tell me.'

'The operation was successful,' Ryan said.

Skorzeny sat back, took Celia's hand in his. The fingers dwarfed hers. Celia winced as he squeezed. 'Tell me.'

'They know about the money,' Ryan said.

A furrow appeared on Skorzeny's smooth brow. 'Money?'

'The money you've been channelling away from the escape fund. Millions upon millions. I've seen the accounts myself. You've been robbing your *Kameraden* blind for years. Skimming off the top, Weiss called it. He had the proof.'

Skorzeny sat in silence for a moment, his mind working behind his eyes. 'So he had proof. What does this matter to me?'

'It matters to your friends in South America. The rest of the Nazi scum you handle the funds for. If they find out you've been stealing from them, there won't be a safe place on God's green earth for you. Not even Franco could protect you.'

'So he would have my *Kameraden* kill me rather than do it himself? Was he such a coward?'

Ryan shook his head. 'I told you, he didn't want you dead. He wanted something far more valuable than your life.'

'What?'

'The ratlines. He wanted to know about every piece of filth you helped get out of Europe, all of them, going right back. Either you turned on your friends, or he'd make sure they turned on you.'

Skorzeny gave a laugh, the sound of it leaping high and shrill from his barrel chest. 'Now Weiss is dead. His proof cannot help him.'

'Oh, but it can,' Ryan said. He spoke slowly and clearly, relishing every tic on Skorzeny's face. 'You see, he told me where to find the information he had on you. This morning,

I took it to his contact at a legal firm in Dublin. They're a front for the Israelis. The mission continues, only with one change.'

Skorzeny released Celia's hand. 'Go on.'

'That if anything happens to me, or anyone close to me, the information will be passed to your friends. If you kill me, they will kill you.'

'Do you think this makes you safe?' Skorzeny smiled. 'Why do you believe I would rather live as a slave to Jews than die by the hands of my *Kameraden*?'

'Because of your pride.'

Skorzeny's head tilted. 'Pride?'

'I think you would rather live under the Mossad's thumb than let your friends know you stole from them. You won't have that stain on your memory.'

'You seem very sure of this, Lieutenant Ryan. Are you willing to wager your life on it?'

Ryan asked, 'Are you?'

They held each other's gaze, Skorzeny seeming to stare into Ryan's soul.

'When they write the books about you,' Ryan said, 'what should the final chapter say? That in the end, you were nothing but a thief?'

Skorzeny sat frozen, his breathing the only sound in the room.

Eventually, he stood.

'You will never be at peace, Lieutenant Ryan. You might be safe for now, perhaps for a year or two, maybe more, but you must know this: one day, I will make you suffer.'

Skorzeny reached for the bag.

'Weiss told me something else,' Ryan said.

Skorzeny paused, his fingers on the handle of the satchel.

'He told me about the raid on Gran Sasso you're so famous for, Mussolini's rescue. He told me it wasn't true, any of it. He told me it was all propaganda, that you've been living a lie.'

Skorzeny went to lift the bag.

'Leave it there,' Ryan said.

Skorzeny paused.

'I said, leave it.'

Skorzeny straightened. 'Now you are the thief,' he said, his voice wavering.

'I can live with that.' Ryan got to his feet. 'You can go now.'

Skorzeny held his ground for a moment, then he smiled at Celia.

'Good day, Miss Hume.'

He left them there.

Celia crumbled, the tears soaking Ryan's shoulder as he embraced her.

EPILOGUE

HERBERTS CUKURS COULD ILL AFFORD THE COST OF A LONG distance call from the hotel, but he had to be sure. He had to hear it one more time.

He listened to the dial tone, the distorted whirr that travelled all the way from a small townland outside Dublin.

'Yes?' the voice said, deep as ever, but perhaps not as strident as it had once been.

'Otto, it's me. Herberts.'

'Yes, Herberts,' Skorzeny said. 'What can I do for you? It's very late at night here.'

Cukurs swallowed. The Uruguayan heat crawled and slithered over his body. He had been in South America for years, but still he could not get used to the climate. He had flown from Sao Paulo that morning, the ticket paid for by his new benefactor, the businessman who wanted Cukurs for a partner.

'Did I wake you?' he asked.

'No,' Skorzeny said. 'I don't sleep well.'

'Nor do I,' Cukurs said. He removed his spectacles and rubbed at his dry eyes.

In those late hours, he often wondered why it wasn't the screaming souls of thirty thousand Jews that kept him from sleeping, but rather the simple idea – no, the certainty – that one day they would come back to take their due from him.

Skorzeny asked, 'My friend, tell me, what can I do for you?'

'I'm in Montevideo. In Uruguay. Anton Kuenzle is waiting downstairs for me. He wants me to go with him to look at properties for our new business.'

'Good,' Skorzeny said. 'I told you he would make you rich. You've been too long in the wilderness, my friend. It's time you regained the success you deserve.'

Cukurs wiped sweat from his brow. 'But can I trust him? He . . .'

'He what?'

'He looks like a Jew.'

Skorzeny laughed. 'Herberts, listen to me. I've known Anton since before the war, back in Vienna. We joined the Party together. Believe me, you can trust him.'

Cukurs let the air wheeze out of his lungs. 'I'm sorry. Of course I can trust him. You made the introduction, after all.'

It had been fifteen months ago in Buenos Aires, at a dinner party held to celebrate the assassination of President John F. Kennedy in Dallas.

'Please don't apologise, Herberts. Go on, go and see him. Let him make you rich.'

'One day they'll come for me,' Cukurs said. He clamped a hand over his mouth, too late to trap the words inside.

'But not today,' Skorzeny said. 'Life is too short to live in fear.'

Cukurs felt the urge to weep, the tightening in his throat, the heat in his eyes.

Skorzeny said, 'Trust me.'

Albert Ryan stretched out on the smooth pebbles, felt the sun on his bare legs and chest. Forte Vigliena rose up above, the ancient lookout with its bleached parapets standing guard over the Mediterranean. The small cove's beach was barely large enough for two people, tucked beneath the eastern sea walls of Ortigia, the tiny island off the coast of Sicily where Ryan had wandered as a young soldier.

Celia sat on a rock reading a paperback, her lower lip pinched between her teeth in concentration, her feet bathed in the clear water. Schools of small silvery fish plotted courses through the rocks. Celia's naked shoulders glistened in the light, shining with the water she had splashed across her skin to cool herself. A wide-brimmed hat shaded her face.

A transistor radio sat on the pebbles next to Ryan, tuned to the BBC World Service. The newsreader spoke about Herberts Cukurs, the infamous slaughterer of thousands of human beings, who had been assassinated in South America. He read a statement that had been anonymously delivered to news agencies in Berlin and Bonn.

'Taking into consideration the gravity of the charge levelled against the accused, namely that he personally supervised the killing of more than thirty thousand men, women and children, and considering the extreme display of cruelty which the subject showed when carrying out his tasks, the accused Herberts Cukurs is hereby sentenced to death.'

All but a confession by the Israelis. When Ryan searched his soul for pity for the dead man, all he could find were the images of children and the flies on their dead lips.

The newsreader continued:

'Accused was executed by those who can never forget on the twenty-third of February 1965. His body can be found at Casa Cubertini, Calle Colombia, Séptima Sección del Departamento de Canelones, Montevideo, Uruguay.'

Ryan wondered who had sent Cukurs to his death, who had set him up. But in his gut, he knew.

'What are you listening to?' Celia asked, wading towards the pebbles. Water beaded on her long and slender legs.

'The news,' Ryan said.

'Good or bad?' She sat down beside him, her skin cool and slick against his.

He did not answer.

Ron wondered who had sent Connor to his death, who had set him up. But in his gut, he knew.

'What are you thinking?' Cilla asked, walking towards the pool. Water beaded on her long and slender legs.

'The news,' Ron said.

'Good or bad?' She sat down beside him, her skin cool and slick against his.

He did not answer.

ACKNOWLEDGEMENTS

ONCE AGAIN, I HAVE MANY PEOPLE TO THANK FOR THEIR HELP in writing this book.

All the publishing professionals who have offered guidance, support, friendship, and on various occasions have prevented me from making a complete fool of myself: Nat Sobel, Judith Weber, and all at Sobel Weber Associates; Caspian Dennis and all at Abner Stein Ltd; Geoff Mulligan, Briony Everroad, Alison Hennessey, and all at Harvill Secker and Vintage Books; Bronwen Hruska, Juliet Grames, and all at Soho Press.

Those who have been so generous with their knowledge and experience in helping me research this book: Ruth Dudley Edwards for her first-hand accounts of the Irish corridors of power, and for acting as a wonderful sounding board; Mary McVeigh for her insights into the Dublin of the early 60s; James Benn for pointing me in the direction of some invaluable historical information, as well as being a great travelling and shooting companion; Jay Faulkner for the fencing tips; Armagh Branch Library and the Irish & Local Studies Library for giving me a place to write and research. Any errors or liberties taken with historical reality are entirely my own.

My friends and family for their constant support: my lovely wife Jo, who somehow puts up with me, even when I least deserve it; our daughter Issy for helping me finally understand the point of it all; the wider Neville and Atkinson clans for being such supportive families; my best friend and go-to poetry consultant, Dr James Morrow; Betsy Dornbusch, without whom I would have given up writing years ago; David Torrans and all at No Alibis in Belfast for running one of the best bookstores on the planet; Hilary Knight for working so hard on my behalf; my many friends in the crime fiction community whose kindness knows no bounds; our faithful, excitable and hairy friend Sweeney, who took me on many long walks while I figured out what to do next.

The following books are just a few that have helped enormously in researching this novel:

Fugitive Ireland: European Minority Nationalists and Irish Political Asylum, 1937–2008, by Daniel Leach, Four Courts Press.

Commando Extraordinary: Otto Skorzeny, by Charles Foley, Cassell Military Classics.

Rescuing Mussolini: Gran Sasso 1943, by Robert Forczyk, Osprey Publishing.

Haughey's Millions: Charlie's Money Trail, by Colm Keena, Gill & Macmillan.

JFK in Ireland: Four Days that Changed a President, by Ryan Tubridy, Collins.

News from a New Republic: Ireland in the 1950s, by Tom Garvin, Gill & Macmillan.

Finally, I must thank the late Cathal O'Shannon, whose documentary *Ireland's Nazis* first planted the seeds of this story in my mind.